Adrienne Chinn was born in Grand Falls, Newfoundland, grew up in Quebec, and eventually made her way to London, England after a career as a journalist. In England she worked as a TV and film researcher before embarking on a career as an interior designer, lecturer, and writer. When not up a ladder or at the computer, she can usually be found rummaging through flea markets or haggling in the Marrakech souk.

www.adrienne-chinn.co.uk

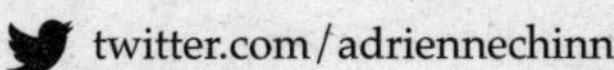

twitter.com/adriennechinn

facebook.com/AdrienneChinnAuthor

instagram.com/adriennechinn

## Also by Adrienne Chinn

*The Lost Letter from Morocco*

*The English Wife*

*Love in a Time of War*

# THE PARIS SISTER

ADRIENNE CHINN

One More Chapter
a division of HarperCollins*Publishers* Ltd
1 London Bridge Street
London SE1 9GF

www.harpercollins.co.uk

HarperCollins*Publishers*
Macken House, 39/40 Mayor Street Upper,
Dublin 1, D01 C9W8, Ireland

This paperback edition 2023
1
First published in Great Britain in ebook format by
HarperCollins*Publishers* 2023



A catalogue record of this book is available from the British Library

ISBN: 978-0-00-850163-1



Printed and bound in the UK using 100% Renewable Electricity
by CPI Group (UK) Ltd

*For my sisters Judith Anne Chinn and Carolyn Patricia Chinn*
*There in all seasons*

*'Sweet is the voice of a sister in the season of sorrow.'*

– Benjamin Disraeli

# Cast of Characters

CLOVER BAR, LONDON, ENGLAND
Gerald Fry – *the sisters' father (deceased)*
Christina Fry – *the sisters' mother*
Hettie Richards – *Christina's housekeeper*

SWEET BRIAR FARM, WEST LAKE, ALBERTA, CANADA
Celie (Cecelia) Fry Jeffries – *the eldest sister*
Frank Jeffries – *Celie's husband*
Lulu (Louisa) Jeffries – *Celie and Frank's daughter*

ALTUMANINA, CAIRO, EGYPT
Jessie (Jessica) Fry Khalid – *fraternal twin of Etta*
Dr Aziz Khalid – *Jessie's husband*
Shani Khalid – *Jessie and Aziz's daughter*
Madame Layla Khalid – *Aziz's mother*
Zara Khalid – *Aziz's sister*
Marta Tadros – *the Khalids' cook and housekeeper*

VILLA SERENISSIMA, CAPRI, ITALY
Etta Fry Marinetti – *fraternal twin of Jessie*
Carlo Marinetti – *Etta's husband*

Adriana Marinetti – *Etta and Carlo's daughter*
Stefania Albertini – *Christina's cousin, owner of Villa Serenissima*
Liliana Sabbatini – *Stefania's housekeeper and confidant*
Mario Sabbatini – *Liliana's grandson*

OTHER KEY PLAYERS

Britain

Harold Grenville, the 6th Earl of Sherbrooke – *Christina's ex-lover, father of Celie*
Henrietta Bishop – *Christina's aunt*
Ellen Jackson – *Christina's friend*
Dorothy Adam – *Christina's acquaintance*

Italy

Marianna Marinetti – *Carlo's first wife (deceased)*
Paolo Marinetti – *Carlo's son from his first marriage to Marianna*
Carolina, the Marchesa Ludovisi – *Carlo's mother-in-law*

Egypt

Lady Evelyn Herbert – *Jessie's friend in Egypt*
Ruth Bellico – *American photojournalist, Jessie's friend*

Paris

François DuRose – *Etta's art dealer*
Zelda Fitzgerald – *Etta's friend in Paris*
CJ Melton – *American journalist in Paris*

Alberta

Mavis Wheatley – *Celie's friend*
Fred Wheatley – *Mavis's husband and Frank's friend*
Ben Wheatley – *Lulu's friend*
Hans Brandt – *Celie's student in Alberta*

Germany

Max Fischer – *Celie's ex-fiancé*

# Part I

1919

# Chapter One

## Christina

**London, England – September 1919**

'*Cioccolato, signora?'*

'*Grazie, Giulia.* You know that chocolate cannoli is my favourite.'

'*Si, sempre il tuo preferito, signora.*'

Christina Fry pays out the coins and collects the paper bag of cannoli stuffed with the chocolate cream she loves. An indulgence for tea, she knows, what with her daughters gone back to their lives in all corners of the world, but she must put on a good show for Ellen Jackson, who will no doubt gloat about her election to the presidency of the local branch of the Women's Institute, and the bridge ladies tomorrow.

She packs the bag into her straw shopping basket with the parmesan and olives and waves at the shop assistant. '*Grazie. Ciao, Giulia.*'

'*Prego, Signora Fry.*'

Christina opens the door of Terroni's delicatessen and steps out onto Clerkenwell Road. The last of the summer's sun has been swallowed up in a steady drizzle of rain, and she pauses under the shop's canopy to unfurl her umbrella. She heads left toward Farringdon Road and the train station, dodging the puddles and the office workers heading homeward.

At the junction with Farringdon Road, Christina waits for a break in the stream of automobiles and horse carts. Shielding herself from the rain with her umbrella, she then dashes across the road, thankful for the looser coat and shorter, ankle-skimming skirt of the new post-war fashions. They are so freeing after the pre-war hobble skirts and, heaven forbid, the corsets and stays of her youth. She rounds the corner, and, intent on avoiding a large puddle, ploughs directly into a man hurrying from the station.

'Oh, I'm awfully sor—'

'Tina?'

She sucks in a sharp breath. There's no mistaking the blue eyes.

'Harry?'

The man stares at her from under his dripping Homburg hat, his mouth agape. 'My word, Tina, how are you?'

Christina shivers involuntarily. 'I'm ... I'm well, thank you.' Harry Grenville, the man that she never thought she'd see again in this life, the man she'd hoped she'd never see, takes hold of her elbow and steers her under a shop awning.

'You're shivering, Tina, and I'm being an idiot. Come out of the rain.'

She shakes out her umbrella. 'I'm fine. Really. I haven't a drop of rain on me.'

'Always foreseeing every eventuality, as ever, Tina,' he says, fine lines fanning from his eyes as he smiles. 'How many times did I have to carry your gloves and your shawls on our walks around Capri? "In case it gets chilly", that's what you always said, isn't it? Capri never gets chilly in the summer!' He laughs, and suddenly he is the twenty-three-year-old she'd known that Italian summer back in 1891.

Christina looks at the man he has become. His neat moustache and the clipped hair at his temples are salted with grey, and his face is heavier, as if it has sagged from carrying a burden too long. But his eyes, so piercingly blue, are the same. The colour of the Italian sky. Celie's eyes.

'Not every eventuality.'

His smile fades. 'I'm sorry, Tina. I had to leave. We couldn't … There was no way …' He looks away from her at the newsboy shouting the day's headlines across the street. 'How is … he? She?'

'You don't know, do you? You never even tried to find out.'

He looks back at her. 'Yes, I know. I'm sorry. You have no idea how sorry I am about everything. I … I tried to explain in the letter I left for you before I left Capri.'

'Ah, yes. Your letter. I remember every word of that letter, Harry. How your father would disown you if you married me. How you couldn't possibly be lumbered with a wife and child as you pursued your military education at Sandhurst. Oh, and how you were already betrothed to the wealthy daughter of some marquess. A detail you had never seen fit to mention to me, I recall.'

Harry's eyes cloud over and he disappears momentarily into some place far from the sodden London street corner. He shakes his head. 'I'm so sorry, Tina. You have no idea how sorry. I – I wanted to contact you after I left Capri. I started a letter to you so many times, but then I thought how much you must hate me, considering …' He rubs at the lines furrowing his forehead.

'Considering?'

'Well, you know … the circumstances.'

Christina smiles tightly. 'Yes, of course. The circumstances. Cecelia Sirena Maria Fry, by the way. Your daughter.'

'A daughter. Cecelia,' he says, testing out the name like it's an unfamiliar sweet. 'Does she … does she look like you? Does she have your beautiful auburn hair?'

'What does it matter? You'll never meet her.'

'I … I'd like to know.'

Christina sighs. 'She does. And your blue eyes. She's just

married and has emigrated to Canada. I expect she's on a train half-way across Canada as we speak. She doesn't know about you, of course. I married a good man and had two more daughters. He died in the war.'

'I'm sorry, Tina.'

She shrugs. 'I've had a good life. Gerald saved me.' She watches Harry as he shifts on his feet and glances past her at the black-suited men scurrying into the dank interior of the train station like wet beetles. *Have I made you uncomfortable, Harry? It's the very least of what you deserve.*

He reaches into his raincoat pocket and removes a watch. 'Is that the time?' he says, glancing at it. 'I'm awfully sorry, Tina. I'm terribly late for an appointment back at my legal chambers.'

'Of course, Harry, or is it my Lord? I expect you've inherited your father's title by now?'

'I have, but I'll always be Harry to you.' He slips the watch into his pocket and pulls up the collar of his raincoat. 'It was … it was good seeing you, Tina.' A smile hovers on his lips as his eyes sweep over her face. 'You haven't changed in the least.'

Christina watches him as he hurries across the street mindless of the puddles and the splashes thrown up by the beeping motorcars. Her heart thuds in her chest and her cheeks burn. She sucks in a breath of the cool, damp air and, snapping open her umbrella, steps out into the rain.

---

Christina shoves her umbrella into the brass stand and calls out to the kitchen as she unpins her hat.

'Hettie? I'm back and I need a tea. The weather is simply foul and I'm drenched to the bone.'

Christina's housekeeper, Hettie Richards – or household administrator, as Hettie has insisted since she'd joined the Domestic Workers' Union after the war – strides out of the kitchen, wiping her hands on a tea towel.

'Give us your coat, then. I won't be 'aving you dripping all over the sitting room carpet after I've spent all morning on my knees brushing out the crumbs.'

Christina shrugs out of the coat and hands it to Hettie with the paper bag of cannoli. 'I'll have one of these with tea, if you please, Hettie. You may have one yourself, as well. Ellen Jackson can be relied on to be on a reducing diet when she comes to bridge tomorrow and will likely only eat two. You have baked walnut squares as well?'

'Of course, and the scones'll be done tomorrow so they're fresh.'

'Good, we can't have the President of the Women's Institute and the bridge club thinking we're parsimonious.'

''Eaven forfend.'

Christina raises a fine auburn eyebrow as she sweeps her gaze over Hettie's impassive face. 'I shall take the tea in my room, if you please, Hettie. The excursion to Terroni's has quite taken it out of me and I feel the need for rest and solitude.'

Later, once she has fortified herself with tea and the sweet pastry, she sits back against the pillows on the large brass bed as she studies the watercolour portrait unrolled on her lap. She looks at the face of the girl turned forever toward the sparkling turquoise sea, her copper hair lit with strands of gold in the summer sun as she sits in her blue dress amongst the Caprese wildflowers. That day is as clear in her memory as the afternoon's unexpected meeting with Harry Grenville. She rubs her finger over his signature: *H. Grenville.* A confident black slash across the white flowers on the lower right side.

*Harry Grenville. The Earl of Sherbrooke. You'll never know how much I loved you. You never per gave me a chance to show you. You got what you wanted from me, and then you were off. I never would have credited you with being a cad, Harry. You made me laugh on all our excursions around Capri. Even Cousin Stefania liked you, despite the fact you were an Englishman. You have charm, that is a fact. It's stood you well in your climb up the political ladder. The rumour is you'll be the next leader of the Conservative Party. Then what? Prime Minister?*

*There's only one thing that would have cut your climb to power off at the knees, isn't there, Harry? One inconvenient secret. Your illegitimate daughter. How would that have played in the newspapers?* 'Earl's Son Caught in Love Scandal'. *That's why you left me, isn't it, Harry? Alone and pregnant with your child on Capri. You were afraid of the scandal, weren't you? Afraid that your father would disinherit you; afraid that you would be thrown out of Sandhurst; afraid that your name would be dragged through the mud along with all your dreams of standing at the pinnacle of British life.*

*Oh, Harry. Would it have been so terrible for us to marry? My father may not have been an aristocrat, but he was a successful architect, well-respected and admired. And my mother, my beautiful Italian mother, Isabella, was hostess for the most sought-after parties in London, much to Aunt Henrietta's and Aunt Margaret's annoyance. Papa's family had never approved of his marriage to the penniless daughter of an Italian plasterer, but Papa had stood his ground and they'd married, with me arriving seven months later.*

*Then … all was well. I had a good education. I was presented at court. I could have fit into your life, Harry. If you'd had the courage to stand up to your father. We could have found a way if you'd really wanted to.*

She runs her fingers over her ear in a habitual gesture she no longer notices and presses her hand against her fluttering stomach. *I thought I'd never see you again. I thought our past was well and truly buried.* She catches sight of herself in the mirror on her vanity table. Her cheeks are flushed pink and her eyes stare back at her like those of a rabbit anticipating an approaching fox. She rolls up the watercolour agitatedly and secures it with a ribbon. She is being ridiculous. She was simply taken by surprise. Best to forget the whole encounter. Yes, that would be best for everyone.

# Chapter Two

## Celie

### Canada – September 1919

Celie Jeffries leans her forehead against the cool glass of the train window and gazes past the reflection of her new husband to the unbroken horizon line dividing the brown earth spiked with regimented rows of wheat stubble and the blue sky puffed with clouds. Now and then the unyielding flatness of the Saskatchewan landscape is pierced by a thrusting blood-coloured grain elevator, and she has begun counting down the lull between their appearance to pass the time. She has never seen a land so vast. From the Québec dairy farms with their fat black and white Holsteins to the Ontario forests of sugar maples transforming into fiery autumn yellows, oranges and reds, and out into the flat plains of the Canadian prairies, it is like an unravelling ball of wool that appears to have no end.

She wonders if Germany looks anything like this. If things had turned out differently, if there had been no war and she and her university German tutor, Max Fischer, had married as they had both hoped, would she now be settled down in a comfortable house in Heidelberg, the wife of a clever young German lawyer? She rests her hand on her belly and brushes her fingers over the small bump. Would the baby she is carrying be Max's child instead of Frank's?

She glances over at her new husband who is deep into *Modern Methods for British Farmers 1902.* Frank's dark brown hair, almost black with its coat of brilliantine, shines in the early morning light streaming in from the dirty window, and he frowns in concentration as he scribbles a note in the margin. The burn scar on his left cheek from the chlorine gas at Ypres has faded so that it is barely noticeable now, and the nervous anxiety he has carried with him since they embarked on the ship from Liverpool for Montréal has gradually dissipated the farther they travel from Europe and the horrors of the past five years. He has even loosened his tie; she will have to remind him to tighten it when they arrive at West Lake later that day.

If someone had told her that she would marry the dull young auctioneer who'd come to Clover Bar for dinner with his overbearing father that spring night in 1913, she would have laughed at the ridiculousness of the suggestion. In fact, Frank had shown more interest in Etta, but then, Etta was always the star of any gathering. Poor Frank would never have stood a chance with her fickle, effervescent younger sister.

Then the waves of life had thrown her and Frank together again during the war and Frank had begun writing her from his posts in France and Turkey. She'd thought Max was dead … But then Max wasn't dead, he was there in the sitting room in the Fry family house, Clover Bar, in May telling her that he loved her, asking her to marry him, but it was too late because she had just married Frank.

It had been simply too late.

Being married to Frank really isn't so bad. He is considerate and funny in a wry sort of way, and handsome in an unassuming way, though not particularly affectionate which is not altogether surprising given that he is an Englishman. Their first night together as husband and wife in her old bedroom at Clover Bar was a mixture of fumblings and apologies, not helped by the narrowness of the single bed. The nights had improved as they'd grown accustomed to each other, though she had never managed to coax her body to spark into the passion that had come so easily with Max.

Max Fischer. The day the new German tutor had walked into her German class at University College in London back in 1912, slender and so blondly handsome in his new wool suit with the price tag still hanging from the collar, was the day her life had changed. But then the war had to get in the way and ruin everything.

*Oh, Max. Why did the war have to happen? Why couldn't we simply have married and had a happy life together?* She runs her knuckle absent-mindedly over the window glass, stopping abruptly when she realises she is writing out his name.

'Is everything okay, Celie?'

Celie drops her hand into her lap. 'Fine, Frank. Just wondering what time we'll arrive in West Lake.'

'We should be there around three, barring any bears or wolves on the line.'

'Bears or wolves? You're teasing me, aren't you?'

Frank smiles, and his pale brown eyes glint with humour. 'Only a little. Winnie the bear in London Zoo did come from Winnipeg, after all.'

'Where *are* you taking me, Frank Jeffries?'

'I'm taking you through the looking glass to a fantastical world, just like Alice in the story.'

'All this when I would have been satisfied with a larger bed.'

He laughs. 'We'll have that, too, Celie. As big as the one we had in the Windsor Hotel in Montréal.'

'That really was an extravagance, Frank. We needn't have stayed a week in Montréal. We should have got straight on the train and headed west.'

'And miss all of Montréal's delights? The restaurants and the dancing? The bagels and smoked meat sandwiches on Saint Lawrence Boulevard at midnight? Not every English girl is lucky enough to honeymoon in Montréal.'

Celie smiles reluctantly. 'It was rather marvellous.'

Frank pats her knee. 'There you go, old girl. We start as we mean to go on.' He sets the book down on the empty seat beside him and rises. 'I'm off to the dining car to get a tea. Shall I bring you one?'

'Yes, please. Milk, one sugar.'

He salutes her. 'I know.'

Celie smiles as he heads out of the compartment and turns right down the aisle in the direction of the dining car. It will be fine. Perhaps what she had with Max was nothing more than a crush. An infatuation. The kind of romance that exists in novels and in the moving pictures, but that never really works in the real world where it slaps up against the shore of mundanity, familiarity, and the tedium of the everyday. Perhaps it is for the best that she and Max never had a chance to experience their love wilting under the weight of reality.

She has to pack her memories of Max away and lock down the lid. She looks down at the gentle swell of her belly. Soon there will be new memories. Her life now lies ahead of her, not behind her in Britain or Germany. There will be a child; hopefully several. A farm to build and manage. She ran her father's photography studio after he was killed in the Zeppelin attack back in 1917, didn't she? She organised marches for women's suffrage before the war and wrote articles for the *Daily Mirror* about women's lives in London during the war. She speaks fluent German and she plays the piano, not that either of these is of any use now. What matters is that she is resourceful. Even her sister Jessie wouldn't begrudge that fact. Jessie once told her that she could 'make a silk purse out of a sow's ear'. It's true. She has this innate urge to improve things. To do her bit in the world around her. And now God has set her out on this new path, and, come what may, she will do everything to make it work.

---

Later that afternoon, Celie watches the train steam away from the station, the great puffs of steam obscuring, for a moment, the towering red grain elevators beside the rail line. The train whistle pierces the soft whoosh of the breeze, stirring a murder of crows from the prairie grass that stretches out beyond the grain elevators to the horizon. The train station – a modest, maroon-painted wooden building with a pitched roof extending to cover the wooden platform – squats in the sea of yellow prairie grass beside the train track, like a boat that has lost its mooring.

She dabs at her forehead with the back of her hand and tucks a damp strand of auburn hair under her hat. The sun beats down from the wide blue sky, reflecting off the yellow prairie, and she steps further back into the meagre shade of the station canopy. She sits on one of their two trunks.

*So, this is it,* Celie thinks as she fans her face. *Where the next chapter begins.* She glances down at her belly. *You'll be a little Canadian, baby. I wonder what you'll think about all of this? What you'll think of me and Daddy taking you away from busy London to the middle of nowhere? I'll make it good for you, I promise. Your daddy and I both will. You won't miss England, baby. Europe isn't the place it was before the war. It's like Daddy said – there's nothing for us there now. Best to start over afresh.*

Frank steps out of the station office onto the platform, still dapper in his grey suit with his straightened tie and his new straw boater, despite the long train journey from Montréal. The copy of the book he has been devouring on the journey is in his hand, his thumb bookmarking where he's left off. He sucks in a deep breath of the clean air and stretches out his arms.

'Hello, Alberta!' he shouts before the coughing takes hold. He clears his throat and wipes his mouth with his handkerchief.

'Are you all right, Frank? It sounds like it's getting worse.'

'I'm fine.' He turns and grins at Celie, his warm brown eyes lit with excitement. 'What do you think, Celie? Look at that sky. Blue as far as the eye can see. And that prairie – have you ever seen anything like it? Flat as a squashed penny. There's space to breathe here. We can make a life here, in our own house on our own farm. One hundred and sixty acres! Imagine that. With our own horses and cows and chickens and fields and fields of wheat. Wheat to the horizon! We'll be free of all the rubbish of the war. I never want to go back, Celie. Never.'

'Surely you don't mean that, Frank. What about my mother? She's all alone at Clover Bar now, what with me here, Jessie in Egypt and Etta in Italy.' Celie rests her hand on her belly. 'I certainly want Mama to see our baby. Maybe she'll finally discover her maternal instinct.'

'Of course, of course. We'll figure all of that out. We can get her out here once we're settled.'

Celie shakes her head at the memory of the arduous journey from England, and an image of her elegant and fastidious mother heaving over a chamber pot on the ship slips into her mind. 'I'm not sure that's such a good idea, Frank. She's not as young as we are. She likes her comforts.'

He bends down and gives her a peck on her cheek. 'First things first, Celie. We need to build a house and a barn and stock up on livestock and seed. I've read that the winters here are rough, so we'll need to sort ourselves pretty sharpish before the snow comes. House first, I'd say.'

'There's no house? I thought ... You led me to believe ... Doesn't the Soldiers' Land Settlement Scheme provide a house?'

'Of course it does. Well, a loan for the land, a house and all the rest. We'll need to pay it back eventually, but it's only $7,500 at five per cent interest.'

'Seventy-five hundred dollars? Frank, that's a fortune! Why wouldn't you tell me? You said ... well, you implied that the land was free.'

'Celie, you don't need to know these things. It's my role to provide for my family, and I'm providing. Don't fret. I have the money from my father's estate and this is the world's breadbasket.

This land grows the best wheat on earth. We'll pay back the loan in no time.' He taps his book. 'I intend to run the most efficient farm in Alberta, with the help of this.'

Celie eyes the book's tattered and stained blue cover. 'Isn't that meant for farming in Britain, Frank? And it is almost twenty years old.'

'Britain, Canada, what difference does it make? Everyone knows Britain's science and industry leads the world. Land is land, and British agricultural methods are so advanced that a mere twenty years isn't going to change much. No, this is my new bible, Celie. This is going to make us rich.'

She smiles and nods. It is no use contradicting him; she'd learned that quickly enough on their trip from Britain. According to Frank, they had more than enough money to get started, were about to take ownership of over a hundred acres of fertile land, would build themselves a big house for all the happy children they would have … all without any setbacks or complications. She was simply being a 'Negative Nelly' when she urged for a prudence that Frank felt impinged on his dream.

'Of course, Frank. It's a new start, as you've said.' She peers down the tracks. 'Where do we go now?'

'I rang into town. The stationmaster gave me the name of the fellow who runs the garage. He's coming to take us and our luggage to the hotel. We'll head out tomorrow to look at the land. We'll need to find a room to rent until the house is built, but that's all work for another day. I say we freshen up and have a slap-up dinner at the hotel this evening to celebrate our new life.'

'Is that wise, Frank? We're going to have a great deal of expenses. The journey here was dear enough, let alone that week in Montréal.'

'There you go again, Negative Nelly. Life is for the living, Celie. I think we'll have a lot of fun here.'

She scans the wind-blown grass, the four gigantic red grain elevators and the train track slicing through the landscape like a cut. 'Of course, Frank. I'm sure we will.'

---

The flatbed truck pulls up outside the West Lake Hotel & Café, which stands pride of place in its yellow clapboard glory in the centre of the run of shops along the west side of the town's gravel-strewn main road. The driver, a thickset, ginger-haired man of about thirty in a flat cap, dungarees and a loose-fitting grey wool jacket, shuts off the engine. The vehicle lurches to a stop. He pushes up his cap and scratches his head.

'There ya go, best hotel this side of Edmonton. Only hotel this side of Edmonton, come to think of it. Lucky ya landed in West Lake and not some place like Boyle. Drove a Scottish fella and his family out there last week. Settlement soldier, just like you. I warned him, I sure did. Told him there wasn't a hotel or lodging house there or anythin'. Wouldn't hear a word of it. Said he was gonna stake his claim before anyone took the land away from him. Stubborn as Tom Philby's mule, and that's sayin' somethin'. His wife gave him an earful all the way there.'

'Oh, dear,' Celie says as she struggles with the truck's door handle. 'What happened when you arrived there?'

He shrugs. 'Dropped them off. Haven't heard anythin' since. Must be sleepin' in somebody's barn or somethin'. Expect to see her roll up here with the kids any day on the back of someone's truck.'

'No doubt they'll work things out,' Frank says as he reaches for his wallet. 'A wife's place is with her husband.' He hands the driver a two-dollar bill. 'Thanks for your trouble. Will you help me carry the trunks into the hotel?'

The driver sucks in through his teeth. 'Can tell you're fresh off the boat. You're overpayin' me a hundred per cent, there. Train station's not that far. Ya gotta get your head around the exchange rate or Ol' Man Forbes in the general store'll take you for a ride, if ya get my drift.'

Frank tucks the bill into the driver's shirt pocket. 'They're heavy trunks.'

The man grins under his ginger moustache. 'Right ya are, then. Name's Fred Wheatley if ya need anything. You can find me down at the garage most days.'

Celie gives the door a shove and it swings open, almost depositing her on the road.

'Careful, there, missus,' Fred says. 'Door sticks sometimes. Same thing happens to my wife, Mavis, all the time. Should probably fix it, seeing as I run the garage, but ya know what they say, the shoemaker always wears the worst shoes.'

---

The following afternoon, Frank kicks a stone into the well of a dried-up puddle and slaps his straw boater against his leg as he surveys their new plot of land. The wind buffets the flat landscape, whipping leaves off the briar brushes and scrubby trees, and he folds up the collar of his coat against the sudden chill. He looks over at Celie, who surveys the landscape of prairie grass, tree stumps, stones, briars and the occasional wind-stunted tree in silence, her expression pensive.

'So, Celie, what do you think?'

She turns to him and smiles, and he thinks again how attractive she is, with her cool blue eyes and the auburn hair, just like her mother's, though she makes no show of it in her sensible clothing and practical manner. It is no wonder Max Fischer fell in love with her before the war. But that's over now. She's Mrs Frank Jeffries now, and, though he knows she isn't in love with him, he will do everything in his power to make her happy. Everything he can to ensure she doesn't regret her decision.

'It's perfect, Frank. We'll make it perfect.'

'It will be hard work.'

'I'm not afraid of hard work.'

'I know. But it'll be physical work. Not writing articles for the papers, or running your father's photography studio, or all the other things you did back in London. Honestly, Celie, you were the busiest person I knew.'

She steps over the stones and grass and stands in front of Frank. She reaches up and caresses the cheek that still bears the shadow of the chlorine gas burn. 'That was my old life, Frank. I couldn't just stay home and play the piano and do needlepoint all day. I'm happy, Frank. I made my decision.'

'No regrets?'

She glances at a crow cawing on a mangled tree branch, the unasked question sitting heavily in the air. She looks back at him and squeezes his hand. 'I'll find my feet here. I'm your wife and we have a farm to build and a family to raise. And that's what we shall do.'

'I worry that you have regrets, Celie, or that you will.'

'No. Never. We'll move forward, Frank. It will be 1920 soon and I'm glad of that. A fresh new decade.' She pats her belly. 'We have everything to look forward to.'

Frank leans forward and kisses her. She wraps her arms around him as he presses her tightly against him.

'I love you, Celie. I want to make you the happiest woman in the world.'

'Let's get back to town and plan out our next steps, Frank.' She nods toward Fred Wheatley's flatbed truck. 'We can't keep poor Fred out here all afternoon. He has a garage to run.'

Frank nods. 'We can look through the Eaton catalogue I picked up in Edmonton. They have Land Settlement kits – houses, barns, equipment ... everything.'

Celie loops her arm through Frank's as they walk back to the truck. 'Isn't that something? Fancy buying a house from a catalogue.'

Frank pulls open the passenger door, and Fred Wheatley snorts awake. He yawns and stretches his arms. 'Ya all done for today? Nice piece of land ya got there. It's black as coffee under those stones and grass. Wheat grows like weeds in it.' He rubs his thumb and forefinger together. 'You'll be a rich man come five years, Frank Jeffries, or I'll eat my hat.'

Frank slides onto the seat beside Fred and helps Celie in beside him. 'I'll hold you to that, Fred.'

Fred turns the key in the ignition and the truck roars to a start. 'Don't know about you, but I'm starved. What say ya come along to the house for supper? Mavis is a fine cook, and there's always more than we can eat. You can meet the kids.'

'That's very kind, Fred,' Celie says, 'but we wouldn't want to impose—'

'Impose?' Fred says as the truck bumps down the dirt road. 'There's a word for ya. Mavis'll like ya. Someone intellectual to talk to. She's always got her nose in a book from the travellin' library. I'm a huntin' and fishin' man myself. You hunt or fish, Frank? We'll get ya out there. West Lake's just six miles north of here. The town used to be closer, but they moved it when they put the railroad in. Carted over the post office on the back of a horse wagon, can ya believe that? We can get some good fishin' up at West Lake. Full of pike, perch, salmon, trout, minnows, ya name it. Lots of other places around here, too. Alberta's got as many lakes as Swiss cheese's got holes.' He jabs Frank with his arm. 'Whaddaya say? Supper? I'll pick ya up at the hotel in an hour. Mavis'll be tickled pink, havin' guests.'

---

A little over an hour later, Fred parks the truck in front of a neat white-painted clapboard house about a mile beyond the modest collection of buildings that make up the hamlet of West Lake, Alberta. A profusion of late-flowering purple asters and carnival-coloured dahlias flutter in the chilly wind along the gravel path to the covered porch where a swing seat creaks as the wind pushes it back and forth. The screen door opens and a tall young woman with large grey eyes and hair the colour of a lion's mane steps onto the porch, followed by two children of about five or six who push past her and jump into Fred's arms, screaming and giggling.

'Well, hello, there!' the woman says, smiling broadly as the group clambers out of the truck's cab. 'I'm Mavis,' she says, waving. 'Those two little monsters are Molly and Arthur. Come in and take a load off. Fred's been telling me you're fresh from England. You'll have to tell me all about your trip. I've never been past Edmonton, let alone London, England.'

Celie climbs the steps to the porch and extends her hand to Mavis. 'Thank you so much for having us to dinner at such short notice. I hope we haven't inconvenienced you, but Fred said you wouldn't mind. If it's inconvenient, we can always come another t—'

Mavis laughs, her face as open and guileless as a child's. 'A handshake, is it? I don't stand on such formality.' She enfolds Celie in an enthusiastic hug. 'I hope you like mutton pie. I'm trying out a recipe from *The Canadian Home Cook Book*. It was my birthday present from Fred this year.' She rolls her eyes and laughs. 'The book, of course. Not the pie!'

Celie smiles, unable to resist the young woman's cheerfulness. 'That sounds absolutely delicious. I'm an awful cook myself. Mama had a cook, so my sisters and I never had much practice. Poor Frank doesn't know what he signed up for, marrying me.'

'Don't worry about that,' Mavis says as she opens the screen door and ushers Celie inside. 'I can teach you. I love cooking and baking. You can learn along with Molly and Arthur. Fred wasn't sure about Arthur learning to cook, but I put my foot down. No reason a boy can't learn to cook as well as a girl, I said. Just like a girl can learn to fish as well as a boy.' She ruffles her daughter's messy plaits as she runs by into the house. 'Molly caught us a big trout last time, didn't she, Fred?'

'Sure did. Put me to shame, for sure.' Fred pats his sturdy belly. 'Mavis is the best cook in Alberta, and that's no lie. Ya couldn't have a better teacher.' He takes Frank's hat and tosses it onto a hat stand by the door. 'We'll get some weight on ya, Frank. Ya'll need it for the winters we have here. The wind can blow a hole right through ya, if you're not careful. A little bit of fat'll keep ya grounded.'

'Where's your manners, Fred?' Mavis admonishes. 'Get the poor man a beer. Molly! Arthur! Set the table, please! You can play Cowboys and Indians later.' Mavis pats her belly. 'Heaven knows what this place will be like when the next one comes.'

Frank's eyes light up. 'Beer? I thought Alberta was dry.'

'Don't believe everythin' ya hear, Frank,' Fred says as he heads toward a shut door. 'Rules are meant to be bent. Mavis makes the best bathtub beer in West Lake, and that's sayin' somethin'.'

'Don't you dare tell Emma Philby in the Women's Christian Temperance Union that, Fred, or I'll be out of the treasurer job,' Mavis says. She looks at Celie. 'I get a stipend for that. It's not a lot, but every penny helps, especially when you have a husband with an appetite like Fred's.'

She beckons towards a doorway from which a scent of warm bread and roasting meat wafts. 'Come with me, Celie. I'm half-way through making bird's nest pudding for dessert. It's Fred's favourite. You can cut up the apples while you tell me all about you and merry old England. I can't tell you how nice it is to have a young woman my age nearby. And a reader, too, Fred says! I'll get you signed up to the travelling library when it comes through next month. I can tell we're going to be great friends.'

---

Celie and Frank stand outside the yellow frontage of the West Lake Hotel and wave at Fred's truck as it trundles down Main Street back toward his house.

'Well, that was interesting,' Frank says.

'It certainly was.'

'I can't say I'm unhappy to find someone who has beer.'

Celie laughs. 'You're an Englishman through and through, Frank Jeffries.' She takes hold of Frank's arm as they head up the steps to the hotel's front porch. 'Sweet Briar Farm. What do you think of that?'

'Sweet Briar Farm?'

'The name of our farm,' she says as she follows him into the hotel's spartan lobby. 'The land's full of briar bushes. The roses will be out in the spring, and they smell lovely.'

'They're weeds, Celie. I'll need to clear them out.'

'Not all of them, Frank. Let's keep some around the house. Papa had some in the garden at Clover Bar. They remind me of him.'

'All right. Just around the house,' he says as he collects the room key from the hotel clerk.

They climb the stairs to the first floor. 'I liked Mavis very much,' Celie says. 'She's the most cheerful person I've ever met. She's expecting as well, did you hear that? In March just like me. Mama would say it's a sign from God that we're meant to be here.'

Frank inserts the key into the lock and pushes open the door to their room. 'Your mother tends to attribute the most innocuous things to God's will. It probably explains a lot about her.'

# Chapter Three

## Etta

### Poggioreale Prison, Naples, Italy – October 1919

Etta Marinetti, twenty-five but looking much younger with her delicate porcelain-white features, hazel eyes, and the mass of dark blonde hair tucked under her wide-brimmed navy hat, follows the guard down the narrow hallway of the prison, her footsteps clicking on the grimy cement floor. The walls are a dull green, or had been once, though the crumbling grey plaster is eating away any nineteenth-century attempt at institutional decoration. The guard's keys dangle from his belt, jangling against his hip as he strides ahead. Etta takes a double-step to catch up and almost careers into him as he stops short in front of a closed door.

He unclips the keychain and shuffles through the keys. Jabbing one into the keyhole, he then pushes open the door. He gestures to her impatiently. '*Entrare. Entrare.*' He thrusts his chin toward the back of the room crowded with inmates and visitors. '*Lui è lì in fondo.*'

Etta nods and slips the agreed *lire* into the guard's hand. *'Grazie.'*

*'Solo dieci minuti. È un assassino bastardo.'*

Etta bites her tongue. Carlo is no murderer. Of that she is certain. She nods curtly. *'Dieci minuti. Grazie.'*

She enters the room and hears the door slam behind her. A thickset guard sitting in a chair by the door eyes her boldly. He leers at her and wets his lips beneath his thick black moustache. *'Ciao, tesoro. Vieni a trovarmi più tardi.'*

She glares at him. 'I don't speak Italian,' she lies. She scans the heads of the room's occupants; wives and mothers and their incarcerated men huddle over the narrow tables, whispering and weeping. Carlo is there, alone at a table at the back. His dark eyes meet hers, and she can see the pain of his suffering in them.

She pushes past the chairs and tables. He stands to kiss her and the guard shouts out *Don't touch!* in Italian.

*'Cazzo,'* Carlo swears under his breath. He gestures to the visitor's chair. 'Come, sit, *Etta mia*. The trip from Capri was fine? You are like the sun shining through a dark cloud. Imagine that I kiss you and I will do the same.'

Etta sits on the hard chair and studies her husband across the table. Dark circles press into the skin under his eyes, and his dark hair curls over his collar and falls across his forehead. His handsome face – the face she has loved since the day they first met at the art exhibition in London before the war – is rough with a month's growth of facial hair. The prison barber isn't keeping up with his job. 'You look tired, my darling. Are you sleeping all right?'

Carlo laughs. 'If only I could. I am squeezed into a cell with three other murderers. They do not make the most comfortable of bedfellows.'

'You're not a murderer, Carlo. Don't say that.'

He sits back in the chair. 'Are you so certain, *mio bell'angelo*? Everyone else seems to think so.'

'You would never be able to do such a thing to your poor wife in that lunatic asylum.'

Carlo frowns. 'Not a lunatic asylum. It was a sanitorium. The best in southern Italy.'

'I'm sorry. Yes, of course. A sanitorium. Why do they think Marianna was suffocated? Maybe … maybe she simply died in her sleep. You said she hasn't been well for years. Besides, someone in the sanitorium would have seen you if you'd been there.'

'They did see me.'

'Yes, but they saw you in the afternoon, and she was still alive when they brought her supper, wasn't she? So, you couldn't have done it.'

'Oh, Etta, it puts me at the sanitorium on the day of her death. It is enough for them to build a case against me. I had a motive, didn't I? I wanted my wife dead so that I could marry the mother of my love-child. It is a solid case as far as the prosecutor is concerned. *Un delitto passionale*. A crime of passion. I am only happy that your cousin Stefania has managed to keep your name and Adriana's out of the newspapers.'

'Cousin Stefania appears to have a few friends in high places.'

Carlo frowns, his eyebrows drawing together. 'I love you, Etta, but I have failed you and Adriana in so many ways.'

Etta reaches her gloved hand across the table, but curls her fingers as she remembers they mustn't touch. 'You haven't, Carlo. I love you with all my heart, and you have such a beautiful little daughter who loves you too.' She digs into her pocket. 'I have something for you.' She smooths out a much-folded piece of paper on the table. 'Adriana drew it for you. She insisted I give it to you today. She can be quite a little madam for a four-year-old. Cousin Stefania and Liliana spoil her terribly.'

Carlo strokes the vibrant scribbles of a yellow-haired girl and an orange cat sitting under a purple tree. 'Adriana and Alice the boy cat.'

Etta shrugs. 'She loves *Alice in Wonderland*, and the cat doesn't care one way or the other. Who's to say a boy cat can't be named Alice, nor a tree be purple?'

Carlo smiles. 'Spoken like an artist. We must be free to perceive the world as we wish.' He folds up the drawing and tucks it into his trouser pocket. 'I miss her. I miss you all so much, my darling. To survive all the years of the war on the Italian Front in the mountains only to be jailed six months after returning to you … on our wedding day! It is like God is a cat and I am a mouse He enjoys torturing.'

'I *will* find a way to get you out of here, Carlo.'

'*Etta mia,* the only thing that will work is money, and this we do not have.'

'You're wrong, Carlo. You're in the newspapers. You're famous.'

'Infamous. Notorious. This is not the fame I wished for. And what does fame matter, anyway? It is like a puff of air on a cold day.'

'There are people out there who support you, my darling. You said it yourself, Carlo. Everyone believes it's a crime of passion, and people love a tragic love story, don't they? Celie's written me from Canada and said the story has even reached the papers out there.'

She leans forward and lowers her voice. 'Carlo, listen to me. I've contacted several art dealers in Paris, and they've told me their clients are clamouring for your paintings and are willing to pay a great deal of money for them. We have every chance of being quite rich.'

Carlo huffs. 'Finally, I will be a rich and successful artist while I rot away in the Poggioreale for a murder I didn't commit. It is true when they say you must be careful what you wish for.'

'No, Carlo, it's not like that. Hear me out. Your trial is in May, and the prosecutors have no proof you killed Marianna except that one of the sanitorium staff saw you in her bedroom earlier that day. Once I sell your paintings, we will have money to pay whomever we need, and that, combined with the lack of proof …

you see, don't you, my darling? They will release you. They will have to.'

'I am not so certain, *cara mia*. You don't know what the police here are capable of.'

'This is why we must make as much money as possible while your name is in the papers.' Her smooth forehead wrinkles as she frowns. 'There's only one problem. I could only find eight finished paintings from your old flat here in Naples. The landlord had stored them in his shed with the onions, can you believe that? Surely you must have more in storage somewhere?'

Carlo runs his hand through his hair and sighs wearily. 'I left a few with your cousin Roger at the Omega Workshops, the work I'd done when I was in London. I have no idea if he still has them. Anything else was sold before the war, and now, with my hand …' He rubs his scarred and useless right hand with the fingers of his left. 'Thanks to the Germans I cannot paint any longer. I am finished. I have tried painting with my left hand but it is pointless. Adriana's efforts are better than mine.'

'*Due minuti, Signora Marinetti*!'

Etta nods at the guard. '*Si! Si!*'

'*Ah, tu parli italiano!*'

Etta rolls her eyes and looks back at Carlo. He frowns at the guard. 'What is that about?'

'Nothing. Ignore him.' She unbuttons her kid gloves and pulls them off. She drops her hands into her lap and reaches her right hand under the table until she touches Carlo's knee.

He clasps her hand and rubs his thumb over her fingers. 'I love you so much, *Etta mia*. I am so sorry for this. All I wanted was for us to be a happy family together, and now I have ruined everything.'

She curls her thumb around his. 'You've done nothing, my darling. We will prove it. I will find a way.'

They need money now. The defence lawyers have already eaten up most of her modest inheritance from her father, and, this time, there's no one else to turn to for help. She has always been one to float through life like a feather on a breeze, without a thought or care for the consequences of her actions, relying on others to solve any problems that arose – her sisters, her mother, Cousin Roger, Cousin Stefania, Carlo. Even her twin, Jessie, had called her selfish and irresponsible on more than one occasion.

Perhaps they were right. Running off with Carlo to Italy, three months pregnant, in the middle of a war was possibly not the wisest of ideas, but they'd been so in love, and she'd thought they would marry, but then she'd found out about Carlo's poor, mad wife Marianna and had lied to her parents about the marriage, and then he'd signed up for the army … It had been a mess on every front. Thank goodness her grandmother's cousin Stefania had taken her into her villa on Capri. It was not the first time Cousin Stefania had rescued a pregnant Fry woman, she'd discovered, though of course her mother wasn't a Fry then. That was a secret she needed to unravel one day.

She squeezes Carlo's hand under the table as an idea unfurls in her mind like a blossoming flower. *I don't see what's wrong with wanting what one wants. And I want you back, Carlo. I've waited all the years of the war for you to return. I wasn't meant to be alone with a child. I want us all to be a family. I'm not going to lose you again. Maybe you can't paint, Carlo, but I can. I'm every bit as good as you are. I will paint the paintings and take them to Paris to sell under your name. The dealers will be queuing to buy them, I'm certain of it. I will get you out of this place, no matter what it costs and whom I have to pay off. I will do it for you and me and Adriana. No one can take our perfect future away from us. I won't permit it.*

---

The bell jingles as Etta pushes through the door into the Giosi art supply store on Via Constantinopli opposite the Accademia di Belle Arti di Napoli. The manager, a man of about fifty with an extravagant moustache and round, flushed cheeks, greets her in Italian from behind the large wooden counter.

'Good morning, *signorina*! So nice to see you again. Isn't it a lovely day? October is so much better than the summer months, don't you think? One can breathe, at least! Are you here for more paint? I have some excellent grade linen canvases. Fifteen threads per square centimetre. Our great Neapolitan Vincenzo Irolli cannot get enough of them.'

'Excellent,' Etta responds in fluent Italian. 'I shall require six canvases to start with – I shall look at the sizes – rabbit glue, linseed oil, several new brushes both round and flat, turpentine and more paint, of course. I have quite a list, I'm afraid.'

'Of course, of course,' the manager says as he pushes past a young, eager-eyed assistant to join Etta beside the palette knife display. 'The *signorina* may be interested in our red sable brushes? Or, perhaps, our very best quality Kolinsky sable brushes made from the hair taken from the tail of the rare Siberian weasel—'

Etta tilts her chin and smiles from under the wide brim of her hat, fully aware of the effect of her dimples on susceptible men. 'Oh, how I would love some sable brushes, but I'm afraid I must resign myself to hog hair. Unless … no, I couldn't possibly.'

The manager's face flushes an even deeper shade of crimson as he ushers her toward the rear of the shop. 'We shall see, we shall see … I may be able to do something. Come, *signorina,* let me show you our latest paints.'

Etta tucks her hand into the crook of the manager's arm. 'You take such good care of me, *signor*.'

'Fabiano.'

'What a strong Italian name. It suits you perfectly, Fabiano. You will apply your best discount, won't you? I would be so very appreciative. The one you give Vincenzo Irolli?' She holds her gloved hand up to her mouth and whispers conspiratorially. 'I heard it is twenty per cent.'

Fabiano splutters. 'This is a very special discount, *signorina*. Irolli is Napoli's greatest modern painter.' His moustache twitches as he takes in the sight of Etta's quivering lip. 'But, for you, of course, of course. Twenty per cent, but please don't say a word to anyone. *Signor Giosi* would be most displeased.'

Etta turns her head so that Fabiano enjoys the full effect of her dimples. 'I promise not to say a word, Fabiano. On credit, of course, and free delivery to Capri.'

# Chapter Four

## Jessie

**Altumanina Health Clinic, Cairo, Egypt – December 1919**

'You look tired.'

Jessie Khalid raises a hand over her mouth to stifle a yawn, with little success. 'Oh dear, excuse me, Zara,' she says to her sister-in-law as she follows the final patient out of the clinic's examination room. 'I haven't been sleeping all that well. There's so much to do here, and not enough hours in the day. If only we had a full-time doctor, it would make a huge difference. Aziz does his best, but the hospital and these government negotiations take up so much of his time.'

Zara ushers the young pregnant patient out the clinic's ornately carved door and shuts it behind her. 'Why do you not ask him to train you in some procedures? You are as good as any doctor.'

'If only that were true, Zara. I saw a lot nursing in the army hospitals during the war, but that was patching people up. Dealing with illnesses is something else altogether. Honestly, if I were in England, I would train to be a doctor myself, but there isn't a chance of that here in Cairo.'

She picks up an envelope from the wooden desk. 'The Gezira Sporting Club sent us another letter today.'

'You cannot blame our patients for wanting to eat their lunches on their lawn amongst the trees and flowers, Jessica. In Islam, gardens are meant for rest, reflection and contemplation, not simply to gaze at from afar. It was good of Aziz to turn over Altumanina's gatehouse to us, despite Mama's disapproval, but I think some of our patients pretend they are sick as an excuse to spend a day out in the Sporting Club's gardens by the river away from the dust and noise of the city. Gezira Island is like an oasis in the middle of Cairo.'

Jessie unfolds the letter and perches on the desk. She reads out the letter. '*Once again, we must remonstrate with you about the influx of your patients onto the lawns of the Gezira Sporting Club, which are for the use of our private membership exclusively. Further incursions will result in our having to take up the issue with the local authorities and may to lead to the enforced closure of your establishment.*'

She drops the letter onto the desk. 'Can you believe that, Zara? Our "establishment" is here for the critical care of the local population who otherwise would have extremely limited access to health care. They make us sound like a gin joint. I wager it was that awful black satin and pearls set complaining. Those women never did like the fact that I married an Egyptian.'

'I should not worry, Jessica. Aziz will sort it out.'

'Aziz will sort what out?'

The two women look over at the tall, dark-haired figure of Doctor Aziz Khalid in a smart three-piece black suit in the doorway. He shuts the door as Jessie picks up the letter and tucks it into the envelope.

'Just another letter from the Sporting Club, Aziz. They're upset about our patients eating lunch on their lawn. We can add it to the ones from the Anglo-American Hospital and the Albanian Embassy across the road.'

Aziz greets his sister in Arabic and bends to kiss Jessie on her cheek.

'A kiss on your wife's cheek, Aziz! In front of your sister! You are becoming British,' Zara teases.

'I will never be British, Zara.'

'Mama would not mind if you were. She has no love for the nationalists. Not like you or I. She abhors the thought of Egyptians ruling Egypt one day. The riots this spring and summer quite unnerved her.'

'Our mother is from the old Turkish and Albanian ruling class, Zara. She hasn't a drop of Egyptian blood in her veins. She tolerates the British because they keep the Egyptians under their thumb, just as her uncle, the old Khedive, did. She is happy as long as she can continue enjoying a life of privilege. It is why she hates the Egyptian nationalists so much. If they get into power, she fears she will no longer enjoy the status to which she has become accustomed.'

Zara tuts, her gold earrings swinging beneath the blue scarf she has wrapped around her head like a turban. 'If Mama only knew ...'

Jessie glances from Zara to Aziz. 'Your mother doesn't know that you're both involved with the Egyptian nationalists?'

Aziz shakes his head. 'She knows we are sympathetic, as many Egyptians are, but not more than that. She thinks that I am spending all my extra time at the hospital. It is best that way. She has some dubious friendships. It would not be wise for the wrong people to hear of our involvement in the Wafd Party.'

'Yes, of course,' Jessie says. 'How did the meeting go with Lord Milner today? At least Lloyd George appears to understand that the British government must meet the Egyptian nationalists half-way to stop the riots that have been going on this year.'

Aziz sits on the desk beside Jessie. 'I was pleasantly surprised. He seemed open to what the Wafd Party leaders had to say.' He shrugs. 'We shall see what his report says when it is released. I believe he understands the British Protectorate cannot go on as it has. Over eight hundred people have been killed in the riots since the spring. This must stop or the country will descend into anarchy.'

Jessie slides off the desk and brushes out the wrinkles on the grey skirt of her nurse's uniform. 'A state into which the Gezira Sporting Club seems to believe the country has already descended.'

Aziz picks up the envelope and tucks it into the breast pocket of his jacket. 'I shall have a word with them. My father was a founding member and I fund the annual cricket trophy. I have no doubt a mutual agreement can be reached.'

---

Jessie steps out onto the marble balcony off their bedroom and looks up at the crescent moon. A brace of doves coos in the trees by the river and the cicadas fill the night with a low-pitched hum. The palm leaves rustle in a gust of wind and the scent of the climbing rose beside the bedroom window drifts through the air. She breathes in the cool air and wraps her dressing gown more closely around her body. Somewhere out there it is Christmas Eve, but not here. Not, at least, until January 6th for the Coptic Christians, like their cook, Marta, who is currently in the middle of her pre-Christmas fast.

Her mother will have decorated the tree in Clover Bar this evening, hanging the delicate glass baubles that Papa had bought from Liberty's every year: the jolly Father Christmas; the snowman with his stovepipe hat; the silver swan which was Etta's favourite; and the perfect red sphere the size of a grapefruit which was her favourite. It would be the first Christmas when none of her daughters would be with her. The third Christmas since Papa's death.

'You can't sleep again, *habibti*?'

She turns to see Aziz shrugging into his dressing gown. 'I can't seem to settle.'

He wraps his arms around her and rests his chin on her shoulder. 'You are working too hard. You need to rest.'

'I enjoy working. I could never be one of those ex-pat women playing bridge all day at the Sporting Club.'

He chuckles. 'Oh, I know. What is it that you said to Lieutenant-Colonel Purvis's wife at the cricket ball?'

'I said she was a pinch-nosed bigot. I'm sorry, Aziz, but she is.'

He turns her in his arms and kisses her. 'It is one of the many reasons why I love you, Jessica. You are forthright and uncompromising. I am more than happy to control the damage left in your wake.'

'Am I that bad?'

'Not all the time.'

Jessie smiles. 'Sorry. I should be more circumspect. That's what Mama always told me. "Be circumspect like Cecelia. She never gets herself into spots of bother the way you do, Jessica." Poor Celie. I hope she's managing all right out in Alberta. I imagine she's missing home tonight.'

'Ah, yes. It is Christmas Eve.'

'Maybe that's why I couldn't sleep. I'm thinking of home.'

'That is entirely understandable, *habibti*. I studied in London, remember? I know how important Christmas is to you.' He whispers in her ear. 'Turn around and close your eyes.'

'What?'

He laughs. 'Just do it. Don't argue.'

'All right.'

'Don't look until I say.'

'I won't.'

Jessie feels something cool drape around her neck. 'Happy Christmas, my love,' Aziz says as he fixes the clasp. 'You may look now.'

Jessie looks down and strokes the gleaming strand of black pearls. 'They're lovely, Aziz. I've never seen anything like them.'

'They are unique, like you, my lovely, green-eyed wife.'

'I have a present for you, too.'

'You know that's not necessary.'

She takes hold of his hand and rests it on her belly. 'I'm expecting, Aziz. Almost three months. Finally, after two-and-a-half years—'

'You're pregnant?'

She laughs. 'Yes.'

'*Habibti*!' He pulls her into his embrace. 'I love you, Jessica.' He covers her face in kisses. 'I love you with all my heart. You have made me the happiest man on earth. Finally, we will be a family. It is everything I have ever wished for.'

He hugs her against him, and she feels his heart beating against her breast. She shuts her eyes and lets the moment of happiness float about her, knowing that as soon as she reaches to catch it, it will fly out of reach like a bird taking flight.

# Part II

1920

# Chapter Five

Jessie

**Cairo, Egypt – February 1920**

Zara slips her hand into the crook of Jessie's arm as they amble through the crowds jostling in the narrow lanes of Cairo's sprawling Khan el-Khalili souk. She stops suddenly and points to an open-fronted shop. 'Oh, Jessica! They have new shoes over there. Come, let us have a look.'

'Another shop, Zara? Haven't you bought enough already? Mustapha's donkey cart is overflowing. We're meant to be shopping for the new nursery, not for shoes.'

Zara rolls her striking amber eyes above her face veil. 'My mother says a woman can never have enough shoes, Jessica, and on this one subject, I agree with her.'

'Well, my feet hurt, I'm thirsty as a camel, and I need to … I need to use the facilities. The baby's sitting on my bladder.'

'Oh, my goodness! I am so sorry, Jessica. How could I forget about the little one? You cannot tell at all with that coat you are wearing.' She grabs Jessie's hand. 'Look, there's a *sobia* stand. Let us have a drink there first.'

'What's *sobia*?' Jessie asks as Zara pulls her along the alley.

'It is a delicious drink made of rice and coconut milk. You will like it very much.' She slaps away a shop seller's wandering hand and stops abruptly in front of an open doorway hung with clattering beads. A hand-painted wooden sign of a palm and the words *Fortune-Teller* in several languages hangs over the door. 'Oh, Jessica! Let us have our fortunes told.'

Jessie frowns at the sign. 'It's a racket for money, Zara. Let's just go home. I don't think I can last much longer.'

Zara tugs Jessie toward the shop. 'We will ask to use the fortune-teller's facilities first. I like this word "facilities". It is very polite. I will remember this for the future.'

---

The fortune-teller runs her finger along a line on Jessie's right palm. She is Greek, possibly forty or sixty years old, or anywhere in between, with the pale olive skin and thick black hair of the Greek seamstress in her mother's favourite haberdashery shop in Lewisham. The woman's dark eyes sweep over Jessie's face.

'You are far from your home.'

'Well, yes. I'm English. I don't imagine that's too difficult to guess.' She glances at Zara, who has removed her face veil and sits in rapt attention. 'Really, I'm most appreciative that you allowed me to—'

'Use your facilities,' Zara interjects.

'Yes. I really don't need a reading. Zara, why don't you—'

The woman arches one of her thick black eyebrows. 'You have a sister who is your twin, but you are not alike in any way.'

Zara nudges Jessie's arm. 'She is right, is she not?'

'I have a twin sister. That's true. We're fraternal twins. We don't look alike.'

'There is another sister as well. Older than you.' The woman draws her black eyebrows together. 'She is not altogether your sister.'

Jessie grunts. 'Of course she is. That's Celie. She's a year older.'

The woman shakes her head, setting her gold coin earrings jiggling. 'She is older than that. Two years, I think.' She bends over Jessie's hand and taps a line. 'Yes, two years older.'

Jessie rolls her eyes at Zara. 'I'm afraid you're quite wrong.'

The fortune-teller looks across the table which is spread with a purple cloth and a stack of worn tarot cards. 'You do not believe me. You believe life is only what you can see.'

'Of course. I'm not a fantasist, unlike my twin Etta.'

'Your twin sister sees the other elements which shape this world.'

'I think Etta views herself as a heroine in a tragic romance. I'm more practical.'

The woman raises a long finger. Her fingernail glints bright pink in the dimly lit room. 'You must not tell me anything. It is for me to tell you.'

Jessie glances at Zara and raises her eyebrows. 'Right. Sorry.'

A whisper of a smile slides across the woman's face as she traces her finger along another line. 'There is a man, an older man. He is a man who works very hard. He cares very much for people.'

Zara nods, her lapis earrings bobbing on the shoulders of her black cotton cloak. 'That is my brother and her husband. He is a doctor.'

The woman reaches for Jessie's right hand and holds it palm upright. Jessie's skin tingles at the warmth of the woman's hand and she resists the urge to pull away.

'This man … this man …' The woman shuts her eyes and sucks in a deep breath. 'There is a child, as well.' She opens her eyes and regards Jessie with a hawkish intensity. 'You are with child.'

'Yes, yes! It is true,' Zara says, her bracelets jangling as she swivels in her chair.

Jessie throws her sister-in-law a cross look. 'Zara!'

'I am sorry, Jessica. She is very good.' She looks at the woman. 'You are very good.'

The fortune-teller folds her fingers over Jessie's hand. 'I am sorry. It will be difficult.'

'Of course, I know that labour is meant to be difficult. I've never understood why that's the case. Poor design, if you ask me.'

The woman shakes her head. 'There is a path which divides in two: one direction leads to great happiness and the other to great sadness. You hold the answer as to which path to take.'

'I hold the answer? I thought you were meant to be the one telling me my fortune.'

The woman slides her hand away and sits back in her chair. 'I can tell you the answer, this is not an issue. But you would not believe what I have to tell you.'

Zara looks over at Jessie and back at the fortune-teller. 'Is it my turn? Will I marry and have many children? Please tell me I shall be my husband's only wife. I do not wish for other wives in my household. It is enough I have Mama to live with.'

---

The elegant figure of Madame Layla Khalid rises from the wicker chair on Altumanina's shaded terrace like an elegant flower unfolding. The musty pine scent of frankincense mixed with the heady perfume of roses and sweet earthiness of patchouli wafts around her like a cloud. She reaches for the ornate silver teapot and pours out a stream of fragrant tea into two delicate tea glasses.

'You are late for tea.'

Zara kisses her mother on her cheeks. 'I am sorry, Mama. You know how busy the Khan el-Khalili can be.'

'Indeed, I do not. It is a place of filth and thieves. I shop only in Zamalek where one can rely on quality and service.'

'Oh, we went there as well, *Madame Khalid*,' Jessie says as she sets her packages on a table. 'I'm afraid my feet will never recover.' Jessie takes the tea glass Zara offers her and sits on the plump chintz cushions in a wicker chair. 'I had forgotten that Zara treats shopping like an Olympic sport.'

Layla Khalid sits down in her chair and observes Jessie with her kohled amber eyes. She strokes her long pearl necklace with her slender fingers. 'A woman in your condition should not be traipsing around the Khan el-Khalili. I am certain Aziz will be quite unhappy once he learns of this.'

Zara picks up a small butter cookie sprinkled with powdered sugar. 'He does not need to know, does he, Mama?'

Her mother huffs. 'At least with the clinic closed today, I did not have to suffer half the population of Cairo eating *falafel* and *mahshi* on our lawn. In case you have not noticed, our lovely garden has become the preferred picnic spot of your patients since the Sporting Club chased them away. What sort of impression do you think those filthy people crowded outside the gatehouse every morning makes on our neighbours? I dare not show my face at the Albanian Embassy next door any longer. The ambassador must look out of his window in disgust at the sight.'

'Mama, it is not as bad as all that. Our patients are extremely respectful and thankful.'

'Zara, I never agreed to this clinic in our gatehouse and am still incredulous that Aziz permitted such a thing.' Layla Khalid sighs dramatically. 'I am now nothing but a visitor in my own home. I must acknowledge that my place as Altumanina's chatelaine has been usurped by my son's wife.'

Jessie chokes on her tea. 'Madame Khalid, this is most certainly not the case. I could never have created such a beautiful home with all these antiques and draperies and what-have-you. I'm much more comfortable in the clinic. I wouldn't know the first thing about running a house of this size.'

Layla Khalid nods her turbaned head graciously. 'It is well you remember that your comforts are the result of considerable work and organisation.' She shrugs under her black silk *jellabiya*. 'At any rate, the clinic will not be an issue for much longer. As soon as the child arrives, you will have your duties as a mother to attend to.'

Jessie stares at her mother-in-law. 'Excuse me?'

Layla Khalid smiles over her tea glass. 'Really, Jessica, you cannot possibly continue working in the clinic once the child is born. Think of the diseases you might expose the poor baby to! My son and I have spoken about this, and he is in absolute agreement with me. The clinic will shut when the baby is born.'

'I beg your pardon! It most certainly will not shut.'

Her mother-in-law sets down her tea glass. 'It most certainly will. Speak to Aziz about it. You will see that I speak the truth.'

---

Jessie switches on the bedside lamp as Aziz quietly shuts the door and enters the bedroom. He sits on the side of the bed and kisses her.

'I am sorry, *habibti*. There was an emergency at the hospital. Another road accident. Something must be done about the state of the traffic. It is chaos at the best of times.' He unlaces his shoes and drops them onto the carpet. 'Did you and Zara have a nice day off shopping? Did you find anything for the nursery?'

'We had a lovely day, and, yes, Zara helped me negotiate a good price with a carpenter to make a crib for the baby.'

Aziz undoes his tie. 'It will be good to have the nursery back in its proper use. You will have no need of the room as your study once the baby is born.'

Jessie sits up against her pillows. 'I've been hearing quite a lot today about the shape of my life after this baby is born. Why wouldn't I need my study? It's where I do my work outside the clinic.'

He stands up and unbuttons his shirt. 'You will be busy with the baby, and besides—'

'I'm not closing the clinic, Aziz! I've worked too hard for it. I'm a nurse. It's what I've trained to do. It's what I *want* to do.'

'Jessica—'

'What exactly have you and your mother been discussing

about me and the clinic? Don't you think I deserve to be part of the conversation? And what about Zara? She's the practice manager. She's affected by this as well.'

Aziz sits on the bed. 'Jessica, please. Let me speak. I do not know what my mother told you, but we will not close the clinic.'

'Really? She said—'

He takes hold of her hands. 'Once the baby is born, I will increase my hours at the clinic, and we will bring in another nurse—'

'Another nurse? If you think I'm going to stop working at the clinic—'

'We will bring in another nurse until you feel ready to get back to work.'

She withdraws her hands. 'Why would your mother tell me that you would shut down the clinic?'

'Perhaps she misunderstood me.'

'That is rather magnanimous of you.'

He shrugs. 'My mother wishes to hear what she wishes to hear.'

She picks at a loose thread in the bedcover. 'What about my study?'

'We will move it into one of the spare bedrooms. It is not an issue.' He smiles and his dark eyes shine with amusement. 'I know better than to stop you from doing what you want in your life, Jessica. You are a stubborn, passionate woman, and I love you for that. You remind me of your mother.'

'My mother? Oh, good heavens, I hope not. She can be the most unreasonable woman. You have no idea the arguments we had when I signed up to be an army nurse.'

He leans over her and kisses her – long, deep, probing kisses that turn her blood to honey. The heat rises from her belly and slides over her body like a warm splash of water in the women's *hammam*.

'You are my life, Jessica. I will do anything for you.'

She reaches her arms around him and presses her body against his warmth. 'Anything?'

He looks at her, his eyes lit with an intensity she has only ever seen when they are alone. Sitting up, he pulls away the bedcover. He runs his hand along her leg, pushing the silk nightgown up her body as his hand travels higher and higher. 'Tell me what you want, *habibti*, and I will do it.'

---

The next day, as Jessie reaches up to lock the bottle of aspirin in the medicine cabinet in the clinic's examination room, a jab spears her belly like a knife thrust. She cries out as the aspirin bottle crashes onto the tiled floor.

Zara pushes open the curtain. 'Jessica?' She gasps when she sees the bloodstain on Jessie's skirt. She grabs hold of Jessie's arms. 'Jessica, sit. Quickly. Let me help you.'

Jessie gasps as another pain stabs her belly. She looks at Zara. 'Get Aziz. Quickly. It's the baby.'

# Chapter Six

## Christina

### Clover Bar, London – March 1920

Hettie enters the dining room, sifting through the post which she's just collected from the hallway floor. 'Looks like you've got a letter from Jessie,' she says as she sets the post on the table beside the rack of cooling toast. 'It's been a while, 'asn't it? Nuffing since Christmas. I'd be expecting a letter a fortnight if she was my daughter off in Timbuktu.'

Christina sits back in her chair and arches a fine eyebrow. 'Thank you for your unsolicited opinion, Hettie. Cairo is hardly the middle of nowhere. Now, if you can be bothered to bring me my boiled egg, I will ponder whether to go down to the Salvation Army office to find myself a new housekeeper.'

Hettie huffs and grabs the handle of the china teapot. 'I suppose you'll want the tea 'eated up as well?'

'That would be appreciated. We are not Americans. We do not appreciate cold tea and warm toast.'

After Hettie has left, Christina picks up the letter postmarked Cairo and slits it open with her knife.

*Altumanina*
*Cairo, Egypt*

*March 8th, 1920*

*My Dearest Mama,*

*I don't know how to start this letter, so I will simply write it down without any of the pleasantries and niceties you might expect. I have lost the baby. Aziz and I are heartbroken.*

*I became ill quite suddenly one afternoon in the clinic. It happened so quickly. Fortunately, Aziz was nearby at the Anglo-American Hospital and Zara ran to fetch him, but by the time he reached me it was too late. I'd lost a great deal of blood and I'd passed out on the clinic floor. When I woke up, I was in a bed in the hospital, but I was not well, Mama. I was weak and I contracted a fever. I've been here in the obstetrics ward in the hospital for the past fortnight. I made Aziz promise me not to telegram you as I didn't want you to worry. He has been by my side every minute he's been able, and Zara has been here reading the American fashion magazines she's 'borrowed' from the waiting room.*

*I am feeling much better now, and I shall be released tomorrow morning. I've had quite enough of all the fussing, poking and prodding, and I intend to be back working in the clinic within a few days. My doctor has warned of relapses and all that nonsense if I do so much as lift a finger for the next month, but what use is it to be British if one can't employ the famous British stiff upper lip when required? I've got to get on with things. No use crying over spilt milk and all that.*

*Aziz has not taken this at all well. He is so very sad, Mama. He tries to conceal it, of course, chivvy me along, but I can't help but feel that something has broken between us, and that it's my fault. I know that's ridiculous, even more so as I write it down, but it's what I feel. That I've disappointed him somehow, and I don't know how to fix it.*

*I am sorry if I am gloomy. I don't believe in wallowing in things, as you know, unlike Etta who lives for drama. And Celie hasn't had it easy this winter either, expecting a baby and freezing in a cabin in the Canadian wilds. She puts a brave face on it in her letters, of course; when she sets her mind to something, she has a determination I can only admire. What is the saying? She is 'an iron fist in a velvet glove', whereas I tend to whack people over the head with my bluntness. I know she and I have had our run-ins, but I do admire her. I always have.*

*There, it's said and done. I do feel better for having written everything down and for having you there to read it all. I know we are quite different, Mama, and that you have often (always?) questioned my choices in life, but I am happy that you got to know how wonderful my husband is when we were in London last May when you were ill with the flu. I love my life here in Cairo, Mama. My work is fulfilling, Zara is a lovely and supportive sister-in-law, and Aziz is everything anyone could ask for in a husband. There must of course be a weed in every garden, and his mother, Layla, is my dandelion amongst the roses. She never came to see me in the hospital, of course. Apparently, she has an aversion to sick people.*

*All my love to you. Do try not to alienate Hettie. You are a terrible cook.*

*Jessie*

'Everyfing all right, ma'am?'

Christina looks up from the letter. 'I beg your pardon?'

'I asked if you wanted me to refresh your tea and I got an earful of nuffing.'

Christina nods. 'Yes.' She forces a weak smile. 'Please.'

Hettie raises her eyebrows as she pours the hot tea into Christina's teacup. 'Everyfing all right wiff Jessie?'

Christina folds the letter. 'Couldn't be better. Pass me the sugar, Hettie. Where is that egg?'

# Chapter Seven

## Celie

**Sweet Briar Farm, West Lake, Alberta – April 1920**

Celie looks up from the kitchen table where she is peeling and cutting apples into a pie shell. 'Supper will be ready in a quarter of an hour, Frank.'

Frank shuts the door against the frigid April wind blasting across the fields where hillocks of grey snow are slowly dissolving into Sweet Briar Farm's muddy earth. 'Smells good. I could eat a bear.'

'I've cooked up a stew with the rabbit Fred dropped off yesterday. Mavis lent me her cookbook. I don't know how we would have managed this winter without those two.'

Frank sinks down on one of the two old wooden dining chairs Fred had managed to wangle off Ol' Man Forbes at the general store in return for a gallon of Mavis's bathtub beer. He doubles over as a coughing jag racks his body.

Celie pours him a glass of water from a pitcher on the table. 'You really should take Fred up on his offer to find you a local man to help you, Frank,' she says as she watches him drink. 'You shouldn't be trying to do everything yourself, what with your lungs.'

'My lungs are fine.'

She takes the empty glass from her husband. 'You know I'd be out there, too, if it weren't for the baby.'

He shucks off his muddy boots onto a newspaper Celie has spread out on the wooden floor. 'The man will have to wait. I have to buy a horse and a plough first so I can sow the wheat next month. Between Mr Eaton Catalogue and Ol' Man Forbes, I'll be lucky to have two cents to rub together before long.'

'I did try to say we needed to be careful with our money when we were in Montréa—'

'Enough about Montréal, Celie,' he says sharply. He rubs his forehead and huffs out an exhausted sigh. 'I'm sorry. I'm just tired.' He blinks his eyes and yawns. 'Where's Lulu?'

Celie points her paring knife at a cradle beside the pot-bellied stove. 'She's good as gold now that her daddy's home. She was cranky all day. She takes after her grandmother. She's not one to suffer in silence if she's displeased about something.'

Frank strides over to the cradle in his stockinged feet. He smiles down at the baby who is bundled up under a quilt, fast asleep. A tuft of dark hair has escaped from her cap and curls on her forehead.

'Hello, angel,' he whispers as he bends over the cradle. '"There was a little girl, who had a little curl, right in the middle of her forehead. When she was good, she was very good indeed, but when she was bad, she was horrid."'

Celie smiles as she watches Frank rock the cradle. The district midwife had had a busy couple of days at the end of March. First little Benjamin Wheatley on the twenty-sixth and Louisa not twenty-four hours later, just a week after she and Frank had moved from the one-room cabin Frank and Fred had thrown up in a week in October, into a new one-storey white clapboard house with a red-shingled roof.

Practically twins, Fred had called the babies, as he and Frank had 'wet the babies' heads' with Mavis's beer. *Funny how men do that,* Celie muses, *getting drunk after their babies' births, while their wives lie exhausted and damaged in their beds. You would have thought the men were the ones who had done all the work! Still, it was good to see Frank so happy, instead of frowning over the account book.*

'Lulu's going to be a daddy's girl, isn't she?' Celie says as she lays a grid of dough on top of the apples.

'I have every intention of spoiling her. If that makes her a daddy's girl, so be it.' Frank picks a slice of apple out of the pie shell and pops it into his mouth. 'There were times during the war … that I never thought—'

He clears the catch in his throat. 'I'll go wash up. That stew does smell good, Celie. I'll make a farmer's wife out of you yet.'

---

Frank shuts the bedroom door and stands for a moment, turning his head to listen to Celie move around the kitchen on the other side of the door. He moves past the brass bed with its crazy quilt on loan from Mavis and pours out water from the dressing table pitcher into a large china bowl. Rolling up his shirt sleeves, he splashes his face with water and scrubs his hands with soap and a nail brush from Forbes's store and dries them on a fine linen towel Celie brought from Clover Bar. Then he kneels by the bed and reaches underneath for the leather case.

He takes out his keyring and unlocks the brass lock. Reaching inside the case, his hand closes on the brass tin. The metal is cold in his palm. He sits on the bed with the tin and flips open the lid. Removing the syringe, he then selects a slender vial from its slot and fills the syringe with the colourless liquid. He stretches out his arm and taps at the crook of his elbow until a vein rises. He glances at the door, then he slides the needle into his vein.

The Harrods's advertisement for the soldiers' morphine / cocaine kit in *The Times* back in 1916 had been spot on. 'The perfect present for friends on the Front'.

He had bought it as his Christmas gift to himself that year when he was on leave in London. It had made the war and the pain of his injuries almost bearable.

The war may be over, but the morphine is his loyal companion, a perfect present for a new father trying to build a farm in a country thousands of miles away from the place of his birth with a wife he knows doesn't love him.

# Chapter Eight

## Christina

### Clover Bar, London – April 1920

*The sun is high in the blue, cloudless sky, and the wide turquoise sea sparkles where the sunlight kisses the crests of the rippling waves. Far below her, the waves crash against jagged limestone rocks at the base of the cliff, and gulls emit shrill cries as they swoop on invisible insects. She lifts her face to the sun and closes her eyes, inviting the warmth to penetrate her skin. She has taken off her hat, which her Cousin Stefania would disapprove of, warning her that the sun will bring out freckles on her nose, but she doesn't care in the least.*

*'There you are, my lovely siren. Are you singing to lure unwary travellers to their doom?'*

*She spins around and smiles at the boy at the top of the path. A smile lights up Harry's square face and his dark, brilliantined hair falls over his forehead. His blue eyes glint with amusement as he waves his straw boater at her. She smiles as he lopes down the path, easily negotiating the stones and tufts of scrub grass with his effortless athleticism.*

*'It worked, didn't it?'*

*He laughs as he throws his arms around her and lifts her into a twirl. 'If having you means my fate is sealed, so be it.'*

*He sets her down and leans in to kiss her. She giggles as she pushes him away. His eyes cloud over. 'What is it? Is something wrong?'*

*'No, silly. Everything is exactly as it's meant to be. I'm a siren, remember?' She thrusts her foot behind his leg and watches him as he teeters on the cliff's edge. His eyes – as blue as that wide Italian sky – widen as he flails, and his sturdy body, in its fine Savile Row linen suit, arches back as he falls away from the path, past the invisible insects and the crying gulls, until it splashes into the sparkling waves of the turquoise sea.*

*She picks up the straw boater that has landed at her feet and brushes off the dust. Setting it on her head, she then looks out at the idyllic Italian day and smiles.*

Christina opens her eyes. The room is dark, and she is momentarily confused. She sits up in her bed and reaches for the glass of water Hettie has left for her. She sips at the tepid liquid as the dream floats around her mind like a lost thought.

She'd been with Harry at the ancient Roman ruins of the Grotta di Matermania on Capri, where they'd met so many times that summer. Where she'd been so happy. So happy, until the day she'd told Harry of her pregnancy – the last day she'd seen him until the day in September outside Terroni's delicatessen.

His abandonment of her and her unborn child had been devastating. To have had to return to her father and her two aunts in Marylebone, alone with a baby in her arms, had been a fate she could never have imagined. Her aunts had been only too happy to exacerbate the humiliation of it with their snide comments and disdain of her 'Italian blood'. Worst of all, the disappointment on her father's face. And all the lies that he had been forced to construct on her behalf – that she'd married an Italian doctor from Capri whom she'd met through her late mother's relatives; that he'd died of the Russian flu shortly after the baby's birth; that she was now the widowed Mrs Christina Innocenti with their fatherless child, Cecelia Innocenti. *I lived in shame until Gerald rescued me and Cecelia from the lie.*

*Did you think of me after you abandoned me, Harry, pregnant with your child on Capri? I thought about you. I followed your progress in the Conservative Party in the newspapers. Read of your failed marriages, with you casting off your barren wives, one after the other, like a twentieth century Henry VIII scrabbling for a male heir. Poor you, Harry. You made a mistake leaving me on Capri, and now I see that you have been paying for it all your life.*

*It was a shock to see you so unexpectedly, but I've had time to deal with it now. You are just a man. Nothing more nor less. It's true that I was obsessed with you for quite some time. Through my whole marriage, much to my shame. It is possible that if we had married, we would be living separate lives now, as so many of your class do. There would have been no divorce, of course, with me being Catholic, so perhaps we would have descended into a mutual antipathy, passing each other in the hallways of our stately home on the Scottish Borders with a curt nod before escaping to our separate lives. Or perhaps we would have been happy, but for my own peace of mind, I won't dwell on that any longer. If I am to think of anyone, I will think of my dear late husband Gerald, who loved me despite knowing the truth, and whom I never loved enough.*

*All because of you.*

# Chapter Nine

## Etta

### Castel Capuano Courthouse, Naples, Italy – May 1920

Etta paces the marble floor in the enormous vaulted hallway of the Castel Capuano courthouse, which is crowded with lawyers and police and vocal Neapolitans, and exclaims crossly at a hefty bowler-hatted lawyer who ploughs into her as he argues with a client.

'*Scusi*,' he says, eyeing her like she is a stain on his expensive suit. '*Devi guardare dove stai andando.*'

The anxiety and frustration of the past months rise up inside Etta and the words tumble out in a stream of Italian. 'What do you mean *I* should watch where I'm going, you big lumpen ox? I think you've broken my toe, you idiot.'

The lawyer explodes in a barrage of Italian too rapid for Etta to understand, and is quickly joined by his client and several curious onlookers.

A hand clutches Etta's elbow.

'Come, *cara*. Come, sit. It shouldn't be too much longer before the judges make their decision.'

Etta nods at her cousin, Stefania Albertini. The older woman, though diminutive in height, takes control of the scene by dint of her queenly bearing and the solidity of her black-clad figure. A large maroon hat with a long turkey feather sits like a saucer on Cousin Stefania's bouffant pompadour – still jet black despite the fact that Stefania has reached her seventy-first year. The feather thrusts through the air like an epée whenever she turns her head, causing the incandescent men to duck and parry it with their elbows.

Etta cocks her chin at the men. 'You're right, Cousin Stefania. Let's get away from here before I break his toe, the stupid jackass.'

Stefania steers Etta down the hallway past the opulent painted frescos to a bench under a row of marble busts. They sit and Stefania pats Etta's hand. 'They are certain to release Carlo, do not worry. We will all be home at Villa Serenissima for our supper tonight.'

Etta expels an exhausted sigh. 'I hope so. You know, I left England with Carlo five-and-a-half years ago, and we've spent only twelve months together in all that time.'

Stefania pats Etta's hand. 'How can we know why the Good Lord shoulders us with such trials? You will come out of it stronger, I have no doubt.'

'Do you think so?'

'Of course. Look at you, *mio angelo*. You were a helpless, romantic girl about to give birth to her first child when you came to Capri. And then … well, you were ill for such a long time. I worried for you and for little Adriana—'

'I would never have done anything to hurt her.'

'Not intentionally, of course. But you weren't always conscious of your actions. I thank the Good Lord every Sunday that you came through it. Stronger, so much stronger. You've been a good mother to Adriana, and a good teacher to Liliana's grandson, Mario. He has applied to the Accademia di Belle Arti di Napoli, did he tell you?'

'I had no idea!'

'Mario may have wished to surprise you. His family is so proud of him. He will be the first Sabbatini to go to college. Liliana is beside herself with pride.'

'I'm so pleased. Mario has a great deal of talent.'

'But no one noticed this until you. He was simply my housekeeper's grandson, destined to shepherd his father's goats or join his uncle on a fishing boat. You nurtured his artistic talent and gave him the key to a bigger life. You saved him and now you are saving Carlo.'

'What do you mean?'

Stefania's eyes narrow as she regards Etta. 'I found your paintings. In the old shed at the end of the garden.'

Etta looks at Stefania as her stomach drops. She should have found a safer hiding spot. *Stupid, stupid mistake.*

'You were in the shed?'

'Villa Serenissima is my home, Etta. I sometimes have cause to visit its hidden corners.'

Etta looks across the great hall and stares absently at a giant wall painting of a classical goddess. She turns back to Stefania.

'So? I had to do something to keep myself occupied since Carlo's arrest.'

'And I've been delighted to see you so engaged with your art. I had worried that you might slip back—'

'I will never slip back to those days, Cousin Stefania.'

Stefania scrutinises Etta with her dark, probing gaze. 'I particularly liked the view you painted of the Faraglioni. It was nothing like the polite dabblings I have seen the tourists produce. It is bold and passionate. Do you remember I commented on it when you were working on it on the balcony?'

'I remember.'

'The thing is, *cara,* you signed that painting with his name. *Carlo Marinetti.* I looked and I found that they all were signed with his name. I can think only that you intend to sell them as Carlo's paintings.'

Etta purses her lips.

'All right. It's true. You won't say anything, will you? Carlo doesn't know. We need the money, Cousin Stefania. I've used up the money I inherited from Papa, though it wasn't a great deal anyway. The money from the paintings is our only income. The art dealer in Paris wants more, you know. He's already sold the ones I had Uncle Roger send him from London. Luckily Duncan Grant and Vanessa Bell had taken them down to their farmhouse in Sussex when Cousin Roger closed the Omega Workshops last year. The money will help pay for Carlo's legal fees—'

'Don't, Etta. Carlo will be released soon and he can paint them himself. I will not permit you to stoop to fraudulent activities.'

'But his hand—'

'He will simply have to learn to paint with his left hand. You should be painting your own work. It is not right to hide in Carlo's shadow. You are better than that. We can manage. My dear Federico left me well provided for, which is more than I can say for your husband.'

Etta narrows her hazel eyes. 'You don't like Carlo very much, do you?'

'I can see that he and Adriana adore each other, and that he claims to love you, and, of course, I know you love him. More than is wise. In my experience, it is always best for the man to love the woman just that bit more than the woman loves the man. It is a better balance.'

'You think Carlo doesn't love me as much as I love him?'

'I think, Etta, that he was wrong to make you love him when he was still married to another woman. For this, I cannot forgive him.'

---

Etta and Stefania settle onto wooden chairs in one of the courtrooms that has been carved out of the grand salons and ballrooms of the old palace. As the five judges file in, she glances around the room which has filled with reporters and the curious of Naples. On the opposite side of the room, Marianna's parents sit – the old Marchese Ludovisi, rigid-backed and sour-faced in a tailored grey suit, and the glamorous Marchesa Ludovisi, though the Marchesa's rumoured beauty is obscured by the wide brim and black veil of her hat. Beside her, a slender boy of about seventeen in a dark suit sits with his arms crossed, his handsome face a cloud of impatience. *Paolo,* Etta thinks. *That must be Carlo's son, Paolo.*

The room hums with murmurs and the scraping of chair legs on the marble floor. A door opens and Carlo is ushered into the room and over to a stand. The suit she'd brought him for the trial hangs off him, and his newly-cut hair and shaven face reveal the lines and hollows the months of sleepless nights and worry have etched. She glances at his hands, which he holds in front of him as the metal of the handcuffs gleam in the room's electric light. He looks over at the gallery, scanning the faces until his eyes rest on Paolo. His son turns his head away and whispers to his grandmother, who shakes her head and puts a black-gloved finger to her lips.

Carlo's eyes find hers, and again, like all the times before, her heart leaps. His brown eyes look into hers – the eyes of a wounded animal, of a creature resigned to its fate. The judge slams down his gavel, and the courtroom falls silent.

Etta watches the proceedings as if through water. The judge blurs and his words ebb and flow, now quiet, suddenly loud, then quiet again. She sees Carlo raise his hands to his face and shake his head. A policeman takes hold of his arm and leads him toward a door. She stands and hears herself cry out, and he turns his head.

'*Ti amo, Etta mia,*' he shouts. Then he is gone.

# Chapter Ten

## Christina

### Lincoln's Inn Fields, London – May 1920

Christina sits on a bench under the spreading, pink-flowered branches of a hawthorn tree and eyes the black door of a handsome red-brick building on the northeast corner of Lincoln's Inn Fields. Florid-faced barristers in curled white wigs and black gowns hurry in and out of the doors of the elegant Georgian buildings surrounding the London square, oblivious to the beauty of the peonies and forget-me-nots and the flowering hawthorns of the fecund oasis.

The bell of the Church of St Anselm and St Cecilia chimes one o'clock, and the doors of the buildings housing London's most prestigious legal chambers begin to open and close in a flurry as barristers and legal clerks rush out in search of a café or pub for their lunches. She glances at the address on the slip of paper she holds in her white-gloved hand and back to the building on the corner. She shouldn't be here; it's not too late to leave. But since that unexpected meeting in September, Harry has been haunting her mind like a spectral memory, waking her from her dreams at night. Perhaps if she sees him one more time, she can exorcise the ghost of their past. As it is, she can't close her eyes without seeing his face – the handsome face of the twenty-three-year-old boy she once loved.

The black door opens, and suddenly he appears, his black gown flying around his body as he hastens down the steps, though he has replaced his grey wig with his Homburg hat. She tucks the paper into her pocket and, rising, walks past a hawthorn tree to the entrance gate. If she times it just right …

'Oh, I'm terribly sorry!' Harry reaches out to steady the woman with whom he has just collided. 'Tina? Good heavens. What are you doing here?'

'Oh, my word! Harry? Fancy bumping into you again!'

He shakes his head in puzzlement. 'Do you have a meeting in one of the law chambers?'

'No, no, I was just on my way to Sir John Soane's Museum. I'm having to give a talk at the WI next week on Piranesi of all things.' She rolls her eyes. 'Our president, Ellen Jackson, visited the museum last month and saw the Piranesi drawings there. She thought they would make a scintillating subject for our June meeting and volunteered me to deliver the talk. So, off I go like a diligent student.'

Harry glances at his wristwatch. 'Look, why don't I join you? I have an hour before my next appointment. I … I feel I owe you an apology after our last meeting.'

'Do you? I feel I was the one who was rather, well, less than civil. I … I was taken by surprise.'

'Yes. Yes, indeed. I understand completely.' He extends his arm. 'Let me escort you to the Piranesis and we can catch up properly, shall we?'

Christina rests her hand on his arm. 'All right. That sounds perfect, Harry.'

---

Harry grabs hold of the brass knob on the wall panelling in the Picture Room of the Sir John Soane Museum and tugs at it. The large panel swings open with a groan.

'Now this is what you should talk to the WI about,' Harry says. 'Hogarth's *The Rake's Progress*. The tale of poor fictitious Tom Rakewell's journey from riches to rags in eight paintings.'

Christina stuffs her notebook into her handbag and peers at the collection of bawdy art. 'Goodness, I had no idea there were more pictures behind the wall panels.'

'Oh, yes. The more interesting pictures.'

She leans forward and reads the inscription below one of the paintings. 'Heavens. Does it really say "The Orgy"? Goodness, is he in a house of ill repute?'

Harry laughs as he shuts the panel. 'Those Georgians got up to quite a lot of naughty business.'

'I should say.'

'Have I shocked you? Should I not have shown you these?'

'Oh, no! I'm rather tempted to do my talk on Mr Hogarth's paintings rather than Mr Piranesi's decaying Roman ruins.'

Harry chuckles. 'I should like to see that.'

'Not as much as I would like to see Ellen Jackson's face if I presented the WI with a talk on "The Orgy".'

Harry laughs, and she sees the young man he once was in the curve of his mouth and the sparkling blue of his eyes.

'Have you seen everything you need to here, Tina? I should be getting back.'

She waves her notepad at him. 'I have all the notes I need. It's been lovely doing this with you.'

'Yes, it has. And thank you for telling me about Cecelia and your late husband and your other daughters. It sounds like you've had a good life. I'm very glad of that.'

'Thank you, Harry. From what I've read in the papers, you've done exceptionally well yourself. They're saying that you've every chance to be the next Prime Minister once Lloyd George is out.'

'Yes, well, I need to win over the Conservative Party first.'

'And I hear you're to marry again soon. You must be looking forward to that.'

'Yes. Yes, of course. Rose McClellan. A lovely girl. A soup heiress of all things. She has red hair, like you, though she is quite different.' He smiles wanly. 'More's the pity.'

A light-hearted response dies on Christina's lips. Her heart thuds like a drum in her chest and she feels her blood rise through her body. She must compose herself. She must keep her head.

They stand alone in the silence of the Picture Room, the quiet like a wrinkle in time. Then she is in his arms, and it is like all the years of their separation fall away, until they are just Harry and Tina, back on Capri in the magical summer of 1891.

# Chapter Eleven

## Celie

### Sweet Briar Farm, West Lake, Alberta – July 1920

Celie sings softly as she rocks the baby in her arms. *'Let me call you sweetheart, I'm in love with you. Let me hear you whisper that you love me too. Keep the love light glowing in your eyes so true. Let me call you sweetheart, I'm in love with you.'*

She brushes the soft brown curls off her daughter's forehead. 'You're a sweet little one when you choose to be, aren't you, Lulu?'

The baby stares at her with big blue eyes rimmed with long black lashes. She looks up at the ceiling and waves her chubby arms in the air as she emits a sound between a gurgle and a coo.

Celie glances at the ceiling and scans it for leaks as the rain pelts against the roof. 'Yes, I know. That's rain, sweetheart. It's been raining for days and days. Do you think we need to start building an ark? Maybe Mr Eaton has one in his catalogue. Wouldn't that be a good thing?'

Rising from the chair, she strolls over to the cradle. She lays Lulu down and draws the sheet up to the baby's chin. The baby yawns and squeezes her eyes tightly shut. Celie smiles as she rocks the cradle. How did she create such a little creature, as precious as a tiny bird, yet as wilful as a mule? She is sure Fred Wheatley can hear Lulu at his garage all the way in town when the baby decides it's time for a feed.

She wanders over to the kitchen table and picks up Frank's copy of *Modern Methods for British Farmers 1902*. She thumbs through the pages until she reaches the dog-eared chapter on 'Cultivating Barley in Norfolk and Suffolk'. She shuts the cover and sets the book back on the table. Wheat isn't barley, and the Alberta prairie isn't the soggy marshland of eastern England. She's told Frank as much, but he won't hear a word of it. 'English agricultural methods are the best in the world, Celie. Barley and wheat are both grains, and the Canadian prairies and Norfolk broads are both flat and fertile. Trust me, I know what I'm doing.'

She shrugs. Maybe he's right. What does she know about growing wheat? It's hard enough coaxing the carrots and potatoes out of the ground, what with the rabbits and the deer.

She glances out at the rain sheeting against the window. Thunder rolls overhead and crashes like the drums and cymbals of a percussionist at the crescendo of a symphony. The leaden sky flashes white, and a crack like the sky breaking in two reverberates through the wooden house. The air is heavy with humidity that the rain only seems to worsen, and she fans her face to cool her damp skin.

Frank is out in the fields with Fred, doing their best to rescue the young wheat from the battering rain. This weather isn't doing his lungs a bit of good; it's nothing like the gentle spring rains of England. Everything here is bigger and louder and harsher. The winter had shocked her to her core, her English coat and neat buttoned boots from Selfridges no match for the thigh-deep snow and grey spring slush. She'd had to telegram her mother to wire Frank's bank account fifteen pounds from her share of Papa's legacy money for new boots and a heavy coat from the Hudson's Bay Company, and for warm clothes and bedding for Lulu, but she isn't going to do that very often, even though Frank suggested she have the entire two hundred pounds of her inheritance wired to his bank account. He'd been quite cross when she'd refused, arguing that the money is of no use to them in England. But she feels better knowing that it's there. Just in case. It was their first big argument.

She looks back at Lulu, who is as peaceful as a doll in her cradle. Life on the Alberta prairie isn't at all what she'd expected. Oh, she'd known it would be hard work setting up the farm, and it is. No electricity. No plumbing. A well for water. A stove for heat. The cold that freezes your words in your throat; the wind that almost cuts you in two. Chickens and pigs to feed, eggs to hunt for, the two new cows to milk, the vegetable patch to tend, the water to draw from the well, meals to cook, the cleaning, the baby … She falls into bed half-dead by nine and is up at five to light the stove and start another day. How had she ever once had the time to study German, work in her father's photography studio, fight for women's suffrage, write newspaper articles, and play her mother's piano?

She misses the piano.

And she misses Max Fischer. She wanders over to the sink and looks out at the rain pelting against the window.

*'Please, let me help you.'*

*She looks over her shoulder into the blue eyes of the new German tutor as she shifts the pile of books in her arms. 'Oh, thank you, Herr Fischer. I'm afraid I overindulged at the library.'*

*He relieves her of several of the books. 'Ah, Goethe.* Wilhelm Meister's Apprenticeship. *You are in Professor Obermeyer's literature class.'*

*They head down the path toward Euston Road. 'Yes. I think he was rather shocked when I turned up in the class last week. He asked me if I had meant to join the German music appreciation class next door which he said was more suitable for ladies. I simply asked if this was the nineteenth-century German literature class, and when he said it was, I said, "Wonderful. I'm in the right place, then", and sat down at the desk right in front of him.'*

*Max laughs. 'What was his reaction?'*

*'I think the word is "nonplussed". He sputtered and harrumphed and grumbled something to the effect of "What is the world coming to? Women in my class!"'*

*'Oh, dear. I am very sorry for that. On behalf of my countrymen, I apologise.'*

*'No, no, no. I'm quite used to dealing with affronted men. I help in my father's photography studio. Some of our gentlemen customers can be quite … discourteous when faced with a capable working woman.'*

*'This is a pity. But we are in a new century of aeroplanes and motorcars. Women's roles will surely progress as well.'*

*'If I have anything to do with it, they certainly will. I'm one of those awful women fighting for women's right to vote. I haul my two sisters off to our local suffrage meetings every week. We shall overcome!'*

*'Ah, such passion and conviction! You would have my vote, Fräulein Fry.'*

*'Would I, Herr Fischer?'*

*He smiles. 'Without question.'*

*She stops at the omnibus stop. 'Here we are. The omnibus is just down the road. I shall relieve you of your burden.'*

*He hands the books back to her. 'It was my pleasure, Fräulein Fry. I shall see you in class tomorrow. I am afraid it is declensions.'*

*'Declensions? Oh, dear. Thank you for the warning, Herr Fischer. I shall brush up on them this evening.'*

*'You're welcome, Fräulein Fry. And, please, call me Max.'*

*She looks at the handsome young man in his black bowler hat and new grey suit. 'Then you must call me Celie.'*

Turning away from the window, she sits down in a kitchen chair and rubs her forehead. Where has that Celie gone? The Celie full of self-belief and convictions, looking to carve a future for herself that mattered. One where she could influence and encourage other women to have bigger dreams and claim the rights that should be theirs. Encouraged and supported by men like Max. No, not men *like* Max.

*Max.*

She is trying to be a good wife to Frank and a good mother to Lulu, but she is losing herself. Maybe this life would have been easier if Max *had* died in the war. She would have been able to lock away her past into the store of memory, and start over with Frank properly, the way she had intended.

She had been happy to marry Frank when she'd thought Max was dead. Frank had always been kind to her, thoughtful … and he loved her. She had convinced herself that she could love him, too, over time. But then, seeing Max again just a few weeks after her wedding, all the feelings she had suppressed through the long years of their separation during the war had risen to the surface.

She drops her head into her hands. She has to forget Max. Every time she thinks of him, her heart throbs with the pain of loss and her body shakes with longing. Longing for the feel of his hair under her fingers, the touch of his lips on hers, the warmth of his body pressing against her in the warmth of a summer night, the sound of his voice murmuring in her ear: *Ich liebe dich, Schatzi.*

I love you too, Max. I will always love you, and I hate myself for it.

# Chapter Twelve

## Jessie

**The Nile, Egypt – November 1920**

Jessie leans on the freshly painted white railing of the SS *Sudan* and watches a pair of *feluccas* slide past the steamship, their triangular white sails as graceful as swans' wings. Beyond the two small wooden boats, palm trees, reeds and a thirsty gazelle pass by as the steamship chugs down the great river toward Luxor. Behind her, the chatter of voices, the clink of glasses, and the occasional burst of female laughter filter over to her from the white-cushioned wicker chairs clustered along the railings.

The fortune-teller had been right. Her pregnancy had been difficult, the baby lost. The thing that had wrong-footed her had been Aziz's pain. The sadness he tried so hard to conceal, but that still clung to him like a scent. She had never really understood how much he wanted children until they'd lost theirs. He'd buried himself in his work at the Anglo-American Hospital, just as she'd filled her days with her work at the clinic, until they had become strangers sleeping in the same bed, the sensuous explorations of their early married life abandoned. Was this what the fortune-teller had meant when she'd said that there is a path which divides into one of great happiness and one of great sadness, and that the power to choose which path to take lay with herself?

She wants them to be happy again, the way they'd been when they'd first married. She'd thought that if they escaped from Cairo, away from the clinic and the hospital and Aziz's mother and the political meetings that Aziz and Zara slipped away to in the late evenings, they would have a chance to put the grief behind them and start over. Perhaps this was the good path the fortune-teller had spoken about; the path that she could choose. She had mapped out their long-delayed honeymoon to the temples of Luxor in minutes stolen from the clinic, burying herself in maps and the latest Baedeker guide to Egypt up in her study that was never a nursery, and had told Aziz to book off the six weeks they would need to travel down the Nile and back. The baby was lost and they had to heal.

They need this trip to find each other again.

---

'Penny for your thoughts?'

Jessie looks across her shoulder at the petite young woman in a stylish navy linen dropped waist dress and huge-brimmed navy straw hat that sits on her bobbed dark hair like a platter.

'Excuse me?'

The young woman grabs the ship's railing and leans over to wave at two young Egyptian fishermen sailing by on their *felucca,* who respond with wide grins and shouts of what Jessie recognises as Arabic endearments. The young woman laughs and glances at Jessie. 'You're not shocked, are you?'

'Why ever would I be shocked?'

The young woman's expressive face lights up and her large dark eyes flash as she graces Jessie with a pearly smile. 'I'm ever so glad of that. I've been watching you, you know. The Lonely Lady of the Nile, I call you. Not to anyone, of course. Just to myself. I thought, how interesting she seems, all wrapped up in her thoughts up on the deck here every afternoon before drinks and dinner. She's someone with a past, I thought to myself. I should like to know her.'

Jessie tries, without success, to suppress a smile. 'I assure you I'm not as interesting as you seem to think. I'm here with my husband for a holiday down in Luxor. Hardly mysterious, I'm afraid.'

'Ah, that very handsome Egyptian gentleman I've seen you with at dinner. So, that's your husband? I'd rather hoped he might be your illicit lover squiring you away from your dull army colonel husband whom you'd married at eighteen to escape a tedious life in the English countryside, despite the protestations of your vicar father and your dutiful mother.'

Jessie laughs. 'My, you do have an imagination!'

'So I've been told. It's probably not helped by all the romantic novels I read, nor all the stories of the Egyptian gods and goddesses my father told me as a child.'

She holds out a delicate hand. 'I'm Lady Evelyn Herbert. I'm going down to Luxor with my father, the Earl of Carnarvon. It's my first foray down here. Father's been coming down for years to visit a dig he's financing. We're quite an Egypt-mad family.'

Jessie shakes her hand. 'Heavens, that is all quite something. You have no need to make up stories about anyone else. It sounds like your life is quite exciting as it is. I'm Jessica Khalid. Jessie to everyone but my husband … and my mother.'

The young woman studies Jessie with curious dark eyes.

'I shall call you Jessica, I think. Did you know that Mr Shakespeare invented the name Jessica for Shylock's daughter in *The Merchant of Venice*? Imagine having a name invented by William Shakespeare!'

'I wasn't aware of that.'

'I am a font of facts, Jessica Khalid. My mother says I'm too curious for my own good, but I don't believe anyone can be too curious, do you? I must get that from my father. Curious, stubborn and wilful.'

Jessie smiles. 'I've been accused of those same qualities myself on more than one occasion.'

Lady Evelyn claps her hands. 'Oh, good. I shall look forward to getting to know you, Jessica Khalid. You'll be staying at the Grand Luxor Hotel, of course? Everyone does.'

'Yes, my husband and I are there for a month.'

'Wonderful. I'll be on the dig most days, but we must meet up. It shall be such fun having another wilful young woman around!'

---

**Grand Luxor Hotel, Luxor, Egypt**

'My word, Aziz, this is grand!'

Aziz takes hold of Jessie's elbow and steers her across the polished white marble floor and under the towering gold and maroon Moorish arches toward the Grand Luxor Hotel's bar. 'Come, Jessica. Let us have some hibiscus juice on the balcony before we go up to the room. As lovely as the boat was, I am glad to set foot on solid ground again.'

They pass through the bar panelled in dark wood and *mashrabiya* screens, where British and German tourists dressed in stylish silk dresses and linen suits sip cocktails and smoke, and out onto the large covered balcony. In a corner, a trio of Egyptian musicians in embroidered maroon *jellabiyas* and red felt *tarbouches* play a pear-shaped *oud*, finger cymbals, and a *djembe* drum, while a handful of the more intrepid tourists fan themselves and sip iced drinks in the afternoon heat. Jessie walks over to the green-painted wooden railing and grasps it as she closes her eyes and raises her face to the sun.

Aziz joins her by the railing. 'Be careful or you'll get a sunburn.'

'Who cares about that? I love the feeling of the sun on my face.'

She breathes in and expels a deep breath. She opens her eyes and points at the river. 'Look, Aziz, isn't it glorious? This is the kind of thing I used to dream of when I was a girl in London. Trips to exotic lands.'

Beyond the tall date palms, the Nile gleams in the sun as elegant *feluccas* skim the rippling water. The fringe of green vegetation on the far river bank gives way to a long flat limestone hill and mounds of desert sand.

Aziz nods at the hill. 'The tombs of the pharaohs are beyond the hill. We will need to hire donkeys to get there. You can bring your camera and take pictures for your mother and sisters.'

Jessie rests her hand over Aziz's and squeezes. 'I'm glad we came, aren't you?'

Aziz stares out at the idyllic scene. 'Of course.'

He slips his hand out from beneath hers. 'Let's have that juice, shall we? We can read what Baedeker has to say about the Temple of Karnak.'

# Chapter Thirteen

## Christina

### Clover Bar, London – November 1920

Hettie strolls into the sitting room at Clover Bar, sifting through a stack of letters. She pulls out a stiff cream envelope and grunts as she sets it on top of the pile.

'Looks like anovver one from Lord 'igh 'n' Mighty.'

Christina casts a sharp look at the housekeeper over the top of her reading spectacles. 'The post I receive is none of your concern, Hettie. I would appreciate it if you cease your assessments of it.'

The housekeeper shrugs her sturdy shoulders and passes the post to Christina. 'Just saying. It's a free country.'

Christina sets down her novel and takes the letters. 'There's no need to loom over me like a spectre.'

'There's somefing else.'

'Yes? What is it?'

A rustle of silk as a shadow darkens the doorway. 'Am I to be expected to linger in the draught of your hall to catch my death of pneumonia?'

The black-clad figure of her father's elder sister, Henrietta Bishop, just three years off eighty, stands as proud and imperious as a weathered figurehead on the prow of a ship. She thrusts her umbrella at Hettie as she enters the room, settling herself on the chaise longue like a queen preparing to hold court.

'Aunt Henrietta? Whatever are you doing here?'

Henrietta focuses her watery grey gaze on Hettie. 'Bring us some tea, please. None of that wretched Earl Grey. You do have English Breakfast tea, I assume?'

Christina draws her lips into a tight smile. 'English Breakfast tea for our guest, Hettie. I shall have Earl Grey myself, as is customary.'

Hettie stomps out of the sitting room, but not before Christina catches her shooting a gaze like daggers at the elderly woman's back. Christina bites her lip to suppress a smile.

'Aunt Henrietta, I seem to recall you saying once that you would only deign to travel south of the Thames when the United Kingdom becomes a republic.'

The older woman huffs as she peels off her black gloves. 'With Lloyd George's Liberals in power, we're as good as a republic in my view.' She tosses the gloves onto a side table. 'No, I am here on a serious business matter. You may be assured I would not have made the journey from Marylebone otherwise.'

'I was under the impression that after the furore you caused over Papa's will back in 1912, our business matters had concluded.'

Henrietta Bishop sniffs and dabs at a dribble from her nose with a lace handkerchief that she tugs out of her sleeve. 'You can scarcely blame me for wishing to keep the Bishops' valuable possessions in the hands of the rightful owner.'

'I am my father's – your brother's – only child. *I* am his legal heir.'

'Conceived with an Italian peasant outside of wedlock!'

Christina springs to her feet. 'You are not to speak of my

mother like that! My parents married. I was legitimate. The court agreed with me during your spurious claim on my inheritance.'

'Oh, do sit down, Christina. Stop making a spectacle of yourself.'

Hettie arrives with the tea and hovers in the doorway as she takes in the scene of the two seething women. 'Will you be wanting the tea in teacups, ma'am, or in your guest's lap?'

Christina makes no effort to stifle her laugh. 'Teacups will do, Hettie.'

Henrietta casts a withering glare at the housekeeper. 'How insolent! Christina, you cannot permit such impertinence from a servant.'

'Thank you, Hettie. Just set the tray down on the table.'

Henrietta follows Hettie's exit with a frown of disapprobation. 'If she were in my employ, she would be out in the street post-haste, you can be assured of that.'

'But she's not, so she isn't.' Christina hands Henrietta a teacup and saucer. 'I'm afraid I can't spend very long with you, Aunt Henrietta. I have a WI meeting I must leave for shortly.'

'I have no intention to stay here any longer than is necessary.' The older woman takes a sip of the steaming tea and wrinkles her thin nose. 'You must teach your housekeeper to make tea properly. It's been steeped far too long.' She sets down the cup and saucer. 'My mother's Royal Worcester china, I see.'

'*My* mother's china, you mean.' Christina sits back in her chair and scrutinises her aunt. 'What is it that you've come for?'

Henrietta harrumphs and folds her blue-veined hands in her lap. 'I have decided to sell the Marylebone house and move permanently to the country house in Yorkshire.'

'Why are you telling me this? You wangled that house out of my inheritance, and then insisted on living up in Yorkshire with Aunt Margaret, leaving that poor, lovely house – the house that Papa meant to go to me – empty most of the year.'

'I have not come here to re-tread tired ground, Christina, and I will not have you drag my poor, departed sister into the conversation.' She pulls the handkerchief out of her sleeve and dabs at her nose. 'I have had some interest in the Marylebone house as a girls' school.' She clears her throat and tucks her handkerchief back into her sleeve. 'However, upon enquiries with the family solicitors, it appears that my father bequeathed the family house to my brother's eldest child in the event of the death or the decision to vacate it by my father's last living child, which is me.'

Christina looks at her aunt, the teacup half-way to her lips. 'Are you saying *I* own the Bishop house in Marylebone after all?'

'No, I am not. *I* am the legal owner. However, I am unable to sell it because of my father's will. The house in Yorkshire needs a considerable amount of updating, and I require the funds to do so.' She takes a sip of tea. 'And I have no intention of you inheriting the Bishop house after my death.'

Christina laughs. 'Oh, how delightful! Grandpapa has spoiled your grand plan. You can't sell the house out from under me. I'm meant to have it after all!'

'Your grandfather died before the scandal of your father's marriage to the wanton daughter of an Italian tradesman. He would never have left their child the house had he known of it.'

Christina slams the cup and saucer down on the table. 'I have told you not to speak of my mother that way. Her name was Isabella. Isabella Innocenti Bishop and she was a decent woman and a wonderful mother.'

Henrietta waves her hand dismissively.

'Believe what you wish. However, it is a pity your father never reviewed your grandfather's will properly before he so cavalierly made you his heir in his will. We might have been spared all that unpleasantness after his death had he done so. When all was said and done, it was very clear that the family house was meant to go to my sister and myself, not to you.'

'Fine. Now, why exactly have you come here? According to Grandpapa's will, you can't sell the house, and I'm to inherit it after you die. I can't imagine you came here to give me good news.'

Henrietta purses her thin lips, causing a map of wrinkles to fan into her crepey skin. 'I have no intention of letting that Italian harlot's daughter take possession of our house. I intend to contest my father's bequest.'

'On what possible grounds?'

Henrietta opens the clasp on her handbag and removes a folded document. She sets it on the table beside the tea tray. 'On the grounds that my brother was coerced into the marriage by the Italian mistress who was expecting their child out of wedlock, and her money-grubbing peasant father.'

Christina grabs the document from the table. 'What are you talking about? This is a ruse to steal the house from me.'

'You were born seven months after the marriage, were you not? Not to be indelicate, but it is quite obvious that you were conceived out of wedlock. Just as your daughter, Cecelia, was. The apple doesn't fall far from the tree, does it, Christina? I am confident that I can have the court declare you illegitimate.'

'That's ridiculous. If that were the case, half of London would be illegitimate.'

Henrietta picks up her gloves. 'Be that as it may, I expect that, under the circumstances, you will not interfere with my sale of the house. I don't expect you would wish to have your name dragged through the mud.'

'I have no intention of letting you sell that house from under me.'

Henrietta stands up and pulls on her gloves.

'Temper, Christina. You will permit me to sell the house, because if you interfere, I shall let everyone know your inconvenient little secret. How do you think Cecelia will feel when she finds out she is a bastard?'

'You wouldn't dare.'

'Oh, my dear, I would indeed dare. I have engaged a very thorough investigator to uncover the identity of Cecelia's father.

Rest assured I will leave no stone unturned. If you don't forswear your future claim on the Bishop house, by the time I am through, your reputation will be in tatters. I don't imagine your WI will welcome a whore into their midst with open arms, nor your Catholic priest, for that matter. I shall see myself out.'

# Chapter Fourteen

Jessie

**Grand Luxor Hotel, Luxor, Egypt – November 1920**

Jessie snaps a picture of a hawk circling in the burning blue sky high above their heads. She glances over at Aziz as his donkey plods along the stony trail between the dull sand-grey cliffs of the valley. Ahead of them, their white-turbaned guide sways on a donkey as he idly taps the animal's haunch with a long twig. For the best part of the morning, they've been stopping at excavated doorways into the cliffs, following the guide down the subterranean passageways decorated with mysterious painted hieroglyphs, into empty musty chambers where some grand pharaoh had once laid. She has dutifully photographed their discoveries to send pictures to her sisters and mother, though she is aware she lacks Celie's 'eye' and will likely come in for a ribbing from her sister for her pedestrian efforts.

Since their arrival in Luxor the previous week, she has been doing her best to maintain her enthusiasm, to hold onto the feeling of excitement at their grand adventure, but though Aziz smiles and says the right things, and their nights are filled with murmurs and entwined arms, he withdraws from her to sleep before they engage in the intimacies which she has been hoping the holiday would rekindle. For some reason, a part of him is no longer within her reach.

Jessie fans her face with her straw hat. 'Do you suppose we might find some shade and stop for our picnic soon, Aziz? I'm afraid I'm quite tombed out.'

Aziz says something in Arabic to the guide, who answers with animation in a dialect Jessie finds impossible to decipher.

'He says, "Soon, soon".'

'All of that to say soon, soon?'

'Yes.'

Jessie sets her hat back on her head and sighs. 'Right, then. Soon, soon, it is.'

A quarter of an hour later, they reach a dig where an army of turbaned Egyptian diggers stab at the dull, dry earth with spades as they shout at the boys carrying buckets of water and rubble. The tall figure of Lord Carnarvon, dressed as if for a British garden party in a beige linen three-piece suit and wide-brimmed Panama hat, stands on a hill like a general as he points his polished ebony walking stick and shouts out directives to a harried-looking site manager. Several canvas tents with fly screens are pitched around the dig like a circus.

'There you are!' Lady Evelyn calls out as she pushes aside a fly screen and emerges from a tent. 'I thought you'd got lost in Queen Hatshepsut's temple.' She waves at the archaeologist, who is bent over a set of drawings spread out on a makeshift table. 'Howard, come over here! These are the lovely Khalids I told you about. Send someone up to fetch Father, will you? Fortnum's hamper won't keep for ever.'

Jessie looks over at Aziz. 'Did you know about this?'

Aziz smiles at her from beneath his Panama hat. 'You are not the only one capable of making arrangements, Jessica.'

Lady Evelyn approaches, dressed today in a feminine version of her father's linen suit and Panama hat. 'Slide off that donkey,

Jessica, and come have a gin and tonic. Howard does something to them which is just marvellous. Some secret ingredient he simply refuses to reveal, no matter how much I flutter my eyes.'

The archaeologist, a man of about forty-five with expressive brown eyes and a jaunty moustache, extends his hand to help Jessie off the donkey. 'Howard Carter, Mrs Khalid. I'm running the dig for Lord Carnarvon.'

'Oh, you're far too modest, Howard,' Lady Evelyn says. 'Father would be simply lost without him. Howard is an archaeologist extraordinaire. He and Father have been working together here for years looking for the tomb of a mysterious missing pharaoh. What's his name, Howard?'

'Tutankhamun.'

'Such a mouthful. How one is meant to remember that, I'll never know.' She shakes Aziz's extended hand. 'So pleased you finally made it out to Father's little dig, Dr Khalid. Ah, here comes Father now. Do let's go into the dining tent and have those drinks, shall we?'

---

Lady Evelyn sets down her crystal champagne coupe and focuses her dark gaze on Aziz. 'So, tell me, Dr Khalid, what made you fall in love with Jessica?'

Lord Carnarvon sets the chicken leg bone on the china plate and dabs at his lips with a linen napkin. 'Evelyn, don't put poor Dr Khalid on the spot like that. I do apologise, Dr Khalid.'

'Oh, Father, how am I meant to find out about men and love if I can't ask someone who can tell me?' Lady Evelyn says. 'I'm a debutante now. I should know these things.'

Aziz smiles. 'It is quite all right, my Lord.' He looks over at Jessie who is on her second cucumber sandwich. 'We met on a hospital ship during the war. She was by far the most competent surgical nurse on the ship.'

Evelyn sighs dramatically. 'That's hardly romantic. I mean what made you fall in love with her?'

Jessica raises an eyebrow at her husband. 'Yes, Aziz. I should quite like to know.'

'Besides the fact that my wife is stubborn, opinionated, and wilful?'

Lady Evelyn laughs. 'All excellent qualities in a woman, wouldn't you agree, Howard?'

Howard coughs and reaches for his glass of champagne just as the tent flap flies open and a dark-skinned young woman in jodhpurs, a white shirt, and an old, wide-brimmed US army hat stumbles into the tent, a Brownie camera in her right hand.

'Ah, excellent timing as ever, Ruth,' Lord Carnarvon says as he swats at a mosquito. 'Shut the fly screen, would you? These rotters are everywhere. They'll be the death of me.'

'Ruthie!' Lady Evelyn springs to her feet and embraces the young woman. 'I was starting to think you'd fallen into King Tut's tomb.'

The young woman laughs – a loud, uninhibited belly laugh – and she tosses her hat onto a camp table, releasing a bobbed head of wild black curls which frame her face like a dark halo. 'No such luck, Evie,' she says as she sets down the camera beside the hat, 'though I've got some good stuff about the dig from Howard for the papers back home. The Americans are lapping up your search for the missing tomb. All you need to do is find it and let me be the first one to write about it.'

'Of course, Ruth, my dear,' Lord Carnarvon says. 'You have certainly earned that right after all your work here these past few seasons.' He glances at Howard Carter. 'I wish that we had more to show for it than rocks and camels. My bank is getting quite cross with me. I'm afraid I won't be able to keep this dig going much longer.'

'Oh, Father, poor Howard and I have been hearing you tell Mummy that for years. You won't stop until you find that tomb. If

I'm in England when you do, you must wire me directly and I'll rush right out here. I shall want to be the first one in it.'

'You'll have to fight with Howard for that privilege, my dear.'

Lady Evelyn smiles coquettishly at the archaeologist. 'Howard will wait until I'm here, won't you, Howard?'

Howard clears his throat and rises from the table. 'I'm afraid you must excuse me. I must get back to the dig. Tutankhamun awaits.' He extends his hand to Aziz and then Jessie. 'You must stop by my house for dinner before you leave Luxor. It's just at the entrance to the Valley of the Kings. It's the only house over here. You can't miss it.'

'Just Howard and his dead pharaohs this side of the Nile,' Ruth says as she takes a glass of gin and tonic from Lady Evelyn. 'Don't know how you do that, Howard. It's creepy, if you ask me.'

'It's peaceful, Miss Bellico.'

Lord Carnarvon chuckles as Howard exits the tent. 'Hear, hear, Carter.'

Lady Evelyn looks at Ruth. 'I'm afraid we've frightened poor Howard off.'

'I'm quite certain you did, Evelyn.' Lord Carnarvon says as he rises and collects his hat and his walking stick. 'You two do torture the poor man.'

'We don't mean it, Father. I really do find him quite fascinating. He's taught me so much about Egyptology. I do mean it when I say I want to be here when you open King Tut's tomb. What an adventure that will be!' She squeezes her friend's arm. 'And you shall write about it all, Ruthie, and become famous!'

Lord Carnarvon sets his hat on his head and nods at Aziz and Jessie. 'I'm afraid I must leave you in the hands of these two dubious characters. The pharaoh awaits. We must meet for drinks and dinner at the hotel before you leave.'

After her father leaves, Lady Evelyn grabs Ruth's hand and pulls her over to Howard's vacated chair. 'Come, sit, Ruthie. Meet the lovely Khalids. This is Dr Aziz Khalid and his delightful wife, Jessica. Dr Khalid, Jessica, this is Ruth Bellico of Los Angeles,

America. She gallivants all around the world for the Associated Press. She's quite the best journalist and news photographer around.'

'Tone it down a bit, will you, Evie?' Ruth's large dark eyes flash with amusement as she extends her hand to Jessie. 'I'm a reasonably good journalist who takes functional pictures with a Brownie because, try as I might, photography is just not my thing.' She shrugs. 'Thankfully, the papers don't seem to mind. What do you do, Jessie?'

Jessie stares at the young woman, taken aback by her directness and casual use of her name. 'I'm a nurse. I run a clinic in Cairo.'

'My wife is quite a force to be reckoned with, Miss Bellico,' Aziz says. 'We met on a hospital ship off Gallipoli during the war.'

Ruth raises an eyebrow and scrutinises Jessie. 'Is that so? You'll have to tell me about that sometime. I do love a woman with a story. Are you the same?'

'I beg your pardon?'

'Do you love a woman with a story?'

Lady Evelyn pops the cork on a bottle of champagne and squeals as the cork flies into the tent's ceiling and ricochets off like an errant badminton bird. She hands the frothing bottle to Aziz.

'Would you do us the honours, Dr Khalid? I think we're in for a delicious afternoon. You still haven't told me what made you fall in love with Jessica.'

---

Jessie watches Aziz sway on the back of the donkey ahead of her. He's been quiet since they'd left the Carnarvon dig. It is like something hangs in the air around them, like an oppressive humidity she can feel but can't see.

It has been a pleasant day, as all of their days exploring the temples and sites of Luxor have been. Aziz was in fine form during the lunch, asking all the right questions of

Howard Carter and Lord Carnarvon, and laughing at Lady Evelyn's wry observations and Ruth Bellico's candid comments, even as he fended off their more intrusive questions with gentlemanly good humour. But now that they are alone – except for their guide, who pays them little attention – the feeling of something being off between them settles over her again.

'Aziz?'

'Yes?'

'You didn't answer Lady Evelyn's question.'

'Which question is that?'

'What made you fall in love with me?'

The donkeys' footsteps echo off the cliff walls.

'Aziz?'

He turns around to face her. 'I'm your husband, Jessica. You are my wife. We are together in this life. Isn't that enough for you?'

He turns away. A mosquito buzzes near Jessie's face and she slaps it away. The donkeys' hooves kick at the loose stones, kicking up puffs of dust. Ahead of her, Aziz, in his white shirt and Panama hat, sways on the donkey.

---

Jessie tosses her hat onto the dresser in their opulent Moorish suite. 'What is it, Aziz? Is it something I've done?'

Aziz strides past her and pulls open the double doors to their balcony and steps outside without answering.

Jessie follows him out onto the shaded balcony. 'Aziz? Please talk to me. I feel like I've been walking on eggshells with you ever since we arrived in Luxor. What's going on?'

He presses his fingers against his forehead as he looks out to the view of the limestone hill across the Nile. 'I am sorry, Jessica. It is nothing you have done. It is … it is nothing.'

All the months of frustration bubble up inside her like a pot boiling over. 'Don't be an ass, Aziz. It's something. I know losing the baby was difficult for us both—'

'I don't wish to talk about it.'

'We need to talk about it.' She clutches the railing as she stares out at the late afternoon sun shimmering on the blue water of the river. 'I'm only twenty-six, Aziz. There will be another child.'

'There won't.'

'What do you mean?'

'Jessica …' He shakes his head as he stares at the river.

'Aziz! What do you mean?'

He looks at Jessie, the muscle in his jaw flexing. 'Jessica, you cannot have any more children.'

'What are you talking about? Doctor Shaw told me I'm fine.'

'I told him to tell you this.'

Jessie's stomach lurches and her legs begin to shake. 'He lied to me?'

'Not entirely. He is too ethical for that.'

'I don't understand …' She shakes her head like she is trying to awaken from a bad dream. 'Just tell me the truth, Aziz. I was an army nurse, or have you forgotten? I was at Gallipoli, for heaven's sake! I can take it. Tell me the truth!'

He looks at her with eyes glazed with pain. 'Your womb was weakened by the miscarriage, *habibti*. You can conceive, yes—'

'Thank God. So, we can—'

'Jessica, Dr Shaw told me that there is a strong possibility that another pregnancy will kill you, or the baby, or both of you.'

'He what?'

Jessie grasps for the railing as the glittering Nile, the green palm trees and Aziz's face wheel around her like the view from a carousel spinning out of control.

---

'Jessica? Jessica, how are you feeling?'

Aziz brushes his fingers across Jessie's damp forehead as she opens her eyes. Their beauty – the colour of the purest Chinese jade – never fails to take his breath away. His beautiful, strong-willed, stubborn, passionate, green-eyed wife. He could not bear to lose her. A child is too high a price to pay.

He reaches for a glass of water and holds it out to her. 'Drink this. You will feel better.'

Jessie nods and sits up against the pillows on the large four-poster bed. He watches her as she sips the water. 'My darling, I am very sorry. I have been unfair to you since we lost the baby. I should have told you the truth.'

She hands him the glass. 'Yes, you should have.'

'It is the reason why—'

'Why you won't touch me.'

He sets the glass on the bedside table. How can he tell her how he had cursed the world and all the angels in Paradise for the tragedy that had been visited upon them? That the only woman he had ever loved, he could not now touch for fear of a pregnancy that could kill her? He would not be her murderer.

'I want our child, Aziz,' Jessie says. 'I know you do, too. You've told me often enough how much you are looking forward to being a father.'

Aziz studies his wife. It will not be easy, but, surely, she will come to understand the logic of what he is about to propose. 'Jessica, *habibti*, there is another way.'

'Another way?'

He reaches for her hands and holds them in his. 'I am Muslim. I can take another wife.'

Jessie gasps and pulls her hands away.

'Please, Jessica. It is not my choice, you must believe me, *habibti*. You would be the first wife. The most important wife. I know this is a strange concept for you, but it is a logical solution. Many people do this in Egypt. We can then have children—'

'*You* can have children.' She pushes him away and shuffles off the bed. She glares at him as she paces the carpets that cover the white marble floor. 'I married one man. You, Aziz. I am not of a mind to share.' She grabs her straw hat from the dresser and jams it onto her head.

'Jessica, wait. Let us talk about this.'

'I'm done with talking about this. Don't follow me.'

---

'Jessica! Where are you off to in such a huff?'

Jessie looks over at the stylish young woman sitting on the red velvet ottoman in the hotel's lobby. 'Lady Evelyn? Oh, I'm sorry. I'm rather on the moon. Are you waiting for your father?'

'No, Father's in meetings with Howard and some dreary Egyptian officials. I thought I'd read Ethel M. Dell's latest.' Lady Evelyn flourishes the novel. '*The Lamp in the Desert*. It's all about a passionate love affair in the desert. I thought it apropos.' She glances beyond Jessie's shoulders. 'Where's your handsome husband?'

'In the room. He ... he has some work to attend to.'

Lady Evelyn drops the novel into her handbag and rises to her feet. She tucks her arm through Jessie's.

'A lovers' spat. Marvellous. Let's go for a walk in the garden and you can tell me all about it.' She shrugs. 'Or not. It will be nice simply to have some female company. Ruthie's left for Italy. Someone named Mussolini is stirring up trouble in Bologna, so she's gone to report on it.'

They head across the gleaming marble floor and out the front door. Lady Evelyn takes hold of Jessie's hand and pulls her along a gravel path. 'This way. There's a lovely fish pond under some palms. We can watch the heron eye the goldfish.'

Jessie laughs as she hurries to keep up with Lady Evelyn. 'You remind me of someone I once knew. An Australian nurse named Ivy Roach. She had a knack for shaking me out of my gloom.'

'So, it *was* a lovers' spat! Come, sit. I like this bench the best. No one can see us from the hotel. It would be quite a place for an illicit tryst, don't you think? You should bring your husband here when you make up.'

'You're so sure we'll make up?'

'Of course you shall! He adores you, more's the pity. He takes no notice of any of the bored young daughters and wives who eye him like cats ready to pounce whenever he walks into the dining room. Don't tell me you haven't noticed?'

Jessie smiles. 'Yes, I've noticed.'

'So, tell me. Why so gloomy? You can't be bothered by those silly women.'

'It's not something I really wish to talk about. It's ... it's complicated.'

'Isn't everything?' Lady Evelyn casts her dark-eyed gaze on the grey heron lurking on the edge of the pond. 'He's rather prehistoric, don't you think? I can rather imagine him flying around with the dinosaurs.' She turns to Jessie and squeezes her knee. 'Whatever it is, I would encourage you both to kiss and make up. I see the way he looks at you when you're not aware.'

Jessie gazes at the hulking grey bird. 'Really?'

'Absolutely! Your husband's mad about you. It's plain for everyone to see. My goodness, I *aspire* to be looked at like that!'

'I don't imagine that's an issue for you, Lady Evelyn.'

'You're lovely to say that.' Lady Evelyn shrugs her slender, linen-clad shoulders. 'I simply never know whether it's because of me or because I'm an earl's daughter.'

'If it's any consolation, I would be tripping over myself to get to know you if I were a young bachelor.'

'And I would be flirting with you outrageously here in our little nook!' Lady Evelyn glances past the heron. 'Ah, there he is. I wondered how long it would take for your handsome husband to search you out.'

She rises and extends a delicate hand to Aziz. 'Dr Khalid, I'm afraid I squired away your lovely wife for some sisterly bonding. You must excuse me, but Father should be through with his meeting and will be expecting his gin and tonic in the bar. The sky will surely fall if I'm late for that!'

Jessie waves at Lady Evelyn as the young heiress skips past the heron, setting the bird to flight.

Aziz sits on the bench beside Jessie. 'It is nice for you to find a friend, *habibti*, especially when I have behaved so appallingly.'

Jessie picks at a green paint chip on the arm of the bench. 'Yes, well … yes.'

'Jessica, you do see the logic of what I was saying, don't you?'

Jessie shrugs. 'Logic isn't everything. I simply can't agree to it, Aziz. It's not the way I've been brought up.'

He sighs wearily. 'I understand. I shall move my things into one of the guest rooms when we arrive home.'

'What? Why?'

'Jessica, it is the only way. I can't … be with you. I love you with all my heart, but I refuse to do anything that might hurt you.'

'If you do that, it will hurt me more than anything. How could we even say we're husband and wife if we sleep in separate rooms?'

'Many husbands and wives do not sleep together, *habibti*. My parents didn't.'

'Well, my parents did. We'll find another way.'

'Perhaps.' He rises and holds out a hand. 'Come, we should get dressed for dinner. Lord Carnarvon has invited us to join his table. I expect Mr Carter will tell us all about the day's dig for this elusive pharaoh's tomb. Let us put all of this behind us for now.'

---

Jessie lies awake in the big bed, watching the shadows of the palm trees outside their balcony play on the bed's muslin canopy in the silvery moonlight. Beside her, Aziz breathes softly in his sleep, his body warm and solid under the fine cotton sheet. She shifts her leg against his, and he resettles, trapping her knee between his legs. She looks over at him. The moonlight draws a thread of silver light around the outline of his face. She has the urge to trace the silver line with her fingertips, but thinks better of it. They are at a stalemate.

He will not make love to her for fear of making her pregnant.

She will not agree to his marrying a second wife in order to have children.

She refuses to live an empty marriage. How can she, when she wants to throw herself at him, kissing him until they both go mad with their hunger for each other? Yet, here she is, her fingers itching to touch him even as she balls them into a fist that she presses against her belly.

She will find some French letters, those condoms that she knows the soldiers used on their visits to the Cairo cathouses. She is practical that way. She is a nurse; it shouldn't be too difficult. Surely, Aziz will see the sense of it, though she supposes lightning will strike her if she ever sets foot inside a Catholic church again. But, needs must.

As long as Aziz is in her bed, there is the chance of a pregnancy. She can wait. She is patient.

# Chapter Fifteen

## Christina

**Grenville, Montcrieff & Smith Solicitors, London – November 1920**

Harold Grenville, the 6th Earl of Sherbrooke, looks up from the large mahogany desk in his wood-panelled office as the door swings open. Christina rushes into the room followed by a flustered clerk.

'Chris— Mrs Fry!' he says as he rises quickly to his feet. 'To what do I owe the honour of your visit?'

'I'm terribly sorry, sir,' the clerk says, glaring at Christina. 'I'm afraid she wouldn't be stopped.'

Harry nods at the frantic clerk. 'Thank you, Rupert. Bring us some tea. Shut the door behind you.'

Christina tugs off her leather gloves. 'That's not necessary. I shan't be long.' Once the clerk leaves, Christina sits in one of the brown leather wingback chairs either side of the black marble fireplace and runs her fingers around her ear. 'You should have a fire in, Harry. It's frightfully cold outside.'

Harry kisses her on her cheek and sits in the other chair. 'Tina, I'm not sure it's wise for you to come to my chambers like this.'

'I know. It's just that … something's happened.'

Harry rests his elbows on the chair's arms and steeples his fingers. 'What is it? What's happened?'

'It's my Aunt Henrietta. There's an issue with the Bishop family house in Marylebone. She has decided to sell it and move up to Yorkshire permanently.'

'I'm not following, Tina. What has this got to do with you?'

'That's what I said to her when she showed up at Clover Bar yesterday unannounced. That gave me and poor Hettie a fright, I can tell you. Anyway, apparently my grandfather stipulated that the house be inherited by my father's eldest child after the death of all his own children. As it happens, that is me. It appears that Aunt Henrietta can't sell the house unless I agree. She said she's going to contest the will if I object.'

'On what grounds?'

'On the grounds that I was conceived out of wedlock and that my father was coerced into the marriage by my mother and her father. Aunt Henrietta intends to have me declared illegitimate.'

Harry picks up the poker and prods at a black lump of burnt wood in the fireplace. 'How long ago did your grandfather pass away?'

'Oh, years ago. Before I was born.'

He taps the iron poker against the hearth and sets it back on its hook. 'Then you have nothing to worry about. She's missed the time limit for contesting the will by years.'

'Oh. Good. Well, that's very good, but that isn't the only thing.' She fiddles with the fingers of her gloves. 'Harry, she's threatened to tell Cecelia that Gerald wasn't her father if I don't sign the house over to her. She's hired an investigator to find out who Cecelia's father is.'

'An investigator?'

'It will all come out, Harry. Everything. Maybe I should just sign it over and be done with it.'

A knock on the door and Rupert steps into the office, darting Christina a curious glance. 'Your next appointment has arrived, Lord Sherbrooke.'

Harry waves him away. 'Give him tea and some of those ginger biscuits from Fortnum's. I won't be much longer.'

'Certainly, sir.'

The door shuts behind the clerk. 'Don't sign over the house yet, Tina. You're a widow. It's a good thing for you to build up your financial assets.'

Christina leans forward and rests a hand on Harry's arm. 'Cecelia mustn't find out Gerald wasn't her father. It would destroy her.'

'Of course, Tina. I'll find a way to stop your aunt.'

'Are you sure, Harry?'

He reaches over to Christina and squeezes her hand.

'Absolutely.'

He sits back in the chair and looks at her, taking in her trim figure in the fashionable maroon coat and the black hat with the upswept brim that frames her beautiful heart-shaped face. Her jawline softer now, a few strands of white in her auburn hair, and lines fanning out from her cool blue eyes when she smiles, but still a handsome woman at almost fifty. 'Tina, what do you really want from me?'

Christina's eyes widen. 'What do you mean? I've come to ask for help with Aunt Henrietta.'

He runs a hand over his clipped grey moustache as he studies her. 'It's been five months since that day in the Piranesi Room, Tina. Five months of lunches in hidden pubs, walks in Hyde Park, and tea under the eyes of your scowling housekeeper. We're never alone. You insist we meet where there are other people around. Are we meant to be friends now? Am I your surrogate brother? Is that what you want?'

'No. I mean, I mean—'

Harry leans forward and her body tingles as his hands encircle hers in a warm grip. 'You keep me at arm's length, but that day in the museum, when I kissed you … I know you felt it too, Tina. I've missed you so much. So very, very much. I can't be just your friend. I want more than that. Tell me I'm wrong, Tina. Tell me you don't feel the same.'

She pulls her hands away. 'What about your fiancée? Miss Soup Heiress.'

Another knock and Rupert peers around the edge of the door.

'Blast it, Rupert! What is it now?'

'I'm sorry, sir. Your appointment is becoming quite agitated. I don't believe His Royal Highness is used to being kept waiting.'

'Fine. Fine. I'll be right there.'

Christina is already on her feet and tugging her gloves over her fingers. 'I shall leave with you, Rupert.' She holds out her hand to Harry. 'Thank you, Lord Sherbrooke. You've been most helpful.'

He squeezes her hand. 'You will consider my proposal?'

'I shall give it due consideration. Good day, my Lord.'

---

Christina stands on the concrete stoop of Harry's chambers and exhales a deep breath. Across the street, the leafless trees of Lincoln's Inn Fields grab at the dead white sky like gnarled grey fingers. She wraps her cashmere scarf tighter around her neck and shivers as a gust of wind blows down the street, stirring up the tired leaves that have collected in the gutters.

How has she let herself fall under his spell again? Despite the kiss, she had thought she could keep things cordial and platonic. He was good company. He'd always been good company. He made her laugh, the way she used to laugh all those years ago on Capri. She'd convinced herself it was harmless, that it was innocent because of his engagement to Rose McClellan. But she can't let it continue. Her love for Harry almost killed her last time. She should hate him for what he did to her. To Cecelia. But her body betrays her every time they are together. She despises herself for her weakness, but the desire that fires through her flesh when she is with him burns through every rational thought, every objection. She was a fool to think they could be anything but lovers.

She will have to end it before this love … no, this lust, the Lord help her … this lust consumes her entirely. As soon as Harry has dealt with her aunt and the investigator, she will break off these meetings. For now, she needs him. Henrietta mustn't discover the identity of Cecelia's father. If Harry can convince her aunt to relinquish her claim on the Bishop house, that accidental meeting with him outside of Terroni's delicatessen will have served its purpose, and she will be able to get on with her life.

# Chapter Sixteen

## Etta

### Villa Serenissima, Capri, Italy – December 1920

A bicycle bell in the lane outside Villa Serenissima rings. Inside, Etta applies herself with concentration to the canvas she has set up on the balcony. The sun has transformed the heavy grey winter sky to a soft blue, awakening the chiffchaffs and robins who perch in the branches of the parasol pines twittering. Five-year-old Adriana Marinetti sits at the table in the flowered art smock the housekeeper, Liliana, has made for her from an old dress, frowning over her drawing of the ginger tomcat, Alice, who is curled up on the cushion of a wicker chair.

Liliana Sabbatini comes out onto the balcony, her slippers slapping against the tiles. Her once raven hair, still gathered into the loose bun she has never seen a reason to update, is now almost white and her breasts and hips spread out like pillows beneath her sober black dress and white apron.

'A letter for you from your sister in Canada, *Signora Etta,*' she says in Italian. 'The postman asked if he can have the stamp for his collection.' She leans over Adriana and brushes the girl's soft golden curls with her hand. 'Adriana, I need to go into town to buy some fish for supper before Valentina Borelli and Ilaria Fusco buy up all the best fish. It is Friday, after all, and they are greedy cows.'

Etta laughs as she takes the letter. 'Liliana! That's not a very nice thing to say about your friends.'

Liliana shrugs. 'Your Italian has become too good, *Signora Etta*. Isn't that a lovely picture, Adriana? What is it?'

Adriana turns her dark gaze on Liliana, her round white forehead wrinkling in disgust. 'It's Alice, of course, Lili. I always paint pictures of Alice. Can't you see? This is his tail and these are his whiskers.'

'Oh, yes. Lili needs her spectacles, my angel. Would you like to come to the market with me? We can stop to buy some *stuffoli* from the *pasticceria*.'

'Oh, yes!' Adriana jumps up, her drawing in her hand, and thrusts it at Liliana. 'You can put this on your wall in your house with all the others, Lili.'

'Well, of course, my little mouse. Where else would I put such a lovely drawing of Alice?'

Etta watches her daughter follow her beloved Lili into the villa. If only Adriana would look at her the way she looks at Liliana. It's not like she hasn't tried to engage Adriana in games and stories – and now painting. Anything to regain the bond that has frayed since Carlo's arrest. Perhaps Adriana can sense the pretence of it all, can sense the balloon of emptiness inside her heart that grows larger every day of Carlo's absence.

It wasn't supposed to be like this. She and Carlo were supposed to live 'happily ever after'. She feels betrayed. Isn't love supposed to be enough? Isn't it meant to conquer all? Well, it doesn't. It's a lie, all a lie.

She turns back to the painting. A woman's hazel eyes stare back at her, direct, with a hint of challenge, and the long dark blonde hair flies about her naked body like a cape of silken strands. Behind her the shells and mosaics of the Grotta di Matermania glint in the Caprese sun, while in the curls of the sea a man waves his arms and sucks for breath in a sky hung with musical notes.

'Another painting of a siren, Etta?' Stefania says as she enters the balcony. 'And that grotto again. Why are you so obsessed with that place? Capri is full of lovely sites.'

'I'm painting a series based on the legend of the sirens of the grotto, Cousin Stefania. My next one is of the siren falling in love with a human.'

'That won't end well for either of them.'

Etta regards the painting. 'Why do you suppose it is that one of them must die if a siren falls in love with a human?'

'I imagine it is in atonement for all the sailors whom the siren has lured to their deaths by the sound of her song. Evil must be punished.'

'It doesn't seem fair to me. To be punished for love. If anything, love should be punished. Love is cruel.'

'Etta, I wish you wouldn't speak like that.'

Etta shrugs. 'Why should the sirens conceal the beauty of their voices because of the weakness of men?'

'Because men cannot abide a world where they are at the mercy of women, *cara mia*.' Stefania nods at the letter in Etta's hand. 'Liliana said you had a letter from Cecelia.'

'I imagine everyone on the island will know that within the hour.'

'What does she have to say?'

'I haven't had a chance to read it yet.' She raises a fine blonde eyebrow at her cousin. 'Oh, all right. Let's sit down in the sitting room and I'll read it to you. You're far too curious for your own good, do you know that?'

---

*Sweet Briar Farm,*
*West Lake, Alberta, Canada*

*November 10th, 1920*

*Dear Etta,*

*I am writing my Christmas letter early, as I suspect the post will take some time to travel all the way from Alberta, Canada to Capri, Italy – Jessie would love to be on that adventure, no doubt! I hope you will have a good Christmas with Cousin Stefania and Adriana despite Carlo's absence. Have you heard about whether your efforts for a retrial have been approved yet? It seems to me that you have a strong case, seeing as the evidence against Carlo is less than robust. Don't give up, Etta. I know his innocence will be proven in the end. Though I have never met him, I know he could not possibly be capable of such a thing.*

*Life out here on the Canadian prairie is interesting. The sky is immense and the land as flat and endless as the eye can see. Our little farm is coming together. I have a nice little house courtesy of the Eaton catalogue and we had a barn raising this summer to get our barn up (it's a custom here to help new arrivals put their barn up over the course of a weekend). We have two cows, two huge Percherons to pull the plough, more chickens than I can count, and four pigs. I've made a lovely friend here named Mavis who's been helping me with my new vegetable garden. Do you know that it's quite normal to eat sweet corn here? And I'd thought it was just animal feed!*

*Our Lulu is a sweet little thing, and Frank dotes on her as every father should dote on their daughters. He is eager to have another child soon, but I am in no great hurry. I am quite rushed off my feet as it is with tending Lulu, the housework, farm chores and cooking (Me cooking! Imagine that!). I can't see how I can fit another baby into all of this right now.*

*I do confess to missing my life in London. Sometimes I can't believe I ever was that person. So busy, so … earnest. It seems such a long time ago, but I mustn't complain. Frank is a good man, a good husband and father. I intend to be a good farmer's wife. It seems that is my lot now. I had thought I might write or take photographs for the local paper, but I haven't a moment to myself. To think I used to dream about becoming a German professor at a university!*

*Give my love to Cousin Stefania and little Adriana. Send me a photograph or a drawing! I have a corner in the bedroom where I stick up my favourite pictures of us all. The one of you, me and Jessie at the waterfall up in Yorkshire just before the war is pride of place right in the centre. I wonder when the three of us will be together again?*

*Thinking of you.*

*Your loving sister,*
*Celie*

Etta picks up the black and white photograph that has fallen out of the letter. Frank and Celie, with Lulu in her arms, stand on the front porch of a one-storey white clapboard house smiling at the photographer. Celie is in a plain cotton dress, with her hair pulled back in a low bun, and though she is smiling, there is something in her eyes which resists the happiness she attempts to exude. Frank is thinner than in the wedding pictures, though his smile as he gazes down at his swaddled daughter is the picture of joy.

She hands the photograph to Stefania.

'A lovely family,' Stefania says as she examines the photograph.

'Yes. It sounds like a hard life. But if anyone can manage it, Celie will. She's always been one to dig in and get things done without complaint. Celie was always the dutiful daughter, not the rebel like Jessie nor the romantic like me. I imagine she'll be a dutiful wife, too.'

'Just as you are, Etta?'

Etta jerks her head toward Stefania. 'Yes, of course. What do you mean?'

'I know you have sent the paintings to Paris. They are no longer in the shed.'

'I moved them.'

Stefania smiles wryly. 'Indeed, you did. To Paris. Etta, you forget Capri is a small island. Ilaria Fusco saw Mario loading several large packages onto the funicular last week. She told Valentina Borelli who told Ginevra Guarino in the *pasticceria* who asked me what Mario was taking to the ferry when I went in to buy bread last Thursday.'

'People should mind their own business.'

Stefania laughs. 'We are in Italy, *cara*. Everybody's business is everybody's business.'

'What did you tell her?'

'I told her that Mario was simply taking some of his paintings to the art college in Napoli. You would be wise to tell Mario this in case someone asks.'

Etta rises from the settee and wanders over to one of the large windows overlooking the sea. 'It seems we are a family of liars. I sometimes wonder when we will become so tangled up in our lies that we will end up caught in a web we can't escape.'

'You are talking about Cecelia, aren't you?'

Etta turns to face her cousin. 'The biggest lie of all. My mere fraud pales in comparison, don't you think? You and Mama and Papa hiding the truth about her father from her all these years. I wonder how you can look Father Izzo in the eye when you go to church.'

Stefania's face freezes. 'You haven't told her, have you? Please say you haven't said anything to your sister.'

'Why? Because then Mama would know it was you who'd spilled the secret?' Etta flops back onto the settee. 'No, I haven't told Celie anything. What can I tell her? I don't know who her father is. You wouldn't tell me that.'

'And Carlo? Jessica?'

'No, no one. Yet.'

'Good. Please, don't. It is best left in the past. I have told you too much already.'

Etta looks at her elderly cousin. 'It seems we have reached the end of our negotiation.'

'Negotiation? What are you talking about?'

'I will agree not to say anything to Celie in return for you turning a blind eye to my artwork for the Parisian dealer. You mustn't tell Carlo. Are we agreed?' She holds out her hand for a handshake. 'Cousin Stefania, are we agreed?'

Stefania's shoulders slump. She takes hold of Etta's hand. 'We are agreed.'

# Chapter Seventeen

## Celie

### West Lake, Alberta – December 1920

Celie steps into West Lake's new community hall, which has been strung with coloured paper garlands by local members of the Women's Christian Temperance Union. The hall, by far the largest room she's seen in West Lake, thrums with the sound of voices and the squeals of children playing tag amongst the crowd. On the stage at the front of the hall, a brass band crashes into an exuberant version of 'We Wish You a Merry Christmas' under the direction of the kilted schoolmaster. She clutches Lulu, swaddled in the pink blanket she has knitted, closer against her body as a throng of excitable locals push past her.

'All in good time, chaps. We've ladies with babies here,' Frank admonishes the men, who, judging from their heightened colour and glazed eyes, have indulged in someone's moonshine on the way to the town's Christmas party. The men doff their hats and mumble apologies to Celie and Mavis as they edge past them and head toward the tables spilling over with food.

Fred Wheatley removes his hat and runs his hand through his unruly ginger hair. 'Wouldn't mind some of what they've had.'

'There's plenty of that at home, Fred,' Mavis says as she shifts the papoose carrying Ben on her back. 'Check the baby, will you?'

Fred chucks the round-cheeked baby under his chin. 'He's right as rain, Mave. Thirsty as his dad, though.'

'He'll just have to wait. Now, where have Molly and Arthur gone off to? Honestly, Celie, you'll need to grow eyes on the back of your head when you have more children.'

As if on cue, Molly Wheatley, one of her brown plaits already unravelling – having lost its blue ribbon – peels through the crowd, her face smudged with chocolate icing. 'Mommy, they've got chocolate cake! With sprinkles!'

'Do they now? Is it as good as Mommy's apple cinnamon cake?'

'Better! Arthur's eaten three pieces!' Molly turns as she hears her name called by one of her friends. She waves at her mother and dodges back into the throng.

Mavis looks at her husband. 'Fred—'

'Yes, Mave. I'll go rescue the cake.' He glances at Frank and taps his breast pocket. 'Fancy a nip, Frank? Some of Ol' Man Forbes's best hooch?'

Frank looks over at Celie who rolls her eyes. 'Go ahead, Frank, it's Christmas. We'd be having rum punch at my mother's if we were back in England.'

Mavis points to a pair of empty chairs at a large table of women. 'Come on, Celie. Let's grab those. Your arms must be about to fall off carrying the baby.'

Celie follows Mavis over to the chairs, watching young Ben Wheatley eye her over the top of the embroidered suede carrier Mavis has on her back. Celie nods at the carrier as she adjusts the knitted cap on Lulu's head. 'What did you call that thing Ben's in, Mavis?'

'A papoose. Fred got it for me from the reserve.'

'The Indian reserve outside of town? I've heard it's not safe.'

'Oh, it's plenty safe. That's just the Temperance ladies sowing rumours. This papoose is the best thing ever. You should ask Frank to get you one.'

'I'm not sure what Frank would think about that.'

'What's it matter what he thinks, Celie?' Mavis wiggles her fingers. 'It leaves your hands free.'

Celie nods. 'That's all right, Mavis. We've ordered a baby carriage from Eaton's for Christmas.'

'Good luck with that. Have you seen the state of the roads?' Mavis unstraps the papoose with the sleeping baby and props it against the table leg and sits in a chair.

'What is it, Celie?' Mavis asks as Celie settles in a chair with Lulu. 'You've seemed … I dunno … a bit off lately.'

'Have I? I'm sorry. I'm simply tired, I suppose.'

'We're all tired. It's not that. You and Frank stepped off that train last year ready to take on the world. You had ideas about writing for the local paper and taking pictures again like you said you used to do in England. You haven't even borrowed a book from the travelling library for the past three months. What's happened?'

'Oh, Mavis, I'm not sure I know who I am anymore.'

'You're Celie Jeffries. Look into the mirror and tell yourself that every morning. It's what I do. *I'm Mavis Wheatley, world, and don't you forget it.* Then I make breakfast.' Mavis's large grey eyes light up as she smiles. 'We have a lot to offer this world, Celie. Being wives and mothers, of course, but other things, too. Things that will fulfil *you*.'

She reaches into a pocket on the side of the papoose and retrieves a page ripped from a newspaper. She hands it to Celie.

'What's this?'

Mavis taps the paper. 'You told me you speak German, didn't you? I saw this and I thought of you right away.'

In a small box in the lower right-hand corner of the ripped page, Mavis has circled a classified advertisement in blue ink:

*German-Speaking English Teachers Wanted for Fall Term*
*For schools in Edmonton and Surrounding Communities*
*Apply to PO Box 973, Edmonton Bulletin*

Celie looks over at Mavis. 'A German teacher? When would I have time—'

'Just write to them, Celie. Do something for yourself. What have you got to lose?'

# Part III

1921

# Chapter Eighteen

## Jessie

### Altumanina, Cairo, Egypt – April 1921

'We'll need more Dakin's Solution, silk thread and needles,' Jessie says to Zara as they enter Altumanina and head across the marble-floored hall toward the rear terrace. 'Oh, and a couple more thermometers. I seem to have a habit of misplacing those.'

'Yes, I have noticed, Jessica. You really must be more mindful. My supplier rubs his hands with glee whenever he sees me approach his stall in the souk.'

They enter the cool blue drawing room and skirt the careful arrangements of French settees and armchairs. Zara pushes open the French doors to the terrace.

'Oh, Mama! I am sorry. We didn't know you were entertaining guests.'

Layla Khalid looks over at them from the peacock chair where the ornate twists of wicker frame her elegant form like the throne of an ancient Egyptian pharaoh. She sweeps her languid gaze over

Jessie's creased and stained nurse's uniform and scuffed lace-up shoes.

'That is quite evident, Zara.' She turns to her two guests, a woman of about forty with heavily kohled eyes whose thickening figure has been dressed with some care in an embroidered rose pink *jellabiya,* and a girl of no more than seventeen, with delicate features and large dark eyes that dart around the terrace and the garden as though she is taking an inventory.

Layla Khalid gestures to the guests with a graceful sweep of her hand. 'Allow me to introduce Madame Abdallah and her daughter Zainab. The Abdallahs are a very fine family here in Cairo.' She settles her gaze on Jessie. 'We are discussing the betrothal of Zainab to Aziz.'

Jessie's jaw drops. 'I beg your pardon?'

'Madame Abdallah is most pleased with my proposal that Zainab become Aziz's wife.'

Zara gasps. 'Mama! You cannot possibly be serious.'

'I am most serious, Zara. Once the engagement has been arranged to everyone's satisfaction, I shall be turning my attention to you, although why any decent man would want you at the age of twenty-nine is difficult to imagine.'

'I do not wish to marry just anyone, Mama. Aziz supports me in this.'

Layla raises a black eyebrow. 'You are a terrible embarrassment to me, you are aware of that, Zara? To be unmarried and childless at your age? It simply cannot be permitted to continue any longer, no matter what your brother says.'

*'Madame Khalid,'* Jessie interrupts. 'With apologies to your guests, but Aziz has no need of a wife. *I'm* his wife.'

Layla Khalid smiles at Jessie, though her eyes are void of emotion. 'You are *a* wife.' She picks up the silver teapot and refreshes her guests' tea glasses. She sets down the teapot and spears Jessie with her amber gaze. 'A barren wife.'

A flash of anger flares inside Jessie. 'I am not barren.'

Layla sits back against the peacock fan of the chair. 'Oh? That is not what Aziz told me.' She smiles at her guests and indicates the plate of sweet pastries which Madame Abdallah is only too happy to plunder. 'You will forgive me, Jessica. I have guests to attend to.'

'Aziz told you I can't have children?'

'He did.'

'That's simply not true.'

'Is that so? Why then would *he* have suggested I meet with Madame Abdallah and her lovely daughter to discuss Zainab's marriage to him as a second wife?'

'He would never—'

Layla waves a hand dismissively at Jessie. 'You needn't worry if you are concerned that Zainab may steal away Aziz's affections with her youth and beauty and the children she will bear him. You have told me any number of times of Aziz's great love for you.'

'Aziz would never have suggested this. This is *your* idea.'

Layla Khalid smiles indulgently at Jessie. 'Oh, my dear Jessica. Aziz wants children even more than he wants you, you can be certain of that. He needs an heir to continue our line.' Her face hardens. 'I have every intention of becoming a grandmother, Jessica. I warn you not to impede me in this endeavour. You *will* fail.'

---

'Aziz, I need to talk to you.'

Aziz hands his hat and briefcase to Mustapha and looks at Jessie, who stands in the doorway of his study off the large entrance hall. 'Can it wait, Jessica? I have been on my feet in the surgery all day.'

'No. I need to talk to you now.' She enters the wood-panelled study.

He follows her and shuts the door. 'Yes? What is it?'

Jessie turns around, her arms folded tightly in front of her. 'You bloody well know what it is.'

'Jessica! What are you talking about?'

'What was Zainab Abdallah doing here with her mother today, being vetted as your second wife by your mother?'

Aziz runs his hand over his brilliantined hair. 'Jessica, *habibti*—'

'Don't you dare *habibti* me. I thought it was bad enough when Zara and I interrupted their cosy little tea party, but when your mother said *you'd* suggested it in order for them to discuss Zainab's candidacy as your second wife, I was so shocked I could barely speak.'

'Jessica, my mother has been at me constantly since—' He sighs heavily. 'She simply wore me down. It keeps her occupied. It means nothing. I would still need to agree to the marriage, and I have no intention of doing so.'

Jessie leans against the large mahogany desk. 'I don't know who to believe anymore. Your mother says you need heirs. That you're obsessed with having children.'

Aziz takes hold of her hands. 'I am not obsessed, but I would be lying if I said it isn't a concern of mine.'

Jessie whips her hands away. 'It's a concern of your mother's, too. She told me to keep out of her way and that she has every intention to see you married to Zainab. She wants me out of here, Aziz. You have no idea how much she hates me.'

'She does not hate you.'

Jessie laughs mirthlessly. 'Oh yes, she does. She wants nothing more than to get rid of me. I could feel it from the very first day I met her.' She turns away from Aziz and walks over to the window. She stares out at the wash of yellow and orange in the dusk sky. 'She said you told her that I'm barren.'

'Well, you are.'

She spins around. 'I am *not*! I've been to see Dr Shaw. He's confirmed that I can conceive. He's simply cautioned against it, but that doesn't mean we can't try. I can be careful. I can rest. Zara can manage the clinic; she's more than capable. We can have another child, Aziz. Let's at least try.'

'You will never rest. You will be in the clinic all hours of the day until you go into labour.'

'I won't. I promise.'

Aziz shakes his head. 'I can't, Jessica. What if …' He clears his throat. 'If anything happened to you, I would never forgive myself.'

'But, Aziz—'

'No, Jessica. There is nothing more to say. I will not endanger your life.'

Aziz strides across the room and pulls open the door, slamming it shut behind him.

---

Early the next morning, Jessie knocks on her mother-in-law's bedroom door. 'Madame Khalid? It's Jessica. I'd like to speak to you. It's important.'

The door swings open. Layla Khalid, elegant as ever in her black silk *jellabiya,* with her thick dark hair trailing over her shoulders, turns her back on Jessica and walks back into the room. 'You've spoken to Aziz.'

Jessica follows Layla into the large room, more of a suite than a simple bedroom, decorated in the high French style Layla prefers with an antique Aubusson rug, a Murano glass chandelier, an ornate silver-gilt rococo four-poster bed, and any number of settees and silk-upholstered chairs.

Layla sits on a stool in front of her vanity table and begins dabbing at her eyes with a kohl stick. She observes Jessie in the mirror. 'Yes? What is it? You can see I am busy.'

Jessie sits on a settee and watches her mother-in-law in the mirror. '*Madame Khalid,* I have been to my doctor. He has confirmed that I am perfectly capable of having children.'

Layla flicks her gaze at Jessie in the mirror. 'If that is so, why is Aziz proposing to take a second wife? Perhaps everything is not satisfactory in your marriage?'

Jessie's jaw tightens. 'You needn't sound so hopeful. I can assure you that everything is quite satisfactory. *More* than satisfactory.'

The older woman slips the kohl stick into its jewelled bottle. 'And yet, there is something.'

She has no choice. The only way to solve this problem is to get her mother-in-law on her side. 'There is a … complication. The miscarriage caused some damage. There is some concern … though I believe Dr Shaw is being overly cautious … there is some concern that I may either lose the baby or I may not survive childbirth. Or both. That's why Aziz refuses for us to have a baby.'

Layla turns around on the stool. 'I see.'

'The thing is, I want to have Aziz's baby. I've told him I will rest and be careful. If necessary, I could have a caesarean birth, though that has its own risks.'

'Why are you telling me all of this? It seems that the simplest solution is for Aziz to take a second wife.'

'No. I won't have it. That's why I need your help.'

'*My* help?' Layla Khalid turns back to the mirror and, picking up her silver hairbrush, commences to brush her long black hair. 'What makes you think that I would help you?'

'Because this is in both of our interests. I want you to convince Aziz that our having a child is the best … no, that it's the *only* solution. I want you to persuade him that my health is perfectly robust and that there is nothing to worry about. You want to be a grandmother and I want a child. Aziz will listen to you. You are his mother.'

Jessie meets Layla Khalid's amber gaze in the mirror. They scrutinise each other in silence for a long moment. Layla shifts her gaze back to her own reflection and returns to brushing her hair.

'As you wish, Jessica. I will help you. It is the least I can do for my beloved son's wife.'

# Chapter Nineteen

## Etta

### Villa Serenissima, Capri, Italy – May 1921

*Villa Serenissima*
*Capri, Italy*

*May 4th, 1921*

*My dearest darling Carlo,*

*Adriana has drawn you another picture of Alice, which she has insisted I send to you without delay for you to hang in your 'room'. She is quite cross with me that I forgot to bring it to you on Friday. I believe she thinks you are being kept in a castle tower, much like the characters in her fairy tales, but perhaps it is best that way. She is quite the little artist for a five-year-old! She is missing 'her Mario' awfully since he's gone off to the art academy in Naples and she has now become poor Liliana's shadow in the kitchen, though I can tell Liliana doesn't mind in the least. Adriana has become the queen of Villa Serenissima, and I am little more than a lowly courtier.*

*Stefania spoke to the mayor at the Labour Day festivities this past weekend, whom she says owes her several favours. He has been pursuing his contacts in the Naples judiciary. There is nothing concrete as yet, but the fact that there is no proof of your guilt in Marianna's death other than you being seen in her room that afternoon leaves the possibility open for a retrial.*

*Please, Carlo, tell me. Where were you the night of Marianna's death? Someone must be able to say you were with them, or that they'd seen you. The Marchese said in court that you didn't arrive at their villa to see Paolo until the following day. If only you had come here, my darling, but I understand you wanting to see your son. I saw him in the courtroom. I can imagine you looking like him when you were his age. He has your wild hair, though his eyes are the most intense aquamarine. Did Marianna have eyes like that?*

*There are days when I'm so awfully afraid, Carlo. Why is the world conspiring to keep us apart? I feel the grey wool starting to fill my head again. Liliana's tonic helps, but I don't want to be ill again the way I was after Adriana's birth.*

Etta taps the pen against her lips. How is she going to write this next part? She glances at the Penhaligon's perfume bottle beside the purple African violet on her desk. The tonic. It will help. It always helps.

Setting down the pen, she picks up the perfume bottle and removes the glass stopper. She pours a small amount into a water glass and drinks it in one gulp, shivering as the honey-sweetened laudanum spreads through her body like a warm wave trickling through parched crevices. She replaces the stopper and picks up the pen, chewing her lip as the pen hovers over the paper.

How can she justify leaving for Paris in the morning? Stefania has kept her promise and Carlo has no idea of the deception she has been undertaking with the sham paintings. Monsieur DuRose at the art gallery has sold most of Carlo's paintings from London and Naples, as well as the paintings she'd painted last year under Carlo's name, for excellent prices, and he will receive the new shipment of paintings when she arrives in Paris the day after tomorrow. This time she intends to be there to discuss improved percentages on the sale of the paintings.

There's only one way that she can think of. She will tell a truth and she will tell a lie so, really, it's only half a lie; only one and a half *Hail Marys* after Confession instead of three.

*Carlo, I had my friend Violet send the paintings you left with Cousin Roger at the Omega Workshops in London to Monsieur DuRose at the DuRose Gallery in Paris last autumn.* (This is true enough.) *I have had such an enthusiastic response from him!* (True!) *They are all now sold and Monsieur DuRose is itching to sell the paintings you have in storage in Naples.* (A lie; he's sold most of those now, too, although Monsieur DuRose is eager to sell more of Carlo's paintings, so it's only half a lie.) *I have decided to go to Paris personally with the paintings.* (The new sham paintings, that is. Is it a lie if Carlo misinterprets which paintings I mean?) *I feel that I will be able to negotiate better percentages for us if I am there. I feel so useless here. Liliana won't have me in the kitchen and Stefania is busy with her church activities and ladies' groups. Adriana is in school most of the day now, so there has been little for me to do except putter around and dab at my own paintings, but there are only so many coastal scenes and bowls of lemons I can paint! I simply feel we have no choice. The money I inherited from Papa has run out and we need money if we're to get you out of that awful place.*

*So, Paris. I have made appointments with several dealers and will be gone for just over a week. It's best for Monsieur DuRose to think he has competitors when I undertake the negotiations. I plan to travel to Paris tomorrow* (true) *with your paintings from the Naples flat.* (Yes, well, that's a lie. I'm travelling with the fake paintings.) *I know this is rather sudden and it would have been better to tell you personally, but I have only just received his letter, and everything has progressed so quickly. We must strike when the iron is hot! Monsieur DuRose has booked me into a nice hotel in Paris which is not too dear, and it is easy to eat well in Paris on very little with all their lovely boulangeries and patisseries.*

*Cousin Stefania will visit you next Thursday in my place and bring you some clean clothes and writing paper. I shall ask her to stop by Giosi's for a sketchbook and drawing pencils. You can start practising sketching with your left hand. With some practice, you will be as good an artist as you ever were!*

*All my love always,*
*Etta*

*PS: Mario says to thank you very much for letting him take over the lease of your old flat while he's at the art college in Naples.*

*PPS: I shall visit you as soon as I'm back and tell you all about Paris!*

Etta screws the cap on the fountain pen and blots the letter on the green blotter. *Well, perhaps that was more than one lie. Needs must, Carlo, as Celie always used to say. These 'newly discovered' Carlo Marinetti paintings will make us rich. I'll be able to pay for a retrial and a sympathetic judge, and then we can start our life all over. Just you, me and Adriana in our own house by the sea where we will paint, and love, and have babies, and live happily ever after.*

# Chapter Twenty

## Etta

**Paris, France – May 1921**

Etta examines herself in the mirror above the dressing table and tucks a wayward blonde curl behind her ear. She frowns and glances down at the ladies' magazine she bought at the Gare de Lyon. On the cover, a beautiful brunette beams coquettishly from beneath a cropped bob that ends just below her ears. She'd seen at least a dozen young women sporting the new hairstyle in the train station. It was spreading amongst fashionable young Parisiennes like dandelions sprouting in a lawn, just as their hems were rising – just below the knee! So daring!

She huffs at her reflection and slams her hat on her blonde pompadour. How has she let herself fall so behind the times? It simply won't do. She has one chance to make a good impression on the Parisian dealers, and it isn't going to be as a country bumpkin.

'Madame Marinetti! Such a pleasure to finally meet.'

Monsieur François DuRose of Galerie DuRose on rue La Boétie – the heart of Paris's top-end art galleries, a fact of which Monsieur DuRose is only too happy to remind his artists when they quibble over his commission – rises from his tufted black leather desk chair and extends an elegant, manicured hand.

'I trust your journey was not overly taxing, *Madame Marinetti*? The trains are so much more efficient now, though I am quite partial to taking the Orient Express as far as Milan when I travel to Italy and then changing for the Rome train. The Orient Express cannot be faulted for the quality of its service and its excellent *Filet de bar rôti à la fleur de sel de Guérand*. I can't recommend it enough, particularly paired with a 1900 vintage *Bordeaux blanc*. You must try that route the next time you come to Paris. You will find it most pleasurable.'

Etta graces him with her very best dimpled smile. 'I shall certainly have my travel agent look into that, *Monsieur DuRose*.'

He scans the attractive young woman, who is fashionably turned out in a peach jersey dress, daringly sitting mid-calf, and an austerely elegant hat on her stylish waved blonde bob. He smiles approvingly under his pencil moustache and gestures to a chair in front of the carved Art Nouveau desk.

'*Madame Marinetti*, please have a seat and we will talk about your husband's paintings. We were most excited to receive your latest shipment yesterday. They are quite astounding. His best work yet, if I might say.'

Etta settles into the bends of the bentwood chair and folds her hands in her lap. 'I'm delighted that you received them in good order. One is always worried that they will make the journey from Italy intact, what with the trains and the porters. It's one of the reasons I chose to accompany them this time.'

Monsieur DuRose takes a seat and rings a small bell. A thin young man with slick dark hair and round tortoiseshell glasses appears almost instantly. '*Gaston, le thé avec les madeleines, s'il te plait.*' The young man nods and slips back through a door as soundlessly as he'd entered.

The art dealer looks back at Etta. 'You like madeleines, I trust, *Madame Marinetti*? We are fortunate to have an excellent patisserie nearby.'

'I must confess, I've never had them.'

'Ah, then you are in for a delightful treat.' He rests his elbows on the arms of his chair and regards Etta as he steeples his fingers. 'I've noted from the last two shipments of your husband's more recent paintings that his style has changed quite radically from his pre-war work.'

'Oh?'

'I recall an exhibition of his at the Omega Workshops exhibition in London before the war and noticed some of the early artworks you had sent to me from London were some I'd seen then.'

'You were there? In London? I was there as well.'

'Oh, yes, I know. I saw you on the arm of Carlo Marinetti and your face on many of his paintings. I remember thinking what a lovely and charming young woman you were in both instances.'

'You are quite charming yourself, *Monsieur DuRose*.'

He smiles and brushes his fingers along his thin waxed moustache. 'At the time I felt his work exuded great promise and huge passion.'

Etta smiles and nods in acknowledgement of the compliment. 'I've always thought so.'

'But that it was … derivative.'

'I beg your pardon?'

'His earlier paintings leant rather too heavily on the traditions of Van Gogh and the Impressionists.' He shrugs. 'It is simply my opinion.'

He looks up as Gaston glides into the room bearing a silver tray of the tea and small golden cakes. 'Ah, merveilleux! You must try a madeleine, *Madame Marinetti*. I simply must insist.'

---

Etta bites her lip and feels the colour rise in her face as she watches Gaston set the tray down on the art dealer's desk.

*Derivative! How dare he say such a thing?* She scans the large grey-painted room hung with Cubist art. *Everyone is painting like Picasso now. You can't walk through Montmartre without being accosted by street artists offering to paint your portrait like a cube!*

Monsieur DuRose waves Gaston away. 'Milk? Sugar?' he asks as he hovers the milk jug over a teacup.

'Milk, thank you,' Etta replies stiffly

He offers her a golden madeleine on a delicate china plate. Etta shakes her head. 'One must watch one's figure.'

Monsieur DuRose's moustache twitches as he hands her the teacup. He places the golden cake on his plate. 'You won't mind if I do?'

'Not at all.'

Etta watches him break off a corner of the cake and savour it like ambrosia sent to Earth by the gods. He dabs at his lips with a linen napkin and looks at her.

'Can I be frank with you, *Madame Marinetti*?'

'I expect nothing less, *Monsieur DuRose*.'

'I was curious and intrigued when I received your letter about Carlo Marinetti's artwork. Had you contacted me before the war, I would have sent you a gracious letter declining your offer. However, recent events, unfortunate as they are, have made Mr Marinetti's work a valuable commodity. A commodity which I thought we might exploit during his moment of infamy to our mutual benefit.' He wipes a golden crumb from his lip with his napkin. 'Everyone loves *un crime passionnel*.'

Etta cocks her head and observes the art dealer. His black hair shines blue in the gallery's electric light, and his manicured nails gleam with what she suspects is a coat of nail varnish. She sets down her teacup and saucer on the desk and rises.

'It seems that I have made a terrible error in judgement coming here, *Monsieur DuRose*. I have appointments with other dealers to attend. I will arrange for the hotel to send porters to collect the paintings.'

Monsieur DuRose stands abruptly and gestures for her to sit down. 'Please, *Madame Marinetti,* do not be upset. I am simply putting into blunt language what any other dealer would be thinking. Carlo Marinetti's work is not unknown to us. We have seen it in minor exhibitions here and in Rome and London before the war.' He shrugs, the light catching the emerald-green satin of his bowtie. 'He is a competent artist, certainly. Better than most, even. But he was never one of the true geniuses.'

'*Monsieur DuRose—*'

The art dealer holds up a hand. 'Please, sit down, *Madame Marinetti*. I do not mean to offend you.'

'Do you not?'

'Please.'

He holds up a slender finger as she sits. 'This is what I thought, and the earlier of his paintings that I received did nothing to change my opinion, though I knew his new notoriety would make them appealing to a certain type of customer. As you know, I was proven correct and they sold reasonably well.' He breaks off another corner of the madeleine and pops it into his mouth.

'Then I unpacked the consignment of paintings you sent me in December, and the shipment I have just received. The new paintings … these are genius. The brushstrokes sure and confident. The use of colour remarkable. The blend of modernism and naturalism and images of wild imagination … they are like stepping into a dream that is both ecstasy and nightmare.' His dark eyes gleam with ill-concealed avarice. 'Please tell me, *Madame Marinetti,* there are more?'

*What is he saying? That* she *is a genius?*

Etta reaches across the desk and picks up a madeleine. She bites into the soft, crumbly cake, and she chews. It is delicious. She smiles at the art dealer.

'As I said, I have appointments with other dealers here in

Paris. I am here to negotiate the most favourable percentages on the sale of Carlo's art. If we can reach a mutually satisfactory agreement, then I will cancel these appointments and engage your gallery to represent all of Carlo's work. I can assure you there are many more paintings in storage on Capri. He was very productive before he enlisted in the army. I am vain enough to imagine myself his muse.'

The art dealer pushes the plate of madeleines across the desk to Etta. 'Please, have another

madeleine, *Madame Marinetti.* I shall have Gaston bring us more tea.'

---

**A few days later**

The phone line buzzes and hisses as Etta presses the receiver against her ear.

'Hello? Mama? Mama, it's Etta. I'm in Paris.'

'Etta! My word! Is everything all right?'

Etta twirls the telephone cord around her finger as she looks out through the glass door of the hotel's telephone cubicle. 'Everything's fine. More than fine. I've had a meeting here with a dealer for Carlo's paintings. We'll have more than enough money to arrange a retrial and get Carlo out of that awful prison. It's quite medieval, Mama. I can't bear seeing him in that place.'

'You haven't had an easy time of it since you left home, have you? Honestly, Etta, eloping like that in the middle of a war … the anxiety you caused us. I'm glad your father isn't alive to see what you're going through now. It would break his heart.'

'Don't say that, Mama. You'll make me quite melancholy.' She turns her head to look at a commotion by the hotel's entrance where a stylishly dressed young couple remonstrate with a taxi driver.

'How is Adriana?' her mother asks. 'When will you bring her

to London? Here I am a grandmother to two granddaughters and I've never seen either! It really won't do.'

'You'll be travelling out to Celie and Frank's farm in Canada to see Lulu, then?'

'Good heavens, no. I am far too old for that nonsense.' There's a pause on the line. 'Will you be coming to London? I haven't seen you in almost six years. Not since you chose to run off to Capri with your artist. It's only a short journey from Paris on the train.'

'I'm sorry, Mama. Not this time, I'm afraid. I must get back to Carlo and Adriana. I have rather left Cousin Stefania in the lurch.'

'Of course. Quite.'

'Next time. I promise.'

'Indeed.'

'Mama ... there's something I need to speak to you about. It's been weighing on my mind since I found out.'

'Yes? What is it?'

'Mama ... I know about Celie.' A long pause on the line. 'Mama? Are you there?'

'What do you mean by that?'

'After I was so ill following Adriana's birth, you wrote me that you'd been on Capri before you married Papa. You said that you understood more of my situation than I would ever know.'

'Yes, well, my father had sent me off to Cousin Stefania's after my mother and my brother died during his birth. Papa thought it would be good for me to get away from the trauma. Cousin Stefania was to teach me Italian. What has this to do with Cecelia?'

'I know you met someone there, Mama. A man. I know that Papa wasn't Celie's father.'

A pause on the line.

'Etta! My word, what a fabrication! What nonsense has Cousin Stefania been putting in your head? She should never—'

'Don't blame Cousin Stefania. I forced it out of her after I found out she'd written you to tell you that I'd lied about my marriage to Carlo, and that he was still married to Marianna. I had just had Adriana, and Carlo had left for the war, and I had no idea if I would ever see him again. I didn't want to worry you and Papa. I was so angry at her for writing to you. I demanded she tell me what you meant by writing that you understood my situation.'

'What did she tell you?'

The operator's voice comes onto the line requesting additional payment.

'Mama, I—'

The line goes dead.

Etta leans her forehead against the phone and hangs up the receiver. Maybe she should never have said anything. Certainly not over the telephone. What was she thinking? What business is it of hers anyway? If anyone should be asking questions, it's Celie. But, then, Celie doesn't know that Gerald Fry wasn't her father. Who was? Who did their mother meet that summer on Capri?

Why does she have to be burdened with this secret? All she knows is that it's not her place to tell Celie. It has to come from their mother.

She is pondering whether to ring back when she is disrupted by a pounding on the cubicle door. She looks over to see a young woman with a wild dark blonde bob and painted bee-stung lips waving at her to exit.

Etta pushes open the door. 'Yes? What is it?'

'Hi, doll. You wouldn't happen to have a few francs on you, would you?' The woman jabs a white-gloved thumb toward the entrance doors. 'The cab driver is giving poor Scott a hard time because we haven't had a chance to change our money yet. We're just off the boat from the States. We're good for it, I promise you.'

'Uh … well, all right.' Etta steps out of the cubicle and opens her handbag. She takes out her coin purse. 'How much do you need?'

The young woman cranes her neck to glance into the purse. 'Five, maybe? Or ten? I'm absolutely famished, and we can't get a *sou* till the banks open in the morning. Are you staying here?'

'Yes, till next Thursday.' Etta digs out the coins and drops them into the woman's gloved hand.

'Fab, doll. You're a peach. We'll see you at breakfast. Not too early.' The woman spins around and heads toward her husband and the irate taxi driver.

'Excuse me!' Etta calls out. 'Who are you?'

The woman turns around and holds out her arms like an actress about to take a curtain call. 'I'm Zelda. Zelda Fitzgerald.'

---

A week later, Etta is folding her new purchases into neat piles in her suitcase when there is a staccato rap on her bedroom door. She opens the door to see Zelda Fitzgerald dressed in a cerise satin cocktail dress with a fashionable handkerchief hem and matching satin shoes.

'Hello?'

'Doll, it's me. Don't you remember? The phone box?' She opens the clasp of her beaded evening bag and, fishing out a ten franc note, hands it to Etta. 'Thanks awfully for the loan. Sorry I missed you at breakfast the other day. Bet you thought you'd never see hide nor hair of me again. Scott and I ended up tripping the light fantastic at the opening night of Le Perroquet above the Casino de Paris and the days have simply flown by ever since. We only just got up an hour ago and I'm famished.' She pats her stomach. 'Eating for two now.' She walks past Etta into the bedroom, taking in the half-packed suitcase.

'Oh, crisis!' Zelda exclaims. 'You're not leaving already?'

Etta shuts the door and follows her into the room. 'I'm afraid so. On the eight o'clock train to Rome tomorrow morning.'

Zelda shoves aside a stack of blouses and sits on the bed. 'No, no, no, you simply mustn't. Stay a few more days. Scott is such a bore during the day, scribbling away at his novel, and I know you and I are destined to be great friends. Say you'll change your ticket in the morning and come out to supper and dancing at Le Perroquet tonight. It's absolutely to die for. They're giving away the most charming little *poupée* dolls to the most beautiful ladies. We're both bound to get one.'

Etta regards Zelda as the glamorous interloper pulls a slim cigarette out of a silver cigarette case and commences a choreography of lighting, sucking and expelling streams of white smoke.

'That sounds lovely, Zelda, but I really should finish packing. My family is expecting me back in Capri the day after tomorrow.'

Zelda pulls her pretty face into an exaggerated pout. 'Oh, pooh.' She stubs out the half-finished cigarette in a water glass. 'Wait a minute.' Her face brightens. 'Why not come out tonight and simply not go to bed? Scott and I will get you to the train station in time. Promise!'

Etta chews her lip. Oh, how she'd love to go out dancing. It had been so long. But she really shouldn't. 'When would I sleep?'

'Sleep? Who needs to sleep when Paris is on their doorstep?' Zelda grabs one of Etta's new purchases, a lavender silk sleeveless gown decorated with crystal beading, off a pile. She walks over to Etta and holds it up against her, the cigarette dangling from her red lips. 'Where are you going to wear this in Capri? Doll, this deserves Le Perroquet.'

Etta looks down at the new Jean Patou dress. Zelda's right, of course. She wasn't about to wear it at the Capri market or, Heaven forbid, at the Poggioreale Prison. It had been a terrible extravagance, but she'd simply not been able to resist, and she had been quite gratified by the turned heads and murmurs she had generated when she had entered Le Train Bleu on Monsieur DuRose's arm the previous night.

She takes the dress from Zelda and scrutinises her reflection in the vanity mirror. She catches Zelda's eye in the mirror and smiles. 'I suppose I can always sleep on the train.'

# Chapter Twenty-One

## Christina

### Clover Bar, London – May 1921

Christina sits on the white crocheted bedcover on the large brass bed, her fingers tracing the scrolls and leaves tooled into the diary's green leather binding. She opens the cover and the book falls open to the familiar page.

*August 4th, 1891:*

*How can I ever be the same? I cannot.*

*August 6th, 1891:*

*Cousin Stefania sent me to the market today with a list of items for dinner and a small amount of lire with which to buy everything. Fortunately, she'd written everything in English, so I know what I was meant to be purchasing. In the market I was meant to practise my Italian and negotiate the best prices. I must confess my mind has been far too full of other thoughts for there to be much room left for Italian verb conjugations.*

*I was rescued by Harry as I attempted to buy octopus. I couldn't for the life of me remember the word for octopus, so I was reduced to flailing my arms about as I waggled my head, much to the amusement of the fishmonger. It's* polpo *apparently. I pretended penury, of course, though I don't believe the fishmonger was much convinced, and I believe I paid at least double for it than I should have.*

*Harry and I walked back the long way to the villa, which was lovely. I could barely speak as my heart was beating so heavily. He didn't appear to notice, which was a good thing, and he told me all about Pompeii, which he had visited in May when he'd stayed in Naples for a time. But, as to what he said, if you were to ask me, my mind is a blank.*

*He wishes to finish my portrait. I have agreed to meet him at the grotto on Sunday after lunch. Cousin Stefania always takes a long* riposo *– nap – on Sunday afternoons, and the housekeeper, Liliana, and her husband, Angelo, who is the gardener here, have the afternoon off, so I shall be quite on my own. As long as I am back to the villa by five o'clock, no one will be the wiser.*

*My heart, my heart. We will be alone together again. How I long to feel his kisses again.*

Christina looks out the window at a robin trilling in the branches of the old oak. *How is it possible for you to be so full of joy when life is so full of sadness and disappointment, little bird?* She looks down at the diary. She'd been like that robin once, all those years ago on Capri, when she'd met Harry and it had seemed, for that brief, shining summer, that life could be full of joy and love. But, then—

The bedroom door swings open. Christina shuts the diary and frowns at the intruder. Hettie thrusts a package wrapped in white paper with a black satin ribbon at Christina. 'Just came for you. Airmail all the way from Paris, don't you know? Must 'ave cost Miss Etta a pretty penny. I took off the brown paper wrapping. There's a letter. I tucked it under the ribbon.'

Christina takes the package from the housekeeper. 'You are not required to unwrap my post, Hettie. I should prefer you give it to me unadulterated in future.'

Hettie shrugs. ''Ave it your way.' She heads toward the bedroom door. 'I'm baking scones. They'll be ready in an 'alf hour.'

'Thank you, Hettie. I'll be down shortly.'

Christina slides the envelope out from underneath the ribbon and slits it open with her finger.

*Dearest Mama,*

*Happy Birthday! I know I'm weeks and weeks late, and I should have wished you a happy birthday on the telephone, but I'm afraid it absolutely slipped my mind. I have been running around Paris like a madwoman to meetings and all sorts. I hope you forgive me and enjoy my little gift. It's a perfume from this wonderful Parisian couturier I've discovered named Coco Chanel. Everybody in Paris wants it. It just came out in her shop a few days ago. I bought a bottle for myself as well. She's called it Chanel No. 5. What an odd name, don't you think? It sounds rather like a chemist's tonic. I'm not sure it will catch on.*

*Mama, I'm so very sorry about our little tiff on the telephone last week. It was quite wrong of me to bring up the subject of Celie on the telephone. It is quite properly something which is best discussed in person, but I don't know when we will see each other next. The thing is, I feel awful that Celie is in the dark about you and Papa and whatever happened when you were at Cousin Stefania's that summer. I truly wish I didn't know anything. I am not made to be a keeper of deep, dark family secrets. Please, Mama, write to Celie and tell her the truth. Don't you think she should know? If it were me, I would want to know, but then, Celie and I are quite different, so, oh dear, it's all so confusing. It's just so burdensome carrying this secret around in my head! I feel I shall explode!*

*I must go now. Monsieur DuRose has invited me to dinner at Le Train Bleu this evening and tomorrow I must pack up for the long journey back to Capri.*

*All my love always,*
*Etta*

Christina looks over at the dot of red in the oak's branches. Why did this all have to come out now, after so many years? How could Cousin Stefania have betrayed her trust like this? Now she must put the genie back in the bottle before the secret leaks out to Cecelia.

Rising from the bed, she walks over to her writing desk and settles in the chair. She opens the drawer and removes a sheet of monogrammed paper and her old Waterman fountain pen.

*Dear Etta,*

*Thank you for your thoughtful gift, which is most appreciated. You are quite forgiven for forgetting my birthday. I received a lovely letter and a silk scarf from Jessica and a card and several photographs from Cecelia. I shall be certain to wear the scent to the next WI meeting. Thank you, as well, for your apology with regards to the extraordinary revelations with which you assailed me on the telephone. I am still not quite recovered from the shock of it all.*

*Let me relieve you of the burden of carrying this secret. It has nothing whatsoever to do with you. It is my business solely and it is my decision and mine alone whether or not to reveal it to Cecelia. You are never to say anything about this to anyone; not Cecelia, nor Jessica, nor Carlo. No one. Is that understood?*

*I am sorry if I sound harsh. It is simply that I wish to save Cecelia from the heartbreak I am certain she will experience should she ever discover the truth of her parentage. Your papa was Cecelia's father in every way except that one. In fact, I don't think it was a secret that she was his favourite. I often found it strange knowing that they weren't father and daughter. They were so very similar in so many ways. I do not wish for you to be the agent of destruction for her memories.*

*I shall leave it there. I trust in your love for your sister and I know you shall do the right thing by her.*

*Mama*

# Chapter Twenty-Two

## Celie

### Sweet Briar Farm, West Lake, Alberta – June 1921

'Celie?! Celie, where are you?'

'In here, Frank! In the bedroom. I'm hanging up the new curtains.'

Frank enters the room where Celie teeters on a kitchen chair by the window looping the new floral curtains she's sewn onto curtain hooks. She steps down and stands back, her hands on her hips.

'What do you think? I think the yellow flowers are quite jolly, don't you?'

'I didn't see what was wrong with the old curtains.'

'Oh, those were only temporary. Mavis lent them to me, and I didn't want her to wait too long before I gave them back.'

Frank pulls out the chair to Celie's writing desk and flops down with a heavy sigh. 'I'm just back from Ol' Man Forbes's place. The bill came in from Eaton's. What's with this all this film and developing fluid and photographic paper you're buying? And now you're going off buying material for curtains, too? How much did that all cost? I'm not made of money, Celie.'

'I'm sorry, Frank, but you said we did well from last year's wheat harvest, so I thought I'd take up photography again. The camera materials aren't all that expensive, and I managed to cadge a ten per cent discount on the fabric from Mr Forbes.'

Frank unlaces his boot and drops it onto the wooden floor. 'I don't see why you need to be wasting your time and our money on taking pictures. It's not like you're doing it for your father or the newspapers anymore. At least then you were getting paid for it.'

Celie sits on the bed. 'Frank, I enjoy taking photographs. I need to do something for myself, otherwise it's just housework every day.'

'Yes, well, I've got farm work every day.'

'You chose to be a farmer, Frank.'

'And you chose to be a farmer's wife.'

Celie bites her lip. 'I know, but I didn't think I would have to give up doing the things I love. I'm a very capable person, Frank. I want to do more than wash clothes and hoe the garden. I used to do so much in London, and it made me happy. Taking pictures makes me happy.'

Frank's second boot clomps onto the floor. He looks over at her. 'Are you saying you're not happy?' He sweeps his arm around the room. 'Celie, I'm doing all this for us! Do you think I like breaking my back at the plough, or pulling splinters the size of knitting needles out of my hands when I'm hammering in the new fences? This is all for us! For our future. For our children's future.'

'I understand, Frank.'

'Do you, Celie? For your information, the wheat prices are dropping, and getting this farm up and running is costing more money than I thought it would. I've run through my father's inheritance already. I thought it would last us a good five years. Everything depends on this next wheat harvest now.'

'Frank, I'm sorry. I had no idea. You should tell me these things.'

He runs his hand through his hair and shakes his head. 'It's harder than I thought it would be, Celie.'

She rises from the bed and wraps her arms around Frank, who hugs her against him. 'I know.' She gives him a quick peck on his lips. 'Don't worry about the photography. I can pick it up another time. We'll get there, Frank. We're both hard workers. We'll get there.'

---

Celie tucks the quilt under Lulu's chin, and, after kissing the sleeping baby on her forehead, returns to the letter she is writing to Jessie at the kitchen table.

> *... Two months with Aziz away in London? How will you manage in the clinic? I've always thought you would make a wonderful doctor, Jessie. It's a shame that women aren't permitted to study medicine in Egypt.*
>
> *I must say I was awfully shocked to read the business about the proposed second wife. I can't imagine how you must have felt walking into your mother-in-law's interview of the suggested candidate. Of course, the miscarriage was awful, but you're young and time is on your side. It will happen, I'm certain. Your mother-in-law needs to be patient. Really, what was she thinking?*
>
> *Life here on the farm trundles on. Lulu is growing and is now in a new crib which we have set up between the kitchen and living room as it's too large for our bedroom. Frank hopes to build another storey onto the house eventually and move the bedrooms upstairs, but for now we're cosy in our little bungalow.*
>
> *I had rather a kerfuffle with Frank the other day about the cost of camera film and processing materials. I have been trying to save as much of the money Papa left me as possible as an emergency fund (I have left it in Mama's account in England where I feel it's safest), and so I have been putting the purchases onto our credit account at the local general store.*

*Frank was quite cross with me when he picked up the latest statement. I had no idea our finances were being so stretched; he'd never given me any reason to think so, but of course building the house and the barn and all the rest has cost a considerable amount. He inherited a comfortable sum from his father, so I thought we were fine. It seems I may have been mistaken, and I am feeling terribly guilty. Truthfully, things are rather stressful here currently. Frank walks around like the weight of the world is on his shoulders. Some days I find myself tiptoeing around the kitchen just to keep him from snapping at me. I'm certain it will all improve with a good wheat harvest this year.*

*Have you heard from Etta? She is such an unreliable correspondent! I received a postcard from her from Paris a month ago with nothing written except 'I'm in Paris and I'm having a marvellous time! Lots of love, Etta'. Whatever was she doing there?*

*I must leave you now. Time to make dumplings for the stew! Write soon.*

*Love always,*
*Celie*

Celie puts down the fountain pen and refills her teacup from the small brown teapot. She splashes in milk and a spoonful of sugar and takes a sip of the hot tea. Since the argument with Frank over her camera expenses, she has stored away her camera and the film in a box at the back of the bottom drawer of her dresser. It takes so little to make Frank cross these days, and it is so exhausting when he prowls around the house like a tiger with a thorn in its paw. If she could only pay for these things herself, how could he begrudge her the photography – the one thing that makes her feel herself? There is her father's legacy money, of course, although she has already spent another fifty pounds of that on various of Frank's 'emergencies'. There is only £135 left, and she has earmarked that to go toward Lulu's college education or for a true emergency should one ever arise. She can't touch that, not even for her photography.

If only Jessie were here, or even her mother; someone she could really talk to. She can't burden Mavis with these personal issues. She misses her mother and her sisters so much. Some days she feels like she is losing herself, that pieces are falling off her like roof tiles in a storm. It would be so much easier to cope if they were closer. She can't let herself fall apart.

She looks over at her handbag which hangs on a hook near the front door. Getting up from the table, she retrieves it and takes out the small scrap of paper she has been carrying around in her change purse since the town's Christmas party.

*German-Speaking English Teachers Wanted for Fall Term*
*For schools in Edmonton and Surrounding Communities*
*Apply to PO Box 973, Edmonton Bulletin*

It is likely too late. But if she did take on a class teaching English to German immigrants, she could use the money to pay for her photography and other bits and pieces around the house. Surely, Frank would be happy about that? Maybe Mavis is right. What has she got to lose?

# Chapter Twenty-Three

## Christina

### Clover Bar, London – June 1921

Christina looks up from the piano at the visitor standing in the sitting room's doorway.

'Aziz? Good heavens! What are you doing in London? Where's Jessica?'

Aziz hands his hat to Hettie, who is hovering in the hallway making no effort to return to the laundry in the kitchen. He strides across the Persian rug and, taking hold of Christina's hands, holds them against his chest. 'Mrs Fry, I am so delighted to see you again. I am in London on a government mission from Egypt as a representative of the new Wafd Party. I am afraid I am on my own. Jessica is back in Cairo.'

'She's not with you? What a shame. Why didn't she come? You both could have stayed here. We could have had a lovely visit.'

'She sends her love and apologies. She very much wanted to come, but she has been kept in Cairo by work at the health clinic. With the movement away from the British Protectorate to the proposed Treaty of Alliance between Britain and Egypt, many of the British-run hospitals are closing and the new Egyptian government has not yet had an opportunity to organise the health care situation. Consequently, Jessica's clinic is overrun. One of my colleagues from the Anglo-American hospital has stepped in to help her in my absence.'

'I wasn't aware that you were involved with the new government there. Jessica hasn't mentioned it in her letters.'

He takes a seat on the settee. 'I feel it is my duty as an Egyptian to do what I can to support a peaceful transition to Egyptian self-rule. I am afraid the British thought the delegation would simply rubber stamp the treaty memorandum, which is not in the least what the Wafd government is prepared to do as there are still several contentious issues. There is much still to work through. My British education is seen as an advantage by both factions.'

'Oh, dear. Politics!' Christina says, waving her hand dismissively. 'If it's not one thing, it's another. I find my involvement with the WI is as close to politics as I can manage. The exchanges between our president and the vice-president are quite bloodthirsty enough for me.'

She rises from the piano bench and glances at Hettie. 'Hettie! What are you doing lurking there like a vulture? Bring us the cannoli I bought yesterday with some tea, if you would, please. You haven't polished them all off yet, I trust.'

Aziz smiles at the housekeeper. 'Thank you very much, Hettie. I remember how very helpful you were when Mrs Fry was ill with the Spanish flu. I would not have managed so well without you.'

Hettie's lips twitch and a film of pink spreads across her dour face. 'Glad somebody noticed. I'll fetch the tea then.' She flicks her gaze at Christina. '*And* the cannoli which I 'aven't touched but for one or two.'

Christina glances at Aziz after Hettie leaves. 'Don't mind us. We are quite comfortable in our grumpiness. The truth is I couldn't manage without Hettie, and she knows it. I've grown quite fond of her, though I'm not entirely confident the sentiment is reciprocated.'

'I am certain you are quite mistaken.'

Christina settles into her favourite armchair and fixes her son-in-law with her cool blue gaze. 'So, Aziz. Tell me all about Jessica and your life in Cairo.'

---

Aziz sets down the teacup and saucer on a side table. His eyes stray to the baby grand piano with its collection of family photographs arranged on its lid.

Christina follows his gaze. 'What is it, Aziz? It seems that there is something on your mind.'

He looks back at Christina. 'It is nothing. It is the additional work, as I said. It is keeping us all very busy. Jessica rarely arrives home before eight o'clock in the evening and is out the door by seven most days. I am afraid she will wear herself out. We could do with a full-time doctor on staff, but it is difficult attracting anyone to work in our clinic for the modest salary we could offer.'

Christina wipes her hands on a napkin. 'Jessica has always been mulish when she fixes her mind on something. I don't believe it is the work. Aziz. I am your mother-in-law. You can speak to me candidly. You are family, although I am quite ashamed of the way I behaved toward you when you first visited with Jessica after your marriage.'

'It is of no consequence.'

'It is very much of consequence. I was small-minded and bigoted. I was shocked beyond reason that Jessica had married a Muslim man.'

'I am simply a man, like any other, Mrs Fry. We worship the same God, only under another name.'

Christina runs her hand over her ear and pats her hair. 'I understand that now. I am only sorry that it took almost dying of the Spanish flu for me to discover my humanity. Your care of me, at your own risk, is something for which I can never repay you.'

'There is no need to thank me. I did what any doctor would have done.'

'You did more than that, Aziz. You showed someone who had treated you with nothing but ill manners the meaning of compassion. Let me repay the lesson. What is really bothering you?'

Aziz regards his mother-in-law. She is as straight-backed and formal as he remembers from their first meeting, immaculately dressed in a stylish, low-waisted lavender silk day dress, her wavy auburn hair arranged into a low bun at the base of her neck. Her eyes, the coolest of blues, like ice reflecting the winter sky, pierce him with their sagacity.

'You are quite right, Mrs Fry. There is something else. Jessica wishes to have a child, and I do as well, very much so. But her doctor has advised us that a pregnancy may be dangerous for her. Possibly even fatal. The miscarriage ...' His voice trails off and he shakes his head.

Christina reaches across to Aziz and squeezes his hand. 'Every time a woman carries a child, there is risk. I'm sure you know that, being a doctor. My own mother died giving birth to my brother. Unfortunately, he passed away as well.'

'I am sorry. I wasn't aware of this.'

Christina nods. She reaches for the teapot and refills the teacups. 'It was a very long time ago, but, yes, it was very sad.' She pours a dollop of milk into the cups. 'I, myself, struggled terribly with Cecelia during the birth. But Jessica is a very robust young woman, nothing like me or my mother. What has she said to you about this?'

'She wants us to try for a child. She promises to rest and follow her doctor's instructions to the letter.'

'And you're concerned she won't.'

He smiles ruefully. 'Jessica is not a woman to sit still for very long. She is quite wilful.'

'That is indeed an understatement.' Christina takes a sip of the tea and grimaces at its tepidness. 'It seems to me that if you both decide to go forward with this, Jessica will require a firm hand to keep her in line.'

Aziz frowns. 'A firm hand?'

'I have been called wilful myself on more than one occasion. Should Jessica find herself with child, I will come to Cairo and ensure she follows her doctor's orders to the letter, as she's promised you.'

'Oh, no, Mrs Fry, that is quite an imposition on you. I couldn't possibly take you away from your life here for what may be months.'

Christina selects a chocolate-filled cannoli and drops it delicately onto her plate. 'Aziz, it is no imposition, I assure you. I am her mother. Let me do this for both of you.' She licks the chocolate cream off her fingers. 'She will hate every minute, of course, but that is what mothers are for.'

# Chapter Twenty-Four

## Christina

**Grenville, Montcrieff & Smith Solicitors, London – July 1921**

'Mrs Fry, sir.'

Harry rises from his chair and gestures for Christina to take a seat across from his desk. 'Mrs Fry. I'm so glad you come by at such short notice.' He nods at his assistant who hovers in the doorway. 'Thank you, Rupert. Bring us some tea, would you? The good stuff from Fortnum's.'

Christina waves at the assistant. 'No need for that, Rupert. I won't be staying long.'

When the door is shut, Harry moves around the desk and bends down to kiss Christina on her cheek. 'I'm glad you came, Tina. You've been dodging my invitations for a month. Have I done something to upset you?'

Christina rests her sun parasol against Harry's desk and regards him from beneath the spreading brim of her grey straw hat. It's true; she has been avoiding him. It is ridiculous to encourage any friendship between them, not when all she wants is

— No, she mustn't think about it. Getting involved with Harry again is absolutely out of the question. She will meet him for business, but nothing more.

'Not in the least, Harry. I have simply been quite busy. My son-in-law is in town from Cairo doing some work for their government, and we have been out to dinner on a few occasions.'

'Oh, good.' He shifts a stack of papers to one side and leans against the desk. He smiles at Christina, his blue eyes sparkling with humour. 'I'd thought you'd finally realised what a tedious bore I am and had decided to cut me loose.'

A smile flits across Christina's face. Why did he have to look at her that way? Why does her heart judder like it has been prodded awake whenever she is near him? She runs her hand over her ear and shifts in her chair.

'Of course not, Harry. We both lead busy lives.' She clears her throat. 'Your note said you have news about Henrietta and the Bishop house. I have been wondering what has been taking so long.'

Harry sighs and returns to his chair. 'Yes. I've been contacted by your aunt's investigator, a Mr John Jacob Fincher. A grey little man unremarkable in every regard which, I suppose, stands him in good stead as an investigator. He is hardly one to generate any notice.'

'And? What did this Mr Fincher have to say?'

He slides out a leather ledger from beneath a stack of files and pushes it across the desk to Christina. 'Do you recognise this?'

Christina frowns as she runs her fingers over the initials tooled in gold leaf into the fine maroon leather. *MAB*. She flips open the cover to the first page.

*A Complete Record of the Art of the Bishop Household to 1900*
*Compiled by Miss Margaret A. Bishop*

'I've never seen this before. It was my Aunt Margaret's?'

'Yes. She appears to have been most diligent in keeping a record of all your family's art.'

'I don't understand. What has this to do with anything?'

Harry rifles through the pages until he finds what he is searching for. He taps on the third item.

*Acquisitions in 1892*

1. *'Girl in Velvet Dress with Dog', artist unknown, engraving on paper, gilt and green wood frame, 25 inches wide by 22 inches high.*
2. *Series of sketches of people at work, George Morland RA, 1700s (exact dates unknown), pencil on paper, unframed, 18 inches wide by 14 inches high each (8 in all).*
3. *'Christina', H. Grenville, Capri 1891, watercolour on paper, unframed, 16 inches wide by 20 inches high. (In possession of Mrs Christina Innocenti, née Bishop).*

Christina gasps. 'I had no idea that she'd even seen that picture. I kept it rolled up in my bedroom. She must have gone into my room and gone through all my things. Honestly, I can't believe she would have stooped to such a thing.'

Harry shuts the ledger. 'Well, it seems your Aunt Margaret was a sleuth on par with our Mr Fincher. He had rather a lot of questions to ask me about my movements back in 1891. He appeared to be quite convinced that I was the H. Grenville in question, you see.'

'Oh, Harry.'

'I told him I'd never been to Capri and that the artist of the watercolour could have been any H. Grenville ... a Helen Grenville or a Hugo Grenville. Although Grenville isn't a common name, it isn't altogether uncommon either.'

'Do you think he believed you?'

'No, but this ledger isn't enough proof of anything.'

'That's good, but there is proof, Harry. Cecelia's birth certificate. Her real one. It has both of our names on it.'

Harry draws his eyebrows together. 'Of course. Where is it?'

'I left it with Cousin Stefania for safekeeping. She'll never let anyone have it. I managed to have a British birth certificate drawn up for Cecelia after the war, with Gerald's name on it and a birthdate of 1893 rather than 1892. There was so much chaos going on at the records office at that time what with the local bombings, it wasn't difficult.'

Harry nods. 'As long as the real birth certificate doesn't come to light, everything should be fine.'

Christina frowns. 'You don't suppose he might be following me, do you? What if he's followed me here to your chambers? He'll know that we know each other.'

Harry rises from his chair and stands to one side of a tall window as he scrutinises the men in the park across the street. He turns away from the window and sits back in his chair with a grunt.

'I don't see him, but you're right. We need to be very careful. Henrietta appears to have got the bit in her teeth about all of this.' He chews his lip. 'Tina, are you certain you want to pursue going after the house in Marylebone? Perhaps, given the diligent Mr Fincher, it might be wise to give in to your aunt.'

Christina picks up her parasol. 'Aunt Henrietta and Aunt Margaret stole that house from me after Papa died, Harry. It should have been mine as his heir. I won't give up the claim on the Bishop house. I simply won't.'

'Of course, Tina. I understand. But do you really think your aunt will stop trying to uncover the identity of Cecelia's father, especially if everything is pointing to it being me?'

'Aunt Henrietta is a vindictive old bat. She's never forgiven me for coming home to London with a baby and no husband, just as she never forgave my mother for getting in the family way before marrying my father. She believes we Innocentis have sullied the

Bishop name. She won't let it go, Harry. But as long as Aunt Henrietta doesn't get hold of Cecelia's birth certificate, she won't find any real proof that you're Cecelia's father. As you say, we simply need to be very careful.' She rises from the chair. 'And I want you to get me that house.'

# Chapter Twenty-Five

Jessie

**Altumanina, Cairo, Egypt – August 1921**

'But, Aziz, Premier Adli was quite wrong to try to negotiate the treaty with the British without Saad Zaghloul, who everyone knows is the true leader of the Wafd Party. He is the one who holds the hearts of Egyptians in his hands. Adli is simply a' – Zara Khalid screws up her face as if she has bitten into a lemon – 'a functionary who pushed Zaghloul aside when the negotiations collapsed last year.'

'Zara, Zaghloul's intransigence on the Sudan issue, amongst other things, has infected the whole treaty negotiation. Premier Adli's hands were tied in London. No matter how hard he tried to find a common ground, Zaghloul's insistence on Egyptian sovereignty of the Sudan collapsed the whole negotiation like a house of cards in the wind. We are now at stalemate and Premier Adli is threatening to resign. If Egypt is to move forward as an independent country, we must find a way to work with the British, not against them. We must take small steps, Zara. We cannot take a great leap and expect to be successful.'

'But, Aziz—'

Layla Khalid sets down the delicate tea glass she is holding onto the silver tray. 'Zara, Aziz is quite right. We would all be happier without the British in Egypt, but how are these uneducated Egyptians meant to govern themselves?' She picks up a small honey-soaked cake in her long delicate fingers. 'The British at least have a proper king. There are shopkeepers in Premier Adli's new government, Aziz! Shopkeepers and butchers.' She shudders. 'Oh, for the days of our Turkish pashas. That was when Egypt was a civilised country.'

Zara jumps to her feet and stamps her foot on the terrace's tiles. 'This is the reason the country is in the state it is, Mama! Subjugating ourselves, with our own rich history, to foreigners like the Turks and British! We must follow our destiny to self-rule without compromise, just as Saad Zaghloul says! I am a proud Egyptian and I will do everything in my small power to see our country ruled again by Egyptians, without Britain hovering over us like a watchful uncle.' She storms across the terrace and into the sitting room, almost upending the bemused housekeeper Marta, who carries a fresh pot of tea.

Marta looks from Zara's disappearing figure back to the others. 'She is all right?'

Layla beckons impatiently for the silver teapot. 'It is none of your concern, Marta. It is a family matter.'

Marta exchanges a look with Jessie. Layla clears her throat impatiently. 'The tea, Marta.'

Jessie looks across at Aziz. 'I had no idea Zara felt so strongly about these issues. She can't be very happy working for an Englishwoman in the clinic.'

'You are her sister-in-law, Jessica. You are family. It is not a problem.'

Layla pours out a long stream of steaming tea into the tea glasses. 'Zara is far too high-spirited for her own good. Aziz, it is time we found her a husband. She can channel her energies into having children and running a household. Politics is no place for women.'

'I'm afraid I must disagree,' Jessie says. 'Women all around the world have marched and demonstrated and fought for the vote. Both men and women make up our societies. Politics is absolutely the place for women.'

'This is not yet the case in Egypt,' Layla says as she blows on the steam arising from her tea glass. 'Here politics is left to men. Let it fall to them to be the agents of our country's destruction. Women should be above such things.'

'I'm afraid I really can't agree—'

Layla leans across the arm of her chair and places a hand on Jessie's arm. 'Jessica, you must be exhausted after the long day in the clinic. Why don't you have a rest before dinner? I should like to speak to my son as a mother speaks to her child.' She glances at Aziz. 'He has been away for over two months and when he is here, he works such long hours at the hospital. It is not often that I am graced with his presence. I must take advantage of the situation. I hope you understand.'

Jessie glances from Layla to Aziz. 'Of course. We were exceptionally busy in the clinic today. Sprains and strains all around. I could do with a rest before dinner.'

Aziz makes to rise from his chair. 'I will come with you, Jessica. I will tell you all about my visits to see your mother while I was in London.'

'We can speak after dinner, Aziz. Spend some time with your mother. I think I may take a nap. I am quite exhausted.'

After Jessie leaves, Aziz turns to his mother. 'You have my full attention, Mama. But, please, do not bring up the subject of a second wife again. I have already had enough trouble with Jessica over this.'

Layla waves her hand at her son. 'Never mind about all that.' She sets down the tea glass and folds her graceful hands in her lap. 'I had a great deal of time to think about your situation while you were away.'

'And what have you decided about our situation, not that it is any of your concern?'

'Aziz, this is where you are wrong. It is not simply about you and your wife.' She gestures toward the house. 'This house needs an heir.' She pats her chest, setting her bangles jingling. 'I want to know that *my* blood will continue on this earth after I am gone.'

Aziz smiles. 'It *is* about you. I should not be surprised.'

Layla huffs impatiently. 'It is about all of the Khalids. Do you not wish to honour the name of your father by bringing a son into this world?'

'Ah, a son, now, not just any child.'

'You know what I mean.'

'No, I don't know what you mean. I have had quite enough of this conversation.' He moves to rise, but Layla stops him with her hand.

'Please, Aziz. Hear me out. Then you can go see your precious English wife.'

Aziz sits back against the chintz cushions. 'All right. What is it?'

'Jessica came to speak to me after the debacle with the Abdallahs.'

'I am aware of that.'

'Well, you may not be aware that she told me that she is perfectly capable of bearing a child, and that she wishes more than life itself to give you a child.'

'This is precisely why I cannot agree to it. Did she tell you that her doctor has warned against it? That she may, indeed, give her life for our child?'

'Aziz, my beloved son, she is your wife. She wishes to bear your child. It is not for you to deny your wife this fundamental desire. It is what marriage is for, is it not?'

'Not all marriages produce children.'

'And they are the worse for it. You and Zara were the light of my eyes when you were children.'

Aziz snorts. 'You sent us to boarding school as soon as we were six.'

'As all parents caring for their children's futures would, had they the funds to do so.'

'Mama, it is late and I have just returned from London. I want to talk to my wife. Is there anything else you wish to say?'

Layla eyes her son dispassionately. 'Aziz, please think about this carefully. You, as a husband, have a duty to your wife. It is against Allah and nature to deny her this.'

'And, if she dies, will you take care of the child?'

'She won't die. I will ensure she follows her doctor's directives. If she is ordered to bed, I will lock her in her room if I must. She will hate me, of course, but I know she does already, so it barely matters.'

Aziz laughs. 'It seems that I am outnumbered.'

'Outnumbered?'

'I visited Jessica's mother in London. You both share the same sentiment.'

'Really? Well, it appears she is more sensible than her daughter.'

He rises from the chair. 'If Jessica does fall pregnant, you will have an opportunity to judge this for yourself. You see, Mrs Fry has insisted on coming to stay at Altumanina to see her daughter through the birth.'

Layla's mouth drops open as Aziz rises and disappears through the French doors into the sitting room. 'Aziz? What do you mean, Jessica's mother is coming to Altumanina? I won't have it, Aziz! Did you hear me? I will not have it!'

---

Jessie looks up from the chair where she is reading the copy of *This Side of Paradise* by a new American writer named F. Scott Fitzgerald that Lady Evelyn had sent her from London. She sets down the book and smiles at her husband.

'You escaped.'

He shuts the door and walks over to her as he unfastens his cufflinks. 'It wasn't easy.'

'Mothers are like that.'

'Your mother is charming.'

'Are you sure it was my mother you visited in London?'

He leans over the chair and kisses Jessie full on her lips. 'I am perfectly certain it was her. There was cannoli.' He takes hold of Jessie's hand and pulls her toward the bed. 'I've missed you, *habibti.*'

She turns toward the chest of drawers. 'Shall I get the—'

He tugs her hand. 'No.'

'No?'

He pulls her onto the bed. 'Let us make our child, Jessica, if God wills.'

## Chapter Twenty-Six

Celie

**West Lake School, West Lake, Alberta – September 1921**

West Lake School, in the Vermillion Springs School District, sits like a white clapboard dollhouse in the middle of a flat patch of grass near the crossroads known as Protestant Corner. There, the sturdy red-brick edifice of West Lake United Church faces the yellow clapboard steeple and fine pitched roof of St Andrew's Anglican Church. Celie adjusts her hat and climbs the two wooden steps to the front door. She hesitates for a moment as she ponders knocking but changes her mind. Emma Philby and Rosita Majors from the school's board of governors are expecting her. It's not like she's a guest.

She steps through the door into the small covered porch which is lined with hooks hung with hats, coats and jackets. A gust of wind catches the door which slams behind her with a bang.

'Ah! Mrs Jeffries, finally,' Emma Philby calls out from the front of the classroom. 'Do hang up your coat and hat and come in. We had expected you five minutes ago. Didn't you receive the letter stating an eight o'clock start time?'

Celie hangs up the items and pats her hair as she enters the schoolroom. There is a scrape of chairs and a soft shuffle of bodies – a mix of children and adults – as the students turn in their seats to look at her. The room is simple and functional with white wooden clapboard walls above dark red wainscotting and a pot-bellied stove in the centre, either side of which sixteen desks sit in precise rows. Three narrow sash windows along both sides appear to provide the main light, as there are only two electric bulbs dangling at the end of wires from the ceiling. The two women from the school's board of governors stand, hands clasped in front of them, in their sober Sunday best, behind a table painted the same dark red as the panelling. A large blackboard covers much of the wall behind them.

Celie walks up to the front to join the two women, sensing the eyes following her. 'I'm terribly sorry. My husband's watch must be running behind. I thought I was in good time.'

'No harm done, Mrs Jeffries,' Rosita Majors says. 'We are grateful that you've given up your Saturday mornings to teach our German neighbours English. It's difficult finding teachers who are prepared to teach one class a week outside of the cities. We were delighted when the Board of Education forwarded us your application.'

'The sooner you get started the better, Mrs Jeffries,' Emma Philby interjects. 'We don't wish to encourage the speaking of German in our community. I must say I was most surprised to hear that you spoke it fluently. I wouldn't have thought an Englishwoman would have any interest in German.' Her pale blue eyes narrow. 'You have a German mother, perhaps? Or a grandparent?'

Celie smiles politely. 'No. I simply admire the language and the literature. I had hoped to become a German teacher at one time.'

'How extraordinary.' The woman looks past Celie to the faces watching them from the schoolroom. 'You can appreciate that this is a sensitive matter, Mrs Jeffries, what with the war being such a recent memory. If our government has chosen to accept these immigrants, which is a folly if you were to ask me, then we must do our duty to turn them into fine English-speaking Canadians.'

Celie glances at Rosita Majors who is listening with a fixed smile. 'They have left their homeland and everything they know in order to make a new life here, Emma,' Rosita Majors says. 'I have no doubt they have the motivation to become very fine Canadians.'

'One hopes. At least they are Protestants, Rosita. We certainly don't want to encourage any more Catholics in the area. They are far too high-strung in my opinion.'

Celie raises an eyebrow. 'Then I shall endeavour not to be too high-strung, Mrs Philby, being as I am myself a Catholic.'

The woman clears her throat. 'Quite. Well, that explains your absence from St Andrew's on Sundays. I had thought you were a Unitarian or a Baptist. Had I known—'

'I'm so pleased you have agreed to teach our class English, Mrs Jeffries,' Rosita Majors interrupts. '*I* have no doubt we've made a good choice in you. Mavis Wheatley speaks very highly of you. You should consider joining the Women's Christian Temperance Union. We do very good work for the community.'

Emma Philby huffs. 'Catholics don't join the Union, Rosita. It's a Christian organisation.'

Celie smiles tightly. 'I can assure you, Mrs Philby, Catholics are Christians. We are really not so very different from you.'

Rosita Majors bites her lip to suppress a smile. She takes hold of her colleague's arm and steers her toward the door, smiling at Celie as they leave. 'Good luck, Mrs Jeffries. We're very fortunate to have you.'

---

Celie nods at the tall young boy of about fourteen with the shock of wheat-blond hair sitting in the desk beside the stove. She gestures for him to stand. 'Your turn, now, please. Do you speak any English?'

The boy stands, unfolding like a colt as he rises from his chair. '*Ja, Frau Jeffries.* Yes. A little.'

'Do you want to try telling me about yourself in English?'

He smiles and nods shyly. 'I will try.'

'*Das ist gut.* That is good.'

The boy stands stiffly behind the desk and looks down at his hands which he squeezes like he is juicing a lemon. 'My name is Hans Brandt. I have fourteen years.'

'Hans? I'm over here.'

Hans looks up. 'I am sorry, *Frau Jeffries.*'

'You're doing very well. Now, you said you *have* fourteen years. You should say, "I am fourteen years old."' She looks at the class. '*Ich bin vierzehn Jahre alt.*'

She writes this on the blackboard in both English and German and points to the English sentence with her stick of chalk. 'If you say you *have* fourteen years, it is like you are saying you are holding fourteen years in your hand, or that you own fourteen years, like you would own your clothes,' she explains in German. 'But if you say I *am* fourteen years old, it means that the fourteen years are a part of you which cannot be taken away. Does everyone understand the difference?'

The students nod, and a farmer in pressed overalls and a brown corduroy jacket raises his hand.

'Yes, Mr Berger?'

'*Aber ich bin nicht vierzehn Jahre alt.*'

'In English, please, Mr Berger. Stand, if you would, please.'

The farmer, who barely fits on the chair behind the desk, shuffles to his feet. His face reddens. '*Aber… aber …*'

Celie nods encouragingly. 'But. In English *aber* is but.' She writes this on the board.

The farmer takes a deep breath. 'But I am fourteen years old … *nicht.*'

'Very close. "But I am *not* fourteen years old." How old are you? *Wie alt bist du*?'

'*Dreiundvierzig*.'

'Forty-three. Now say it all in English, please.'

The farmer rubs a meaty hand over his mouth. 'But I am … not fourteen years old.' He swallows and glances at the blackboard.

'Very good. Continue.'

'I have …' He shakes his head. 'I *am* forty-three years old.'

'Excellent. Very good, indeed, Mr Berger. You may sit down.' She turns back to Hans. 'Now, tell us where you are from in Germany, Hans.'

The boy nods, his blond hair falling into his blue eyes. He brushes it back with his hand. 'I come from Heidelberg.'

Celie's heart jumps. 'Heidelberg?'

'Yes. *Es ist eine wunderschöne Stadt*.'

Celie stares at the young German, but all she can see is Max.

'*Frau Jeffries*?'

'I'm sorry. Yes. In English, you would say, "It is a beautiful city."'

'I come from Heidelberg,' the boy repeats. 'It is a beautiful city.'

'Thank you, Hans. That's very good. You may take your seat.'

She sits down in the wooden chair behind the table and stares at the green cover of *English Grammar Book 1*. Her stomach quivers and her heart thuds in her chest. Maybe this has been a mistake. Just hearing the language again stirs up all those memories of her and Max in London before the war. Memories she's tried so hard to suppress. Memories that are now fluttering through her mind like butterflies released from their chrysalises.

She sucks in a deep breath and flips open the cover. 'Please turn to page five, class. We will look at the verb "to be".'

## Chapter Twenty-Seven

### Etta

**Villa Serenissima, Capri, Italy – September 1921**

Etta steps back from the canvas and, after setting down her palette and paintbrush, picks up the embroidered Spanish fan Cousin Stefania has lent her. She fans her face as she examines the half-finished portrait. On the canvas, Stefania observes the viewer from her favourite wicker chair on the terrace, the turquoise sea rippling in a landscape of watery hillocks and valleys behind her, where two mermaids cavort in the waves. Her cousin's ageless black hair sits on top of her head like a helmet, and her dark brown eyes stare down the viewer with their delving perceptivity.

Etta squeezes out more paint onto the palette. Cerulean blue and yellow ochre. Cadmium red and titanium white. Burnt sienna, of course, and a touch of alizarin crimson. She dabs at the paints with a paintbrush until the rich purply red of the roses twining around the terrace pillars appears on the palette.

She hears the soft slap of Liliana's carpet slippers on the sitting room's marble floor, and a moment later the housekeeper emerges onto the terrace with a tray of icy lemonade and fat green grapes. An envelope sits on the tray beside the grapes.

'Something came for you from America,' Liliana says in Italian as she sets the tray down amongst the litter of paint tubes and brushes on the table. 'No return address.'

Etta sets down her paintbrush. 'America? I don't know anyone there.' She picks up the envelope and slits it open with her thumb. She turns over the letter to read the signature. 'Oh! It's from Zelda Fitzgerald.' She looks at Liliana, who is chewing on a grape in the doorway. 'She's a friend I met in Paris. No need to worry. It's not a scandal of any kind.'

Liliana shrugs as she heads into the house. 'What is one more scandal in this house?'

*Home Sweet Home*
*St Paul, Minnesota*
*USA*

*August 29th, 1921*

*Dear Lovely Girl,*

*Hello, sweet Etta from Italy. Scott and I are now safely back in dear old St Paul, USA and I am blowing up like a fairground balloon awaiting our blessed event in October. It was so very gratifying meeting you in Paris in the spring! So sorry Scott and I didn't get you to your train on time! I hope you didn't get into too much trouble for delaying your trip back to Capri by a couple of days. You cheered me up no end, and I can't thank you enough for introducing me to the lovely Mademoiselle Chanel. I spent far too much in her shop, of course, but what's a girl to do when faced with such chic dresses and hats? I am the talk of St Paul, you know (although that isn't saying much). Dear Scott was rather cross at the expense, but I simply told him to hurry up and finish his next book and all will be well.*

*I still laugh when I think about our little escapade in the hotel. You were so naughty to suggest tying the lift in place on our floor with one of*

*Scott's belts. Even I wouldn't have dreamed that up! Really, it was so very tedious having to wait for the lift to reach our floor every day, wasn't it? You were lucky to check out the next morning before the kerfuffle with the hotel manager. He wasn't best pleased with us, I can tell you, and Scott and I were invited to leave. Ah well, it was a laugh, wasn't it? I do so miss you!*

*I do hope poor Carlo is released from that awful prison soon. Anyone with so much talent simply couldn't be a murderer. Scott and I think his paintings are wonderful. Perhaps one day when we are very rich and have a proper home of our own, we shall buy one to hang over the sitting room fireplace. Then you both* must *visit, of course, and we shall all drink gin and tonics and caper about.*

*Sending you kisses from America.*

*Zelda F.*

Etta tucks the letter back into the envelope. What a lark she'd had with the Fitzgeralds in Paris, brief though it was. Zelda had fizzed about like a soda about to spill over, and Scott's appetite for jazz clubs and cocktails had been insatiable. She'd felt so alive in Paris with them. Not like here on Capri. Here it is like she is in her own prison, with eyes everywhere and everyone wanting to know her business. She can't bear it. Some days she can barely breathe for the oppressiveness of it all. And then there are the dreams that steal her sleep and send her reaching for her tonic. The only things that keep her from screaming at the unfairness of it all are the tonic and the painting. Not even Adriana helps. Since Carlo's arrest, she has lost touch with her daughter and can't find the way back to her. Adriana will listen to no one but Liliana and her darling Mario.

She walks over to the black iron railing and leans against one of the terrace's stone pillars as she looks out at the view across the Tyrrhenian Sea to the coast of the Italian mainland. She lifts her face to the sky and lets the late summer heat press into her skin like a hot cloth.

A woman's face slowly materialises in her mind as if it is surfacing through water. The long dark hair floats about her perfect oval face and the woman opens her eyes – the aquamarine of the sea – and looks at Etta. She raises a shapely arm and reaches for her. 'I forgive you,' she says in soft-voiced Italian. *'Ti perdono.'* Etta's eyes fly open and the vision of Marianna's face vanishes. She looks out to the view where several small blue-painted fishing boats bob on the water.

*When will you leave me alone, Marianna?*

Her visit to Carlo in the prison the day before had been awful. The man she loved, the handsome, charming, talented man full of a passion for life and for love who had literally swept her off her feet to Italy, had sunk into a despair that hung off him like a foul odour. She could almost smell it on him – or was she imagining that? She sniffs the air and is sure she catches a whiff of the fetid stench. She rubs her forehead and moves back into the shade. She is finding it increasingly difficult to face the bi-monthly visits, forcing a cheeriness she can't feel only to be met with a brooding man she no longer recognises.

*Oh, Carlo, what has Marianna done to us? She kept us apart as husband and wife when she was alive, and now she keeps us apart when she's dead. I don't deserve this, Carlo. I've done nothing except love you. I've stayed by you through all of this awfulness, but it's so hard. I'm not meant to be alone, my love. I miss the man I fell in love with so much. Come back to me; please, please, come back to me, Carlo. I'm going mad here. I can feel it happening, just like it did after Adriana was born. I don't know how much longer I can go on like this.*

# Chapter Twenty-Eight

## Christina

### The Café Royal, London – September 1921

Christina graces the liveried doorman standing outside the doors of The Café Royal on Regent Street with a courteous smile as he hurries to open the door. Wielding her umbrella like an elegant walking stick, she sweeps into the large lobby where the carved buff marble walls, gilded mirrors and squat white marble fireplaces reflect an opulence more suited to a French chateau than a restaurant in the centre of London's shopping district. She is greeted by an imperious Frenchman in a finely tailored dinner jacket whose haughty set of his hawk-line face softens into obsequiousness at the mention of her luncheon companion, Lord Sherbrooke.

She follows him into the vast restaurant, where the ornate gilded plasterwork and mirrored walls reflect the crystal chandeliers and the exuberant diners in their Savile Row suits, handkerchief-skirted frocks and chic jersey dresses. Harry smiles broadly and rises to his feet as the *maître d'* ushers her to the table.

'Tina, you are a sight for sore eyes, I must say.'

Christina's lips twitch as she hands her umbrella to the *maître d'* and removes her kid gloves. 'I've always found that an odd expression, Harry. I know it's meant as a compliment, but it sounds quite the opposite to me.'

'Well, it's meant as a compliment.' His eyes sweep over her delicate features, the auburn hair arranged in a thick roll at the nape of her neck where her large-brimmed forest green hat allows a glimpse of the smooth white flesh. The jade green silk of her dress glimmers like sea water as she settles into her seat. He leans forward conspiratorially. 'You are by far the loveliest woman here, bar none.'

Christina arches a fine auburn eyebrow. 'Harry, I'm fifty years old. That isn't saying much for the other ladies in the Café Royal today.'

'You have obviously made a pact with Lucifer himself, as you put even the young debutantes to shame.' He flaps out his napkin and drops it across his knees. 'Really, Tina, you must learn to take a compliment rather than batting it away like a tennis ball.'

Christina smiles despite herself. 'Point taken.' She eyes Harry, who is dressed in a perfectly tailored grey wool suit and a burgundy silk tie speared with an onyx tie pin, though the stiff white shirt collar digs into his thickening jawline.

His teeth flash white beneath his clipped moustache. 'Do I meet with your approval? You're looking at me like I'm a horse in an auction.'

She smiles. 'You're a very suitable luncheon companion for an honourable widow.'

'Not too honourable, I hope.'

She presses her lips together and ignores the insinuation. She glances around the crowded dining room. 'Are you sure meeting here is wise? What if that Mr Fincher were to see us together?'

'If Mr Fincher followed either of us here today, Tina, he will, most unfortunately for him, find that there is no table available to accommodate him. The charming *maître d'* and I have come to an arrangement on that score. Should Mr Fincher appear in his dull grey suit, he will make it no further than the foyer.'

He picks up the menu. 'Now, what shall we have for lunch? Have you had the Café Royal chicken pie? I particularly enjoy it with a sweet champagne.'

'I haven't had the pleasure. Gerald and I tended to stay closer to home. Our maid Milly was an excellent cook.'

'Ah, yes, lovely Hither Green. London isn't a patch on it.'

'I have always found Hither Green to be quite comfortable.'

'But rather lacking in the finer aspects of life, I should imagine.' He folds the menu and motions for the waiter. 'Café Royal chicken pie and sweet champagne it is, then.'

After the order has been taken, Christina folds her hands in her lap and regards Harry across the table. The meetings with Harry, usually at obscure restaurants and cafés far away from the West End, where they both make a point of arriving and leaving separately by taxi, have begun to take an unsettling turn – the flirtatious banter, which she's been more than happy to encourage, transforming into suggestions of an illicit nature. She is treading a tightrope, and she is not entirely confident in the sureness of her steps.

'What's happening with my aunt's claim on the Bishop house, Harry? It's been dragging on for almost a year. Please tell me that the investigator hasn't found any proof that you're the H. Grenville who painted my portrait, has he? Is that what this is about?'

'Tina, I have, in fact, had another visit from our Mr Fincher. He was just back from a trip to Capri. He tried to speak to your cousin Stefania who wouldn't have anything to do with him, so he started sniffing around the town. He found the *Pasticceria De Rosa.*'

'The pastry shop where we used to buy our bread?'

'Yes. It seems that the shopkeeper who served us still works there with her granddaughter. She's ancient now, of course, but Fincher showed her my Sandhurst graduation photograph and she recognised me immediately. She called me *"L'Inglese"* – the

Englishman, and then she spoke to him about you with her unfortunately bilingual granddaughter translating. She said you had a fondness for chocolate cannoli. She called you *"la bella ragazza inglese dai capelli rossi"*. The beautiful red-haired English girl.'

'Oh, my word.'

'I know. It's not ideal, but don't worry. It's just the word of an old woman. She must have seen hundreds of tourists go through her shop over the years. There's no real proof unless he gets his hands on Cecelia's Italian birth certificate.'

'That will never happen.'

'So, we should be safe. Hopefully, your aunt will soon realise that her quest to uncover the identity of Cecelia's father is in vain and will abandon this ridiculous vendetta against you. Or, should I say, us?'

Christina runs her hand over her ear and sighs. 'I hope so, Harry. This is all so very tedious.'

'It is indeed.' Harry looks across the table at Christina and clears his throat. 'Tina, that's not the only thing I wished to speak to you about.' He reaches under the table and rests his hand on her knee. 'I have purchased a small flat in Chelsea. For us. Where we can have some privacy.'

Christina's heart jumps and she pushes his hand away. 'What do you mean, "for us"?'

'All those years since Capri, I never forgot you, Tina. Please, correct me if I'm wrong, but I believe you never forgot me either.'

'You're quite wrong, Harry. And Capri was a very long time ago.'

'Not so very long ago, in the scheme of things. What is thirty years? Didn't Einstein suggest that time is relative?'

Christina nods impatiently. 'That the speed at which time passes depends upon one's frame of reference. Yes, I know of it.'

'Ah, yes, I remember. I mustn't underestimate you.'

'A mistake many men make about women.'

The food arrives, and the waiter sets the plates of steaming, thick-crusted chicken pie and vegetables on the table with a flourish. He makes a show of uncorking the sweet champagne and pouring out the fizzing wine into two champagne coupes.

Harry raises his glass. 'To relativity.'

Christina huffs and sets down her glass.

'Tina, I'm sorry if I'm being too forward. One can always dream, can't one?'

Christina arches her eyebrow. 'Being a dreamer has served me no useful purpose in my life. It has only led to disappointment.'

'That is a very sad state of affairs indeed. What can I do to remedy this sad situation, my beautiful siren?'

She looks Harry in the eye. 'Secure me the Bishop house.'

'This is your dream, Tina? The thing you want more than anything else?'

She studies him as his blue eyes burn into her, seeking an answer she wishes she could bury deep within herself. Can he sense the fire that burns through her body when he touches her? Can he hear the thudding of her heart when he says her name? She must gain control of herself or all will be lost.

'It is what I want more than anything else in the world. It is my one connection to my mother and to the girl I was before everything changed. That house is a part of who I am, Harry. I will never be whole until I have it back.'

She raises her champagne glass and touches it to his. 'To making dreams come true.'

# Chapter Twenty-Nine

## Jessie

### British Residency Building, Cairo, Egypt – November 1921

'Jessica! Dr Khalid! There you are!'

Jessie looks over the heads of the other guests at Lord and Lady Carnarvon's reception at the British Residency in Cairo to see Lady Evelyn Herbert waving an ostrich feather fan high in the air as she weaves her way through the glamorous crowd. The embassy staff have outdone themselves decorating the huge ballroom with fan-like palmyra leaves and clusters of papyrus with heads like firework sparklers. A military band plays up on the mezzanine and strains of 'The Sheik of Araby' drift over the chattering mass of Cairo's elite as waiters in red *tarbouches* and white livery slip through the crowd carrying silver trays with coupes of champagne.

Jessie whispers to Aziz. 'I feel a tad underdressed. I had no idea Lady Evelyn's Cairo debut would be such a grand affair.'

Aziz smiles at Jessie, who is self-consciously smoothing the skirt of her simple green silk dress embroidered with jet beads. 'I think you are more beautiful than anyone else here, *habibti*.'

'You would say that, wouldn't you? You are obligated as my husband.'

Lady Evelyn, glittering in diamonds and a froth of cream satin and organza, elbows past the final barrier of elbows and fans with a tall young gentleman in a perfectly tailored tuxedo trailing in her wake. She kisses Jessie on her cheek and smiles impishly at Aziz. 'You both scrub up rather well.'

She eyes Jessie critically. 'I say, Jessica, you've finally bobbed your hair. It suits you terribly. I can see your lovely green eyes now. And your dress is divine.' She flips her hand through the layers of her dress's filmy organza. 'Not like this thing Mummy had her dressmaker throw together for me. I look like one of Diaghilev's ballerinas.'

'My sister Etta sent it to me from Paris.' Jessie looks down at her dress and frowns. 'It's not too plain?'

'It's perfectly plain in all the very best ways, Jessica. You are putting us all to shame in our fripperies.' She grabs hold of the young man's arm. 'Let me introduce Brograve Beauchamp. He's the son of Sir Edward Beauchamp, the Minister of Parliament for … what is it, Brograve?'

'Lowestoft, Lady Evelyn.'

'Ah, yes. Lowestoft, wherever that is.'

'Suffolk, Lady Evelyn.'

'Suffolk, then. Brograve, this is the eminent surgeon Dr Aziz Khalid and his lovely wife Jessica Khalid. Aziz, Jessica,' she says and gestures to her companion, 'Brograve.'

Brograve extends a hand to Aziz. 'Very pleased to meet you, Dr Khalid.' He shakes Jessie's hand. 'Mrs Khalid, a pleasure.'

'Have you seen Ruthie Bellico anywhere, Jessica? She said she'd come, but who knows with her? She could be in Siam now for all I know.'

'I'm afraid not, Lady Evelyn, we've only just arrived.'

'Well, do let her know I'm looking for her if you do. I must make the rounds as Mummy has thrown this party to introduce me properly to Egyptian society.' She rolls her dark eyes. 'I'd much rather be knee deep in sand down at Luxor with Howard looking for King Tut.' She leans forward and whispers in Jessie's ear. 'Do come rescue me later, would you? There's only so much of this *la-di-da* that I can stomach, and I haven't quite made my mind up about Brograve yet.'

---

'Dr Khalid, I had no idea you were such a good dancer,' Jessie says to her husband as Aziz guides her around the dance floor in an energetic foxtrot.

'You can thank my mother for that. She felt that an ability to dance would stand me in good stead in my climb up the social ladder.'

'To charm the wives and daughters of wealthy industrialists and politicians?'

'You know my mother well.'

'I really must be a terrible disappointment to her. A modest Englishwoman who prefers to work for a living rather than gossip, play bridge and swan about at soirées.'

'I would not have it any other way, *habibti*.'

The song ends and they pause on the dance floor to await the next tune. A tap on Aziz's shoulder.

'Mind if I cut in?'

Ruth Bellico smiles at Jessie. Her curly black hair is plastered to her head in sleek waves with brilliantine, and her handkerchief-skirted dress floats around her dark limbs like bright yellow petals.

Jessie releases her hold on Aziz. 'Of course, Ruth. Not at all.'

Ruth reaches for Jessie's hand. 'Not him, silly. You.' She glances at Aziz. 'You don't mind, do you, Dr Khalid?'

Aziz smiles. 'Not in the least. I shall find you some champagne.'

Ruth takes Jessie in her arms as the band starts into a languid Argentine tango. 'Well, hello there, Jessie Khalid.'

Jessie smiles. 'Lady Evelyn is looking for you.'

'She found me. As did her shadow.'

'Mr Beauchamp? I thought he was rather charming. Very polite. And very tall.'

Ruth laughs. 'He is that. Very tall.' She leads Jessie into a series of forward *ochos*. 'What have you been up to since we last met? Running a health clinic, weren't you?'

'I still am. I hear you've been in Italy.'

'Italy, Germany, France ... Back to the States last month to visit my parents for my father's fiftieth birthday.'

'You do get around. Where's home? I know Lady Evelyn said, but I've quite forgotten.'

'Los Angeles. My father's a cameraman for Paramount Pictures. My mother's a make-up artist there. Are you ready to try some backward *ochos*? The tango's all the rage over there right now, what with *The Sheik* with Rudolf Valentino just released in the picture houses. The girls are mad for him.'

'I'm afraid I'm not a very good dancer.'

'You're plenty good, Jessie. I'll go slow. Or is it that you're uncomfortable dancing with a Black woman?'

'Not at all! I'm just worried about stomping all over your nice shoes.'

'My nice shoes can take it. It's my feet I'm worried about.'

Jessie follows Ruth's lead through the backward figure of eights, laughing when she completes the sequence.

'See, what did I tell you? You can dance as well as anyone. And you look very fine tonight too. It's a Chanel, isn't it?'

'How did you know?'

'I did a piece for *Vogue* magazine on Coco Chanel back in February. Bought a few things there myself. Wangled a discount because of the article. I don't have a wealthy husband to buy my clothes for me.'

'Aziz didn't buy this. My twin sister Etta sent it to me as a birthday present. I sent her a red *tarbouche*. I'm not sure it was an equal trade, but she wrote me that she loves to wear it shopping in Naples. She said it livens things up no end.'

'It sounds like I'd like her.'

'Everyone likes Etta. That's her blessing and her curse. She's married to the painter Carlo Marinetti.'

'Really? The one in prison for murdering his wife?'

'I'm afraid so, though he didn't do it, of course. Etta's working on getting him a retrial.'

'And you? What about you, Jessie?'

'I have a few friends. And there's Aziz. Unlike my sister, I don't need the world's adulation. My goodness, if I told Etta I knew someone with connections in the moving pictures, she'd be straight on the boat to America. She used to fancy herself the next Lillian Gish.'

The music climbs to a throbbing crescendo and Ruth sweeps Jessie into a low dip. Jessie giggles as Ruth pulls her to her feet.

'Thank you, Ruth. I shall always remember the night I danced the tango with the famous writer Ruth Bellico in Cairo. A story to tell my grandchildren.'

Ruth squeezes Jessie's hand. 'Here's hoping there will be more stories to tell them one day.' She releases Jessie's hand and weaves through the bodies crowding onto the dance floor until the flash of yellow is obliterated in a sea of black tuxedos and glittering diamonds.

---

'Well, aren't you a revelation, Jessica,' Lady Evelyn says as Jessie joins them at a table, sitting between Aziz and Brograve Beauchamp. 'I had no idea you could dance like that. Everyone was watching you two. If I had a jealous bone in my body, I would have been … well, quite jealous. It is my party, after all.'

Jessie fans her face with her hand. 'It was all Ruth. I simply followed her lead.'

Aziz pours out a glass of fizzing champagne into a delicate

crystal coupe and hands it to Jessie. 'Have some champagne, Jessica. You look flushed.'

Jessie eyes the bubbling wine, the thought of which stirs up the contents of her stomach like a tempest. 'I'd actually prefer a glass of water.'

'Oh, don't be silly, Jessica,' Lady Evelyn says. 'It's Pol Roger. Winston put Papa onto it. Apparently, it's his favourite. If it's good enough for Churchill, it's good enough for Lord Carnarvon.'

Jessie grimaces as her stomach dips and rolls like a boat on a high sea. 'No, really. I would prefer water.' She swallows down the bile rising in her throat. 'Or tea, perhaps?'

Brograve rises to his feet. 'I shall attend to that, Mrs Khalid. I should like some tea myself.'

Lady Evelyn fans her face with her feather fan as she scrutinises Jessie. She drops the fan onto Brograve's chair and leans across the table. 'Jessica! Are you' – she drops her gaze to Jessie's waist – 'are you *enceinte*?'

Jessie glances at Aziz. 'I, uh ...'

Aziz stares at Jessie. 'Are you ...?'

'I was going to tell you next week once I'd reached the end of the third month.' She glances back at Lady Evelyn, who looks about to burst with excitement.

Aziz rises abruptly. 'Please excuse me.'

'Aziz? Where are you going? Aziz?'

'Go after him, Jessie,' Lady Evelyn says, her dark eyes bright with emotion. 'It just took him by surprise. Men are funny creatures. It will be fine. Go.'

---

Jessie heads down the concrete path through the Residency's garden. If she has learned anything about Aziz in their four years of marriage, it is that he will be out here by the river.

Her pace quickens as her eyes adjust to the night sky. The waning moon is a yellow sliver in the dark sky which glitters with thousands of throbbing stars. She sees the black silhouette of a man under a towering sycamore tree by the perimeter wall, the tip of a cigarette in his hand a stab of orange in the gradations of black and grey.

'Aziz?'

Stubbing the cigarette out on the low stone wall, he turns to her. She can barely make out his features, though his eyes glitter in the moonlight. 'I'm sorry, Jessica.'

'Aren't you happy? We'll have a child now. I know how much you wanted a child. It's what I want, too.'

He encircles her in his arms and buries his head against her shoulder. 'I'm afraid, Jessica. I will never forgive myself if anything happens to you or the child.'

Jessie presses her hands against the soft, warm wool of his tuxedo as she clutches his body against hers.

'Nothing will happen, my darling. I promise you. We'll have a child and we will be a family. Everything will be fine, I promise you.'

# Chapter Thirty

## Celie

**West Lake School, West Lake, Alberta – December 1921**

'*Frau Jeffries?*'

Celie looks up from her table in the schoolroom as her students collect their coats and scarves from off the hooks at the back of the room and hurry out into the snowy landscape. She smiles at Hans, who shifts awkwardly on his feet in front of the table. 'Yes, Hans?'

He reaches across the desk and sets a small package wrapped in newspaper and green ribbon on the table. 'Happy Christmas, Frau Jeffries.'

'Oh, Hans!' she says as she picks up the package. 'That's awfully kind, but you didn't need to do that.'

'Please, I wanted to. I enjoy your classes very much. My Aunt Ursula says my English is very much improved.' He smiles shyly, ducking his head away from her gaze. 'I made it for you.'

'You did? May I open it now?'

'Yes. If you wish.' The colour rises in his cheeks. 'It is only a small thing.'

'And a very thoughtful thing.' She unties the ribbon and opens the newspaper, revealing a wooden pen case painted with stylised flowers. She unlatches the tiny brass catch. Inside, a cushion of blue cotton nestles, ready for a pen, and her name – Cecelia Jeffries – has been painted inside the lid in looping calligraphy.

'Oh, Hans. That's lovely! You did all this yourself?'

'*Ja*. I mean, yes. Except my Uncle Klaus helped me with the hinges and the clasp. He was once a clockmaker in Germany.'

She picks up her fountain pen and nestles it into the bed of cotton. 'You know, my fountain pen was given to me by my German tutor in London many years ago. Now I have a perfect place to keep it safe.' She shuts the lid and holds the pen case against her heart. 'I shall treasure this always, Hans, and whenever I open it, I shall think of you both.'

The boy's face flushes. 'I am very happy for that, Frau Jeffries.' He nods several times. 'Happy Christmas.'

Celie smiles. 'Happy Christmas, Hans.' She sets the pen case down on the table. 'Have you heard from your family in Germany?'

'Oh, yes. They are looking forward to my brother returning home for Christmas. He is studying law at university in Berlin. He will go home to Heidelberg for Christmas.'

'Doesn't Heidelberg have a good university?'

'Yes, one of the best in Germany, but he found it difficult to study there after the war. He said it made him think of all his friends who … who are no longer able to study.'

'Of course. I understand. The war was awful for so many people.'

Hans nods. 'It is why my parents sent me to Canada. To be away from these things.'

Celie nods. 'You'd best get home before it gets too dark, Hans. I'll see you in the New Year.' She holds up the gift. 'With my pen case.'

When he has gone, Celie opens the case and takes out the pen, a slim black Waterman's 'Ideal' fountain pen with a pointed brass nib, a gift from Max in 1912 before he'd left for his Christmas holiday in Heidelberg. The first thing he'd ever given her.

*'A Waterman's fountain pen, Max! It's lovely!'*

*Max laughs, his blue eyes lit with delight. 'It is to ensure you write to me when I am away,* Schatzi.*'*

*'I suppose I have no excuse, now, do I?'*

*'Indeed, you do not.'*

*She looks over at the geese and the ducks paddling through the gentle undulations of the boating lake in Regent's Park. A Canada goose honks and flaps at a small boy holding a piece of bread, and he screams and runs back to a plump, middle-aged woman pushing a baby carriage, the bird in hot pursuit.*

*'Drop the bread, Reggie! Drop the bread or 'e'll 'ave your fingers for tea!'*

*The boy abandons the bread and rushes into the woman's arms, weeping.*

*'Now, now, Reggie. 'E was only 'ungry. Let's go get ourselves an ice cream, shall we? There's a good boy.'*

*Max shifts on the bench, his leg brushing against her thigh. She is suddenly conscious of his warmth and she swallows as she debates whether to gently pull her leg away or surrender to the warmth that sends ripples of pleasure through her body. She turns to him abruptly just as he does the same to her.*

*'Celie, I—'*

*'Max, I—'*

*They stare at each other; and the honks of the geese, and the shrieks of the children, and the chatter of the nannies promenading around the chilly park with their charges fade into a distant murmur.*

*'Celie … Schatzi … may I kiss you?'*

*'Please, Max.'*

*As he leans forward, she closes her eyes. His warmth fills her world. And when he kisses her, it is like her life is finally beginning.*

# Chapter Thirty-One

Christina

**Chelsea, London – December 1921**

'Good morning.'

Christina opens her eyes, blinking as she focuses on the face in the bed beside her. Harry kisses her on the tip of her nose. 'Do you realise this is the first time we have woken up in a bed together?'

'It wasn't the first thing I thought of, no.'

He leans on his elbow and rests his chin in his hand. 'What is the first thing you thought of?'

'I thought, what am I going to tell Hettie? I was meant to be back from the opera by midnight.'

He leans over her and nuzzles her neck. 'You don't owe your housekeeper an explanation.'

'No, of course not. Still, I imagine she will *tut tut* me to death if I don't come up with some semi-believable excuse.'

'Tell her I had my foot run over by a taxi and you spent the night in the hospital with me. She will think that you are kind and caring.'

Christina pushes him away and sits up against the pillows. 'No amount of fibbing will ever make her believe that.'

Harry reaches out and grabs Christina's hand as she moves to rise. 'Come back, Tina. I've missed you so much.'

She looks over her shoulder at Harry. Against the white of the sheets, his skin is almost pink, and the grey in his hair, once so black, seems only to highlight the bright blue of his eyes. His body, which had once been sturdy with youthful muscle, has softened, though he has avoided gaining the gelatinous belly of so many of his contemporaries. He is still a handsome man. He is still the man her body wants more than any other.

She has fallen. Again. She should have never agreed to a second glass of brandy after the late supper at Rules. Though, if she were truthful with herself, her fate was sealed the day she ran into Harry at Farringdon Station in the rain. They are like two magnets, which, once near, must connect.

Even so, she should never have agreed to an evening in the West End. They were getting careless. What if Mr Fincher had seen them together? But then, what if he had? Just because she and Harry were acquaintances now, it doesn't mean they'd known each other thirty years ago on Capri. She cannot live in fear of that little grey man.

Now that she has capitulated, she is surprised to feel no remorse. She enjoyed her evening out with Harry at the opera, in one of the best boxes, and the supper at Rules. She had never done these things with Gerald, who had worked so hard in his modest photography studio to make a pleasant life for her and the girls. Pleasant, but not fun. Harry is fun.

They are both adults. They are both free of attachments. Is loving someone outside of wedlock really so very wrong if they are not hurting anyone? Her conscience pricks with Catholic guilt. She must go to Confession on Sunday and confess her sins. It's only been the one time. She will end it, of course she will. He is engaged to be married. Nothing good can come of this. She will end it and then all will be back to normal.

She leans over and kisses Harry lightly on his lips. 'I must wash and get dressed. I'm meeting the church council at eleven-thirty to discuss the final arrangements for the Advent Sunday cake sale.'

Harry throws open his arms. 'I surrender. I am no match for the Advent Sunday cake sale. Don't run off. I'll go downstairs to the café and fetch us some eggs and toast and tea.'

Christina smiles. 'Am I to be waited on hand and foot?'

'It's the least you deserve, my lovely siren.'

---

Harry regards Christina as he chews on a piece of toast covered with marmalade. He drops the crust onto his plate and dabs at his mouth with a napkin. 'Is everything to your liking?'

Christina smiles over her cup of tea. 'Very much so.'

'Good. The café is one of the reasons I chose this flat. That, and the rather good pub across the road. We never have to concern ourselves with cooking.'

Christina scans the large room, which is lit with the morning light streaming in through two tall sash windows, but which suffers from a surfeit of Victorian furniture and dull green wallpaper. Her forehead creases as she frowns at the overstuffed velvet button-backed settee.

Harry smiles. 'Yes, I know it's all rather dull, but I thought you might like the project of decorating it exactly as you wish. I've set money aside for that and have opened an account at Thornton-Smith Decorators in Soho Square.' He reaches into the pocket of his suit jacket and takes out a set of keys. 'These are yours. For the door downstairs and the front door here. Come and go as you please.'

Christina eyes the keyring with its dangling brass keys. 'Am I to be your mistress, then?'

Harrys sets the keys on the table beside the small brown teapot he's borrowed from the café. 'Tina, you and I belong together. I felt it from the first moment I saw you, sitting amidst the wildflowers on a hill overlooking the sea on Capri. But I need an heir or the Scottish estate will end up in the hands of the National Trust or some such when I die. If I had an heir and I were free, believe me, I would be on my knees begging you to marry me right now.'

'You have an heir, Harry. Cecelia.'

'Tina, I need a legitimate heir. A boy, ideally.'

'Yes, of course.' She picks up a spoon and stirs her cooling tea. She drops the spoon onto the saucer. 'I can't do this, Harry. I simply can't.'

He leans across the table and kisses her. 'You can. Please, Tina. Say you can. Say you will. I love you more than anyone else in the world. I always have and I always will.' He reaches for her hands and presses them against his chest. 'Can you feel that? You hold my heart in your hands. It's yours, Tina. No one else's but yours.'

She pulls her hands away. 'What about your engagement? Will you be calling that off or is the prospect of filling your bank account with Miss Rose McClellan's soup inheritance too much to resist?'

'Tina. Please. My engagement to Rose McClellan is nothing more than a business transaction. I need an heir and she is young enough to give me one. I am not impecunious, but the prospect of her dowry and eventual inheritance simply adds an additional shine to the deal. Eighteenth-century stately homes are expensive to maintain.'

'What if Mr Fincher were to discover our love nest?'

'He won't. I have ensured that he would not be able to trace this flat back to me.'

'But if he were to see us—'

'He would need to see us together. We will always arrive and leave at different times.'

'I am not certain I am capable of such subterfuge.'

'You managed well enough in Capri.'

Christina lays her napkin on the table and scrutinises Harry. She should leave now. Leave and never return. It's wrong, all wrong. She is a decent woman, a decent Catholic woman, living a decent life as a respected member of her community in Hither Green. But it is all so dull. The tedious church council meetings and WI talks. The cake sales and the knitting circles and Ellen Jackson's irritating superiority. When she looks forward to the years ahead, all she can see is more of the same. More of the same and then death. It's not enough. Not by a long chalk.

She picks up the keys. 'I am glad to hear your financial future is secure, Harry. I have very expensive tastes.'

# Part IV

1922

# Chapter Thirty-Two

## Etta

### Galerie DuRose, Paris – February 1922

Monsieur François DuRose of Galerie DuRose dabs at his lips with his handkerchief (Gaston having, much to his annoyance, neglected to provide napkins with the tea and macarons from Ladurée) as he eyes the chic figure of Madame Marinetti seated in the chair across from his desk. Her khaki-green tunic top, cape, and side-buttoned skirt are austere in their simplicity, set off only by a wide-brimmed black hat and ropes of pearls, though the colour is not, in his opinion, the most flattering for a fair-skinned blonde such as Madame Marinetti. He sniffs and presses the handkerchief against his nose. She has succumbed to the new scent as well – Chanel No. 5 – which now hangs over the streets of Paris like a cloud of bergamot and civet, and which now wafts through his gallery with Madame Marinetti's every movement.

'Are you certain you do not wish to taste one of the macarons, *Madame Marinetti*? I am particularly fond of the coffee-flavoured ones.' He presses his thumb and forefinger together beside his mouth and makes a smacking sound with his pursed lips. 'They are beyond exquisite.'

Etta smiles at the art dealer. 'Thank you, *Monsieur DuRose*. The tea is sufficient.' She adjusts the folds of her cape. 'What did you think of the latest shipment of Carlo's paintings?'

'Simply divine. There won't be any difficulty selling these, so long as your husband's name remains in the newspapers. I understand the old Marchese Ludovisi is objecting to any retrial on the grounds that your husband is a menace to society.'

Etta's smile fades and she juts out her jaw. 'My husband is no menace to anyone, *Monsieur DuRose*. He is the kindest, most loving man I have ever met. Carlo will get a retrial; you can be sure of that.'

'Helped, no doubt, by the income from the sale of his paintings.'

Etta fixes Monsieur DuRose with a cold hazel green stare. 'Good lawyers are very expensive.'

The art dealer rests his elbows on the arms of his chair. '*Madame Marinetti*, your husband has been in prison for over two years. Obviously, he has been unable to produce any new work since his arrest.'

'Yes?'

'I have been wondering how it is that there appears to be no shortage of supply. I am not complaining, to be sure. We are both benefitting exceptionally well from the sale of his work.'

'I'm sorry, *Monsieur DuRose*, but I fail to see your point.'

'*Madame Marinetti*, I am simply concerned about when the supply will' – he clears his throat – 'dry up.' He leans forward in his chair. 'It would be a great shame for both of us if it did.'

Etta relaxes in the bentwood chair. She had been worried for a moment. Worried that Monsieur DuRose might call her bluff. He knows. He knows that someone else is painting Carlo's artworks, but of course he will never admit it. That would be fraud, and he, of course, is above such a thing.

There is another thing Monsieur DuRose knows. He knows

that as long as Carlo is in jail, and there is a regular supply of 'his' art, they will make money. A lot of money. And this, as he says, is to their mutual benefit. It seems that his greed has rescued her from admitting the fraud. Without Carlo, she is a nobody. Worse than that, she is a female nobody.

If only she could tell the art dealer that *she* is the one who has transformed Carlo's 'derivative' work into art on par with the best of Picasso's and Modigliani's. She bites her lip to keep herself from shouting it out. *It's me! I'm the great artist! It's been me all along!*

She nods her head toward the plate of macarons. 'I will have a macaron after all, thank you. A coffee-flavoured one, as you suggest.'

He offers her the plate and she selects one of the delicacies. She takes a bite and observes him watching her as she chews. She sets the half-eaten macaron on her saucer. 'You are right. It is delicious.'

'I am gratified that you agree.'

She folds her hands in her lap. '*Monsieur DuRose,* I can assure you that I have located a large collection of my husband's paintings and sketches in an old storeroom in Naples. Neither of us need to worry about running out of the supply any time soon.'

The art dealer's fox-like face breaks into a chilly smile under his pencil-thin moustache. 'That is excellent. Very excellent, indeed.' He pushes the plate of macarons across the desk. 'Please, have another macaron, *Madame Marinetti*. I simply must insist.'

# Chapter Thirty-Three

## Christina

**Chelsea, London – May 1922**

*19 Portman Square*
*London W1*

*May 1st, 1922*

*My Lord,*

*You are no doubt surprised to receive this letter from me rather than from my solicitor, but I could not deny myself the pleasure of personally revealing this gem of information to you. It has taken a great deal of time and money, but I am a stubborn woman and I have finally succeeded in my quest to uncover the identity of Cecelia Fry's father.*

*First, permit me to gloat. I am an old woman, and I have not had much opportunity to do this in my life, so I ask that you indulge me.*

*You have met my investigator, Mr John Jacob Fincher. A man, I am sure you would agree, who appears unworthy of notice or attention. This is a demeanour he has done well to cultivate and which has stood him in good stead in this search.*

*How can an individual of such unremarkableness be a threat? Quite the opposite, it appears. The lovely woman – a Signora Guarino — and her granddaughter from the pastry shop on Capri were very taken with Mr Fincher on his first visit there last year, so much so that when he returned to Capri last month, they went so far as to welcome him into the bosom of their family.*

*Ah, what was Mr Fincher doing back on Capri, I hear you ask? As well you might, as it is not an inexpensive trip. He had exhausted all other avenues of investigation, and most of my patience, but I had rather underestimated his talent for persuasion. He had a hunch, he said. A hunch and a photograph of Christina I had recently found in my dear late sister Margaret's effects which I had given him, and which, in the strange way that the world works, was taken by her late husband Gerald in the autumn of 1892 when she had returned to London with Cecelia.*

*When Mr Fincher showed the dear old woman Christina's photograph alongside the one of you from Sandhurst, there was no doubt in her mind that these were the two young people who would visit her shop so regularly all those years ago, Lord Sherbrooke. Or, should I say, H. Grenville?*

*Truthfully, I have suspected as much for quite some time, but lacked incontrovertible proof. I believe you will agree with me that this hurdle has been cleared.*

*Now, what am I to do with this incendiary information? Oh my. I have just had to lay down my pen and fan my face. I am overcome with the emotion of this moment. I do not believe I have ever felt such power in my life. I can see why you have chosen to pursue a career in politics. Power is, indeed, a heady drug.*

*To business. If Christina wishes not to have me reveal the identity of Cecelia's father to Cecelia, she must stop her objections to the sale of the Bishop house immediately. She is to sign over the deed to my name and remove herself and her descendants from any claim on any property or possessions of the Bishop family. In return, I shall take the knowledge of your identity as Cecelia's father to the grave and cease any further investigations into the legitimacy of Christina's birth.*

*You will agree, I am certain, that this is a very generous offer. Given your own interest in this matter, and the damage its reveal will do to your reputation should it reach the newspapers, which I suspect it would via our dear Mr Fincher, I expect that you shall make every effort to persuade Christina to agree to this proposal.*

*I shall advise my solicitor to expect an answer to this offer by twelve o'clock noon on Friday. Any delay will render this offer null and void, and you can expect the newspapers to be running some very interesting headlines on Sunday. I would not credit your chances at the leadership of the Tory Party should they appear.*

*Yours faithfully,*
*Miss Henrietta Bishop*

---

'Syrie, are you certain dipping curtain hems into cement is a good idea?'

The interior decorator Syrie Maugham looks up from the sitting room floor, where she kneels in her black wool Molyneux suit, dipping the hem of a curtain into a bucket of watery cement. Her dark eyes glint like chips of coal in the sunlight streaming in from the window and she brushes the back of a hand across her cheek, leaving a streak of white cement.

'It's the only way these linen curtains will hang properly, Christina. We are striving for perfection, are we not? *Harper's Bazaar* are expecting nothing less for their feature on me and my new shop.'

'Yes, of course. It's why I lent you the money to open your own shop in the first place. People need to see what you're capable of, Syrie. Ernest Thornton-Smith didn't appreciate your unique aesthetic, but I do. I have always had an artistic eye. My daughter Etta takes after me in this regard.'

Christina picks up a white satin cushion and fluffs it into a shape. She frowns as she sets it back on the cream velvet sofa. 'You will ensure my name is kept out of the magazine article? As I've said, I am not one to cultivate publicity.'

Syrie presses a cement-stained finger against her lips. 'Discretion is assured. I will ensure that no one's name is mentioned.' She lifts the curtain hem out of the bucket and gestures at Christina. 'Take the bucket away and slide that piece of cardboard underneath, please. Quick, quick.'

Christina organises the swap as the interior decorator climbs to her feet with a grunt and proceeds to arrange the curtains into perfect vertical pleats. Christina scans the room, its dull green décor now transformed into an oasis of mirrors and white damask-covered walls, creamy upholstery and French antiques stripped of their gilding and painted white.

'You will come to the house-warming party on the nineteenth, Syrie? You're certain to pick up some new customers. Do be sure the white leather dining chairs are delivered by then. I can't have our government ministers and their wives standing about eating and drinking red wine on the new cream carpet.'

Syrie Maugham looks over her shoulder. 'Oh, white wine only, please, Christina. Red wine would be disastrous.'

Christina smiles weakly. 'Of course. And the dining chairs?'

Syrie huffs impatiently. 'They are in hand.' She wipes her hands together and stands back to inspect her handiwork. 'What does Lord Sherbrooke think of the new décor?'

'He's quite pleased with it. He also has an artistic eye. He used to paint when he was a young man.'

'Oh? Did you know him back then?'

'Uh, no, not at all. He's simply told me about it. It's all hanging up in the Scottish house.'

'Perhaps Lord Sherbrooke might consider my services for the Scottish house in due course? I've often thought that those stuffy old piles would benefit from a complete rethink.'

The front door slams and a voice calls out Christina's name from the hallway. The door to the sitting room swings open. 'Tina? Oh, hello.'

Christina gestures to the decorator. 'This is Syrie Maugham, Harry, the wonderful decorator I've told you about? She's ensuring that our flat is on the cutting edge of style and taste.'

Harry shakes Syrie's hand and glances around the room. 'It's rather white, isn't it?' His eyes narrow as his gaze travels down the length of the draperies. 'What's happened to the curtains?'

'Just a bit of cement, Harry.'

He raises his eyebrows. 'Cement?'

Syrie smiles indulgently. 'It's a technique I've developed to help curtains fall in perfect vertical pleats, Lord Sherbrooke.'

Harry glances at Christina. 'Ah, of course. Silly me.'

Christina takes hold of Harry's elbow and steers him toward the hallway. 'Give us a moment, will you? Syrie's just about to leave. She was asking about her bill earlier. You have paid it, haven't you?'

'Not yet. It's extortionate, Tina.'

Christina fixes Harry with an icy blue stare. 'We are not having this conversation, Harry. You said I could decorate the flat how I wish. You are to pay that bill forthwith, or we risk not having chairs for our house-warming supper for your Tory colleagues.'

'Tina, my account was with Thornton-Smith, not this Syrie woman. Ernest and I had … an arrangement. I was not expecting to have to pay retail prices. I'm not made of money, Tina.' He lowers his voice. 'Why else do you think I need to marry an heiress? The Scottish estate is a money pit.'

'The Scottish estate is of no concern to me, and I prefer not to discuss the issue of Miss McClellan. Syrie is a talented decorator whom I am supporting in her new venture. I have invested personally in her shop. I believe the investment will be lucrative in the long term, but only if you pay her bills.'

'You invested in her shop? How much did that cost?'

'Not that it's any of your business, but four hundred pounds.'

'Four hundred pounds! Are you mad, Christina! Where did you get that sort of money?'

'From Gerald. He made some wise investments. He was surprisingly financially astute for a photographer.'

'I see.' Harry sighs. 'Well, I'll see what I can do.'

'We need the chairs, Harry.'

'Yes, of course.'

Syrie Maugham appears in the hallway, adjusting a fox fur around her shoulders. 'All done for today. Don't draw the curtains for twenty-four hours. They need to set.'

---

At breakfast the next morning, Christina refills Harry's teacup and sets down the brown teapot. 'I've been thinking that we should engage a housemaid.'

Harry looks over at her, a spoonful of boiled egg half-way to his mouth. 'A housemaid? There's just the two of us, Tina, and we're only here a few nights a week.'

'The flat doesn't clean itself, Harry, and I'm not about to get down on my hands and knees and scrub the floor. And these dishes? They need washing.'

'We've managed fine so far.'

'That's because I've had Hettie over once a week, but I simply can't take her grumbling any longer. She quite disapproves of us. And I will need a cook and a butler for our house-warming supper as well.'

He tosses his napkin onto the table. 'Tina, I am not a walking chequebook.'

'Harry, I am compromising myself enough by even being here. Believe me, there are times when I feel I must end this ... arrangement.'

'Tina—'

'Do you think it's easy for me when I take Communion on Sundays? To know that I am a sinner in the house of God? Harry, you must meet me half-way. If I am to be a sinner, I expect to enjoy the trappings of my status as your mistress.'

A nerve quivers under the skin of Harry's temple. 'Enough of all this nonsense.'

'Nonsense? What nonsense?'

Harry runs his hand over his moustache. 'Tina, I've received a letter from Henrietta.'

'You did? Why didn't you tell me?'

'That woman was here when I arrived last night, and then' – he expels an exhausted sigh – 'Henrietta knows, Tina. She knows that I'm Cecelia's father.'

Christina's mouth falls open. 'How?'

'That bloody investigator. He went back to Capri with that photograph of me at Sandhurst and one that Gerald took of you in 1892 that Henrietta gave him. He showed them both to that old woman who runs the bakery in the Piazzetta. She confirmed it. One hundred per cent, absolutely. We were the ones she remembered. Incontrovertible proof, as your aunt says in her letter.'

'Oh, Harry. What are we going to do?'

'It's what *you're* going to do, Tina.'

'Me? What do you mean?'

'Your aunt is demanding that you sign over the deed to the Bishop house to her and remove yourself and your descendants from any further claim on any part of the Bishop estate.'

'That house should come to me when Aunt Henrietta finally dies, which I sincerely hope won't be too long. I'll not give in to her, Harry. That house is mine by right.'

'She's threatening to go to the newspapers about this. We will both be ruined.'

'Is that what you're worried about? The loss of your reputation?'

'Tina, she said that she'd tell Cecelia that I'm her father. Is that what you want?'

'No, of course not.' She picks up her teaspoon and stirs her cooling tea. 'I can't believe Aunt Henrietta's doing this.'

'Believe it. I have every reason to think she is serious.'

'I'm to give up every claim on the Bishop fortune in return for her silence?'

'Yes.'

She glares at Harry, her eyes narrowing as the years of suppressed anger, heartache, hurt and frustration bubble up through her body like molten lava.

'This is all because of you, Harry! This is all your fault. You took advantage of me. I was an innocent and you ruined my life!'

Harry stares at her, his face a mask of shock at the sudden attack. 'My fault? I seem to recall you were a willing participant on more than one occasion.'

She glowers at him across the table. 'I thought we would get married. I loved you. I loved you more than I've ever loved anyone, and I hate myself for it.'

Harry pushes away from the table and heads toward the door. 'That's where you made your mistake. I never loved you, Tina. I wanted you, but I never loved you.'

She springs to her feet. 'Harry! Harry, come back here! You're lying! Tell me you loved me. Tell me you still do. I've ruined myself for you, Harry!'

The front door slams. Christina stares at the expensive white china laid out on the table. She swipes her arm across the table, screaming as the plates, saucers, teacups and the brown teapot spill the remains of their breakfast across the white carpet.

# Chapter Thirty-Four

## Etta

### Shakespeare and Company, Paris – May 1922

Etta winces as a fresh spattering of raindrops falls from the surly grey spring sky. *A rotten day to have forgotten my umbrella,* she thinks as she pulls up the collar of her coat. She pushes through the door of a bookshop just as the clouds burst, deluging the street with a thundering curtain of water. She shuts the door behind her as the bookshop embraces her with a welcoming warmth and the scent of leather and tobacco. The walls, where the wooden shelves are not stacked to the ceiling with books, are plastered with framed photographs of living and long-dead authors. A handsome, dark-haired woman of about thirty-five, wearing a brown velvet jacket and silk scarf tied as a cravat, sits at a small battle-scarred table talking to a heavy-set man with glistening black hair and a thick moustache who listens to her in rapt attention.

'… and I'm a firm believer that the Russians are imperative reading,' she is saying. 'Dostoyevsky, Tolstoy and Turgenev, of course. You must read *Fathers and Sons* as soon as you finish *War and Peace*. Then we'll move on to more Joyce and Lawrence. Hadley just borrowed D.H. Lawrence's *Sons and Lovers*. Read it once she's finished it and then bring it back. No rush.'

The woman looks up as Etta brushes the raindrops off her sleeve.

'Oh, hello. Raining cats and dogs, isn't it?' she says in an American accent. 'Come in and have a wander. Stay as long as you like. Can't have you getting drenched out there.'

Etta smiles gratefully. 'Thank you. It is rather a bear out there today. It's lovely and cosy in here.'

'Best place in Paris next to Café du Dôme,' the dark-haired man says as he eyes her. 'Sylvia here is the mother hen of us writers.'

'Oh, are you on the wall?'

The man draws his black eyebrows together into a puzzled frown. 'On the wall?'

Sylvia laughs and points to the wall of portraits. 'On the wall, Ernest.' She looks at Etta. 'He's not on the wall yet, but you can be sure he will be one of these days.'

The man turns back in his chair to face the woman. 'Too right, Sylvia. Now what about those blue notebooks? I'm going to need a good half-dozen for the summer in Switzerland ...'

Etta wanders into the depths of the shop, eyeing the shelves of English language books, art books, travel memoirs, classical literature and poetry, until she finds herself in a narrow aisle devoted to the types of novels of which her mother would never approve. If only Zelda were in town. What fun they'd have reading naughty passages to each other in the stacks. She slides a copy of D.H. Lawrence's *Women in Love* from the shelf and begins reading the first chapter.

'So, you're one of those.'

Etta looks up to see a young man with a slick of dark blond hair crowning a high forehead regarding her with deep-set blue eyes from the opposite side of the bookshelf.

'Excuse me?'

'One of those. You know, people who read books for free in bookshops.' He has the nasal twang of an American.

'I beg your pardon. The lady at the desk said …'

'That's Sylvia all over. Heart as big as a whale. Freeloaders don't pay the rent.'

Etta's jaw drops. 'Are you saying that I'm a freeloader? I'll have you know I am quite able to afford any book in this place.'

The man walks around the end of the bookshelf and picks a book off the shelf. '*Erotic Symbolism.* My, my. It looks like you've found your way into the naughty book section.'

'I have not!'

He nods toward the book in her hands. 'What have you got there, then?'

'If you must know, it's *Women in Love* by D.H. Lawrence. The woman at the front—'

'The owner. Sylvia Beach.'

'Right. Sylvia Beach was talking to a customer about one of Mr Lawrence's books when I came in. Do you think she would be talking about erotic literature so freely when anyone walking into the shop would hear her? I hardly think so.'

'You haven't read any Lawrence, then, I take it.'

'No.' She points to the book. 'That's why I was reading the first few pages. To see if I might like it.'

'And? Do you like it?'

She feels the heat rise in her face. 'I don't know. I was rather rudely interrupted.' She puts the book back on the shelf and moves to step past the man. She glares at him. 'If you'll excuse me.'

He raises his hand to stop her. 'Hold on. Aren't you going to take the book? You'll like it. Trust me. It's very naughty and very well-written. It's a lot better than reading Ethel M. Dell.'

'I'll have you know I quite like Ethel M. Dell. *The Desire of His Life* is one of my favourite books. I like Henry James and Gustav Flaubert as well, but sometimes one does not wish to eat a five-course meal when a delicious pudding will do.'

He chuckles. 'That's me put in my place.' He pulls the book off the shelf and hands it to Etta. 'Do Sylvia a favour and buy the book.'

Etta clutches *Women in Love* against her coat. 'I didn't come in here to buy a book. I just wanted to get out of the ra—'

'Damn, is that the time?' the American says as he catches sight of the ancient wall clock mounted on a ceiling beam. He jams his grey felt fedora onto his head and tips the brim at Etta. 'Gotta go. Deadline calling. Enjoy the book.'

'Yes … right …' She watches him wave at Sylvia and pat the man named Ernest on his shoulder on his way out of the bookshop. The door slams and he disappears down the rain-soaked street.

She walks over to the woman at the desk and hands her the book. 'I'll take this, please.'

'Certainly. Borrowing or buying?'

'Buying.'

Ernest nods approvingly. 'Good choice. Any right-thinking person needs to read Lawrence.'

'So I gather.' She pays for the book and tucks it under her arm.

'Let me give you a bag for your book,' Sylvia says as she bends down to grab a paper bag from a jumble under her desk. 'You don't want Mr Lawrence to get wet.'

'Thank you.' Etta drops the book into the bag. She glances out at the street. 'You don't happen to know who that young man was who just left, do you?'

Ernest grunts. 'You mean CJ? That was CJ Melton. He's a hack for the Associated Press. Could be a proper writer if he put his back into it.' He shrugs. 'Doesn't seem that bothered. Less competition for me, isn't that right, Sylvia?'

'Don't get ahead of yourself, Ernest.' She taps the copy of *Crime and Punishment* on her desk. 'Read first, write later.'

Etta shuts the bookshop door behind her and huddles under the awning of the adjoining shop as the rain drizzles down over the scurrying shoppers.

*CJ Melton. Charles John? Chester James? Christopher Joseph?* She smiles and shakes her head. He was just a man in a bookshop. An impertinent man at that. She will probably never see him again.

# Chapter Thirty-Five

## Jessie

### Altumanina, Cairo, Egypt – June 1922

Jessie stands on the balcony of her bedroom at Altumanina and breathes in the warm morning air, which is heady with the scent of the roses and jasmine that clamber up the walls of the house. She looks down at her bump which presses against the fine cotton of the loose blue *jellabiya*, one of a dozen Zara had bought her in the souk when she could no longer fit into her own clothes. A listless breeze wafts across the garden from the river, barely stirring the leaves of the palm trees and sycamores. Jessie encircles her bump with her hands. *It will be hot later, little one. Is that why you're not coming out? Are you too cosy in there?*

Aziz joins her on the balcony, tying his tie. 'How are you feeling, *habibti*? Shall I ask Dr Shaw to come by later to check on you? Perhaps we should think about inducing—'

'No, no inducing. The baby will come when it's ready. I'm perfectly fine.' She reaches up to brush away a fleck of shaving cream from Aziz's cheek. 'Don't forget that Mama's train is arriving at six. Mustapha may want to take Mohammed to help him. She's bound to have a mountain of luggage.'

Aziz smiles. 'Don't worry. Everything is taken care of. Zara and I are closing the clinic early today so I can leave in good time to meet your mother at the train station. I am glad she is finally arriving. I still don't understand why you refused to have her come sooner.'

Jessie rolls her eyes. 'Aziz, if you had ever lived in the same house as my mother and me, you would be glad I've managed to put her off till now. Mama and I have a talent for rubbing each other the wrong way at the best of times. At any rate, both Zara and Dr Simmonds from the hospital have kept the clinic running smoothly when you've been busy.'

'If we hadn't done so, you would have been in there on your feet every day.'

'I wouldn't.'

Aziz raises a dark eyebrow.

Jessie laughs. 'All right, I probably would have. But I promise I've been keeping off my feet and resting, even though your mother is driving me mad insisting I play backgammon with her every afternoon. She gets extraordinarily affronted when I win, by the way.'

'Jessica, speaking of my mother, she has agreed to have tea and sweets for your mother when she arrives.'

'How did you manage that? Your mother's been in a strop ever since she heard that Mama is coming to stay for two months.'

'It was Zara's doing. She has promised to permit the parents of one of King Fuad's functionaries to ply their son's candidacy as a possible husband in return for my mother being civil to yours.'

'Zara mustn't do that! She can't marry someone she doesn't love.'

'I shouldn't worry about that. Zara is playing a game with our mother. I can assure you she has no intention of marrying this fellow or anyone else to my knowledge.'

'But—'

Aziz kisses Jessie on the cheek. 'Have a good day, darling. I'm just in the clinic with Zara. Stay off your feet and don't do anything to overexert yourself.'

Jessie is kneeling on the grass pulling weeds out of the rose bed when she feels the first sharp pang. She gasps and sits back on her heels. She breathes deeply as she grips the cool grass. It needs a cut, she thinks. I must tell Mohammed.

She rubs her swollen belly as the pain dissipates. *Are you finally coming, baby? You've taken your time about it.*

She lumbers to her feet and has taken only two steps toward the house when a stream of bloody water gushes down her legs. Sinking to her knees, she clutches at her belly.

'Marta! Marta!'

Another stab like a knife plunging into her core. *No, no, no. Not again. Please God, not again.*

---

She is floating. An angel wraps his arms around her and carries her through jasmine-scented clouds. Pink and red rose petals sprinkle down like rain.

The angel lays her down, and she sinks into the cloud until it folds over her. Until she can't breathe. She thrashes against the cloud which is as thick and heavy as damp cotton.

'Jessica. Everything will be fine. Jessica, do you hear me?'

She opens her eyes and blinks as the angel materialises. 'Aziz?'

He is clutching her hand. 'Jessica, the baby is coming. Marta has gone to fetch Dr Shaw. Zara will be here as soon as she shuts the clinic. We will be here for you, *habibti*. It will all be fine.'

Her body seizes as a contraction pushes at her womb. She groans and squeezes Aziz's hand, panting until the seizure spends itself. 'There was blood, Aziz.'

'I know. I found you in time. Don't worry.'

She struggles onto her elbows. 'We're going to lose the baby, aren't we?' Panic rises through her body in a wave. 'Aren't we, Aziz?'

'No, *habibti*. Our baby will be born today and will be healthy, *inshallah*.'

Another contraction wracks Jessie's body and she pants until the cloud encloses her in its soft, suffocating hold.

A woman's voice.

'She's bleeding.'

---

'Jessica?'

'Mama!' Jessie beams at her mother as she cradles the baby in her arms. 'You found us.'

Christina enters the room and thrusts her parasol into Layla Khalid's hands. 'I did. Zara met me downstairs and told me where you were.' She crosses over to the bed and kisses Jessie on her forehead. 'I'm relieved to see you're in one piece.'

'Isn't she lovely, Mama?'

Christina sits on the bed and brushes her hand over Jessie's damp hair. 'She's beautiful. Just like her mother.'

'What are you talking about, Mama? She doesn't look like me at all. She's the spitting image of Aziz with her black hair and dark eyes.' She taps the sleeping baby on her nose. 'You're going to be the apple of your papa's eye, aren't you, my love?' She looks at her mother. 'Her name is Shani Maryam. It means wonderful beloved.'

Layla Khalid drops the parasol on the bed beside Christina. 'It is a pity she is a girl, Jessica. You have had to endure all of this for nothing.'

Jessie frowns at her mother-in-law. 'What do you mean?'

'A daughter cannot carry on the family name. You will simply have to do it all again and hope for a son or Aziz must seriously consider taking a second wife.'

Christina rises and turns to face Layla. 'You are not to speak to my daughter like this.'

Jessie glances from her mother to her mother-in-law, who are glowering at each other like angry cats about to pounce.

'Mama, please. This is Aziz's mother, *Madame Layla Khalid*. I'm sure she didn't mean what she said. We've all had a difficult day.'

Christina purses her lips as she eyes the woman whose physical grace and dark beauty cannot conceal the coldness in her eyes. '*Madame Khalid,* as I am a guest in this house, I shall give you the benefit of the doubt. I should warn you, however, never to speak to my daughter like that again, or you will have to deal with me.'

Layla Khalid arches a dark eyebrow. 'This should worry me?'

Christina graces Layla Khalid with her frostiest smile. 'It should worry you very much indeed. I can be quite vindictive.'

A groan from the bed. The two women turn to see Jessie bent over the baby, clutching at her stomach.

'Something's wrong,' Jessie gasps. 'Mama, take the baby. Find Aziz.' She groans and writhes against the pillows. 'Quickly! Please!'

Christina takes hold of the baby and turns to Layla. 'Where's your son?'

Layla stands at the end of the bed, watching Jessie thrash and roll under the sheets. It had all seemed lost, her dream of Jessica's death in childbirth dissipating like mist in sunlight. But, perhaps, fortune had shifted in her favour.

She looks at Christina. 'I have no idea.'

---

Jessie hears the mumble of voices first. Then, slowly, so slowly, the grey fog of unconsciousness dissolves. She hurts. It is like an elephant has stepped on her body and crushed every sinew. She opens her eyes. Aziz's face appears above her. She feels him slide his hand around hers. It is warm.

'Jessica. *Alhamdulillah*.'

Christina's face appears beside his. 'Jessica. Thank Heaven. You had us worried.'

'Shani?' Her voice comes out as a croak. She swallows. 'Where's Shani?' She feels the bed dip beside her.

'She's here.' Zara's voice. 'In my arms.'

Jessie turns her head to look at the baby. It isn't their bedroom. A white-uniformed nurse hovers in the background. 'What happened? Where am I?'

Aziz brushes a strand of damp hair off her cheek. 'You haemorrhaged, my darling. You're in the hospital. You need to rest.'

'The hospital?' She sees the tube inserted into her arm. 'I just remember … I just remember the pain. And then you carrying me.'

Aziz sits on the bed. 'Dr Shaw had to perform a hysterectomy, my darling. There was no other way.'

'A hysterectomy? I can't have any more children?'

'No, *habibti*. But we have our wonderful Shani. I love you, Jessica. More than my heart can express. You and our beautiful daughter are everything to me. We have our family now.'

# Chapter Thirty-Six

## Celie

**Sweet Briar Farm, West Lake, Alberta – July 1922**

Celie turns the last of the bread loaves out onto one of the cooling racks she has set on the kitchen table and breathes in the yeasty aroma that wafts through the kitchen. If her sisters could see her now, what a ribbing she would get! The girl who barely knew how to boil an egg before the war. She folds the tea towel over the range's handle and slaps her hands against her apron to brush off the vestiges of flour that cling to her palms.

The oak-cased clock that Frank had bought on credit the previous Christmas chimes twice on the mantelshelf over the new brick fireplace. She is still getting used to the new layout, with the old woodburning stove moved into the smokehouse, yet another of Frank's 'improvements', its space filled with a new buttoned chesterfield, again on credit. *Mr T. Eaton really should be sending us a Christmas card every year*, Celie thinks. *The amount Frank spends with his company*!

She sits in a kitchen chair and pulls open the drawer under the pine table, removing a fountain pen, a bottle of ink and several sheets of writing paper. After filling the pen with ink and blotting the nib on a scrap of cotton, she starts to write.

*Sweet Briar Farm*
*West Lake, Alberta*
*Canada*

*July 24th, 1922*

*Dear Jessie,*

*It feels like such an age since we've seen each other. I suppose that's because it* is *an age! I know we've had our moments in the past, but I'm so glad we smoothed everything over back in London before I left for Canada. Do you still have the photograph I gave you? The one of the three of us by the waterfall? I have it here, pinned to the wall above the dresser n the bedroom. Were we ever that young and carefree, Jessie? It seems so very long ago.*

*Dear me. That sounds rather melancholic, doesn't it? I don't mean that in the least. I am more than busy here on the farm, as you can imagine, and Frank's just had a smokehouse built so I am learning how to smoke ham and cheese now. I smell like a chimney when I come out of there!*

*I was so very happy to hear of the news of little Shani's birth. I told Lulu that she has a new little cousin in Egypt and she jumped around the house with her Raggedy Ann squealing 'Baby! Baby! Baby!' for what seemed like an hour. Won't it be lovely for Shani, Lulu and Adriana to meet one day? What a little threesome they will be!*

*Lulu is growing like a little weed. She is almost two-and-a-half now, though she acts like she's twenty some days. She is quite the bossy boots. She is over at my friend Mavis Wheatley's today playing with the Wheatley children. Young Ben is just a day older than her, and he follows her around like a puppy. She has already started pestering me about school, as she sees the older Wheatleys come home with their school books and she thinks it's all very grown up and exciting. I think I may have to start teaching her the alphabet to keep her from fretting.*

*I have been teaching English to German immigrants in the local school on Saturday mornings since last September, though the students are on their summer holiday currently. It has been a lifesaver for me. Frank wasn't at all keen on the idea at first, saying wives are not meant to go out to work. He seemed terribly afraid that it would reflect poorly on his ability to support his family. I managed to win him over when I said I would use the money from teaching to pay for all the extra household things like curtain material and new dishes. I put my earnings in a Fry's Cocoa tin (of course!) and I call it the Sweet Briar Bank. I had been hoping to use some of it toward my photography, but it seems to be rather a sore subject with Frank currently – he says it's a needless expense and a waste of my time – so I've put my camera away for now. Perhaps photography is a part of my old self that is done and over with, and I simply have to accept that.*

*My German students are all ages, from twelve to over forty. They are all very keen to learn English in order to become Canadians, so I do my very best by them. There is one boy in particular who is so eager and helpful. He ensures the stove is lit before I arrive in the morning and insists on putting it out before we leave at noon. He is from Heidelberg and is staying with his uncle's family in a place called Freedom, west of West Lake.*

Celie sets down the pen and sits back in the chair. Just writing that word – Heidelberg – is enough to call up memories of Max. She pushes away from the table and retrieves the bread knife, a plate, butter, and a butter knife from the kitchen. Picking the fattest loaf, she saws into its end, almost swooning with the release of the intense bready scent from the soft white centre. She slathers on a knob of yellow butter and bites into the bread. Too warm yet, she knows, and she'll likely have a stomachache later, but she is only human. She has to do something to distract herself. But it is getting harder. The memories more frequent.

She sits down and picks up the pen.

*Jessie, I have been thinking about Max. Not just occasionally, but I will find myself out in the vegetable patch suddenly remembering a picnic we'd had in Hyde Park, or an afternoon we'd spent walking along the Embankment. I've read and re-read every letter he's ever sent me and can imagine exactly the scent of the roses along the Philosophers' Walk in Heidelberg, or the colour of the sunset on the Neckar River. It's the German boy, Hans, who has triggered it. He is so like I imagine a young Max would have been. So polite, thoughtful and intelligent. So hard-working and eager to learn. And to know he comes from Heidelberg! I have this deep yearning inside of me that no amount of busyness and fatigue can dampen. I have tried so hard to move on from Max, to be a good wife to Frank, a good mother to Lulu, but marriage is quite different to what I'd imagined.*

How can she tell Jessie that she barely sees Frank at all once he leaves the house after breakfast? She is alone with Lulu until he falls into bed smelling of dirt and Tom Philby's moonshine. It's no wonder there hasn't been another child. She takes another bite of the bread and brushes golden crumbs off the letter, frowning as a drop of butter smudges the ink.

*There are days I miss my old life, Jessie. I loved my life in London. I can't believe I used to be a journalist for the* Daily Mirror. *It seems quite impossible that I was ever that person. But that was another time and another place. We all must make decisions in life and hope for the best.*

*My love to you all. Try not to melt in the summer heat over there in Egypt.*

*Your loving sister,*
*Celie*

---

A few weeks later, Ol' Man Forbes hands Celie a telegram when she is in the store buying thread and floral fabric for a dress for Lulu.

'Came for you this mornin', Mizz Jeffries,' he says, his words still buttered with the sleepy vowels of the American south. 'Would you like a chair?'

She takes the telegram from him. 'Why would I need a chair?'

He squints at her through his rimless spectacles. 'Never saw a telegram with good news.'

She smiles. 'Thank you, Mr Forbes. I'm fine.' She looks over at Lulu who has her face pressed against the glass of the candy counter. 'Lulu, please don't do that. You'll leave marks on the glass.'

The old man chuckles. 'Would you like a gobstopper, Lulu?'

'Yes, please!'

'Mr Forbes, you mustn't spoil her. She gets enough of that from her father and the Wheatleys.'

Ol' Man Forbes drops a large black candy ball into a small paper bag and hands it over the counter to the little girl. 'A gobstopper won't do her any harm, will it, Miss Lulu?'

Lulu looks at Celie. 'Please, Mommy?'

Celie sighs. 'Fine. Just this once and don't tell your father. Sit by the window while I read this.'

Lulu pops the gobstopper into her mouth and skips over to a stool by the window as Celie opens the telegram.

9.30 CAIRO EGYPT 15 AUG 22
DEAR CELIE – BE YOURSELF – TAKE PHOTOS –
EVERYTHING WILL BE OK –
LOVE JESSIE

# Chapter Thirty-Seven

Christina & Jessie

**Altumanina, Cairo, Egypt – August 1922**

Marta sets a plate of butter cookies liberally sprinkled with powdered sugar and slivered almonds on the terrace's low brass table. She smiles at the chubby-faced baby who is nestled in a swaddling of their best cotton sheets in Christina's arms, and chucks her under her chin as she coos.

'She is a pretty little bird, just like her mama.' She smiles at Christina. 'I can bring you more tea, *Madame Fry*?'

'Thank you, Marta, I'm fine,' Christina says as she fans her face with a Spanish fan Zara bought her in the souk. 'I'm simply enjoying sitting here with my granddaughter, though I quite underestimated how hot it would be here in August.'

'Yes, it is very hot but better outside in the shade than in the house.'

'I entirely agree. There is such a lovely view of the garden here. Egypt is quite a revelation to me. I thought it was all desert and pyramids. And the food is delicious.'

Marta nods her kerchiefed head, setting her hooped earrings dancing. 'I am cooking *kushari* tonight. It will help Madame Khalid's strength.'

'Madame Khalid?'

'Your daughter. Madame Khalid.'

'Ah, of course. I thought for a moment you were referring to the other Madame Khalid.'

'You mean me, I assume?'

Christina looks up to see Layla Khalid enter the terrace. The black silk *jellabiya* flutters about Layla's slender body as she makes her way to her favourite settee. She has been heavy-handed with the kohl today, Christina observes, an error which calls attention to the fine lines which fan out from her amber eyes.

'I was simply saying that I am unused to my daughter being referred to as Madame Khalid. She will always be Jessica to me.'

Layla Khalid nods as she arranges the folds of the *jellabiya* over her legs, lifting it slightly to expose slender ankles clad in gold slippers. She snaps her fingers at the housekeeper.

'Tea, Marta. Don't stand there lurking like a heron.'

'Yes, *Madame*.'

Layla focuses her gaze on Christina. 'Every time I see you, you have the baby in your arms. This is a task for a nanny. It is best that the child learn independence from family at a young age. It strengthens them for the challenges of life.'

Christina smiles indulgently. 'Shani is a baby. She has no need to be independent. We engaged a nanny for my daughters only when they reached the age of three, to free up some of my time to attend to my numerous responsibilities in the Women's Institute and on the local church council. They have all developed into exceptional young women with strong characters of their own.'

Layla Khalid tuts. 'Having a strong character is of no use to a woman. My own daughter is evidence of that. I blame my late husband entirely for her wilfulness. He indulged her every childish whim, disregarding any effort I made to steer Zara into a proper marriage. Now she is still unmarried at the age of thirty. My aunt was a grandmother at thirty-one.'

Christina's eyes widen. 'That would mean—'

'Ah, Marta, finally,' Layla says to the housekeeper as she enters the terrace carrying a silver tray laden with an ornate silver teapot and delicate tea glasses. 'You would think the kitchen is the other side of Cairo.'

Marta sets the silver tray on the low coffee table and picks up the teapot to pour out the tea. Layla waves her away. 'Go attend to dinner. I shall pour.'

Marta catches Christina's eye as she bites her lip.

'Marta?' Christina asks. 'Would you put Shani in her crib, please? She's had a busy morning with her Nana. I'll come into the kitchen after tea and you can teach me how to make *kushari*.'

Marta smiles as she takes the swaddled baby from Christina. 'Come now, my little dove,' she says as she kisses Shani on her forehead. The baby squirms and yawns. 'Nana Marta will sing you to sleep.'

After Marta leaves, Layla pours the tea and sets a tea glass in front of Christina. 'Marta is a servant. It is a mistake to treat her like a friend. You are obviously unaccustomed to having servants.'

'I assure you that I have been fortunate enough to have servants throughout my life. I was taught to treat servants with respect.'

Layla takes a sip of the steaming tea and sets the tea glass down on the brass table. 'As I was saying. Zara will not be an unmarried embarrassment much longer. She is marrying the son of King Fuad's private secretary, you know. I made the arrangements myself, given that my son has absolved himself of the duties of the head of the Khalid household since his marriage. *This* is what a mother is for. To ensure the best matches for her children, an opportunity I was denied in the case of Aziz.'

Christina sips her tea. 'I am sure *you* shall be very happy.'

Layla stabs Christina with her gold-eyed gaze. 'I can assure you, I shall. As will Zara.' Layla smiles with exaggerated graciousness. 'Speaking of daughters, where is Jessica? Any normal woman would be back on her feet by now.'

'She's resting on Dr Shaw's orders. I shall be staying until she's fully recovered.'

'Aziz has agreed to this?'

'He is the one who suggested it. I will leave after the christening.'

Layla sets down the tea glass and rests her hands on the arms of the wicker chair. 'The christening? My grandchild will be Muslim.'

'I beg your pardon?'

'My son's child will be raised as a Muslim. It is a requirement. There is absolutely no possibility for my granddaughter to be raised as a Christian.'

Christina sets down her tea glass. 'The baby must be christened as a Catholic, without question.'

Layla's bracelets jangle as she swings her arms in irritation. 'This will not happen, Madame Fry. My granddaughter will be Muslim. On this subject I know my son will stand firm.'

Christina rises from her chair and fixes Layla with a cold stare. '*My* granddaughter will be a Catholic, as all of us Innocenti women are. On this, *I* stand firm.'

---

Jessie tucks the sheet around Shani in the cradle that the gardener, Mohammed, and his son, Isham, have made for her, and kisses her on her forehead. 'Good night, my sweet girl. Mummy's little angel.'

The bedroom door opens and Aziz enters. He treads silently across the fine Egyptian carpet and joins Jessie by the cradle. 'She's asleep already.'

'We're lucky. Mama said Etta and I were fusspots.'

'I wouldn't mind if she were a fusspot,' Aziz says as he brushes a finger along his daughter's cheek. 'She is the sun and moon to me.'

'You wouldn't say that if you were sleep deprived.' Jessie heads to her dressing table and sits on the stool. Picking up a brush, she pulls it through her bobbed brown hair, watching Aziz in the mirror as he removes his tie and unbuttons his shirt.

'Aziz, Mama came to me this afternoon to talk about something quite important to her. To me, as well. It's to do with something your mother said.'

'It's best not to listen to my mother, you know that.'

She sets down the brush and turns around on the stool. 'Yes, normally, but I need to speak to you about this.'

He sits on the bed and unties his shoelace. 'What is it? Not this nonsense about Zara's marriage again? You know that is not going to happen, no matter what my mother says.'

'No, not that.' Jessie takes a breath. 'Aziz, Mama wants to have Shani christened as a Catholic before she goes home. She's insisting upon it.'

He looks at Jessie for a long moment, the shoe in his hand. 'I see.'

'She said that your mother told her Shani must be raised as a Muslim because her father is Muslim. I know I'm not a very good Catholic, Aziz. I don't go to church as much as I should. My father was Protestant, you know. He had to promise Mama she could raise all the children as Catholics before she would marry him. I used to prefer to go to church with him, which always made Mama cross.' She smiles. 'Better psalms.' She rises and sits beside him on the bed. 'I don't know what to do. What are we going to do?'

Aziz frowns as he unties his other shoe. 'This is a problem, *habibti*. My mother is correct. It is my duty as a Muslim man to see that my children are raised as good Muslims.'

'I understand, but Aziz, I want Shani to be free to live the life she chooses. I want her to go to university if she wishes, become a doctor or a … a banker or anything she wants to be.'

'She can be what she wishes to be.'

'Like Zara?'

'Zara lives a fuller life than you imagine.'

'Yes, now that she's working in the clinic. Before that she seemed to spend most of her time reading fashion magazines, rejecting suitors and irritating your mother.'

'You don't know everything about Zara.'

Jessie sits against a pillow and crosses her arms. 'I know enough, and it's not how I want our daughter to be raised.'

'How do you wish for our daughter to be raised? As a Christian or a—?'

Jessie presses her fingers against her forehead as a headache gathers force behind her eyes. 'I don't know, Aziz. I don't know.'

---

'*Shani Maryam, ego te baptizo in nomine Patris …*'

The water streams from the ladle over Shani's forehead and the soft tufts of dark hair, spurring her into a shocked squeal. Christina glances at Marta who jiggles the baby in her sturdy, comforting embrace. Marta's bearded husband, Ezra, stands dutifully, though bemused, beside his wife as the priest intones the Roman Catholic baptismal rites in sonorous Latin. *A Coptic Christian housekeeper and a shoemaker as godparents to her granddaughter. Needs must.*

'*… et Filii*' – another ladle of water, another squeal – '*et Spiritus Sancti.*' A final splash of water and an eruption of full-throated umbrage from Shani.

'Amen.'

'Amen.'

How was she expected to return to England with an unbaptised granddaughter? No, she had a duty to secure Shani's immortal soul for the Catholic Kingdom of Heaven. Where Jessica had prevaricated, Marta had stepped forward as an ally. The Lord works in mysterious ways.

She can go home now. Whatever Jessica and Aziz eventually decide is irrelevant. Layla's imperious face flashes into her mind and she smiles. *Never underestimate an Innocenti woman, Layla Khalid. I have won.*

# Chapter Thirty-Eight

## Celie

### The Brandts' Farm, Freedom, Alberta – August 1922

Celie sets the silver dessert fork onto the bone china plate and smiles at Hans Brandt's Aunt Ursula. The older woman, whom Celie guesses to be in her late fifties judging by her generous figure, neat grey bob, and the round tortoiseshell spectacles that hang from a chain around her neck, sits across from her at the dining table she has dressed with fine white linen and a vase of spear-like purple gladioli, watching Celie with some anxiety.

'You like it? It is called *Quetschekuchen*. It is made from plums. When we came to Alberta, I insisted that Klaus plant a plum tree in the garden to remind me of my garden in Heidelberg.'

'I have heard of it. It's delicious.'

Aunt Ursula reaches for the knife. 'Please, you must have more.'

'Oh, no. Thank you so much. I—'

Hans takes Celie's plate and holds it out to his aunt. 'It is of no use, *Frau Jeffries*. Aunt Ursula will not take no for an answer when it comes to her *Quetschekuchen*.'

Aunt Ursula splashes the cake with cream and hands the plate back to Celie. 'You should eat more, I think. Some extra flesh will help to keep you warm in the winter. This is right, Klaus?'

Hans's Uncle Klaus squints at his wife over the top of the *Kanada Kurier* newspaper. '*Was?*'

Aunt Ursula thrusts a second piece of cake at her husband. She smiles apologetically at Celie. 'Klaus does not speak English so well. I tell him he should go to the English lessons with Hans.'

'You speak English beautifully, *Frau Brandt*.'

The woman smiles, her round face beaming like the full moon on a dark night. 'Thank you. I borrow the books from the travelling library and practise with the ladies of the Temperance Union.' She holds up a finger and pushes away from the table. 'One minute.'

Klaus looks up from his dessert plate where he is demolishing the second piece of cake. '*Wohin gehst du?*'

'*Nirgends. Iss den Kuchen.*'

She reappears holding a book with a soiled blue cover, which she hands to Celie. 'I have just finished to read this by Mr D.H. Lawrence. You have read it?'

Celie stares at the gold lettering on the cover, scratched and worn from many fingers. *Women in Love*. She sets down the notorious book, almost afraid to touch it. 'No, I can't say I have.'

Ursula picks up the book and thumbs through the pages. 'It is very excellent, I think. You liked it also, didn't you, Hans?'

Hans sets down the cream jug and licks a drop from his fingers. 'Yes, I did. It was very educational.'

Celie looks at Hans. 'You read *Women in Love*? I – I'm not sure it's quite the thing for a young person to be reading. Or anyone, from what I've heard about it.'

Ursula looks at the book and shrugs. 'I think it is good. I liked it very much.' She sets the book down in front of Celie. 'I will lend it to you. You will like it, I think.'

Celie stares at the book. What will Frank say if he sees one of Mr Lawrence's books in their house? A book about ... she swallows ... fornication? 'I, um, I—'

Ursula picks up the teapot. 'Come, let us sit in the living room. Hans will play to us a song on the violin. I will make more tea.' She looks at her husband, who is deep into the pages of the German language newspaper. 'I think Klaus will stay here. He is not so fond of Sibelius.'

---

Celie glances around the modest room as Hans makes his way through a Sibelius violin concerto. The high ceiling offsets the otherwise compact dimensions of the room, though a low-hanging brass pendant lamp with five glass globe shades and wallpaper densely covered with navy blue roses do nothing to contribute to a sense of spaciousness. A large circular braided rug covers the polished wooden floor, and a mix of sturdy chairs and tables, and a large Victorian settee sprinkled with lace antimacassars, cluster in front of a black iron fireplace.

Hans finishes off his recital with a flourish of the bow, and Celie joins his aunt in enthusiastic clapping.

'That was excellent, Hans,' Celie says as he flops into a wingback chair. 'I had no idea you were so musical.'

'I have had lessons since I was a small boy. My stepmother is very fond of music. She plays the piano every day. She insisted my stepbrother and I learn an instrument.' He taps his violin. 'We chose the violin. He is much better than I am.'

'This is because he is more disciplined, *Igelschnäuzchen*,' Aunt Ursula says. She rises from her seat on the settee and walks over to a table clustered with framed photographs. She picks up one and brings it over to Celie.

'Here is a picture of Hans and his stepbrother in Heidelberg.'

Celie stares at the photograph. There is no question that the younger boy is Hans at around the age of six or seven. He is seated on a twig bench in a white shirt and suede shorts with embroidered braces. Beside him, a young, blond-haired man of about twenty stands tall and straight-backed in a neat grey suit. His face looks out at her from underneath the glass. The face she still loves. Max's face.

# Chapter Thirty-Nine

## Christina

**London, England – September 1922**

Hettie looks up from the hob where she is stirring the water around a poaching egg with a wooden spoon. Christina enters the kitchen, holding the morning newspaper, and sits in a chair by the old pine table.

Hettie eyes the intruder into her domain. 'Can I 'elp you, ma'am?'

Christina looks at the housekeeper, noting that Hettie's new uniform with its shorter black dress and white lace-trimmed cap and apron only serve to highlight Hettie's broad-shouldered, wide-hipped frame. 'I've decided I shall eat my breakfast in here today, Hettie. It seems an affectation to set up a place at the dining table just for one.'

'In 'ere? It's not the done fing.'

'I am quite tired of the done thing. I'll have my tea if it's ready.'

Hettie screws up her mouth as she watches Christina spread the newspaper open on the table.

Christina glances at the housekeeper. 'What is it, Hettie? You look like I've trekked horse manure through the kitchen.'

'Fing is, ma'am, I was expecting to eat my breakfast in 'ere while you ate yours in there.'

'Well, we shall simply have to accommodate each other, shan't we? You are more than welcome to eat with me.'

Hettie drops the wooden spoon into the pot. 'You won't be expecting me to converse, will you? I'm partial to silence when I eat. I 'ad enough of noise when I was growing up wiff eight brovvers and sisters.'

'I should be most amenable to silence, Hettie.' Christina points to the newspaper. 'I intend to read the paper.'

Hettie scoops the poached egg out of the pot and onto a plate. 'Don't see why you couldn't do that in the dining room.'

'I simply wanted some company. I became rather used to it in Egypt.'

Hettie sets the plate and a rack of toast on the table with some utensils. 'Maybe you ought to get yourself a cat if you're lonely.'

Christina picks a slice of toast out of the toast rack and attempts to spread a solid lump of hard butter over the cold toast. 'Do you know that in Egypt they eat a round flat bread with everything? It's quite an unusual texture but very nice. We would eat it with something called *ful* for breakfast.'

Hettie sets the teapot on the table with two cups and saucers. 'Is that right?'

'Yes, I spoke to Jessica's cook, a very nice Coptic woman named Marta. She told me it was made of fava beans cooked with olive oil and salt. We'd eat it with a boiled egg and strong coffee.'

Hettie scowls as she cracks a second egg into the boiling pot. 'You won't be wanting coffee now, will you? Travel puts odd ideas in people's 'eads, if you ask me. If people were meant to travel, we'd 'ave wings.'

'Travel can be most edifying, Hettie. You should try it one day.'

Hettie snorts as she stirs the water around the poaching egg. 'Like that'll 'appen. Travelling isn't for the likes of people like me.'

She ladles out the cooked egg onto a plate and joins Christina at the table. After lathering a slice of toast with marmalade, she takes a bite and chews as she watches Christina read the newspaper. 'You know I was all set to become a conductorette on the buses during the war?'

Christina looks up from her breakfast. 'No, I wasn't aware of that, Hettie.'

'I was, but I got turned down because they were oversubscribed. That's what they said, "oversubscribed", so I took the job wiff you until somefing better turned up. 'Cept it never did. Seems women were climbing over each ovver to get out of service and get to work in the factories, on the trams and trains and in banks and such. For a minute it looked like we'd found a way to earn a real wage and do what we wanted wiff it. Get an education, go travelling, whatever.' Hettie takes another bite of toast, washing it down with a drink of tea. 'Fing is, the minute the war was over, we got booted out of our jobs. Men wanted 'em back, you see. Woman's place is in the 'ome, and all that.' She stabs her fork and knife into the egg. 'Doesn't look like I'll be travelling any time soon.'

Christina's teacup clatters in the saucer.

Hettie looks over at Christina. 'You all right?'

Christina pushes the newspaper across the table and points to a small notice in the lower right-hand corner of the page.

Hettie holds up the paper and squints at the small print.

*The marriage of the Rt. Hon. Harold Grenville, the 6th Earl of Sherbrooke, only son of the late Cecil Grenville, the 5th Earl of Sherbrooke and the late Countess of Sherbrooke (née the Hon. Bettina Buchanan), of Craigmore Hall, Peebles, Scotland, with Miss Rose Elizabeth McClellan, eldest daughter of Mr John McClellan and the late Mrs McClellan of Morecroft Hall, Bedale, Yorkshire, was solemnised in St Gregory's Church, Bedale, Thursday afternoon. The church was decorated with lilies and palms, and the service was choral. The bride wore a gown of white silk draped with Brussels lace with which the train was entirely covered. The veil was of chiffon, attached to the hair with a diamond half-moon, her father's gift, and she wore a pearl and diamond necklace, a gift of the bridegroom. The reception was held at the residence of Mr John McClellan, the bride's father, at Morecroft Hall, Bedale, Yorkshire.*

Hettie looks over at Christina who is staring unseeingly at the half-eaten egg. 'Oh, ma'am. 'E's a shit.'

---

Christina sets down her pen on top of the letter she is writing to Cecelia as she listens to the key jiggle in the door of the Chelsea flat. She hears the door fly open and slam shut. Harry enters the sitting room, shaking out his umbrella.

'Oh, you're here, Tina. I didn't know you were back from Egypt. Didn't you hear me trying to get in?'

'I did.'

He drops the umbrella into the chrome umbrella stand and tosses his hat on a table. 'Why didn't you open the door?' he says as he shrugs out of his wet coat and throws it over the back of an antique French chair.

She eyes him icily. 'I was busy.'

Harry joins her by the desk and picks up her unfinished letter, scanning it.

'What is it, Harry? Are you hoping to catch me out writing to a lover?'

He drops the letter onto the desk. 'It seems that it's simply motherly advice to a daughter who is in love with someone other than her husband. Something about which you know a great deal.'

'You think a great deal of yourself, Harry. I loved Gerald. Very much.'

'I'm sure you did.' He settles into the comfort of the sofa cushions. 'Do you still have the whisky I brought from Scotland?'

'It's wherever you left it. You know I don't drink anything other than sherry and wine.'

Harry gets up and walks over to the sideboard. After locating the bottle of Laphroaig and a glass in the cupboard, he pours himself a generous measure. He shuts his eyes as he savours the peaty alcohol. 'Ah, ambrosia of the gods. You really should try some, Tina.'

'Thank you, Harry, but I'm not so inclined.'

He sits on the sofa with his drink and looks over at Christina. 'It's good to see you, Tina. You're looking well. You were in Egypt for ages.'

She turns around in the desk chair to face him. 'Is it? Good to see me? I would have thought your eyes would be full of the vision of your sweet young wife.'

'Ah. You've heard.'

'Of course I've heard. The announcement was in *The Times* for all to see. Didn't you forget something before you married her?'

'Excuse me? Forget what?'

'Informing me of your plans, perhaps? Didn't you think you owed me that much, given as how I've compromised my immortal soul to be with you?'

'I don't remember forcing you into this arrangement, Tina.' He gestures to the room with his whisky glass. 'Haven't I given you free rein to do what you wanted with this place? Don't I bring you out to nice restaurants and the theatre?' He takes a sip of whisky. 'Admit it. You were bored to tears in that house in Hither Green. I've given you the life you've always wanted. Why else would you be here?'

Christina juts out her chin. 'I'm here because it's convenient for Harrods and Harvey Nichols. In fact, I'm rather surprised to see you here. I would have thought you would be staying at your club now that you're a respectable married man.'

'As it happens, I have become rather fond of this white palace and those odd concrete curtains. It certainly cost me enough.'

He sets down his glass on the mirrored coffee table and looks over at Tina. 'I didn't mean it, Tina. You must know that. Those things I said before you left for Egypt. I loved you back in Capri and I love you now. I lost my temper. It was unforgivable. I'm sorry. Believe me, I wish I could take it all back.'

'Do you?'

He rubs his forehead. 'Yes, I do. I wish I could take back everything. I regret leaving you back in Italy. There hasn't been a day that's gone by that I haven't thought about you.'

Christina stares absently out the large window. 'I said things as well. I was so angry about Henrietta and her threats and I took it out on you. I wrote to Henrietta to agree to her terms. She has the Bishop house now, to do with as she sees fit.' She shrugs and looks back at Harry. 'I didn't have a choice. I can't ever let Cecelia find out the truth of her birth.'

'I know, Tina. Your aunt did me the courtesy of writing me a letter gloating about her "triumph".'

Harry rises and grabs the bottle of scotch and a second glass from the sideboard; he splashes a generous measure into the two glasses and holds one up to Christina who shakes her head. Shrugging, he sets the glass down onto the desk and returns to the sofa. 'I wish you'd spoken to me first.'

'Why? You'd just told me that you'd never loved me. I felt like an idiot. A stupid naïve fool. You were the last person on earth I wanted to speak to. I couldn't get away to Egypt fast enough.'

'Tina, Henrietta had paid Mr Fincher a tidy sum to leak our secret to the papers. I called him into my chambers and I paid him a greater sum to keep quiet in return for his signature on an extremely official-looking affidavit. I threatened to have him arrested for blackmail should he reveal what he knows. I also promised him some lucrative work with my firm. He won't be bothering us again.'

He takes a sip of whisky. 'It's another reason why I had to marry Rose so quickly. I need access to her money.' His lips twitch as he regards Christina. 'You've been expensive, my lovely siren.'

Christina feels the blood rush from her head, like a lead weight dropped from a great height. 'You mean I … I didn't need to sign over my claim on the house?'

'No, you didn't.'

She drops her head into her hands. 'Good Lord.'

Harry chortles. 'That doesn't sound like the language of a good Catholic.'

Christina eyes him balefully. 'I shall have to add it to the list of all my sins when I go to Confession on Sunday.'

He holds up his glass. 'Here's to forgiveness.' He gulps down the whisky and pours out another measure.

'Not so fast, Harry. I'm not so forgiving. Why did I have to find out about your marriage from the newspaper? Can you imagine how that made me feel?'

'Look, Tina. Jack McClellan was pressuring me to marry Rose or break off the engagement, as apparently there were several other extremely eager candidates in the wings. The church was booked, the banns read ... I had no choice. Honestly, Tina, it couldn't have been a total surprise. I never kept the engagement a secret from you.'

'It most certainly was a surprise. Poor Hettie thought she'd have to give me the kiss of life.'

'All right. I'm sorry. I should have warned you, but in my defence, it all happened very quickly. And you'd run off to Egypt.'

'Yes, very convenient of me, wasn't it?' She brushes an invisible crease out of her green skirt as she fights back the anger rising inside of her.

'Nothing's changed, Tina. Rose is either up at the house in Scotland or at her parents' estate in Yorkshire, and I'm in London for the most part. We have this flat now. This lovely, extremely expensive, extremely white flat. I don't see any reason why we can't continue as we always have.'

Christina reaches for the whisky glass and moves to one of Syrie Maugham's denuded French chairs. Sipping at the drink, she fixes Harry with a frosty stare.

'Oh, Harry, you are so exceptionally self-absorbed. Why did I never see that before? You're just like all the rest of your Eton and Oxbridge set. Privileged and entitled. I worry for our world with people like you in power. Self-important men with not an ounce of compassion for those you consider weaker than yourselves. Which is pretty much everyone.'

'Tina, what are you talking about?'

She takes another sip of whisky. 'What makes you think I wish to be the mistress of a married man?'

He runs his fingers over his moustache. 'Rose isn't you, Tina. She doesn't laugh like you, or get cross at me like you do, or look at me with those eyes the colour of ice. She doesn't feel like you when I touch her. You've haunted me since the first day I saw you sitting amongst the wildflowers on Capri. I love you, Tina. It will always be you.'

Christina scrutinises Harry as her heart thuds against her ribs. She sets down the whisky glass. 'If you feel that way, why did you marry her, Harry?'

'I need an heir, Tina. A legitimate heir. That's the long and short of it, but you're the one I love, my lovely, impossible siren. You're the one I will always love.'

Christina looks into the eyes which are still the same sharp blue as the Italian sky. The same blue as Cecelia's.

It's over. Just like that, the love and the passion for Harry that had eaten into her peace of mind – her happiness – all these years have evaporated like mist in sunlight.

He'd robbed her of contentment in her marriage, of loving her husband and her daughters like she should have. His abandonment of her had left her cold and empty, full of self-loathing for the love she had still felt for him through all those long years. He'd stolen from her an ability to be affectionate and light-hearted. He'd made her a liar to her husband and her whole family. He'd made her a fool for returning to him.

She rises from the chair and picks Harry's hat off the table. She takes his umbrella from the umbrella stand and holds out the items.

'Get your coat, Harry. You are invited to leave. Don't come back.'

# Part V

1925

# Chapter Forty

## Jessie

**Altumanina, Cairo, Egypt – February 1925**

*Altumanina*
*Cairo, Egypt*

*February 3rd, 1925*

*Dear Etta,*

*I haven't heard a word from you since Christmas, so I thought I'd act the responsible older sister (albeit by only a few minutes) and be the one to break the silence. I've heard from both Mama and Celie – Mama says you're back in Paris again. Aren't you worried about Carlo? What is happening about his retrial? Your poor husband, Etta! And what about Adriana? Cousin Stefania has written Mama to say Adriana runs about the island like a wild thing when she's not disrupting the school room. I'm all for Adriana's adventurous spirit, but she's only a little girl and needs to have a parent's guidance. Do you remember all the scrapes I got in before I decided to study nursing? I shudder to think what trouble my impatient mind might have got me into if I hadn't found a channel for that energy.*

*There, I've said my bit upon Mama's behalf (and for once I must agree with her).*

*Let me bring you up to speed with our little family here in Cairo. Shani is the joy of everyone here at Altumanina and loves nothing more than to play with the animals on the lawn (we have any number of cats and dogs now; I have quite lost track) and ride about on her father's shoulders in search of the Nile toads. Zara dotes on her as does our housekeeper, Marta, although Aziz's mother does her best to find fault, which has resulted in some tension between us, as you can imagine! Fortunately, I have had quite a lot of practice standing my ground with Mama.*

*You have no doubt heard from Mama about her latest visit here. She is becoming a regular fixture at Altumanina, much to my mother-in-law's dismay. Mama has settled in very comfortably with the ladies at the Gezira Sporting Club where she spends her afternoons playing bridge and drinking scads of Earl Grey tea.*

*Imagine a house with two imperious queens, and you will be able to paint yourself a picture of life at Altumanina when Mama is here. Poor Aziz has found himself caught in the middle of an argument on more than one occasion and escapes out to political meetings with Zara most evenings after dinner. The main nationalist party here, the Wafd, of which both he and Zara are members, has been in a mess since the assassination of the governor general of Sudan in Cairo in November. General Allenby is demanding all sorts of reparations from the nationalists which is causing a fuss. There have been riots and arrests, and the Wafd Party leader has resigned, which I am certain the British here are very pleased about as they have no desire to see a fully independent Egypt. The dear British have no intention of losing control of the Suez Canal, you can be sure about that!*

*It is an odd thing to be an Englishwoman married to an Egyptian here. The Brits and the Europeans regard me as a fallen woman, and the Egyptian upper classes look down upon me as a woman of dubious morals. I don't seem to suffer the same ill regard from the local people who come to the clinic, although I am certain Zara and Aziz help smooth the waters. I am fortunate in the love and support of both of them, although my relationship with their mother is another story entirely.*

*I miss my friend Lady Evelyn Beauchamp, poor Lord Carnarvon's daughter. She wrote me such a jolly letter after Howard Carter finally found King Tutankhamun's tomb after all those years. She was the very first one inside the inner chamber, did you know that? She, her father, and Howard Carter scrambled inside the tomb the night before the official opening which was to take place in front of Egyptian officials. Because she was the smallest, she went in first. Isn't that something? I'll wager you will never read that a woman was the first one in King Tut's tomb.*

*Poor Evelyn was quite devastated when her father died just a few months later of an infected mosquito bite. Such a shock! And only six months before her wedding to Brograve Beauchamp. I'm happy that she's found Brograve. I met him at Lady Evelyn's coming out reception in Cairo some years ago. They're expecting their first child this summer. I wish she were here in Cairo, as she is jolly good company, but she hasn't been back since her father's passing.*

*For my part, Zara and I are run off our feet in the clinic, and Aziz and Dr Simmonds from the Anglo-American hospital come in several times a week to help, although I know it is an awful additional pressure on their time. If only I were back in London, I would apply for medical school myself. I am every bit as capable as a man and it is beyond frustrating not to be permitted to train as a doctor here simply because I am a woman. Still, what can I do? My hands are tied, and I simply have to accept this ridiculous restriction, as much as it incenses me.*

*I said I have heard from Celie. She confided in me that she has met Max Fischer's stepbrother. Yes, that Max Fischer! His name is Hans Brandt and he is one of her English language students. He has been staying with his uncle and aunt in a nearby town for the past few years helping on their farm. She saw a photograph of Max and Hans together when she was invited to tea at their house some time ago and she said that she has been quite discombobulated ever since. She says that she is consumed by her thoughts of Max, about all the lovely times they had together before the war, and that she dreams about him as well. She is feeling terribly guilty. I don't think it is stretching the truth to say she has become obsessed with him.*

*I can't help but wonder if her marriage is under strain. I don't imagine she would be so fixated on Max if she were entirely happy with Frank. But Celie isn't one to give in to self-pity or contemplate anything so drastic as a divorce. She is so hard-working and dutiful. I have no doubt she will get through this sticky patch and plough on forward.*

*She wants to tell Hans that she knows his stepbrother, but I've written back to tell her to leave well enough alone, and that Max is in her past. I hope she listens. I know if it were you, you wouldn't! You've rarely been one to ask anyone for advice, have you, Etta? You know you can if you need to. Celie and I are always there for you. We are sisters after all!*

*That's all the news for now. Go back to Capri and visit your husband. Carlo and Adriana must miss you terribly. You have responsibilities, Etta. Don't ignore them. And write me!*

*Your loving twin,*
*Jessie*

# Chapter Forty-One

Christina

**Clover Bar, London – March 1925**

Christina glances across the table at Ellen Jackson. The president of the WI perches on the edge of the chaise longue in the sitting room of Clover Bar, sipping from a china teacup as she thumbs through a notebook. Always three sips before returning the cup to the saucer on the side table.

There Ellen goes again; three sips, a pause, then setting the cup down on the saucer, leaving a red lipstick imprint on the teacup's delicate Royal Worcester flowers like a tattoo. It is enough to make her want to throttle the woman until her fashionable navy hat with its peacock feather falls into Hettie's Victoria sponge cake.

Christina smiles politely as she regards the WI president over her teacup: the tailored navy suit with its white piping pressed to perfection, the starched white blouse with its mother-of-pearl buttons, the jaunty red silk bowtie tied just so. Peeking out from underneath the hat, a glimpse of the grey wave of Ellen's newly cropped bob. Christina runs her hand over her ear and pats the thick bun of auburn hair at her nape. How could any woman cut off all her hair? Particularly women of their vintage who should surely know better?

She sets down her teacup and saucer. 'I thought I would speak to Mrs Thompson at the Girl Guides about having some of the girls demonstrate knots and semaphore before the annual meeting.'

Ellen Jackson shuts her notebook and gives the black leather cover a satisfied tap. 'Good. It's important to get the girls involved in the WI early on to encourage their civic spirit.' She glances at her wristwatch. 'I must be going shortly, Christina. My son and his wife are in town from Bristol and they're coming to supper with the children this evening. I must oversee the removal of anything breakable from the sitting room and dining room. We had an unfortunate incident with a Staffordshire dog figurine the last time they visited.'

'Are you certain you wouldn't like more tea before you go, Ellen? It's freezing outside. I wouldn't be surprised if we have snow.'

'Well, perhaps a splash,' Ellen says as she helps herself to the teapot. 'One must fortify oneself.'

Christina clears her throat. 'There is, actually, something else I wished to speak to you about. I thought I might give a short talk about my recent trip to Cairo. My daughter runs a medical clinic there, you know. They eat quite interesting food—'

'That won't be necessary, Christina. Mildred Chadwick's niece has volunteered to give a talk on the archaeological dig she's just back from in Iraq. That's quite enough sand, don't you think?'

'Oh. I rather thought—'

'If the Girl Guides go over well, we can think about expanding the Guides' participation in the Christmas tombola. We can have them patch some people up to show off their first aid skills or some such. I'm thinking I shall ask Lord Sherbrooke's wife to be our guest speaker, that is if we can tempt her away from the pottery studio that I hear she's set up on their Scottish estate. I suppose she had to do something to fill her days, what with Lord Sherbrooke down in London all the time in Parliament. No doubt things will change if they ever have children.' She leans forward and lowers her voice to a whisper. 'Some people say he's incapable, you know ... of having a child.'

Christina smiles tightly. 'Do they?'

'Imagine being on your third marriage. It must be extraordinarily exhausting, all that courting and other nonsense. One husband is quite sufficient for me.' Ellen Jackson takes her three sips of tea and sets down the teacup in the saucer. She glances over her shoulder at the hallway and then leans toward Christina. 'I have heard that Lord Sherbrooke in fact does have a child.'

'What?'

The woman regards Christina with her hooded steel-blue eyes. 'I can't reveal how I heard this, but suffice to say, it comes from an informed source.'

'Yes?' Christina says, conscious that her voice is a croak.

'He's been seen visiting a flat in Chelsea where he's met at the door by an attractive red-haired woman.'

Christina opens her mouth to speak, but the syllables stick in her throat.

Ellen pats her grey bob in an unconscious gesture. 'There is a rumour that he has a weakness for red-haired women because of some early romance which broke his heart. Some fancy created by a gossip columnist in one of the cheaper papers, I expect, but you know how people love these kinds of things.'

Christina watches the woman cut herself another sliver of Victoria sponge. 'What ... what about this love-child?'

Ellen dabs at her lips with her napkin. 'Well, it appears the woman is an actress. Not in the league of Phyllis Neilson-Terry, of course, or it would be common knowledge by now.'

'An actress?'

'Yes. Lord Sherbrooke's last wife was a showgirl. He appears to favour women of loose morals, though, of course, the latest

Countess of Sherbrooke is beyond reproach. She's the McClellan Soup heiress, you know.'

'Who is this actress? Do you know?'

Ellen purses her lips. 'I'm not sure I should be saying all of this. You can imagine what the papers would be like if Lord Sherbrooke were revealed to have a love-child.'

'Oh. Of course. Particularly now that he is married … again.'

'I shall be terribly surprised if this marriage lasts. Men like that are incapable of fidelity.'

Christina swallows down a mouthful of the tepid tea. 'Who is she, Ellen? I promise I won't tell a soul.'

---

Christina slips behind a large oak tree in the square opposite the row of modest terraced houses in a less-favoured part of Chelsea. It had taken her no longer than fifteen minutes to walk from the flat Harry had purchased for their assignations, yet the dirty stucco and peeling paint of the house frontages on this street point to occupants more concerned with surviving than exhibiting their comfortable existences with polished brass doorknobs and glossy black doors.

She steps across the road and climbs the three concrete steps to the front door of one of the houses. After pressing the doorbell, she stands back on the stoop and waits.

The door opens and a young woman of about thirty stands in the doorway. She wears a cheap green cotton dress in the latest drop-waisted fashion, and her auburn hair is bobbed and waved in the Ina Claire style. The woman flicks her pale green eyes over Christina.

'Yes?'

'Miss Adam? Miss Dorothy Adam?'

'Yes?'

Christina extends her hand. 'I'm Mrs Christina Fry. I believe we have a mutual acquaintance.'

The young woman edges back into the hallway. 'I'm sorry? I don't believe—'

'I am given to understand that you know Lord Sherbrooke.'

The woman's eyes widen. She glances past Christina down the road. 'I'm afraid you've been misinformed.'

'Don't worry. No one's followed me. I'm not with the newspapers.'

'I'm sorry. I don't know Lord Sherbrooke.' The woman moves to shut the door.

Christina steps into the doorway. 'We have something in common, Miss Adam.'

She eyes Christina's stylish suit and cloche hat. 'I doubt that very much.'

'Christopher.'

Dorothy Adam stares at Christina for a long moment. She pushes open the door. 'You'd best come in.'

---

Christina sets her handbag on the chintz-covered settee and takes a seat. The sitting room is small, easily a quarter of the size of the sitting room in Harry's Chelsea flat, but it is clean and bright, with cheerful floral curtains and slipcovers over the furniture. Dorothy pushes a cat out of an armchair and sits down. 'How do you know Christopher?'

'Through an acquaintance of mine. It seems that the son of her husband's tailor is in Christopher's class at school. Children talk. Tailors gossip.'

'As simple as that.'

'As simple as that.' Christina cups her hands and rests them in her lap. 'I know that Christopher is Lord Sherbrooke's son.'

Dorothy Adam's face blanches. 'I'm afraid you're quite mistaken—'

'Miss Adam, I have a child with Lord Sherbrooke as well. A

daughter. I was very young. He took advantage of my innocence. It seems he has a predilection for such things.'

Dorothy Adam scrutinises Christina with her pale eyes.

'I'm right, aren't I?'

The woman sighs and nods. 'Yes. I was only eighteen. He came to the theatre and saw me in a play. He sent me a red rose after every performance for a week until I agreed to meet him. He was married, you see. To his first wife. He told me the match had been arranged by their parents years before and that he'd never loved her. He said he would leave her.' She shakes her head. 'He did, but not for me.' She shrugs. 'More fool me.'

'He left you when he found out you were expecting.'

'Yes. I was soiled goods, you see. He never intended to leave his wife for me. I was just an amusement. I have come to learn that many men are ... amused by women. Or would be if they could get away with it. My friend Sheila learned from my mistake. She played the long game and became his second wife just after Christopher was born, and she squeezed him for a good sum of money when they divorced a year later. It didn't do her a lot of good. She became an alcoholic and drank herself to death by the time she was thirty.'

'I'm sorry.'

Dorothy nods. 'Now, I work as a typist four days a week and I teach drama in the local church hall on Saturday afternoons. Harry pays Christopher's school fees at a good school and sends me support money from time to time.' She rises and walks over to a chest of drawers. Opening a drawer, she takes out a photograph and hands it to Christina as she sits back down in the armchair.

'He dropped by out of the blue the day Christopher started school. One of the other mothers took a picture of us all at the school gate. I said he was my brother.'

Christina looks down at the black and white photograph. A small dark-haired boy in a school uniform looks at the camera with a serious gaze as Harry and Dorothy stand stiffly behind him. She sets the photograph down on the side table. 'He looks like a lovely boy.'

A whisper of a smile flits across Dorothy's face. 'Harry said he would support us and pay for Christopher's schooling on three conditions.' She counts off the conditions on her fingers. 'That I never speak to anyone about my relationship with him, that I never tell Christopher who his real father is, and …'

'And the third condition?'

'That I name our son Christopher.' She narrows her eyes. 'He's named after you, isn't he, Christina?'

'I … I couldn't possibly say.'

Dorothy laughs hollowly. 'It's not how I thought my life would turn out. I wanted to be the next Gladys Cooper. A star of the London stage.' She shrugs. 'So much for schoolgirl fantasies.'

The entrance door to the flat slams against the hallway wall. A boy's voice says, 'Mummy! I'm home!' Another bang as the door slams shut.

Dorothy glances at Christina. 'I'm in the sitting room, darling. Come in and say hello to my guest.'

A dark-haired boy of about ten or eleven, in the maroon jacket, striped tie, cap and grey shorts of a school uniform, enters the sitting room. He gives his mother a kiss on the cheek and walks over to Christina. He extends a small hand.

'I'm very pleased to meet you. I'm Christopher Adam.'

Christina gives his hand a shake, but she can't drag her eyes away from Christopher's face. The pale skin, the dark hair, the bright smile. It's all Harry. Especially the eyes. Harry's blue eyes. Cecelia's blue eyes.

A boy. Harry's heir.

# Chapter Forty-Two

## Celie

**Sweet Briar Farm, West Lake, Alberta – March 1925**

'He's here!' Lulu shouts from her perch on a bare branch of the maple tree in the front garden. 'Hans is coming!'

Ben Wheatley squints up into the tree at Lulu's dangling feet as he sucks on a lollipop. 'Come on, Lulu! You promised you'd play marbles with me in the barn.'

Celie steps out onto the porch, wiping her hands on her apron. 'Lulu Jeffries, get down out of that tree this instant.'

Mavis joins Celie on the porch and hands her a glass of lemonade. 'Let her climb trees if she wants to, Celie. The view up there is good. Why should only the boys see it?' She shivers as a chill wind sweeps over the yard. 'Besides, the snow is there if she falls.'

'Lulu's as headstrong as a mule in mud. She won't listen to anything she doesn't want to hear. She's just like her Aunt Jessie.'

'She's got some spark, that daughter of yours, that's for sure, Celie. Poor Ben can't keep up with her.' Mavis eyes the tall young man walking up the road. 'My, is that Hans Brandt? Hasn't he grown up!'

Celie watches as Hans approaches the gate. At eighteen, he is a young man. He is as tall and blond as Max, and when he smiles … No, she can't think like that.

She nods. 'He certainly has.'

Hans unlatches the gate of the picket fence and sets the large straw basket he is carrying on the gravel path as he waves at Celie. 'Hello, *Frau Jeffries*! I am sorry I am late. I hope I did not miss Lulu's birthday cake.'

Ben Wheatley stomps across the melting snow toward the porch. 'Not just Lulu's birthday cake,' he grumbles. 'It's mine, too. My birthday was yesterday.'

Hans nods politely at Ben. 'Well, a very happy birthday to you, too, Mr Wheatley.'

Lulu shouts from a branch, waving at Hans with both hands. 'Hans! Look, I'm in the tree!'

'Oh, for heaven's sake, Lulu!' Celie shouts as she hurries down the steps. 'If you insist on climbing trees, hold on!'

Hans picks up the straw basket and heads toward the tree. 'I have something for you, Lulu, but you must come down to see it. It's a birthday present.'

'I'm coming! Wait! I'm coming!'

Lulu jumps down into the snow and runs over to Hans. The straw basket jiggles under Hans's arm.

'The basket moved!'

Hans draws his blond eyebrows together in a frown. 'Are you sure? That's impossible.' He glances at Celie, who has joined them under the tree's grey branches with Mavis and Ben, and smiles. The basket jiggles again and emanates a whimper.

Lulu shrieks. 'It moved again!'

Hans sets the basket down. 'Perhaps you should open it to see, Lulu. It is your present, after all.'

Lulu kneels down on the snow and unlatches the basket. She gasps as the scruffy black and white head of a border collie puppy pops out of the basket, its tiny body vibrating with joy as it climbs into her arms.

'Mama! It's a dog!' She hugs the wriggling body and kisses it on its head. 'I love you, I love you, I love you!' She beams at Hans. 'This is the best birthday present ever in a million years.'

'What about the yellow marble I gave you?' Ben protests. 'I had to give Jimmy three blue ones for it.'

Lulu rolls her eyes. 'A dog is way better than a marble, Benji.'

Hans hunkers down on the grass beside Lulu. 'I'm glad you like him. You will have to teach him manners. He's very naughty. He chewed my slippers to pieces last night.'

'What's his name?'

'Ah, this is a sad situation. He doesn't have a name. I think you must choose it.'

'Call him "Marble", Lulu,' Ben says as pushes his way between Hans and Lulu. 'He looks like a black and white marble.'

'That's a silly name, Benji. I'm going to call him "Kip".'

Hans pets the dog's head. 'I think Kip is a very fine name, Lulu.'

Celie watches the young German chat to Lulu as Ben glowers between them. He is so much like Max. How she longs to ask Hans about him. *Is he well? Is he a lawyer now? Is he … married?*

'Celie? What is it? Where did you go?'

She looks over at Mavis. 'I was just thinking that that roast chicken will be leather if Frank and Fred don't get here soon.'

---

Celie is taking a photograph of everyone on the porch steps, with Lulu in the centre clutching Kip, when Fred Wheatley's truck pulls up on the road outside the farmhouse. The cab doors slam as Frank and Fred step down onto the muddy dirt road and head around to the rear of the truck. Lulu breaks away from the group and runs down the path to the gate.

'Daddy! Daddy! Hans got me a dog for my birthday!'

Frank grabs hold of the blue bicycle as Fred offloads it from the truck's flatbed. He sets it on the ground and beeps the bike's horn.

'Happy birthday, Lulu.'

Lulu stares at the bicycle. Ben runs up beside her. 'Oh, boy, Lulu! A bike!'

Fred hops down from the truck and hauls down a red bike. 'She's not the only one, Ben.'

'A bike? For me, Daddy? Oh, wow!' Ben runs over to his new red bicycle and climbs onto the seat. 'Thank you, Daddy!' He looks over at Lulu. '*This* is the best present in a million years.'

Celie joins the group as Fred jogs down the road with his hand on the bicycle seat as Ben wobbles over the muddy lane. Frank nods at the camera in her hands. 'You've got your camera out, I see.'

'Yes. I thought it would be nice to take a few pictures of Lulu and Ben's birthday party.'

Frank grunts. He gestures to the blue bicycle. 'Why don't you get on the bicycle and have a go, Lulu?'

Lulu glances down at the dog who has settled its head against her shoulder. 'I don't know how.'

'Give your mother the dog and come along. I'll teach you.'

'Maybe later, Daddy. I think Kip is hungry.' She looks up at her mother. 'Mommy, can I give Kip some cake?'

Celie glances at Frank. A vein ticks at his temple as he stands in the middle of the road gripping the handlebar of the abandoned bike.

'Are you sure you don't want to try out that lovely new bicycle?'

Lulu squints at the bicycle. 'Maybe later,' she repeats.

Celie rests her hands on Lulu's shoulders and steers her toward the porch. 'Dogs don't eat cake, Lulu. Let's go inside and find something else for Kip to eat.'

# Chapter Forty-Three

## Etta

### Tiberio Palace Hotel, Capri, Italy – March 1925

Zelda Fitzgerald waves at Etta from the lawn chair on the large balcony of the Fitzgeralds' hotel suite at the top of Capri's Tiberio Palace Hotel.

'Etta! Sweetie! You don't know what it's like to see a friendly familiar face! Come over here and let me give you a hug! Is that Adriana? Oh, my, aren't you a wild little sprite! Come meet Scottie. She's three, but she's a clever three, aren't you, sweetie? You can pretend you're sisters. I met the lovely Mario earlier. He's brought all the paints and easels and what-have-you. We've got it all set up and ready. I can't say how much I'm thrilled you'll be teaching me to paint, Etta. I've always sketched, of course, but I think I have the character of an artist. I have to find something to do while Scott labours away on the *Gatsby* proofs. It's coming out next month, have I said? We have great expectations, and we need the money, though I still think Scott should make Tom Buchanan the main character. Jay Gatsby's so awfully vague in my view. I'll have the hotel send us up some biscuits and cake, shall I? They call it *dolci* here, don't they? We loved our *dolci* in Rome, didn't we, Scottie? I'm afraid I've been overindulging since we arrived in Italy, but I haven't been terribly well since the operation in December and it was so awfully cold in Rome. If you can't have *dolci* in Italy, then life isn't worth living, is it?'

Etta bends over the lawn chair and gives Zelda a kiss on her pale cheek. 'Oh, Zelda, how I've missed you! Life has just not been the same without you. I'm absolutely thrilled you've come. You'll be your old self in no time under this sun. I'll have you painting like Rembrandt before you know it.'

'Oh, no, not grim old Rembrandt. I want to paint like an Impressionist, but a more' – Zelda waves her hand as she searches for the word – 'expressive kind of Impressionist. Yes, that's it. *Expressive Impressionism*. That's me to a T.'

'Perfect. We'll have a jolly time.' Etta holds out her hand. 'Come on then. Get on your feet. If I'm to make you a great painter, there's no time to waste.'

---

Etta wipes her paintbrush on a paint-splattered cloth and drops it into a glass jar on a metal café table. She looks over at Zelda and watches her friend sweep sky blue paint across the canvas, above a surrealist white skyline of Capri's rooftops. She is pleasantly surprised to see that Zelda has a unique eye and a natural skill with line and colour; maybe if Zelda applied herself, she could move out from Scott's shadow and make a name for herself as an artist in her own right.

'You're good, Zelda. That's really good.'

Zelda flashes Etta a bright smile. 'Don't sound so surprised, honey. I used to paint in school. I'm awfully talented at so many things, much more so than Scott, but I just can't decide where to spend my energies.'

'You just need to make a decision and focus on it, Zelda.'

Zelda laughs. 'That's the problem! I can't make up my mind!'

She points her paintbrush at the half-finished painting on Etta's easel. 'You're awfully good yourself. You're every bit as good as Carlo. Even better, I'd say. Have you ever thought about mounting your own exhibition in Paris? You should, you know. I'd come to it and drag along all of Scott's friends.'

Etta glances over at her painting, where the sky awaits her brush. 'I've thought about it. Once upon a time. I studied fine art at the Slade in London before the war.'

'Did you? Well, aren't you full of secrets, Etta Marinetti!'

Etta glances at Adriana, who is being uncharacteristically patient as she guides Scottie's small hand in feathery brushstrokes as they paint a palm tree onto Scottie's miniature canvas. 'When I had Adriana … things changed.'

'I get that. I used to write, you know. Diaries, short stories, magazine articles. I even helped Scott write a play called *The Vegetable* which was an enormous flop. Scott and I went to a bar before the last act. It closed on the first night. Then, I had Scottie.' She shrugs. 'I have to be a good mama.'

'Scott's lucky to have you, Zelda. He'd be awfully dull and serious without you.'

'That's for damn sure!' Zelda glances at the two little girls and presses her lips together. 'Oops, sorry. Must mind my p's and q's. We can't have the girls sounding like sailors.'

She reaches over to a plate of almond and lemon biscuits and, grabbing two, hands one to Etta. She takes a bite, observing Etta as she chews. 'Please say you'll be coming back to Paris soon. We're going back at the end of April. Say you'll come. *Gatsby* will be out and there's sure to be parties.'

Etta sighs. 'Oh, I'd love that. I get so awfully bored here. But there's Carlo over in that prison, and Adriana to look after, so my family keep reminding me. I've just had a letter from my sister Jessie chastising me for being irresponsible for going off to Paris so often.'

Zelda swats away Etta's concerns like they're a bothersome fly.

'Don't mind them. You have to live your life, Etta. Look, Carlo's not going anywhere and Adriana seems fine to me.'

'She's been skipping school, Zelda. She gets bored and picks fights when she gets impatient with people.'

'So? I did, too. Never did me any harm.'

Etta laughs. 'I was a truant. I loved sneaking off to watch the moving pictures at the local picture house.'

Zelda nudges Etta with her elbow. 'There you go. Adriana will be fine. Look, I've heard they're putting on a big design exhibition in Paris this summer. There's going to be pavilions from all sorts of countries, and loads of people, and parties ... You simply must come to Paris this summer, Etta. Promise me you'll come. We'll have such fun!'

Etta chews her lip. What would the harm be in going back to Paris for the summer? Adriana will be on holiday and can run about the island to her heart's content, and, as Zelda said, Carlo isn't going anywhere.

What's more, the migraines had begun to return, the ones that sent her to bed with the curtains drawn as multi-coloured zigzags throbbed against her eyelids. She only ever had them here on Capri, when the pulsating anxiety that often kept her from sleep began to invade her days. When only Liliana's tonic of laudanum and honey would calm her nerves. She has to get back to Paris or she is afraid she will lose her mind. She can't let that happen again.

She smiles at Zelda. 'I will. I'll come to Paris in June. I promise.'

# Chapter Forty-Four

## Celie

**West Lake, Alberta – April 1925**

The white sheet flaps around Mavis Wheatley in the warm chinook breeze sweeping down from the Rockies over the Alberta prairies. It snaps like a sail in the April wind as Mavis struggles to peg the sheet to the clothesline.

'How is the English teaching going, Celie?' Mavis asks as she grabs a damp pillowcase out of the laundry basket. 'Are you making good Canadians out of the Germans? Arthur says Hans is helping out with the Boy Scouts now. Arthur also says he's awfully good at knots and Kim's Game.'

Celie's stomach drops at the unexpected mention of Hans.

'It doesn't surprise me. Hans is helping me tutor the new students in the school, and he's been coming over to the house to help with farm chores twice a week since January. You've seen how Lulu adores him, especially now that he's given her Kip. He makes her daisy chain crowns which she refuses to take off until they fall off. I'm forever picking wilted daisies out of the rag rugs before Frank comes in for supper. He hates mess.'

Mavis laughs. 'I'm glad Fred's not particular. I don't want to think what my three kids track into the house.'

Celie takes a couple of clothes pegs out of a cloth bag and pegs up a pillowcase. 'I've been helping Hans prepare for the entrance exams for the University of Alberta. He's hoping to start in September. He says he wants to be an engineer and work on aeroplanes. He's very clever, just like M—' She shuts her mouth before the name slips out.

'Aeroplanes? How modern! I read in the newspaper that air travel will take over from sea travel one day. Can you imagine, Celie? Flying from Alberta to England over the ocean? That would scare me to death.'

'I suppose anything's possible. Things are changing so quickly. Aeroplanes didn't even exist when we were born.'

'Well, I prefer to keep my feet on solid ground.'

Celie looks over at her friend as she pegs up a tea towel. Ever since Lulu's birthday, when she'd got out her camera for the first time in ages, she's been thinking about taking up photography properly again, but she needs Mavis's help. Frank has been in a mood since Lulu's lacklustre response to the bicycle, compounded by seeing her with her camera. She had quickly packed it away in her drawer before it triggered another argument.

'Mavis, did I ever tell you that I used to be a photographer? I used to write for one of the London newspapers, too. The women's pages. During the war.'

'Celie Jeffries! Well, you are a keeper of secrets. No, you never told me that.'

She shrugs. 'Now that Lulu's in school, I've been thinking of taking it up again.'

'Well, why don't you?'

'It's Frank. He thinks it's a waste of money and my time. He doesn't see the point of it.'

'Celie, your time is your own. He doesn't own you.'

'I know. I think it's more than the money. We're doing well enough now since they started up the Alberta Wheat Pool and I've been teaching. I think the photography reminds him of my life before we married ... of what I've given up by marrying him.'

'If you love taking pictures, there's no reason to give it up.'

'You're right.' She chews her lip. 'Mavis, I've been wondering if you might ... if I could ...'

Mavis laughs. 'Spit it out, Celie. If I could what?'

'If I were to give you the money for the film and any other materials I needed, would you order them for me from Mr Forbes? I don't want Frank to know. Not yet, anyway.'

'Is that all? Of course, Celie! I've got a room where I bottle my beer behind the pantry. I can keep everything for you there. Heavens, you can even use it for processing your pictures if you like. It hasn't got a window and Fred and the kids are banned from going in there.'

'Really? You'd do that?'

Mavis picks up the empty laundry basket and balances it on her hip. 'Sure. That's what friends are for, isn't it?'

Arthur Wheatley, at ten years old a younger, freckled version of his father, ploughs through a gap in the sheets with his sister's favourite doll in his hand, shouting *Pow! Pow!* as he wields a stick like a gun. Ben Wheatley and Lulu Jeffries burst through the gap squealing as they shoot at Arthur with their fingers, the puppy Kip barking at their heels. Eleven-year-old Molly Wheatley parts the sheets and stomps out onto the grass.

'What's the matter, Molly?' Mavis asks. 'Don't you want to play with the others?'

'They're acting like children, Mommy. Lulu stole Margaret Ellen and gave her to Arthur and now he won't give her back.'

'Arthur Wheatley, give your sister back Margaret Ellen or there'll be no apple dumplings for you tonight.'

'Ah, Ma!'

Celie looks at her daughter, frowning. 'Lulu Jeffries. Did you steal Margaret Ellen? You know she's Molly's favourite doll.'

Lulu giggles as she yanks the doll from Arthur's grasp and teases Kip with it.

'Lulu Jeffries! Do I need to take you home without milk and cookies?'

Lulu screws up her face. 'No.'

'Well, then, tell Molly you're sorry and give her back her doll.'

She stamps her foot. 'But *I* like Margaret Ellen, too.'

'I like Margaret Ellen as well, but she belongs to Molly. You can't always have everything you want in life, Lulu. Best you learn that now.'

'I can!'

'Louisa Isabella Jeffries! Give Molly back her doll at once!'

'Molly, you thank her politely when she does,' Mavis says. 'Then we can all go inside and have cookies and milk.'

'Cookies!! *Pow! Pow!*' Arthur yells as he charges up the gravel path to the house, Ben galloping behind on an imaginary horse. The two girls make a graceless exchange and run up the path, screaming for the boys to wait, Kip bounding up the path after them.

'I'm sorry about Lulu, Mavis. I worry for poor Miss Evans when she starts school in September.'

Mavis slips her arm around Celie's as they head toward the house. 'She'll be fine. I wish Ben had half the spirit she has. He's such a sweet, compliant little boy. Makes life easy for me, but I worry that he's the type who'll find life bruising when people disappoint him, as they inevitably will.'

'And I'm afraid Lulu is the type to do the bruising.'

# Chapter Forty-Five

## Etta

### Grand Palais, Paris, France – June 1925

Against the black night sky, the curved glass canopies of the Grand Palais glitter with the reflected sparkle of a thousand electric lights at the gala of the Exposition Internationale des Arts Décoratifs et Industriels Modernes, so that the vast glass palace appears to Etta like a ship floating amongst the twinkling stars. All around her, the palace hums with the sound of chattering voices, the clink of crystal glasses, the sudden peals of feminine laughter, and the syncopated rhythms of a jazz band. She watches the American dancer Loie Fuller waft by in a gown of impertinent sheerness, arm in arm with the iconic singer Mistinguett in her glittering diamond stage costume.

'They're both past fifty, can you believe it?' Zelda whispers into Etta's ear. 'I hope I can cause a stir like that when I'm their age.'

'Oh, we will, Zelda. We'll be partners in crime.' Etta waves her hand at a waiter in a peacock blue waistcoat and blue silk turban. 'More champagne! We're parched over here!'

Zelda waves at her husband who is weaving his way through the heaving crowd. 'There's Scott. It looks like he's got the Hemingways in tow. Hadley's all right, but Ernest is a crashing bore. It's always all about him, him, him. Just you wait and see.'

Etta watches F. Scott Fitzgerald and his two companions negotiate a path to their table through a throng of ballet dancers in white tutus. Her eyes widen as she recognises the bullish man with Zelda's stylish blond husband.

'Zelda, here he is, the man himself,' Scott says. 'Found him at the bar with Hadley.'

Zelda rolls her eyes. 'Lucky us.'

The large man smiles coldly at Zelda. 'Nice to see you too, Zelda. Finished any paintings yet?'

'Finished any novels, Ernest?' Zelda looks over at Etta. 'Etta, this is Ernest Hemingway, a newspaper hack and aspiring writer and his wife, Hadley. Hadley's a peach. Ernest not so much. Hadley, Ernest' – she gestures at Etta – 'the divine Etta Marinetti.'

Scott pulls out the chair beside Zelda. 'Zelda, honey, give Ernest a break for one night, please?' He throws open his arms and looks up at the glittering glass dome. 'We're in a palace of decadence in the city of glamorous excess and I intend to enjoy it.'

Ernest leans across the table and extends his hand to Etta who gives it a confident handshake. He laughs a deep-throated laugh. 'That's what I like. A woman who shakes hands like a man. None of this namby-pamby limp-wristed stuff.' His eyes narrow. 'I know you, don't I?'

'You do. We met in Sylvia Beach's bookshop a few years ago. You were buying *Crime and Punishment* and I was buying—'

'*Women in Love*. I remember.'

'Ernest wasn't buying *Crime and Punishment*, he was borrowing it,' Hadley Hemingway says as she extends her hand across to Etta. 'Awfully nice to meet you, Etta. Isn't Sylvia a lovely person? She's been advising us on our reading.'

Etta regards the broad, handsome face of Hadley Hemingway, framed by short wavy dark hair. She has eschewed any embellished headdress, unlike the majority of the women at the gala, herself included, and her gown is a simple, though admittedly elegant, dress of violet silk crepe which highlights the soft, pale blue of her eyes. Etta glances down at the diamante glitter on her own apricot silk Paul Poiret gown and wonders, for a brief instant, if her breathtakingly expensive dress and feathered headband had tipped her from exquisiteness into vulgarity, but then decides that she is being unduly self-critical.

She bestows a bright smile on Hadley. 'It's lovely to meet you, Hadley. Perhaps we ought to meet up and compare notes on our reading.'

'Oh, that would be terribly fun. You can come around to our apartment for tea, if you don't mind a baby underfoot. I'm rather stuck at home most days. Bumby is only eighteen months old.'

'Bumby?'

'It's Jack, actually,' Ernest interrupts. 'We just started calling him Bumby for some reason and it stuck.' He grabs a champagne bottle from a passing waiter and, after filling his and Hadley's glasses, skirts around the table to sit beside Etta. He splashes the fizzing wine into Etta's glass and thrusts the bottle at Scott.

'Entertain the ladies, Scott, while I find out about the lovely interloper.'

Etta arches an eyebrow at Ernest. 'Interloper? That doesn't make me feel very welcome, Ernest.'

'Don't mind me. Hadley says I have a habit of saying things in order to make people feel uncomfortable.' He takes a drink of champagne. 'If I do, it's only to check their mettle.'

Etta sips at the champagne. 'And how is my mettle checking out?'

Ernest grins under his moustache. 'You're checking out just fine. What did Zelda say your name was? Etta?'

'Etta Marinetti. My husband is Carlo Marinetti, the painter.'

'Ah, yes. The painter who murdered his first wife to marry his second.' His dark eyes sweep over Etta. 'I can see why.'

'He didn't—' She clears her throat. 'Carlo is not a murderer.

I'm working on obtaining an appeal. They have no concrete proof.'

'Sure. Just a beautiful mistress and a besotted lover with a demented wife. Plenty of motive there.' He sets down his glass and holds out a beefy hand to Etta. 'C'mon. How about we have a whirl around the dance floor?'

Etta glances at Hadley, who waves back. 'Go on. Just watch his left foot.'

Etta treats Ernest to her best dimpled smile and holds out her gloved arm. 'I'd be delighted, Mr Hemingway.' He takes hold of her hand as she rises from her seat, but she turns suddenly and grabs her champagne coupe. 'Mustn't waste good champagne.' She downs the contents in one gulp and hands the glass to Ernest.

He sets the glass on the table. 'There's a girl after my own heart.'

The room spins and undulates around her as Ernest leads them through the foxtrotting dancers.

'Oopsie,' she says as she stumbles over his foot. 'Sorry about that. Zelda and I started on the champagne back at the hotel.'

'Don't worry, honey,' he says as he takes her into his solid grip. 'I've got you.'

'Oh, you think so, do you, Mr Hemingway? I'll have you know I'm a very honourable person.'

He guides her along the dance floor. 'With Zelda Fitzgerald as your Paris guide? You're bound to find yourself down some dubious side roads involving booze and drugs.'

'Don't say that. Zelda is a peach.'

'Sure. Soft and fuzzy on the outside, and hard as stone on the inside.'

Etta stops short and pushes Ernest away, knocking him into several dancers who shout out their protests in angry French. 'Zelda's my best friend. Don't you dare speak about her like that!'

'Are you being an arse again, Ernest?'

Etta looks over her shoulder into the large brown eyes of an attractive Black woman in a white fringed gown. A sequinned headband crowns her slicked black hair and a kiss-curl curves over her right cheek like an invitation.

'Ruth, what do you think you're doing?' Ernest protests. 'We were in the middle of a dance.'

Ruth Bellico takes hold of Etta's elbow. 'From which I am going to rescue Mrs Marinetti before it turns into a free-for-all.' She tugs Etta through the dancers until they are safely away from the argument Ernest is fomenting with several of the disgruntled dancers.

'Who ... who are you?' Etta asks as she is pulled through the crowd.

'That looks like it was a close call,' Ruth says, ignoring the question. 'I didn't want you to get caught in the middle of another Ernest Hemingway incident.'

'An incident?'

'The last time I saw Ernest in the Dingo Bar, Zelda threw her plate of spaghetti into his lap.'

Etta giggles. 'No doubt he deserved it.' She waves down a waiter and takes two glasses of champagne off his tray. She hands a glass to the mysterious woman. 'Who did you say you are?'

'I didn't.' The woman sips at the fizzing champagne. 'I'm Ruth Bellico. I'm a journalist for the Associated Press. I live here in Paris when I'm not away on assignment, which is most of the time. I was making the rounds and heard someone call you Etta Marinetti. I know your sister, Jessie.'

'You know Jessie?' Etta sways and grabs hold of Ruth's arm. 'Sorry. I think I've had a bit too much champagne.'

'Come on, let's sit.' Ruth steers them back to Etta's table without any major incidents and only minor spillage of champagne.

Etta sways as she flops into a chair. 'Where is everybody?'

'Hadley's gone to rescue Ernest and the Fitzgeralds are dancing.' Ruth pours out a glass of water from a jug. 'Drink some water. Time to ease up on the champagne.'

Etta focuses her eyes on Ruth. 'How do you know Jessie?'

'I met Jessie on Howard Carter's dig in Egypt some years ago. We've bumped into each other a few times in Cairo since then. I'm there quite regularly because of the political situation. She told me she has a twin sister named Etta who's married to the painter Carlo Marinetti. I heard someone call out your name and came over to introduce myself, but Ernest whisked you away to dance and chaos ensued, so I swooped in. And here you are, every bit exactly how Jessie described you.'

'Am I? How did she describe me?' Etta takes a silver cigarette case out of her handbag and offers a cigarette to Ruth, who declines. She selects a cigarette and waves down a passing partygoer for a light.

'She said that everyone likes you and that it's your blessing and your curse.'

'What an odd thing to say.'

'She also said you used to fancy yourself the next Lillian Gish.'

Etta laughs. 'That's true enough. I wore my hair long with ribbons and swanned around with fans and shawls and did quite a bit of swooning. Mama despaired.' She frowns at the water glass and picks up the champagne coupe. 'How is Jessie? We write but it's been years since we've actually seen each other.'

'Jessie is …' Ruth smiles. 'She's quite something really. She knows what she wants and she goes after it. She doesn't take no for an answer. She reminds me of me.'

Etta smiles as she empties the champagne coupe. 'That sounds just like Jessie.'

'Etta! Sweetie!' Zelda shouts as she swoops down upon the two women. She grabs Etta's hand. 'Come on! Josephine Baker's dancing the Charleston with Mistinguett and Kiki de Montparnasse. They're up on some tables. You have to come!'

Ruth rests a hand on Etta's arm. 'Etta? Are you sure—'

Etta leaps to her feet and throws Ruth an air kiss as Zelda pulls her into the crowd.

'Lovely to meet you, Ruth! Tell Jessie I miss her and that my life is simply marvellous!'

# Part VI

1926

# Chapter Forty-Six

## Christina

### St Saviour's Church, Lewisham, London – February 1926

Christina takes a seat in a pew near the curtained confessional box in the church. A woman's stockinged legs and the scuffed soles of her patent leather shoes protrude from beneath the short purple damask curtain, and the woman's confessional mumblings filter through the limp fabric into the nave's musty air.

It has been a long time since she's come to Confession. Not since she'd ended it with Harry. She should have felt relieved to be free of an immoral relationship, happy to have her sins with Harry absolved finally and for ever. But she hadn't been able to face her weakness, her absolute failure to live up to the high standards of decorum she had set for herself the day she married Gerald Fry. The Christina Fry she had constructed so carefully – the devout Catholic, the strict but loving mother of three daughters, the respected member of community organisations – was nothing, she had discovered, but a veneer concealing the real

Christina. The naïve, romantic, trusting Christina Bishop whom she had thought she had left on Capri in 1892.

She was weak then, and she is still weak, and she despises herself for it. Had she learned nothing since the summer of her downfall on Capri? How had she allowed herself to be lulled into the belief that Harry had fallen under her spell again? He could never have loved her, despite all his declarations of undying love. He would never have left her with child on that island if he'd loved her, and he would never have married Rose McClellan. She hadn't intended to fall in love with him again, but she had. Even after ending the affair, she has not been able to forgive herself for her weakness of character, so how could she have expected God to forgive her?

She has to pull herself together. She has been mired in self-loathing and guilt for over three years, made worse by her stupidity at signing over her claim on the Bishop family home to Henrietta when Harry had dealt with her aunt's accomplice, the duplicitous Mr Fincher. And then to discover that Henrietta had never intended to sell the house at all and was now the legal owner of it! She has lost everything – her great love, her family home, her self-respect, even her daughters who have fled from her all across the world – and it is destroying her.

She shuts her eyes and leans back against the hard pew; she breathes in the lingering scent of frankincense and myrrh from the morning service. It's time to stop it all. To admit defeat. To give in and live out her days as a genteel widow sewing needlepoint cushions, writing letters to her absent daughters, and submitting to Ellen Jackson's thwarting of her ambitions at the WI. If only she had never gone to Terroni's that day for cannoli. If only it hadn't been raining and she hadn't been blinded by her haste and the umbrella …

She opens her eyes and stares up at the sweeping curves of the church's vaulted ceiling. Could it be that she has it all wrong? Perhaps it happened for a reason. Perhaps she and Harry were meant to meet again. Perhaps Harry was put in her path so that she could atone for the sin of conceiving Cecelia out of wedlock by making him acknowledge his obligations to his daughter. Yes, that's it. Of course, it is. Why has she been so blind?

Ever since she'd met Dorothy Adam and Christopher, she's felt a growing disquiet about how Harry had so cavalierly discarded his inconvenient children and their mothers. It wasn't fair and it wasn't right. There is nothing she can do for Dorothy and Christopher, though she sympathises, of course. They are Harry's problem, not hers, though it niggles her that should Harry have no more children, Christopher would be his heir, not Cecelia. A son trumps a daughter every time. Even an illegitimate one.

Given her own experience as a rejected woman with a fatherless baby, she sees clearly the hazardous path a woman treads in a man's world, particularly if that woman were revealed to be illegitimate or 'ruined' by the attentions of a man. Even when she was seeing Harry in London, she was only too aware that her reputation and her standing in her community would have been destroyed if someone like Ellen Jackson had found out about their illicit relationship. The burden of sin was always put on the woman's shoulders, while the man could slide back into his normal life, taking up where he'd left off.

*Not this time, Harry. You have an obligation to Cecelia as her father, and I'm going to see you fulfil it. The question is how to do it without revealing your identity as her father to Cecelia.*

The purple curtain draws aside and a plain-featured woman in a cheap brown coat and horn-rimmed glasses steps out of the confessional. She glances at Christina before she hurries down the aisle clutching her handbag against her chest.

Christina looks at the vacant cubicle. She collects her handbag and, rising, follows the woman out of the church.

---

Christina sits on a bench under the bare grey branches of a towering London plane tree in Portman Square. She smiles at her foresight at having made a copy of the key to the private garden when she'd lived in the house that she's now watching from her seat. The Bishop house. The house that should have been hers as her father's heir. The house that her aunts Henrietta and Margaret had stolen from her.

She loves every red brick, every polished floorboard, every marble mantelpiece in that house. She remembers how the sash of her bedroom window would stick, and she would have to shove it with her shoulder to ease it open. She remembers the coolness of the Carrara marble mantelpiece in the drawing room when she would run her fingers along its classical urns and reeded jambs, and the way the Portland stone floor tiles in the entrance hall dipped from centuries of wear just as you entered.

And now, since she'd been forced to sign over the deed to the Bishop house to her aunt to buy her silence, Aunt Henrietta has her beloved childhood home. And her aunt hadn't sold it to a girls' school; she hadn't sold it to anyone. No, Henrietta had sold her Yorkshire house and moved into it lock, stock and barrel.

Everything had been a ruse to get her out of the way once and for all. She'd been robbed of her birthright, just as Harry had robbed her of her innocence.

The glossy black door swings open and the old woman steps onto the tiled stoop. Still ramrod straight and thin as a stick at the age of eighty-two. Christina watches as her aunt adjusts her hat and switches her walking stick from one hand to the other. Henrietta glances at her wristwatch and then steps onto the pavement, heading left toward Baker Street.

She won't allow her aunt to get away with the injustice of it. Just as she would see that Harry would pay for abandoning her and Cecelia.

She knows now what she has to do.

# Chapter Forty-Seven

## Jessie

**Cairo, Egypt – February 1926**

Jessie wags her finger at the spice seller who holds up a large scoop of cayenne pepper.

'*La! La!* The other one.'

She points to a huge cone of orange powder.

'Paprika.'

She racks her brain for the Arabic translation Marta had taught her.

'*Falifuli … falifuli …*'

'*Falifuli 'ahmar*.'

She looks over her shoulder into the smiling face of Ruth Bellico. 'Ruth? Good heavens! What are you doing in Cairo?'

Ruth kisses Jessie on her cheek. 'I'm in town to cover the election. I always like to go where the action is.' She gestures to the paprika. 'How much do you want?'

'Oh, uh. Half a pound should be fine.'

'Half a pound of paprika?'

'I know, but our cook Marta uses it like salt.'

Ruth grins and gives the order to the spice seller, who scoops the powder into a small cloth bag. Jessie hands over a coin and drops the spice into her straw shopping bag.

'Anything else?' Ruth asks. 'Some cumin, perhaps. A titch of powdered ginger? I'm partial to titches of ginger.'

Jessie laughs. 'No, I'm all done.'

Ruth slips her hand through the crook of Jessie's free arm. 'Excellent. Then you can have coffee with me and tell me all about your life in Cairo and I'll tell you all about meeting your sister Etta in Paris last summer.'

---

'... So, what with the King dissolving the Wafd parliament last March as soon as it was elected, and the horrendous lack of welfare for the general population, not to mention labour disputes springing up like fires all over the place, life here in Cairo has been rather eventful, Ruth. Aziz and his sister Zara are both involved with the Wafd Party, though they don't see eye to eye. Aziz believes in working with the King and the British, but Zara and the majority of the younger members want to throw the King and British out once and for all. It makes for some rather heated discussions around the dinner table.'

Ruth nods and wipes a butter cookie crumb off her lip with her fingertip. 'At least they're involved. I respect that. Too many people go about their lives expecting other people to sort out society's issues. I don't just mean here; I mean everywhere. If you ask me, wilful ignorance by the employed and well-fed is the root of evil, not money, nor the love of money. I've found money to be quite useful.'

Jessie sips the sweet black coffee, fragrant with the scents of cardamon, cloves and nutmeg. 'I wish I could do more, Ruth. If only you could see some of the people who come to the clinic. It's shocking. There are so few places for them to go when they're ill or hurt. I don't mean people with money – they can afford the doctors and hospitals, but the poor ... Sometimes I think ...' Jessie shakes her head. 'Never mind.'

Ruth reaches across the table and rests her hand over Jessie's. 'Sometimes you think what?'

'Sometimes I think that if I still lived in London, I would find a way to study medicine. I'd love to be a doctor. I know I'd be good at it, but it'll never happen here. The university doesn't admit women.' She shrugs. 'I've checked more times than I can count.'

Ruth threads her fingers through Jessie's and gives her hand a gentle squeeze. 'Things change. They're bound to admit women one day.'

'When I'm a grandmother.'

Ruth laughs. 'For what it's worth, I think you'd make a great doctor. Don't give up on your dreams, Jessie. Just be ready when the door opens.'

'Don't worry, I'll be there with bells on.'

'I have no doubt.'

Jessie pops the last of her butter cookie into her mouth and swallows it with a sip of coffee. 'So, you met Etta.'

'I did. She was everything you said she was. Vibrant, charismatic, the life and soul of the party.'

'That's Etta all over.'

'Look, Jessie, I probably shouldn't say this, but she seems to have gotten herself involved with a louche crowd in Paris.'

'What do you mean a louche crowd?'

Ruth picks up a spoon and stirs her coffee. 'Paris is full of high-strung creative people with big dreams, little money and a love of liquor. Etta is in the middle of it, and I don't mean that figuratively. She was rather worse for wear at the Art Deco Expo party last summer. I had to pull her off the dance floor before a brawl broke out.'

'A brawl?'

'It's a long story. It was fine. She was fine.'

Jessie frowns. 'I know she's been going to Paris fairly often to meet with Carlo's art dealer, but I really had no idea about all this.'

'Look, I don't want to get Etta into trouble, but she needs to be careful. People can and do burn out quickly in Paris. It has every temptation on tap.'

Jessie nods. 'I understand. Thanks for telling me.'

'Sure.' Ruth glances at her wristwatch. 'Sorry, Jessie. I have a meeting at the Egyptian Parliament in half an hour. I have to go.'

'Absolutely.' Jessie watches Ruth as she stands. 'Ruth, you will let me know if you hear anything else … about Etta … when you're in Paris?'

Ruth smiles. 'Of course, Jessie.' She touches her forehead with a finger in a salute. 'Until next time.'

---

*Altumanina*
*Cairo, Egypt*

*February 25th, 1926*

*Dear Etta,*

*I haven't much time today, so I will say what I need to. I met Ruth Bellico today in the Cairo souk. She said she had to rescue you from an altercation at a party in Paris last summer and that you're running with a dubious crowd – louche is the word she used. She also said you were 'rather worse for wear'. Oh, Etta.*

*Etta, it's not my place to lecture you about how you spend your personal time in Paris, though I'd truly like to throttle some sense into you. You are a wife and a mother and you're running away from your responsibilities to Carlo and Adriana with these long stays in Paris. The money you're making from Carlo's paintings, which you said was to go toward his retrial, must be running through your fingers. Please, please go back to Capri and live the life you chose when you eloped with Carlo before it's too late.*

*Papa is no longer around to rescue you if it all goes wrong.*

*Your loving and very concerned sister,*
*Jessie*

# Chapter Forty-Eight

## Etta

**Paris, France – March 1926**

'Like that, Etta, just like that. Don't move.'

Dust motes drift through a beam of white sunlight pushing through the tall grimy windows into the studio apartment cluttered with camera paraphernalia and ancient furniture from the flea market at Saint-Ouen. Etta focuses on the dancing dust as the celebrated photographer Man Ray clicks the camera. Her mind drifts back to her father's photography studio, to the days when she would pose for him in front of backdrops of sylvan scenes she'd paint with her sisters as he tried out new photography techniques. Celie and Jessie were restless sitters, but she loved playing to the camera, discovering the most flattering angles of her face, learning to smile just so while gazing dreamily into a far-off distance or boldly into the camera's all-seeing lens.

The photographer slips out from beneath the black cloth and walks over to Etta. His dark eyes under his thick black brows observe her with the concentration of a hawk eyeing its prey, and he reaches over to her and tilts her head until her neck is exposed in a long, fluid line. His hand traces the line until it is stopped by the collar of her jersey dress. He slips his fingers under the fabric and tugs until her shoulder emerges, naked and white, from the confines of the material.

She catches his eye, and a smile flashes across his face. He reaches for her chin and runs a finger along her jaw.

'Much better. A line of beauty.'

Her blood rises and she feels the warmth spread up her neck and into her cheeks. She shivers.

'Are you cold?'

His eyes shine black like lacquer, and the heat from his body pushes against her skin.

The studio door slams open and the photographer turns abruptly. A woman enters the room and weaves her way through the clutter toward them as she peels off long black gloves. She arches a pencilled eyebrow and stares down her long, straight nose at Etta.

'Well, well, Etta Marinetti,' she says in a thick French accent. 'It appears I owe 'emingway ten francs.' She brushes the gloves against Man Ray's cheek. 'You will pay 'im, won't you, Manny? You know I never carry money.'

'Kiki, what are you talking about? François DuRose has commissioned me to take Etta's portrait for the next exhibition of Carlo's paintings.'

Kiki reaches across and pulls Etta's dress back over her shoulder. She looks Etta in the eye.

'No 'arm in a portrait, you would agree, Etta Marinetti?' She grabs Man Ray's arm and, pulling him into her embrace, kisses him full on his lips. She releases him and laughs at the smudge of red lipstick she has left on his mouth.

'I 'ave branded you, *mon amour*. Must I spray you wizz my scent as well?'

Etta rises from her perch on a stool. 'You and Hemingway bet on me?'

Kiki shrugs. 'It was 'is idea.'

'What kind of bet?'

Man Ray rubs his forehead. 'I think we're done for the day, Etta. I'll print up the contact sheet and Kiki and I can meet up with you at Café Flore tomorrow afternoon to choose the shot you like best.'

'Wonderful. I'll ask Zelda and Scott to come along. Zelda will definitely want to put in her two cents worth. Four o'clock isn't too early for cocktails, is it?'

Kiki holds up a cigarette to Man Ray to light. 'We are in Paris, *ma chère*.' She blows out a stream of smoke. 'It is always time for cocktails.'

She picks up Etta's coat and hat from a chair and hands them to her with a smirk on her red-painted lips. 'It is such a shame your 'usband is in prison. I will find you a paramour. I know everyone in Paris. I will find you someone you will like very much.' She stabs Man Ray with her green-eyed gaze. 'Someone ozzer zan Manny. 'E is a man like any ozzer and cannot be trusted.'

Etta takes the clothes and grabs her handbag from the chair. 'That's not necessary, Kiki. I'm a happily married woman.'

Kiki grunts. 'Everyone needs a paramour, Etta Marinetti. 'Ow else is one an 'appily married woman? Or an 'appily unmarried woman like me? *C'est vrai, oui*?'

---

'Madame Marinetti!'

Etta looks over at the concierge who is waving at her from the hotel's reception desk as she yanks at the buttons of her new Jean Patou wool coat. 'Yes?'

The concierge smiles obsequiously under his waxed pencil moustache. 'Excuse me, *madame*. You 'ave *un lettre*.' He extends the envelope to Etta with a self-consciously graceful gesture.

'*Merci*,' she says as she takes the letter. 'Would you have someone bring me up some aspirin? I have a terrible headache.'

'*C'est dommage, madame*. I will see to it immediately.'

'A glass of champagne as well, please.' She shrugs. 'When in France.'

The concierge smiles and nods, his slick of dark hair gleaming in the electric light of the lobby's chandelier. '*Bien sur, madame*. Pol Roger?'

She smiles coquettishly. '*Naturellement*.'

In her hotel room, Etta tosses her hat, coat and handbag on a chair and throws herself down on the large bed. She rolls over and ponders the envelope as she holds it above her head. Cousin Stefania's handwriting. No doubt more complaints about Adriana's bad behaviour. First Jessie's letter, and now one from Cousin Stefania. Was there to be no end to all this haranguing?

She tears open the envelope and takes out the letter.

*Villa Serenissima*
*Capri*

*March 15th, 1926*

*Dear Etta,*

*I am sorry to be the bearer of more bad news about Adriana. She was sent home from school today for pushing over the daughter of the mayor in the playground, leaving the poor girl with a bloody nose. This is a disaster, Etta. I have been working hard to persuade the mayor to follow up with his contacts in the Naples judiciary for Carlo's appeal. He had promised to meet with the mayor of Napoli to discuss the matter, but now I will have to rescue the situation.*

*You have no idea how families are here in Italy. It will be as if Adriana has started a war. The mayor's wife just turned her back on me at the fish stall in the Piazzetta when I wished her* Buongiorno.

*You must come home as soon as possible. You are spending far too much time in Paris when your responsibilities lie here in Italy. I can't imagine the money you are spending in Paris on hotels and restaurants and all your new clothes.*

*What has happened to you,* mio angelo*? When you are here, you ignore your daughter and paint Carlo's paintings like a madwoman, or stomp across the fields scaring the goats. Or you lie in bed with the curtains drawn, refusing so much as a lemonade or a sip of soup. I am worried about you,* cara mia. *I have seen you ill before, after Adriana's birth, and I do not wish to see you fall into that chasm again.*

*You say the paintings are still selling well, but the well will run dry one day. If they ever find out that you are the artist rather than Carlo, you will be finished. You may even find yourself in prison for fraud, have you considered that?*

*No, of course you haven't. You only think of yourself. It is a great disappointment to me. I once hated your husband for his lies and his promises of marriage to you when he already had a wife and a son. Now I think he has met his equal in lies and subterfuge. I feel pity for you both.*

*I visited Carlo last week at the prison. He is like a broken man, Etta. He asks why you don't visit him more often, and why you are spending so much time in Paris. What can I tell him? What can I say that will make him feel that you haven't abandoned him?*

*Carlo has written a note for you, which I have enclosed. I have not read it, have no fear of that. I made that mistake once before, and I have lived to regret that, as you well know.*

*You can see that I am cross. I make no apology. I am done with politeness. I will leave that to your sisters and your mother. If you come home to stay at Villa Serenissima, I will put all of this behind us and we can start afresh. Please, Etta, look to your conscience. Failing that, look to your soul. I know you are enamoured of your life of parties and gaiety in Paris, but you must rise above your selfishness and come back to your family where you belong, and where you have responsibilities as a wife and as a mother.*

*Stefania*

Etta rubs her temples. *Where is that aspirin? And the champagne?* Humiliated by Kiki de Montparnasse in front of Man Ray and now reprimanded by Cousin Stefania like she's a naughty child. It's too much to bear in one day.

She rolls off the bed and roots around in her handbag for the metal flask. She unscrews the cap and drinks down the dregs of the laudanum and honey mixture.

A knock on the door.

'Just leave it outside!' Etta calls out.

A muffled *'Oui, madame.'*

Etta screws the cap back on the flask and picks up Carlo's letter from the bed. She kicks off her shoes and pads in her stockinged feet across the carpet to the door. Outside, a silver tray with a bottle of aspirin, a coupe of fizzing champagne, and a bud vase with a single white rose sits on the hallway carpet. She drops Carlo's letter down beside the vase and, picking up the tray, re-enters the room.

---

Etta takes another sip of champagne and curses herself for not ordering a bottle. In for a penny, in for a pound, isn't that what Zelda always says? She sets the glass on the bedside table and presses her finger and thumb between her eyes, blinking until the kaleidoscope of zigzags slowly fades away. Sighing, she picks Carlo's letter up from where she'd dropped it on the bedcover and re-reads it.

*My darling Etta,*

*Have I done something to offend you, Etta* mia*? Why is it that you have stayed away for so long? Stefania gave me a calendar at Christmas and I cross off the days between your visits. It has been 58 days since your last visit in January. She has said that you have been in Paris working hard to sell the paintings. I worry about you there. It is a city of temptations and there are many who would take advantage of a beautiful woman like yourself. Please come home. Come to see me. I miss your lovely face. I miss the touch of your hand under the table, the pressure of* *your knee against mine. How I long to hold you against me and kiss you until you weep of happiness. I think about the days of our love in my little hut in the woods at Asheham House in England. How happy we were then, weren't we, my darling? I know I was. I know we can be happy like that again.*

*I like to imagine you guiding the hands of your art students in the garden of Villa Serenissima or sketching the Faraglioni from the hilltops covered with wildflowers. I think of you brushing Adriana's golden hair in the sunlight and drinking tisana with Stefania on the balcony in the late afternoon sun. You are behind my mind's eye. You are in my blood. I am infected with the disease of love. Please, do not make me wait so long to see you. Every day without you is a torture to me worse than anything this horrible hell of a prison can do to me.*

*Come to me soon,* mio angelo. *I am waiting for you.*

*Your adoring husband,*
*Carlo*

Etta looks around the hotel room from the yielding comfort of the bed, at the bedside lamps and their fringed *eau de nil* silk shades, at the soft peach moiré wallcovering and the Louis XIV chairs upholstered in aqua velvet. Her steamer trunk stands open on the carpet spilling scarves and necklaces, and a collection of shoes has been aligned at the foot of the bed by some invisible maid.

She likes her life in Paris. She likes the parties and the music and the high-spirited crowd that she has found her way into. Paris is the centre of the world and she is at the centre of it. She picks up the champagne coupe and swirls the bubbling yellow liquid around in the glass before she finishes it off in one gulp. She sets the glass back down and looks at the letter.

Her cousin Stefania is right, of course. She should be back in Capri dealing with Adriana. She should be there doing everything she can to free Carlo, the man she once loved so much that she left England for a life in Italy with him. What has happened to her?

She is not a wide-eyed ingenue anymore. She is thirty-one years old, a married woman with a child. A married woman with a husband in prison for a crime he didn't commit.

She runs her finger along the lines of Carlo's handwriting. He loves her like no one else has ever loved her. She shuts her eyes and remembers the feeling of his hands on her skin, of his lips on hers. The sound of his voice as he whispers his love in her ear. How has she allowed herself to forget? She loved Carlo once. With every fibre of her being, she loved him. She simply needs to remember it, remember how she used to feel whenever they were together.

Perhaps there is some truth to what Jessie and Cousin Stefania have been saying. It has been easier in Paris, living in the soft-focus world of alcohol and laudanum, where the leaden depression that dogs her on Capri is chased away by nights of liquor-fuelled euphoria and days sleeping like the dead. But despite how much she has tried to escape from the waves of erratic energy and troughs of brain-numbing despair, it has been of no use. The headaches have returned, worse than ever, and there are days when even the promise of a party with the crème de la crème of Paris isn't enough to drag her from her expensive hotel bed.

She folds the two letters and slides them back into the envelope. Jessie and Cousin Stefania are both right. She is an adult woman with responsibilities to her husband and daughter. She must go home to Capri before it's too late.

# Chapter Forty-Nine

## Christina

**Grenville, Montcrieff & Smith Solicitors, London – March 1926**

Harry slams his hand on the large mahogany desk in his office.

'This is outrageous, Tina! I shall never agree to this … this blackmail!'

Christina raises her eyebrows as she twists the end of her ebony walking stick into the thick pile of the Persian carpet. 'I would suggest that it would be in your best interest to comply, Harry. How would your dear young wife react to the news of your two love-children?' She laughs coldly. 'And all this time I thought I was special. How wrong I was. It seems you have been spreading your affections about like a virus.'

'How did you find out about Dorothy? She's none of your business.'

'Secrets have a way of coming out eventually.' She eyes him dispassionately. His face is florid with rage and he looks about to burst out of the constrictions of his Savile Row suit. 'Do you think it was right for me to learn of your marriage from the local gossip,

Harry? I thought' – she stabs the walking stick into the carpet, leaving a dent in the plush pile – 'I thought I meant something to you.'

'You did. You do. But this? What am I supposed to think about you … us now?'

'Harry, there is no *us*. I was foolish enough to let myself imagine we might have a future when we became involved again. But a leopard never changes its spots, does it? I was a fool. I should have known better.'

'I didn't go looking for you, Tina. You were the one who doorstepped me outside of my chambers in Lincoln's Inn Fields. It was no accident, was it?'

Christina shrugs. 'You're right, Harry. I engineered that meeting. I was obsessed. After we met that day by Farringdon Station, I couldn't get you out of my mind. I … I couldn't stop myself.'

He rises from his chair and rounds the desk. He takes hold of Tina's free hand and sandwiches it between his. 'I wanted you, too, Tina. I've always wanted you. You don't have to do this. God knows I don't love Rose. She's as docile as a sheep and about as interesting. I married her simply for the money and to have children.'

'You have children.'

'*Legitimate* children.' He takes the walking stick from her and rests it against the desk.

'Disarming me, are you?'

'Shouldn't I?'

'I would if I were you.'

He folds his arms and looks at Christina. 'Nothing needs to change, Tina. We have the flat in Chelsea. The most expensively decorated flat in London. Why don't you move into town? We can see each other more often then. Honestly, I can't see what the problem is.'

'I'm glad you mentioned the flat. I want you to put it in Cecelia's name.'

He laughs and returns to his chair. 'Let me see if I understand this correctly. You want me to buy your aunt's house and give it to you? Oh, *and* give the Chelsea flat to Cecelia? That's rather avaricious of you, don't you think?'

Christina sweeps her cold gaze over Harry. 'I hardly think so. The house is mine by right and leaving Cecelia the flat is a small way for you to recognise and acknowledge your obligations to her as your daughter.' She shrugs. 'It's the very least you can do.'

'Won't she wonder how the flat has come to her out of the blue?'

'She won't know because you will put my name on the leasehold documents. I shall leave the flat to Cecelia in my will. I shall, of course, move into the Marylebone house and rent out Clover Bar for additional income. I shall use the Chelsea flat as my London pied-à-terre and for my daughters whenever they visit.'

'What makes you think your aunt will sell the house to me after all the fuss she made to have you sign it over to her?'

'You will make her an offer which will be impossible for her to refuse.'

Harry raises a thick black eyebrow. 'Will I now?'

'You will offer to buy the house for a sum above market value and permit Henrietta to live there until her death for a peppercorn rent, at which point you sign over the house to me.'

'And if I refuse, you will leak the details of my affair with Dorothy and the existence of Christopher to the press?'

'I shall.'

'It would destroy them, you know.'

Christina runs her hand over her ear. 'That would be unfortunate, but my concern is for you to do right by Cecelia. However—'

'Tina, hasn't it occurred to you that, if you reveal my relationship with Dorothy, she may well tell the papers about you and Cecelia in retaliation?'

'I'm not worried about that.'

'Why not?'

She smiles. 'As I was about to say when you interrupted me, you won't take the risk of having either of our stories revealed to the papers. If you were exposed as a callous womaniser with two illegitimate children, it would end your career, and quite likely your marriage.'

He leans back in the desk chair and huffs. 'You haven't any real proof that links me with either of you or the children.'

'Mr Fincher—'

'Mr Fincher's findings in Capri are based on the arguably faulty memory of an octogenarian, if the poor woman is even still alive.' He shrugs. 'The portrait signed by H. Grenville proves nothing—'

'My diary—'

'Contains nothing but the fantastical musings of a besotted young girl.'

Christina presses her lips together into a tight line. She opens her handbag. 'It wasn't my intention to use this, but you have forced my hand, Harry.' She takes out the photograph of Harry with Dorothy and Christopher in front of the school gates.

He reaches for it, but she pulls it away.

'Where did you get that?'

'Does it matter, Harry? All you need to know is that it exists and I have it, along with Cecelia's Italian birth certificate. I have no doubt the newspapers would be more than happy to publish it with the story.'

'You wouldn't dare.'

Christina rises and grabs hold of the walking stick. 'You have until five o'clock next Friday to decide. I shall be at Clover Bar. I urge you not to be late with your answer.'

# Chapter Fifty

## Celie

**Sweet Briar Farm, West Lake, Alberta – April 1926**

Celie picks a wooden spoon out of a ceramic jar and stirs bunches of fresh parsley and thyme from her windowsill pots into the bubbling vegetable soup.

'Doesn't the soup smell good, Lulu? We'll have it for supper with fresh bread. Won't your Daddy love that?'

Lulu nods without looking up from the colouring book where she is intent on colouring a duck a violent magenta.

Celie goes back to the patient stirring, watching the foaming soup slowly thicken into a rich fragrant broth. Her days are mostly this now: cooking, sewing, cleaning, tending the vegetable garden, milking the cows, feeding the pigs and the chickens. It is difficult for her to believe that she had ever thought she could make a difference in this world, have an impact, make things better. London had seemed so big and dense and important, the centre of everything, and she had been a part of it all. Still, her first article for the local paper was coming out today, encouraging people to contribute to the building of a new hospital. It was something. It was a start.

She had wanted to tell Frank about it; had opened her mouth to say something about the article for the past two weeks, but the words wouldn't formulate. Why has she become so afraid to tell him things? She huffs at the bubbling soup. That was easy – because he grumbled and barked at her whenever she brought up anything that wasn't about the farm. It was as if he resented the idea of her having any sort of life outside Sweet Briar Farm.

She takes the pot off the stove and wipes her hands on her apron. Opening a tin decorated with the British Houses of Parliament, she takes out a molasses cookie and places it on a plate which she sets on the table in front of Lulu. The little girl looks up, her blue eyes fringed with long, dark lashes.

'Thank you, Mommy.'

'You're welcome, sweetheart.'

Lulu looks down at the dog curled under her feet. 'Can Kip have a cookie?'

'Of course. Just a little bit, but don't tell your father.'

Celie runs her hand over Lulu's soft brown hair. Her life has changed; she simply has to accept it. She had made the decision to marry Frank when she knew it meant leaving the life she had loved; when she had thought Max was dead, and the thought of starting afresh with a man who loved her in a country of opportunity was as shiny as a bauble on a Christmas tree.

The kitchen door slams against the wall and Frank stomps across the new green linoleum, mindless of the mud he is tracking across the floor. He slams a newspaper onto the table in front of Celie and jabs his finger on the paper.

'What do you call this?'

Celie wipes her hands on her apron. 'What do I call what?'

Frank picks up the paper. '"Nursing Sisters appeal to residents to donate to the construction of new hospital" by C. Jeffries.'

Celie frowns. 'Rex Majors promised he'd use my full name in the byline.'

'I was just laughed out of Forbes's store by Tom Philby and Ol' Man Forbes for sending my wife out to work and you're worried about your byline? You made me look like a fool, Celie.'

Celie glances at Lulu who is watching them, wide-eyed, as she chews on the cookie. 'Frank, please. Not here.' She nods at their bedroom door and walks through the kitchen toward it.

Frank follows her into the bedroom and shuts the door. 'What's this all about, Celie?'

'For heaven's sake, Frank, it's only a short article in the local paper. During the war, women packed ammunition shells and drove trams. We're entirely capable of doing things other than raise children and bake bread.'

'That was during the war. Women don't need to do those things anymore. It's *my* responsibility to bring in the money in my household.'

'You don't mind me teaching.'

Frank laughs. 'Is that what you think? My wife going off to teach Germans every Saturday when just a few years ago they were doing everything they could to kill me? I mind, Celie, but we needed the money.'

'And now?'

'Now, the money helps pay for the extra things you need in the house, but you don't need to make a habit of picking up odd jobs all over the place. It makes us look desperate. It makes it look like I can't support my family.'

Celie shakes her head. 'I remember when you used to go to the suffragist marches in London and hold banners, Frank. What's happened to you?'

'That was about women having the vote, not about women taking jobs away from men.'

Celie stares at her husband. Scarcely a day goes by when she doesn't bite her tongue to keep from arguing with him. Frank has an opinion on everything – from the way she plants the runner beans, to how to wax the furniture, to how long or short the curtains should be.

It's all going wrong. There are still occasional days when Frank is close to his old self, when he'll offer to knead the bread, or dig over the potatoes, or even borrow Fred's truck to take her and Lulu for a drive to the lake for a picnic when the weather is nice. Where he'll play 'hide and seek' with Lulu and Kip and skip stones across the water while she sits on a tree stump and suns her bare legs. But those days are sliding away like water down a sinkhole.

She rubs her forehead. 'It was hardly a front-page story for the *Edmonton Journal,* Frank. Most people won't even notice who wrote it.'

'That's not the point, Celie. You went to Rex Majors behind my back. I shouldn't have had to find out about it from Ol' Man Forbes.'

'I wanted to tell you, but …'

'But what?'

She sits on the bed. 'If I'd told you, you would have told me not to do it.'

'Exactly.'

She sighs heavily. 'Frank, you knew the kind of woman I was when you married me. I need to be involved. I want to make a difference, no matter how small. It's just the way I'm made. Do you have any idea how many hours a week I spend washing clothes and cleaning the house? Every day it's the same tedious ritual of cooking and cleaning … The only time I have for myself is when I'm teaching English to the Germans.'

Frank paces across the wooden floor, slapping his hand with the newspaper. 'But, Celie … your name in the newspaper. It makes me look like I'm putting you out to work, especially on top of the teaching job. It's embarrassing.'

'That's ridiculous, Frank. The wheat harvest last year was better than ever. We're doing fine, aren't we?'

'Damn it, Celie, that's not the point!'

He thrusts the paper in the direction of the town. 'Those people are my friends! I care what they think.' He slaps the newspaper down on the bed. 'I don't want my wife writing for the paper, and that's the last I'm going to say on the matter.'

Celie's jaw begins to ache from her clenched teeth. 'Fine.'

'Good.' He picks up the newspaper and heads for the door.

'If it's all the same to you, I'd like to keep the newspaper, Frank. Especially if it's to be the only article I'm to write.'

Frank tucks the newspaper under his arm and opens the door. 'Best not to torture yourself, Celie. Give up on those old ideas. They'll only frustrate you, and the last thing I need is a frustrated wife. You're a farmer's wife now, not a journalist. West Lake isn't London.'

The door slams behind him.

Celie stares at the door, anger roiling up inside her. *Just like you're not Max.*

---

*She lies alone in her bed in the dark room. Her eyes have long adjusted to the shadows, and a silver light from the half-moon throws the square-paned shapes of the window against the far wall. The house is soft with silence, the stillness broken only by the creaks and gurgles of the building.*

*A floorboard squeaks and the doorknob turns. Max stands silhouetted in the doorway, holding his boots in his hands. He closes the door and sets his boots on the rug. She sits up against the pillows, watching his grey shape as he moves across the room toward her. He kneels by the bed and reaches out to stroke her cheek.*

*'How are you, Schatzi?'*

*'I'm happy now that you're here, Max.'*

*He kisses her, and she closes her eyes and reaches for his head, burying her fingers in his cropped hair.*

*He stands up abruptly and she watches as he undresses and neatly lays his clothes over the armchair under the window. As he moves, the moon's silver light slides over the contours of his smooth body like water sliding over stone.*

*She throws back the bedcovers and he comes to her and presses his warm body against hers. She is impatient with the barrier of the thin cotton lawn of her nightdress and pushes him away. Her breath is heavy and a heat has risen in her body, though she knows it has nothing to do with the heat of the summer night.*

*'Schatzi?'*

*'Take it off me, Max.'*

*She shifts her body to help him as he lifts the nightgown over her head. He sits back and she watches as he reaches out to caress her breasts and the smooth skin of her belly. His fingers wander lower and twine themselves around the curls below her belly, and then lower still. She sucks in her breath and reaches out for him.*

*'Are you sure, Schatzi?'*

*'Yes, Max.'*

*He wraps his arms around her and covers her face with kisses. 'I love you, Schatzi. I've always loved you.'*

*'I love you, too, Max.'*

*He moves over her and her body opens to him. Their breath unifies until she no longer knows whose heart beats so loudly in the silent room.*

---

Celie's eyes fly open. Frank lies in the bed next to her, snoring softly. She turns her head toward the window where the moonlight streams into the room, just like in her dream. She slides her hand under the sheet and down her body, slowly inching her nightgown up her legs until her fingers touch her skin.

She shuts her eyes as her fingers caress her body. *'Oh, Max. I love you, I love you, I love you.'*

# Chapter Fifty-One

## Christina

### Clover Bar, London – April 1926

Christina tosses the needlepoint canvas she is working onto the settee. The mantel clock's persistent tick pricks at the torpid silence of the late afternoon, and she rises restlessly to her feet. She has been pacing across the Persian carpet for several minutes when Hettie appears in the sitting room doorway, carrying a tea tray.

'You'll wear an 'ole in the carpet if you carry on like that.'

'Thank you, Hettie. It's my carpet. If I choose to wear a hole in it, it's my business.'

Hettie sets down the tray and faces Christina with her hands on her broad hips. 'That's all well and good, ma'am, but seeing as I would be the one lugging it out to the rag an' bone man's cart, I 'ave an investment in the continued 'ealth of the carpet.'

Christina huffs and sits down on the settee. 'Fine.' She watches Hettie pour the tea and add the perfect amount of milk and sugar.

'You've checked the postbox?'

'An 'alf dozen times.'

'And no one's come to the door?'

'You would know that as well as me, ma'am.'

Christina takes the teacup and saucer from Hettie. 'Thank you, Hettie,' she says automatically.

'You're waiting on Lord 'igh an' Mighty, aren't you? If you don't mind me saying—'

'I mind, Hettie.'

'No good'll come of it. Just saying. I can smell a rotter a mile away.'

'And yet you can't smell the cake burning in the oven.'

'Oh, tosh.' Hettie hurries toward the doorway just as the doorbell rings. 'You want me to get that?' she calls out from the hallway.

Christina is already on her feet. 'No. I'll answer it.'

At the door, a bicycle messenger boy of about twelve in a flat cap and dusty knickerbockers waves a large brown envelope at Christina. He holds out his palm and eyes her saucily. 'Give us a tanner, will ya, missus? It's a long way from 'olborn.'

'Six pence! Certainly not.'

The boy shrugs his skinny shoulders. 'No skin off my nose. I'll just toss it in the river. Company pays me just the same.'

'Why, you little tinker! Just a minute.' Christina picks up her handbag from the hallway table and, fishing out her coin purse, removes a thruppence coin. She holds it up in front of the boy's freckled face. 'Satisfied?'

The boy grabs the coin, tipping his cap as he pockets it. He thrusts the envelope at Christina. 'Much obliged, missus. You don't 'ave a biscuit for an 'ungry boy, do ya?'

'Indeed not! You may be sure I shall complain about you.'

He laughs. 'Nah, ya won't. They all say that and they never do.' He waves his hand in a salute. 'Pleasure doing business, missus.'

Christina slams the door shut and draws the curtain across it with an agitated tug. Hettie comes out of the kitchen, a dishcloth in her hand. 'Thought I'd 'ave to throttle the little shit.'

'Today's youth have no respect for their elders, Hettie. I fear for humanity.'

'Waste of time. We're bound to fuck it all up eventually. It's 'uman nature.'

'Hettie, really. Language.'

Hettie shrugs. 'Looks like you got what you were waiting for.'

Christina looks down at the envelope with her name scrawled across it in Harry's impatient handwriting. 'That remains to be seen.'

---

Christina settles herself on the settee and sets her reading glasses on her nose. Taking a deep breath, she slices open the envelope with the handle of a teaspoon. She slides out a sheaf of papers and scans the first few pages.

The leasehold to the Chelsea flat. Hers for the remaining seventy-five years on the lease agreement. *Well done, Harry. That's a step in the right direction.*

She flips through the documents and finds a note from Harry.

*Dear Tina,*

*It is in situations such as this that I find 'Dear' an odd way to start a note, as it seems a vacuous use of what is meant to be an endearment. I suspect you harbour similar sentiments in this regard.*

*I am sorry, although not surprised, that things between us have ended on such a sour note. I have found that most relationships, whether they be business or romantic, end in dislike, enmity or ennui. One hopes, of course, to 'beat the odds', but, alas, most of us humans appear content to settle either for the security of boredom or revel in the passion of high drama. I have found myself to be the former type of human, while it is obvious to me that you are the latter.*

*Seeing that we have reached our end point, I surrender the leasehold of our love nest to you for Cecelia, as you desired, my dear siren, as I retire to the languorous, and one hopes fertile, embrace of my dull young wife.*

*As to the matter of your Aunt Henrietta's London house, this is a rather more complex situation. She is, as you know, aware of our little secret, and I have no doubt she would not hesitate to leak the identity of Cecelia's real father to the newspapers (is blackmail a Bishop trait?) should she feel it is in her interest to do so. I have engaged a colleague to open up negotiations for the purchase of the property on my behalf to ensure my anonymity, but I am sure you appreciate this will take some time.*

*At this stage I can see you frowning, and I implore you to desist as I find the wrinkles between a woman's eyebrows most unbecoming, and I would not have you mar your flawless complexion.*

*You will simply have to trust me in this matter, Tina. If I catch a whisper of any allusion to a love-child, whether Christopher or Cecelia, I will cease any effort to purchase the house, and you may consider us at war. Be very certain that your estimable reputation as a paragon of propriety in Hither Green will be destroyed. It is an unfair fact that a fallen woman is considered far more abhorrent than a dallying man, but such is the world we live in. My reputation would recover. As a matter of fact, I would expect some pats on the back and offers of free port at the club; men are like that, you see. And women, well, they will be swarming around me like bees to nectar. You and poor Dorothy, I fear, would enjoy no such admiration.*

*I, of course, wish to save you both this fate; so, in acknowledgement of our intimate acquaintance, and your determination that I 'honour my obligations' (I must confess, your argument on this matter has pricked my conscience, and I acknowledge my failure in this regard), I will do my utmost to secure the Portman Square house as you requested. I will be in touch once the sale has been completed. Consider it my parting gift to you, the only woman I have ever truly loved.*

*Harry*

# Chapter Fifty-Two

## Etta

**Villa Serenissima, Capri, Italy – May 1926**

Etta shuts the iron gate to Villa Serenissima and heads up the stone steps, pausing beside the potted lemon tree to breathe in the fresh citrusy scent of the white, star-shaped blossoms. She removes her straw hat and fans her face with it as she skirts the small patio, noting that her cousin's favourite scarlet pelargoniums already need a dead-heading and the marble cupid in the fountain could use a clean. She'll get Mario onto it during his next visit, although his new job teaching at the art academy in Naples is keeping him away longer than either his grandmother Liliana or Adriana like. Perhaps she'll do it herself. It would be better than trying to paint on the balcony while Cousin Stefania castigates her about her absences in Paris and her poor mothering skills.

She steps under the shaded loggia and enters the villa. She hangs her hat on the hatstand beside the hall table. A stack of post sits in the painted ceramic dish from the potteries of Vietri sul

Mare down the Amalfi Coast, and she flicks through the pile, pulling out a letter postmarked Paris.

'Ah, you've found your letter,' Stefania says as she enters the hallway from the sitting room, a watering can in her hand.

Etta watches her cousin approach. Stefania has grown quite stout over the past winter, finally abandoning the wide leather belt that had once been as ubiquitous an embellishment as the tortoiseshell combs in her impressive pompadour. But these, too, have succumbed to the march of modernity, with Stefania's adoption of a permanently waved bob, still raven black despite her seventy-six years.

'Yes. It's from Monsieur DuRose at the art gallery.'

'Ah, excellent. Another cheque, I hope? Carlo's lawyer is very expensive.'

'What are we paying him for, anyway, Cousin Stefania? He's done nothing to move the retrial forward after all these years. I think we are simply funding his holiday house in Sardinia.'

'Carlo is a convicted murderer, Etta. It is not so easy to get this overturned. There are many people who need to be … spoken to, and with Mussolini's Fascists in power, everything is even more complicated.'

'It's been six years since Carlo was found guilty, Cousin Stefania. Am I meant to wait for ever? I've heard the whispers. *La vedova triste*. I'm not a widow, nor am I sad. Angry, yes, but not sad.'

'It is always about you, *cara*, isn't it? What of Carlo? You have been back from Paris a fortnight and you still haven't visited him. And what of Adriana? I hope you haven't forgotten it's her birthday next Monday. Do you even remember how old she will be?'

'Of course I do. She'll be ten.'

'Eleven, Etta. Adriana will be eleven, and she resists any attempt to educate her. Sister Maria Benedicta at the school despairs of her ever learning her multiplication tables.'

'Adriana's a free spirit. I don't want to crush that.'

'Without parameters, one cannot fully appreciate freedom.'

'You're talking in riddles. And I'm going to see Carlo tomorrow.' Etta rubs her forehead. 'I have a headache. It was hotter than I thought on my walk this morning. I'm going to go lie down.'

---

Etta flops onto her bed and tears open the envelope. She scans past all the niceties until she finds what she has been waiting for.

> *… Thank you for sending samples of your own work. While it is obvious that you have an eye for form and colour, these paintings are very much a woman's work. What I mean is that they are, by turns, utterly pure and utterly pernicious. They are, I am sorry to say, pale imitations of your husband's work, in particular his work since the war.*
>
> *I am sorry to be the bearer of disappointing news, but I cannot see any advantage to either of us of trying to sell these to my clientele. At best, your work will be seen as the dabs of an eager amateur hoping to benefit from an association with a genuine artist; at worst, you will be labelled a talentless gold-digger exploiting your husband's misfortune. This would certainly harm Carlo Marinetti's esteemed artistic reputation and could possibly even result in a devaluation or even a boycott of his own work. This, I am certain you agree, would not be to the advantage of either of us.*
>
> *Madame Marinetti, I entreat you to set aside your own artistic aspirations and concentrate your energies on the promotion of your husband's work. It is in this endeavour that we can both be assured of mutual benefit.*
>
> *Sincerely,*
> *François DuRose*
>
> *PS: I trust you will be able to find further works of your husband's in storage in Naples? There is no immediate urgency; however, I should*

*like to organise an exhibition of this 'newly discovered' work next spring. This should give you ample time to locate them and enable me to whet the buyers' appetites with hints of more of your husband's treasures to come. I confess sometimes I wish that all my artists were involved in a crime of passion! I have come to learn the value of notoriety.*

Etta crumples the letter and throws it onto the tiled floor. That horrible, horrible man! Getting rich off of *her* paintings! Not Carlo's! Hers! Paintings that aren't even as good as the ones she'd just sent him under her own name. The paintings Monsieur DuRose refuses to sell because he's afraid of devaluing 'Carlo's work'.

The headache pounds at the back of her head like a hammer. She blinks as a pinprick of pulsing colour in her vision slowly expands into a circle of snaking zigzags. Rising from the bed, she then staggers over to the dressing table and reaches for the Penhaligon's perfume bottle. She sits on the stool and glances into the mirror, but the rainbow-coloured zigzags throb where her face should be. Removing the stopper, she tilts back her head, shuddering as the honey-sweetened laudanum slides down her throat.

---

Carlo leaps up from his chair behind the table in the prison's visitors' room and enfolds Etta in a hug.

'Etta, *cara mia! Cara mia!*'

'*Ehi! Fermo!*' the guard yells out from his post by the door.

'*Si. Si.*' Carlo squeezes Etta's hand and sits down in the chair. His eyes drink in the vision of his wife in her stylish pale blue jersey dress and the cloche hat below which her short blonde hair curls under her ears. 'It seems a man is not permitted to even hug his wife in this hellhole.'

Etta sits down in a hard chair opposite him. 'Don't mind him,

Carlo. I'm here. I'm sorry it's taken me so long. I've ... I've been ill. I must have caught something on the train back from Paris.'

Carlo's forehead creases with worry. 'You do look thinner, *mio angelo.* How are you feeling now?'

'Better. I've just been having headaches and haven't been sleeping very well. Maybe the travel and the stress of everything is simply taking its toll.'

'I understand, my darling. I am so, so sorry. You are certain you are feeling better now?'

'Yes. Much better, my darling.'

Carlo smiles and his dark eyes light up. 'It is so long since I have heard you say that.' He reaches under the table and rests his hand on her knee. 'You look beautiful, *Etta mia*.'

Etta brushes her hand nervously over her dress. 'Yes, well, I can't exactly wear last year's dresses to Monsieur DuRose's exhibitions in Paris.'

He looks down at his shirt that was once, in some long-distant past, white. 'I wonder what the Parisian elite would think of my attire? Would it pass muster, *Etta mia*?'

'Carlo. Don't, please. It's so hard for me to see you like this. Cousin Stefania said she brought you clothes when she visited and sent clean clothes to you in the post when she couldn't come.'

He laughs. 'The clothes she brought me have long since been stolen in the laundry.' He slaps his chest. 'Do you think I would be wearing these if I had received clean clothes in the post? They are probably on the back of one of the guards' sons.'

'Oh, Carlo, I'm sorry. I'm so sorry. I'll go and buy you new clothes and bring them the next time I visit. I'll bring you clothes every time I visit, if I need to.'

Carlo sits back in his chair. 'When will that be? Two months? Four months? Six months? We are still husband and wife and yet the only contact we have had since January has been the letters you sent me from Paris.'

'You know I must spend time in Paris. I have to be there to promote you and help Monsieur DuRose sell your paintings.'

'*My* paintings? Don't you mean *your* paintings?'

'What do you mean?'

Carlo leans his elbows on the table and presses his fingers against his forehead. 'I know what you're doing, Etta. I have been in this prison for almost seven years. The paintings I had in storage would have been sold long ago.' He sits back and waves his hands in the air. 'And yet, new paintings keep being "found".'

Etta wets her lips with her tongue. 'I had to do it, Carlo. We need the money if we're to get you a retrial.'

He presses his fingers against his eyes, then he drops his hands and looks at her, his eyes glistening with tears. 'I didn't do it, Etta. I didn't kill Marianna.'

Etta reaches across the table and takes hold of Carlo's hands. 'I believe you.'

'*Non toccare*!' the guard shouts.

Etta releases his hands and sits back in the chair.

Carlo probes Etta with a penetrating gaze. '*Cara mia*. It wasn't ... it wasn't you, was it?'

'What?'

His shoulders slump. 'I am sorry, Etta. I have spent so much time thinking about this. I have had nothing but time. You had new paintbrushes from the Giosi shop here in Napoli when I arrived back from the war. You said that you had just bought them. It was around the time that Marianna died. You could have—'

'Carlo, I never—'

'*Cara mia,* you, of anyone, had a motive. As long as Marianna was alive, we could never marry.'

'Do you think I could do such a thing and then let you rot away in this place knowing I was the guilty one? How can you think such a thing of me?'

Carlo runs a hand through his hair. 'I want to believe you, my darling. Believe me, I do.'

Etta stares at her husband, at the too-long hair, the shadows under his eyes, the stubble on his face, and her heart wrenches.

How has it come to this? That they each can believe the other capable of Marianna's murder? And now she is a fraudster as well, cheating people out of their money with fake Marinettis while her daughter runs around like a wild thing and her husband wastes away in prison. How has she become so selfish, so self-centred, so distracted by her life with the fast set in Paris? Is she that shallow? That fickle and selfish?

A sob pushes its way up her throat. 'I'm so, so sorry, Carlo. I'll stop. I won't go back to Paris, I promise. I'll … I'll stay at Villa Serenissima and make sure Adriana goes to school.' Her shoulders shake as the sobs burst from her throat. 'I'll be a better mother. I'll visit you every week. I'll be a good wife, my darling. The best wife. I'll get you out of here. I swear I will.'

'*Cara mia—*'

She reaches across the table and grabs his hands, ignoring the shouts of the guard. 'I love you, Carlo. I love you with all my heart. You are my life and I want you back.'

# Chapter Fifty-Three

Jessie

**Altumanina Health Clinic, Cairo, Egypt – May 1926**

Jessie slots the key into the door of the health clinic, but finds it unlocked. She glances over her shoulder at the shadowy trees and the swathe of grass as black as velvet beside the grey curve of the marble gravel drive. Soft yellow light glows from the windows of the big house, but this only emphasises the darkness of the moonless night.

She pushes open the door. 'Hello? Is someone there?'

Something scrapes across the tiled floor in the examination room. She flicks on the light. 'Hello? Who's there?'

A figure steps out from behind the examination room's curtain. 'It is me.'

Aziz's sister stands in front of her, her slender figure hidden by a black cloak. Only Zara's amber eyes are visible above the black veil. In her hands she holds a bulging drawstring kitbag.

'Zara? What are you doing?'

Zara slings the kitbag over her shoulder. 'I am sorry, Jessica. I cannot say.'

'What's in the bag?'

'Medicine. Bandages. We have more than we need in the clinic.'

'I don't understand—'

'It is not for you to understand.'

'But, Zara, we need our supplies.'

Zara juts out her chin. 'I am not a thief, Jessica. We have enough for our purposes in the clinic. I am merely taking what is necessary. They will be put to good use.'

Jessie frowns. 'Does this have anything to do with the riots?'

'It is for a clinic the Egyptian Feminist Union has set up in the al-Baghlah district.'

'Al-Baghlah? In the middle of the night? Zara, it's not safe. You know I have to tell Aziz.'

'Jessica, you cannot stop me. There are many of the poor who will not come to a clinic in a grand house like this that's run by an Englishwoman. You do well, and I appreciate it, but we Egyptians must solve our own problems. It is not for foreigners to come here and tell us how to live. I and many of my Egyptian sisters have learned our power in the EFU. The leader Huda Sha'arawi is an amazing woman, much like your Emmeline Pankhurst.' She smiles. 'I do not simply stay home and drink tea and gossip.'

'I never thought that, Zara.'

Zara raises an eyebrow. 'Did you not?' She shrugs. 'You mustn't tell Aziz about any of this. Promise me, Jessica. As my dear sister, please promise me this.'

'How can I promise that? What if something were to happen to you?'

'Jessica, please. Isham is with me. He is tall and strong and we are careful. We will be safe.'

'Isham? The gardener's son?'

'Yes.'

Jessie sits down in a reception chair, shaking her head as she regards her sister-in-law. 'We can treat people here in the clinic—'

'No. You do not understand, Jessica. It is not just the poor people we treat. There are others who do not wish to be traced. People who are fighting for a truly independent Egypt. *My* people.'

'Aziz is fighting for that too, but peacefully.'

Zara grunts. 'Talk, talk, talk. That is all he and the other accommodationists do. And the British are still here. We have a powerless government and a puppet king and the British pulling all the strings. Nothing will happen without action.' She shifts the kitbag to her other shoulder. 'I am sorry, Jessica. I must go. Isham is waiting for me in the car.'

She moves past Jessie and heads toward the door.

'Zara, please—'

Zara pauses at the door. 'It is best you know nothing of what we are doing, Jessica. That way, if you are ever questioned by General Allenby's men, you need not lie. Please, I beg you as my beloved sister-in-law, promise me you will not tell Aziz you have seen me tonight.'

'If anything happens to you, I will kill Isham myself.'

'Nothing will happen to me. I promise.'

She slips out through the doorway and shuts the door behind her.

Jessie jumps to her feet. 'Zara! Zara, wait!' She runs to the door and out onto the gravel path, but Zara, in her black cloak, has melted into the velvet night.

# Chapter Fifty-Four

## Etta

### Mount Tiberio, Capri, Italy – August 1926

Etta trudges up the goat path, kicking her way through the dry summer grass which scratches at her ankles like sandpaper. The sun beats down on her, though a cool breeze rising from the sea far below caresses the hill, setting the bushes and umbrella pines into gentle undulations. The distant *baas* of mountain goats and the harsh cries of gulls drift up Mount Tiberio on the wind with the faint scent of lemons, and though Nature is gracing the day with her charms, Etta's heart is as heavy as the boulders she skirts on her way up the hill.

She reaches the crumbling walls of the Roman ruins and leans against a vine-covered wall to catch her breath. She removes her straw hat and fans her face. It will be noon soon. What had she been thinking, hiking up Mount Tiberio in the heat of mid-day, with nothing but a flask of water and a pear for a snack? But she'd had to get away from the villa; away from her cousin's overbearing solicitousness, Liliana's disapproving glances,

Adriana's sauciness, and the claustrophobia that presses down on her there until she can barely breathe.

She loves Carlo. Of course she does. Even though the handsome, athletic man he had once been is fading into a shadow of himself, when she meets his eyes and feels the touch of his hand on hers underneath the table in the prison, her heart still quakes. But it is so hard. Every time she walks away from him down the depressing, stinking halls of the prison into the streets of Naples, she feels something inside of her wither and crumble.

*Oh, Carlo. Why does it have to be like this? Why can't we just be together and love each other? I don't know how much longer I can live like this. You're not the only one in a prison, my love.*

She picks at the thin cotton of her dress where it sticks to her body and flaps it in the breeze. Slipping the flask out of her pocket, she unscrews the cap and takes a long gulp of the tepid water. She wipes her lips with the back of her hand and screws on the cap.

She should have brought the honey and laudanum tonic. It is the only thing that gets her through the tedious, empty days. How is it that she can be in this beautiful place, and yet be so unhappy? Is this how her mother had felt when she'd found herself alone and expecting a baby on the island all those years ago? Had she wanted to scream at the world for its unfairness? For its cruelty?

When she left England with Carlo, she thought she was embarking on an exciting new life with her handsome Italian fiancé; a life where they would both be artists in a lovely Italian villa full of their beautiful, happy children. She knows now that dreams and reality rarely mirror each other. But her dreams have turned to nightmares since she stepped onto this wretched island. Yes, she eventually got what she'd wanted – a wonderful husband, a beautiful child, and a lovely villa in which to live. But even in her wildest hallucinations in the darkest days of her illness after Adriana's birth, she'd never imagined a life with a husband in prison for murder, a spoiled and undisciplined child, and a home that is not her own.

She walks over a stone step where thousands of feet over the centuries have worn a divot in the limestone, and through the remains of a doorway into a small roofless room. The stone walls are cool to the touch, and she settles herself in a corner and takes the pear out of her pocket. She bites into the taut skin, her teeth sinking into the ripe flesh. Juice dribbles down her chin and she takes another bite without wiping it away.

She eats the pear down to its core, the juice bathing her face with its sticky sweetness. Then, removing her hat, she takes her flask and tips it over her head, turning her face to the sun as the water streams over her skin.

She shakes her head, spraying the water over her dress. She can't go on like this. She will not be a victim of circumstance. She is a proud and capable Fry sister, every bit as capable as her sisters no matter what anyone thinks, and she will create her own fate.

# Chapter Fifty-Five

## Celie

**Sweet Briar Farm, West Lake, Alberta – October 1926**

'There you are, Frank!' Celie says as Frank enters the kitchen. 'Just in time to carve the turkey.'

'Thought we'd have to start without you, Frank,' Fred Wheatley says as sets down the carving knife and fork and shifts over to his own chair. 'Stomachs grumblin' all around here.'

'Kip's is the loudest,' Lulu says as she chews on a bread roll.

'Like thunder,' Ben Wheatley chips in.

'What's thunder in German, Hans?' Molly Wheatley asks Hans, who sits at the table sandwiched between twelve-year-old Molly and six-year-old Lulu.

'*Donner*, Miss Wheatley,' Hans answers. 'And lightning is *blitzen*. Just like the reindeer in the Christmas poem.'

'I know that poem,' Ben says.

Lulu frowns at Ben. 'I know that poem, too, Hans. I know all the reindeer names.' She looks over at Ben. 'Benji can't remember them.'

'I can!'

'You can't.'

'I can!'

'You can't! You can't! You can't!'

'For God's sake, children!' Frank barks as he carves into the turkey.

Celie glances across the table at Mavis as she sets down bowls of carrots and brussels sprouts gleaming with slicks of melting butter. 'That's enough, you two. Be nice to your guest, Lulu.'

Hans's Aunt Ursula helps herself to a generous spoonful of carrots. 'Don't be worrying, please. Children will be children. I remember how talkative Hans's stepbrother was when he was a boy. Talk, talk, talk, that is all Max did. It is right that he becomes a lawyer now.'

Celie's ears prick up at the mention of Max's name. 'The young man in the photograph I saw in your house? He's a lawyer now?'

Ursula scoops two helpings of roast potatoes onto her husband Klaus's plate. '*Ja.*' The elder woman's forehead wrinkles in a frown. 'I do not know where is that photograph. *Klaus, hast du das Foto gesehen?*'

'*Welches Foto?*'

'*Mit Hans und Max.*'

Her husband shakes his bald head, then nods at the offering of a turkey leg from Frank.

Ursula shrugs. 'Never mind. I must have put it somewhere.' She taps her forehead. 'I will forget my head one day!'

Celie smiles as she watches everyone help themselves to the abundant food. She slides her hand under the table and along the smooth navy cotton of her dress until she feels the soft paper of the photograph in her pocket.

'I'm sure it will turn up one day, Mrs Brandt. I'm forever misplacing things, isn't that right, Frank?'

'Quite right. Terribly annoying. Have you found my shoe black yet, Celie?'

'I wasn't the last one to use it, Frank.' Celie looks around the table at the people who now make up her world. 'Shall we say grace?'

Lulu glances at Hans. 'Can I say it, Mommy?'

'Of course, Lulu.'

Lulu presses her hands together and bows her head as she squints in concentration. '*BlessusohLordforthesethygiftsabouttoreceivethybountyamen*.' She looks up at Hans and smiles shyly.

'That was excellent, Lulu. You have a wonderful memory.'

Her smile broadens to reveal a missing front tooth. 'My teacher says that, too.'

Celie watches Hans entertain the two young girls across the dinner table as everyone tucks into their Thanksgiving feast. Her stomach knots as her memories of Max flood through her mind, robbing her of her appetite. She glances at Frank, who is deep into a conversation with Fred about the Edmonton Eskimos' chances in the new Prairie Hockey League, and Mavis, who is querying Ursula about her apple strudel recipe.

She catches Hans's eye. 'Have you heard from your brother, Hans? Is he back in Heidelberg?'

'Yes. He has joined a good law practice there. He is a criminal lawyer.'

'A criminal lawyer? My goodness.'

'Yes,' Hans says, smiling. 'As my aunt says, Max likes to talk. Now he can talk as a profession.'

'And … uh … he has a family, I imagine?'

'A family? Oh, you mean is he married? No, not yet, but he has a girlfriend named Anneliese. They have known each other for many years. I expect they will marry soon.'

Celie's stomach drops. 'Oh. Yes. Of course.'

Of course, Max has moved on from her. How could she have expected him not to, given that she herself has married?

'Will you,' she clears her throat, 'will you be going back to Germany for the wedding?'

'Oh, yes, of course. Perhaps it will be next summer. I shall send you a photograph of us all when I am there.'

Celie forces a smile. 'That would be lovely.' She takes a deep breath and looks around the table, surprised that the world hasn't fallen through the floor with her heart.

'Would anyone like some more turkey?' she asks, wondering if anyone else can hear the hollow pitch of her voice. 'We have plenty, but save room for Mavis's pumpkin pie.'

---

'What was that all about at dinner, Frank?' Celie asks as she dries the last of the dishes. 'You didn't say a word to Hans or his aunt and uncle the whole time. You weren't exactly a welcoming host.'

Frank sucks in the smoke as he lights his pipe at the kitchen table. 'They're German.'

'And we're English.'

He coughs out the tobacco smoke. 'You want me to be friendly to Germans when they killed my brother *and* spent five years trying to kill me? I have them to thank for my lungs.'

'Smoking doesn't help, Frank.'

'I'll smoke if I like, Celie.'

Celie puts away the last plate. 'The Germans killed my father, Frank. You're not the only one who's suffered.'

'I told you I didn't want them in my house, but it seems my opinion carries no weight.'

'Frank, it's Thanksgiving. If there was ever a day to forgive—'

'Don't talk to me about forgiveness! You weren't there. You didn't see what I saw.'

'I know. I'm sorry for what you've seen … what you've experienced, Frank. I saw terrible things, too, in London. But the war has been over for eight years. You have to let this go and move on.'

Frank looks up at Celie. His brown eyes glint with pain. 'I can't, Celie. I can't be that good man. I will never be able to forgive the Germans for what they did to us. And I can't forgive Max Fischer for being the man you love.'

'Is this what this is about, Frank? Max Fischer?'

Frank sucks on his pipe, then expels a puff of smoke. 'It's always been about Max Fischer.'

# Chapter Fifty-Six

Etta

**Paris, France – New Year's Eve 1926/7**

*Clover Bar*
*Hither Green Lane*
*Hither Green, London*

*December 25th, 1926*

*Dear Etta,*

*I am sitting at home early Christmas morning, having just returned from midnight mass. As much as I am loathe to admit it, the choir under Ellen Jackson's tutelage acquitted themselves very well this year, with Mildred Chadwick managing the higher notes of 'Oh Holy Night' without her voice cracking.*

*It has been dreadfully cold and windy all day, and I shouldn't be surprised to see snow on the ground in the morning, which would be a nice change from the dispiriting drizzle. Hettie has prepared a pheasant breast for me to roast with vegetables for my Christmas lunch and I shall treat myself to a small glass of your papa's port. She has gone off to*

*Worthing to spend Christmas Day with her sister's family but has promised to be back for Boxing Day, for which I am thankful. One day of attempting to communicate with the cooker is quite enough for me.*

*I received Jessica's Christmas letter yesterday and she mentioned her concern that you intended to extend your stay in Paris through the Christmas and New Year holidays because of the expense of travel during this time. Etta, what is more important than being with your child at Christmas?*

*I understand that you have business to undertake with the art gallery there, but surely this can be done without these extended stays? When you returned to Capri in the spring, you said that you would be limiting your visits to Paris to a couple of times a year, but I had not appreciated that these visits would be months long! Do I need to remind you that you are a mother and a wife? These roles bring responsibilities, Etta, which I fear you are shirking. I know that life has not turned out as you most likely thought it would, but in my experience, it rarely does. It is quite wrong that you are not with your family at Christmastime, and that you have left Stefania to, once again, mother your own daughter. To be frank, I am quite ashamed of you.*

*Forgive me for these strong words, but I am your mother, and it is my duty to point out your lapse in your own duties to your family. I am no great champion of your husband's, as you well know, but even I feel empathy for a man left to sit in prison through Christmas and the New Year wondering why he hasn't been visited by his wife.*

*It appears to me that you have been thinking very much of yourself at the expense of Carlo and Adriana. The new year is approaching and I entreat you to step into the year as a responsible wife and mother.*

*Your loving mother*

Etta sets the letter down on the dressing table and stares into the mirror for a long moment. An automobile backfires in the street outside her window and she blinks as her eyes focus on the reflection of the attractive, blonde-haired woman. A thirty-two-year-old woman, though she could pass for much younger, but for how much longer? A woman with a husband in prison so long that, when she is not sitting in that chair in the visitors' room where his presence sparks alive her every emotion, she barely remembers what it feels like to love him. A woman whose daughter ignores her and whom she can't control, whose sisters and cousin send her letters castigating her. A woman whose own mother is ashamed of her. If only Papa were alive; he'd understand her. He'd always understood her.

Is she meant to waste her life away in a villa on Capri dabbing at paintings of flowers and Italian sunsets to sell for a pittance to the tourists and social misfits who find their way to the island? A life of emptiness, where one day rolls into another, without shape or urgency? A life of waiting and wanting? Is that a life at all?

No. That is not her life. She is an artist, a good artist. Possibly even a great artist. She deserves recognition for her talent, for her work. Paintings with her name on them. She will not hide under Carlo's shadow any longer. There are no more 'Carlo Marinettis' in storage in Naples. She wants Monsieur DuRose to mount an exhibition of her own work, and she intends to get her way. As for Carlo and Adriana? She cannot live their lives for them. She will do what she can, of course, to fund Carlo's retrial and steer Adriana's creative energies to productive endeavours, but this is *her* time. She has a plan, and she will enjoy her life. She has wasted enough time.

She smooths a curl over her ear and adjusts the mauve feathers in her diamante-encrusted headband. Uncapping her lipstick, she draws on a perfect cupid's bow. She tucks the lipstick into her satin evening bag and pulls on her long white opera gloves. Giving herself one last glance in the mirror, she picks up her bag, collects her fur-edged wrap from the bed where she'd tossed it earlier, and heads to the door.

---

'Etta, darling! You look a dream! Come, give me a kiss!'

Zelda Fitzgerald wafts through the ebullient atmosphere of the Café du Dôme shining like a gold lamé sun, and, throwing her arms around Etta, presses scarlet kisses on her cheeks. She laughs, her voice light as a bell, and wipes the lipstick off Etta's cheeks with her white-gloved fingers, oblivious to the scarlet smudges on the fine satin.

'Oh, dear! It seems I've branded you with Coty Scarlet Flame. You're all mine now, doll.' She grabs Etta's hand. 'Come on, let's have a twirl.' She leads her to a spot between the tables where couples shuffle to the strains of the musicians' tango music.

'Scott's having a "Who's the better novelist?" argument with Ernest,' she says as she takes hold of Etta's hands and leads her into an *ocho milonguero*. 'Hadley and Pauline look fit to claw each other's eyes out. Pauline's elbowed dear old Hadley right out of Ernest's bed, you know. What they see in Ernest is anyone's guess. All hunting and horse racing and "girlie" and "doll". He's as phoney as a rubber cheque. I'll have to rescue poor Scott after our dance before they start throwing champagne over each other.'

She laughs her bell-like laugh. 'How silly of me. Scott would never waste good champagne on Ernest. Bad champagne either. He's not particular as long as it goes down his gullet. Oh, look! There's that artist Tamara de Lempicka. Isn't she glamorous? She rather looks like Greta Garbo, don't you think?' She whispers in Etta's ear. 'They say she has a passion for beautiful women.' She giggles. 'If I wasn't hooked up with Scott, I might give it a go.'

'Zelda, you're all talk,' Etta says as she leans into Zelda's embrace and follows her skilful lead through the dancers. The café crowd suddenly erupts in clapping, hoots and whistles as a stunning Black woman in a fringed black dress and a headband with an enormous black ostrich feather makes an entrance. A thick choker and bracelets of what look like diamonds glitter as she waves and smiles at the appreciative crowd while striking a series of exaggerated poses.

'My word, Zelda, it's Josephine Baker.'

'Yes, isn't she divine?' Zelda waves at the glamorous woman.

'Josephine! Josie, sweetie!' She blows the celebrated dancer a kiss, which is reciprocated with an extravagant double-handed air kiss.

'You know Josephine Baker? She's the biggest star in Paris.'

'We met her at the Art Deco Expo party, remember? Oh, sweetie, you don't remember, do you? You passed out at the table and Ruth Bellico bundled you in a cab and took you back to your hotel. I know everyone, and *everyone* who's *anyone* in Paris is here tonight.'

She nods at a striking couple smoking cigarillos at a nearby table, setting the white feathers in her headdress bouncing. 'There's Picasso and Olga in town from Barcelona with Man Ray and Kiki de Montparnasse. Isn't Kiki awfully attractive? She's not just an artist's model, you know. She's a very clever painter. She told me she's planning an exhibition of her work in the new year. It's probably why she's cosying up to Picasso. Man Ray doesn't look too pleased.'

Etta catches Man Ray's eye as Zelda steers her around the floor. 'He probably wants all the fame to himself. He's rather full of himself, if you ask me.'

'Aren't they all? Scott wouldn't have a career if he didn't lift pages and pages from my diaries for his books. He tells me he's the novelist and I'm the novelty. I'd like to see him write without me around. I'm the one who gives him all the ideas. Without me, there'd be no Daisy Buchanan.'

She sighs as she leads Etta into a series of *ganchos*. 'Shame no one wants to buy *Gatsby*. Scott's cut up about it and I'll bet you Ernest is rubbing his nose in it, especially with *The Sun Also Rises* being such a big hit. Sometimes life's like reaching your hand in a cookie jar only to find someone's taken the last cookie.'

'I thought *The Great Gatsby* was wonderful.'

'You and the critics. Pity no one's actually buying it. Oh, well, Scott will simply have to write another one. I'm going to be a famous ballerina, did I tell you?'

'A ballerina? I thought you were going to be a painter.'

'I've decided I'd rather be a dancer. I met a lovely girl named

Anaïs at my flamenco lessons ... she has a dreary banker husband but she's terribly fun and she writes naughty stories. She dragged me along to a ballet lesson just before Christmas and I *adored* it.' She laughs and pulls Etta into a hug as the music fades. 'I think she went because she has an eye for the ladies.'

'Maybe you should introduce her to Tamara de Lempicka.'

Zelda squeals, and, releasing her hold on Etta, throws herself at an attractive young man. 'CJ! Darling! How wonderful you've come!' She kisses him on the cheek and pulls Etta into the embrace as the other dancers shuffle around them.

'Etta, meet the amazingly talented journalist CJ Melton from Wilmington, Delaware. CJ, meet the beautiful, darling Etta Marinetti, one of my very best friends in Paris.'

Etta stares at the man – the high, domed forehead, the slick of dark blond hair and the deep-set piercing blue eyes. 'It's you.'

'It is.'

Zelda claps her gloved hands. 'You know each other? How divine! Has Scott persuaded you to come to Hollywood with us to work on the flapper picture at United Artists, CJ? You simply must. What a gay time we would have.'

Etta's eyes widen. 'You're going to Hollywood, Zelda?'

'Yes! Didn't I say? That's me all over. We're off next week for three months. Scott's not that keen, but the truth is, we need the money, what with *Gatsby* being such a bomb. Maybe I should get into the pictures. What do you think, CJ?' She throws her head back and strikes a dramatic pose. 'Zelda Fitzgerald, movie star. I think it has rather a ring to it.'

'I can see your name in lights already, Zelda.'

'Oh, CJ, aren't you a doll?'

Zelda glances over at a table where Josephine Baker has just begun to dance a Charleston amongst the champagne glasses. 'Oh, look! I simply must go.' She waves at the exuberant dancer. 'Josie! Josie, wait for me!'

Etta watches Zelda as she melts into the crowd. 'I love Zelda, but sometimes I feel like I've been swept up in a tornado.'

'That's Zelda for you. She swallows up everyone in her path.' He leans toward Etta's ear. 'I was going to ask you to dance, but the Charleston isn't really my thing.'

'That's a shame. I love the Charleston.'

He takes hold of Etta's elbow. 'Come with me.'

'What? Go with you where?'

'Don't you want to see?'

Etta looks into CJ's teasing blue eyes. She smiles. 'Sure. Why not?'

He takes hold of her hand and she follows him through the crowded tables. He pushes open the swing door to the kitchen and waves at the shouting chefs as he leads her out through a door into a back alley.

Etta laughs. 'Good heavens, CJ Melton, where have you taken me?'

'It was noisy in there.'

Etta squints as her eyes adjust to the dark night. Somewhere nearby two cats squall in a standoff. She shivers and rubs her bare arms. 'At least it was warm.'

CJ unbuttons his jacket and places it over Etta's shoulders. 'Better?'

'Yes. Thank you.'

He smiles as he reaches into his jacket pocket. 'You're nothing if not polite, Etta Marinetti. Your parents raised you well.'

'I'm not certain I can say the same for you.'

Chuckling, he takes out a pack of Lucky Strike cigarettes and a lighter. He lights a cigarette and hands it to Etta.

She wrinkles her nose. 'I don't smoke.'

'No? It's a new year in' – he glances at his wristwatch – 'nine and a half minutes. It's as good a time to start as any.'

Etta eyes the cigarette and takes it between her fingers. 'You'll have to teach me how.'

'It's easy. Just suck it in and blow it out.'

He holds the lighter under the cigarette in his mouth and sucks until the tip glows red. He blows a stream of fragrant white smoke into the cold night air.

She sticks the cigarette she's holding between her lips and sucks. The hot smoke burns her throat and she doubles over, coughing and gagging.

'You're a rank amateur.'

'I told you I don't smoke,' she croaks.

'Take it nice and slow. Try it again.'

'All right. Here goes nothing.'

CJ watches her as she takes a circumspect pull on the cigarette and blows out a thin stream of smoke. Her face breaks into a jubilant smile. 'I did it!'

He reaches for her face and brushes his lips against her cheek. She inhales his scent, of soap, and sandalwood, and the sweet, smoky fragrance of tobacco. She reaches her arms around his neck and, pulling him against her body, turns her head and presses her mouth against his.

He kisses her – her face, her eyes, her neck, her mouth. The world is his warmth and his scent and the scratch of his face against her skin and his arms pressing into her back. It is so long since she's been kissed like this.

She pulls her face away.

He looks at her, his blue eyes like beacons in the dull night of her existence. 'Do you want me to stop?'

A smile flits across her lips. 'No. I want you to kiss me, CJ Melton. I want you to kiss me until I lose my mind, and then I want you to kiss me some more.'

# Part VII

1927

# Chapter Fifty-Seven

## Etta

### Luxembourg Gardens, Paris, France – February 1927

*Our Own Little Bungalow*
*The Ambassador Hotel,*
*Los Angeles, California*

*January 22nd, 1927*

*Dearest darling Etta,*

*I am writing you this little note with a teacup of bootleg champagne while I sun myself in the marvellous California sun. Scottie is splashing in the pool and John Barrymore's monkey, Clementine, is running about the hotel's patio stealing toast and bananas from the breakfast tables. The waiters are all in a huff about dear little Clementine, and I have half a mind to squirrel her away in my luggage when we leave.*

*Etta, Hollywood is* the *place to be! United Artists have put us up in a bungalow here at the new Ambassador Hotel which is just the bee's knees while Scott works on the* Lipstick *picture for them. It's simply divine. Gloria Swanson and John Barrymore are neighbours, and, oh, my, the parties that go on here! Everyone who is anyone in Hollywood comes to the Ambassador and the Cocoanut Grove nightclub. We've made so many new friends! Just last night we had Clark Gable, James Cagney, Tallulah Bankhead, Gloria of course, Charlie Chaplin, Dougie Fairbanks and sweet Mary Pickford all crowded into the bungalow. Tallulah brought scads of bootleg champagne and we all had a super night. Scottie slept through the whole thing, bless her. Scott and I were at another party last week where we thought it would be a laugh to boil Ronald Colman's and Constance Talmadge's expensive watches in tomato sauce in the kitchen. Oh, my, they were cross!!!*

*I expect we'll be heading back to Paris once Scott's contract on the picture is finished at the end of March. Make sure you're there and not away in Capri! We can go drink champagne to our hearts' content at the Dôme and go clothes shopping. Wouldn't that be fun?*

*I miss you terribly. What an awful lot of fun we would have if you were here!*

*Kisses,*
*Zelda*

Etta stuffs the letter into her handbag and leans back against the wooden bench. If she could hop on a boat to America this minute, she would. Life is so dull without Zelda. Nothing in her life has turned out the way she'd expected. She is a talented artist, and pretty, and popular, none of which do her any good hidden away on Capri. And in Paris? Here there are so many pretty, popular and talented girls. When will her own star shine? If she had never met Carlo, maybe she would have gone to Hollywood. Papa had always said she had a dramatic flair and she *had* shone as Ophelia in the Prendergast Grammar School's production of *Hamlet*. Hollywood would have appreciated her.

Across the path, a lone boy prods at a small toy sailboat with a long stick in an effort to launch it across the water of the park's Grand Basin, oblivious to the raindrops which have begun peppering the pond. She opens her umbrella and sits on the bench as the rain taps against the umbrella's black canvas. She hasn't been back to Capri since November, and she is in no rush to return. Adriana is well cared for at Stefania's and there isn't anything that she can do for Carlo there that she can't do here in Paris. Besides, Stefania is taking care of all the 'negotiations' with lawyers and judges back in Italy. The important thing is to sell 'Carlo's' paintings to fund the retrial, and Paris is the best place to do that.

The boy's boat has suddenly set off across the pond, pushed by a gust of wind. She watches him as he shouts, '*Oy, oy, oy! Arrête!*' and chases it around the concrete pond, waving his stick. Maybe she should send Adriana to boarding school in England in the autumn. It would free her from her mother's and Jessica's haranguing letters. Thank goodness Celie isn't so judgemental when she writes. Alberta sounds so wonderful, with its big sky and the jolly winters. A place where you could be free, away from all this … this judgement. Celie is so lucky to be away from all the crushing tedium of family expectations.

CJ's face materialises in her mind and she smiles as she remembers the feel of his lips on her skin, his arms pressing her against the warmth of his body in the alley on New Year's Eve. It had seemed like a lifetime in that midnight minute when everything was him. His warmth, his scent, his breath, his lips. She could have stayed there for ever, but for the drunken partygoers who'd stumbled out of the kitchen and into the alley, looking for somewhere to consummate the new year.

That was over a month ago. Then … nothing. Not a word. Not a message. Not a flower. Nothing. It shouldn't matter; she's married, after all. If only she could stop CJ's face from haunting her thoughts, from invading her dreams. A flare of anger flashes through her body.

*How rude! How dare he be so rude? To her! If I ever see him again, I'll … I'll—*

She hears a splash and glances over at the pond. The boy is knee deep in the shallow water of the pond, wading out to rescue his recalcitrant boat which has settled itself solidly in the middle as if at anchor.

She closes the umbrella and lifts her face to the soft pelting rain. To hell with everyone. It's her life and she will live it. She will see CJ Melton again. She will make sure of it.

# Chapter Fifty-Eight

Christina

**Brompton Cemetery, London – March 1927**

Christina watches the vicar throw a handful of dirt into the grave, wincing as it hits the coffin with a thud. Her mind drifts as the vicar intones the burial prayers, his voice as solemn as the cold, grey March day.

She thinks about Gerald, dead now almost ten years. How is that possible? How could she have had a life with someone for twenty-five years who is now nothing but a fading memory? Sometimes, when she glances at one of his photographs on the piano, the face that had once been as familiar as her own seems as foreign as a stranger's. It's on those days that she has found herself back on her knees in the confessional at St Saviour's Church in an attempt to absolve herself of the sin of forgetfulness. To somehow assuage the guilt that clings to her like a winter cold.

Today, there is no guilt nor sadness. Today is a day of joy. She would dance about the headstones while singing 'Joy to the World' if she could. Today she sees Henrietta Elizabeth Bishop interred in the earth for all eternity. And good riddance.

The mourners are as sparse as she had expected. A few elderly servants in sombre black, no doubt attending out of a misplaced sense of duty. The vicar's wife. A few choristers.

*You reap what you sow, Aunt Henrietta. You were a mean, misanthropic woman, and what did it get you? A huge house empty of life, a bank account of money unspent, and not a soul on earth who will miss you. Why am I here, you ask? I would never have denied myself the pleasure of this day, Aunt Henrietta. And there's nothing you can do about it.*

The burial service ends and Christina watches as the others disperse into the rising mist like crows into a cloud. She hears a step behind her.

'Christina.'

She spins around. 'Oh, it's you.'

Harry stands there, his black wool coat and Homburg hat filmy with damp. 'Don't sound so enthusiastic.'

She shrugs. 'For a moment I thought I was being haunted by the vengeful spirit of Aunt Henrietta. That it's you is both a relief and a disappointment.' She gestures to the grave. 'Have you come to pay your respects?'

'I'm here only insofar as your aunt is one less adversary with whom I need to be concerned and I wished to thank her for lessening that load. I also suspected I would find you here, though I expect I shouldn't call you a mourner.'

'She was my beloved aunt. Of course I've come.'

Harry harumphs. 'You should be on the stage, Tina.'

Christina smiles. 'No doubt Aunt Henrietta is glowering at us both from Hell. As far as your purchase of the London house goes, you can stop that now, Harry. I don't need you any longer. Apparently, Aunt Henrietta died without a will; so, as her only living relative, I will inherit everything, once the government takes its healthy share, of course.'

Harry tuts. 'Your poor aunt. She must be turning in her grave. Not to have made a will when she so desperately wished to cut you out of the inheritance. The hubris of one who believes they will live for ever.'

'May she rot in Hell.'

'Tina, that's not very Christian of you.'

'I'll go to Confession and wipe the slate clean with a few Hail Marys.'

'So, it appears that you had no need to resort to blackmail. I have to say, I was most disappointed to see you stoop so low—'

'How dare you—'

He holds up a hand. 'The thing is, you won't inherit everything.'

'What do you mean?'

He digs into his coat pocket and holds up a key. 'I bought, through my intermediary, your aunt's London house, including all the furniture and what art she hasn't sold. She is … was a shrewd negotiator. That's why it's taken so long. In the end, I was forced to make her an offer that was impossible for her to refuse. The sale went through a week before she died.'

Christina's mind scrambles in confusion. 'So, it's my house now? As we agreed?'

Harry smiles and shakes his head. 'That was the intention, but with Henrietta's death, I no longer have the worry of her revealing my identity to Cecelia. And as for you or Dorothy going to the newspapers, well, I have provided you both with flats, and I pay for Christopher's very expensive schooling. I don't believe either of you would benefit from the revelations of our dalliances being made public.'

'But—'

Harry shrugs. 'Don't worry, Tina. I have taken care of my obligations to my children, which is, ultimately, what you wanted, isn't it? I have signed your beloved Marylebone house over to Cecelia and Christopher in my will as an "anonymous bequest".'

Christina's mouth drops open. 'Oh. I see. Of course. How clever of you.' She eyes the key. 'What about the house now?'

He curls his fingers around the key and returns it to his pocket.

He reaches into the breast pocket of his coat and takes out a thick folded document and his fountain pen.

'What's this?'

'It's a legal document in which you and Dorothy Adam agree never to reveal the true parentage of Cecelia and Christopher so long as I, Rose, or any children we may have are alive.' He hands it to her with the pen. 'You will see that Dorothy has already very kindly signed it.'

Christina frowns as she inspects the document. 'You expect me to sign this now? I haven't even read it.'

'It's now or never, Tina. Do you or do you not want Cecelia to be a benefactor in my will? It is a one-time only offer.'

'Will I … will I be able to move into the house now? If I sign?'

Harry shrugs. 'Why do I need another house now that Rose and I use the McClellan villa in Hampstead when we're in London?' He nods at the document. 'The decision is quite literally in your hands, Tina. Do you or do you not wish to have our daughter inherit your precious Bishop family house upon my death … with Christopher, of course.'

Christina uncaps the pen and scribbles her signature at the bottom of the document. She thrusts it at Harry with the pen. 'You know, of course, Harry, that I never wish to see you again.'

Harry chuckles as he takes the key from his pocket and drops it into Christina's hand. His blue gaze sweeps over her face as he tips his hat.

'Goodbye, Tina. I shall miss you, my lovely siren.'

He steps away. Just as the mist is about to swallow him, he turns around to face her. 'Oh, I don't expect that you've heard, Tina, but Rose is expecting a baby. I shall finally have my legitimate heir.'

# Chapter Fifty-Nine

## Celie

### West Lake, Alberta – April 1927

Mavis knocks on the door of her bottling room. 'Celie? Would you like a cup of tea?'

'Come on in, Mavis. The processing's done.'

Mavis opens the door to see Celie pinning up dripping photographs with clothes pegs to a string she has stretched across the tiny room.

'Perfect timing, Mavis. I'm just hanging up the final lot I took out at the Indian reserve. It was good of Fred to drive us there.' She frowns as she wipes her hands on her apron. 'He won't say anything to Frank, will he?'

'Fred knows better than to say anything if he wants to sleep in my bed, Celie. Don't you worry about a thing.'

Mavis hands Celie the mug of tea and wanders over to the drying photographs of portraits and landscapes from the Cree reserve. 'These are incredible, Celie. You have a real eye. You see things other people miss.'

'Thanks, Mavis. I love photography. In a way I think images

are like a window into my thoughts. They're how I express the things I can't say.' She shrugs. 'Especially now that Frank's banned me from writing for the newspaper.'

Mavis turns around and folds her arms. 'You know, that makes me so cross. What harm does it do him for you to write for the local paper? That article you wrote to encourage people to donate to the new hospital brought in a couple of hundred dollars!'

Celie sighs as she leans against the wooden counter. 'He thinks it emasculates him. He doesn't like being teased about having a wife supporting him.'

'Men and their egos. I thank Heaven every day that Fred doesn't have an ounce of pride in him. He'd pack my lunch and drive me to the *West Lake News* office himself if I wanted to write for them!'

Celie smiles at Mavis over her mug. 'Fred's a diamond, Mavis.'

Mavis grunts. 'A rough diamond, maybe.' She chews her lips as she scrutinises Celie. 'Is everything okay with you and Frank? He seemed a bit … I don't know … a bit tetchy at the kids' birthday party last month.'

'I know. I think he feels like the weight of the world is on his shoulders. I think he thought we'd have an amazing new life out here in Canada, but it's been awfully hard work. And everything costs money, especially when you're starting from scratch. At least the wheat prices have been going up these past few years. At this rate, we should be able to pay off our mortgage and some of our bigger debts within the next five years or so.'

Mavis nods. 'Maybe earlier, if the stocks Frank's invested in come good.'

Celie's eyebrows rise. 'Stocks? Which stocks?'

'Oh, there's me and my big mouth. I assumed you knew. Fred said Ol' Man Forbes has got some of the men here investing with his stockbroker down in Edmonton. Frank and Rex Majors and Tom Philby, lots of men here, have been investing for a couple of years now. Fred won't touch it, mind you. He only buys land. He says land never goes anywhere.'

'Oh. I see.'

Mavis squeezes Celie's arm. 'Don't worry. From what I hear, people are making lots of money on the stock market, though don't ask me how it all works. I haven't a clue.'

Celie nods. Leaving her father's legacy money back in England out of Frank's reach was definitely the right thing to do. 'No. Nor do I.'

'Celie, would you be up for coming to the Nellie McClung talk on *Are Women Persons in Canada?* at the United Church Hall on Wednesday afternoon?'

'The woman politician from Calgary?'

'Yes, that's the one. Well, she lost her seat in the last provincial election, but that's not stopping her from fighting for the rights of Canadian women. Lord knows we women need all the help we can get. Do you know that women aren't permitted to sit in the Canadian Senate?'

'No. Why is that?'

'Because in our constitution, the British North American Act of 1867, only "persons" can be elected to the Senate, Celie, and women are apparently not "persons" in Canadian law. Oh, it makes my blood boil!'

'You can't be serious, Mavis.'

'I am. And Mrs McClung and several other lady activists in Edmonton intend to do something about that.'

Celie feels her stomach leap in a way she hasn't felt since her days campaigning for women's suffrage in the UK. 'Absolutely, I'll come, Mavis.'

Mavis grins. 'Wonderful.' She picks up Celie's camera from the counter and hands it to her. 'Bring your camera. I think you might want to take some pictures.'

'Oh, I'll do more than that, Mavis. People need to know about this. I'll write about it for the newspaper.'

'What about Frank?'

Celie juts out her chin. 'I'll use a pseudonym. What Frank doesn't know won't hurt him.'

# Chapter Sixty

Christina

**Portman Square, Marylebone, London – April 1927**

Christina walks along the wet flagstone pavement in Portman Square, past the black railings fronting the elegant Georgian brown brick townhouses, careful not to slip on any lingering autumn leaves, and stops in front of the Bishop house. She smiles up at the classical pediment over the entrance portico, where her father once had to rescue her cat Ozzy after he'd refused to climb down. *Home! I'm home! Hello, my darling house. I'm back where I belong.* She collapses her umbrella, shaking it out onto the pavement, and takes a step onto the tiled stoop. She is turning the key in the lock when the door is pulled open.

The two women stare at each other in wide-eyed surprise. 'Miss Adam?'

'Mrs Fry?'

Christina frowns. 'What are you doing here?'

Dorothy shakes her head. 'I could ask you the same question.'

Christina holds up her key. 'I was coming to see what furniture I needed to have moved here from Clover Bar next week.'

'I think there must be some kind of misunderstanding—'

Christina feels the colour rise in her cheeks. 'I don't see how. Harry gave me the key last week at my Aunt Henrietta's funeral. He bought the house from her.'

Dorothy nods. 'Well, Harry gave me a key as well a fortnight ago. He suggested I move in here with Christopher rent-free. He even paid for our move, though I didn't need to bring much. It's beautifully furnished. We have everything we could possibly need.'

'I beg your pardon? This is *my* house.'

'Mrs Fry, Christopher and I have moved in.'

Christina eyes the young woman, taking in her stylish silk sheath dress and freshly waved auburn bob. 'This is my family's house, Miss Adam. I grew up here. I expect Harry didn't mention that, did he?'

'No, I'm afraid he didn't.'

Christina huffs impatiently. 'Must we discuss this out here in the rain? I should very much like to come in to see my house.'

'You mean *my* house. I have a signed rental agreement.'

'You're renting it for no money! You don't own it, Miss Adam. *I'm* meant to live here.' She jabs the key at Dorothy. 'I have the key!'

Dorothy steps back behind the door. 'I'm afraid you'll need to take this up with Harry. He told me he had been reminded to take responsibility for his obligations, and that's why he offered me the house to live in at no cost. I expect he felt guilty about the way he'd treated me and my son.' She smiles and shrugs. 'Who would have thought a tiger could change its spots so late in life?'

'It's a leopard. Tigers have stripes, Miss Adam.' Christina stamps her umbrella onto a stone tile. 'A leopard like Harry certainly does not change his spots.'

She regards her usurper, who appears to have settled into her new life with ease. 'You are aware that Christopher and Cecelia are in Harry's will to inherit the house when he dies?'

'I'm aware of that, yes. The thing is, Mrs Fry, by then I expect

Christopher will consider this his home, and, being a male, would have some prospect of claiming the house for himself.'

Fury rises through Christina's body like the steam in an awakening volcano. 'This will never happen, Miss Adam,' she says through gritted teeth. 'This is the Bishop family house, and one day it will be Cecelia's. Don't cross me, Miss Adam. If you do, you and your son will most certainly live to regret it.'

---

Christina throws her umbrella and her gloves down on the kitchen table.

'He double-crossed me, Hettie. Harry Grenville did me out of my lovely house! He's got that strumpet, Dorothy Adam, living in there now.'

Hettie drops the wooden spoon into the mulligatawny soup she is cooking on the hob and sets her hands on her hips. 'The bastard.'

'Too right. He's an absolute b—' Christina shuts her mouth before the word flies out.

'Go on. 'E's a bastard. Just say it. You'll feel better.'

'Bastard, bastard, bastard!'

'Now, sit down and I'll get us a cuppa and you can tell me what the bastard's done now. Then you'll just have to make a plan to get it back.'

Christina flops into a kitchen chair. 'You're right, Hettie. I'll get it back. I swear I will.'

Hettie sets two cups and saucers on the wooden table. ''Course you will. Two spoons of sugar today?'

'Yes. You're a good friend, Hettie.'

'Friend's a strong word, ma'am. Lapsang Souchong all right? We're all outta Earl Grey.'

'How can you run out of Earl Grey, Hettie? It's really quite inexcusable.'

Hettie grunts. 'You won't be wanting any of the cannoli I had delivered from Terroni's, then?'

'Chocolate?'

'Of course.'

'Good. Excellent. Then send a boy out for some Earl Grey. You know Lapsang Souchong gives me wind.'

# Chapter Sixty-One

Jessie

**Altumanina, Cairo, Egypt – May 1927**

'I was thinking we might plant the bird of paradise and the cannas I bought at the Orman Flower Show over in the beds by the river,' Jessie says as she and Altumanina's gardener, Mohammed, stroll out of the greenhouse. 'They'll add such lovely colour amidst all the greenery, don't you think, Mohammed?'

The old gardener nods his head under his wide straw hat. 'It's a good idea.'

Jessie shields her eyes from the sun with her hand and squints at the house. 'I thought the cassia tree might do well near the terrace. It will give us some shade from the afternoon sun once it grows.'

She looks around for Mohammed's son, Isham, who has been transferring her Flower Show purchases from the boot of the car to the back garden.

'Isham, where did you put the cassia tree? We didn't lose it, did we?'

Isham Ali sets down two large pots of poker red cannas and

wipes the perspiration off his forehead with the back of his hand. 'It is on top of the automobile still.'

Jessie nods at Isham, who, with his fine-boned face, deep-set eyes and his tall, athletic frame, is a youthful version of his father. Ever since Zara had told her that Isham drives her to the late-night meetings, she's wondered if there might be more to their relationship than politics. Wondered if she should say something to Aziz. But she hasn't. Zara and Isham are adults. Whatever is going on between them isn't her business.

'Fine. Best retrieve it and plant it over there by the terrace.'

'Of course.'

'Thank you. Mohammed, shall I help you plant the cannas?'

The old man shakes his head. 'There is no need.'

'Fine. I'll let you both get to it then.'

She watches the two men disperse in their opposite directions, still, after all these years, unsure as to whether their terseness is a simply a character trait or a veiled indication of a mutual antipathy toward her and her Englishness.

She looks over at the terrace where the exuberant squeals of four-year-old Shani and her aunt Zara precede their energetic exit from the house. She smiles at her sister-in-law, usually so placid and neat in silk trousers and a *jellabiya* with a *hijab* framing her beautiful face, tumbling over the lawn with Shani. She steps back into the shadow of the greenhouse and watches the two as they giggle and settle into a game of 'Ging Gang Goolie'.

How hard things would have been for her at Altumanina without Zara. Her sister-in-law had been her guide into the feminine side of Cairo life, introducing her to her friends over tea and biscuits, showing her the best places to buy clothes, managing the health clinic, and smoothing the waters during her regular altercations with Layla. And Zara has always been there for Shani, the doting aunt whom Shani adores.

A breeze off the river catches the palm leaves and they flutter and rasp in the fresh May air. The scent of roses wafts over to her from the flower beds by the house. Shani laughs and the sound floats on the air like a feather.

She is so very lucky. How has all of this happened? Even in her wildest dreams as a girl in London she had never imagined a life like this. A wonderful marriage, a beautiful daughter, Altumanina, the health clinic, Egypt. All these things that have come to her since she signed up for the Queen Alexandra's Imperial Military Nursing Service in 1914. If she'd done what her mother had wanted her to do and stayed as a nurse in London, none of this would have come to her. How one decision can change a life. She is happy. If only …

No, she will never be a doctor here. She must let go of that dream.

Jessie is suddenly aware that the giggles and hand-clapping game have stopped. She looks over at Zara and Shani to see Zara tying her *hijab* over Shani's dark hair. The little girl sits patiently as her aunt tucks and drapes the fine cotton scarf around her head.

Zara holds a small cosmetic mirror up to Shani, who presses her hands against her cheeks in delight as she examines her reflection. Zara takes Shani into her arms in a joyful hug and the two tumble onto the grass.

Jessie's heart judders. She hastens over the lawn and holds out her hand to Shani. 'It's time to go in and review your spelling, Shani. Playtime is over for today.'

'Mama, look at my hair!'

'I can't see your hair, darling.'

Zara smiles at Jessie. 'Doesn't Shani look nice in her *hijab*?'

'She's a little girl, Zara. She doesn't need to wear a *hijab*. She may never wish to wear a *hijab*.'

Zara's smiles fades. She quickly unties the *hijab* to Shani's protests.

'I am sorry, Shani, your mama is right. It is time for your lesson and time for me to put on my *hijab*.'

Jessie takes hold of Shani's hand. 'She's only four, Zara.'

'Of course,' Zara says as she ties on her *hijab*. 'There is time. When you are ready for her to pray, Jessica, I am here to help.'

'Shani says her prayers every night before bed. The same prayers I learned growing up. Catholic prayers.'

Zara looks at Jessie, her amber eyes serious. She nods. 'It is good that she prays.'

# Chapter Sixty-Two

## Celie

**Sweet Briar Farm, West Lake, Alberta – May 1927**

Mavis Wheatley jumps off her bicycle and leans it against the picket fence. She pushes open the gate and runs up the gravel path to the house waving a newspaper.

'Celie! Celie! It's out!'

Celie pushes open the screen door and steps out onto the porch. 'Oh, wonderful! Let me see!'

Mavis thrusts the copy of the *West Lake News* into Celie's hands. 'Rex didn't publish your name, just as you asked. Frank will never know.'

Celie smiles ruefully when she finds her article on page 5. 'No byline at all. I seem destined never to have my full name in the paper.'

'Never mind that, Celie. There's the lovely picture you took of Mrs McClung with Emma Philby and Rosita Majors. You're writing and it's being published and Frank can't say a word about it.' She presses a hand against her mouth. 'Oh, fiddle. He's not around, is he?'

'Don't worry. He's down in the south field sowing wheat. He won't be back till late.'

'Good. I thought I'd let the cat out of the bag there for a minute.' Mavis taps on the newspaper. 'Go on, read it out loud.'

Laughing, Celie clears her throat.

*Are Women Persons in Canada?*

*Reformer and former member of the Alberta Legislative Assembly, Mrs Nellie McClung, visited West Lake in April to discuss the ongoing issue of whether women are considered 'persons' in Canada.*

*During a talk hosted by the Women's Christian Temperance Union in West Lake United Church Hall, Mrs McClung discussed the ongoing government debate as to whether women are indeed 'persons' as defined by the Canadian constitution, also known as the British North American Act of 1867.*

*Apparently, despite the fact that women have now won the vote and can be elected to Parliament, women are not 'persons' under our constitution. The issue first came to the fore in 1922 when Mrs Emily Murphy, Canada's first woman judge, was proposed for a position in the Canadian Senate. Her appointment failed when she was judged not to be a 'qualified person' as the British North American Act had neglected to define 'persons' to specifically include women. This was not the first time Mrs Murphy had met with this prejudice.*

*On her first day as a judge in 1916, a lawyer challenged her on the basis that she was not a 'person' and therefore was not qualified to be a judge. To the gentlemen who drafted the Act in 1867, 'persons' were legally understood to refer only to men. To this day, the Canadian government has interpreted 'persons' in Section 24 of the Act to include only men.*

*Owing to the response of the ladies in attendance, it was felt that this egregious situation must be addressed without delay. Mrs McClung concluded her talk to assure the attendees that she and other women activists are joining forces to contest this inequity. She ended by asking for the support of all right-thinking Canadians, be they men or women, in this fight for the inclusion of women in the definition of 'persons' in Canadian law.*

'That's just great, Celie. You should be proud of yourself. You can be sure Rex Majors wouldn't have covered this for the paper. Now everyone in the district will read about it.'

Celie smiles as she folds the newspaper. 'I'm happy I wrote it, Mavis. It felt good, even if I had to lie to Frank about meeting Emma Philby and Rosita Majors about the education board stopping the funding of the Saturday English class in order to go. He was dead set against me going to the talk, you know. He said I had no business as an Englishwoman poking my nose into Canadian politics.'

'Oh, never mind Frank. Men have all sorts of queer ideas. The important thing is that you did go and you ended up doing something you loved by writing about it. Just like how I love making beer. I'm darn good at it and I'm even experimenting with mead, now, did I tell you?'

'You didn't, but I'm sure Frank will make a dent in it when it's ready.' Celie holds up the newspaper. 'Can I keep this, Mavis? I want to send it to my mother. I'd like her to see what I've been getting up to, other than feeding pigs and milking cows.'

'Sure. I've bought a few extra copies. I'll keep them in the beer room for you where they're away from prying eyes.'

Celie looks at her friend, at her kind grey eyes and the sweep of unruly tawny hair. What would she have done here without Mavis Wheatley and her generosity? Mavis has been there for her through everything, cheering her along when it had all seemed too much some days. She's almost become like a sister to her. Sisters are everything.

She loops her arm under Mavis's. 'Come on, then. I've just made a strawberry shortcake. Best to eat some before Frank and Lulu get home. Strawberries are their favourite.'

# Chapter Sixty-Three

## Etta

### Galerie DuRose, Paris, France – May 1927

Etta winds her way through the throng of stylish Parisians and a motley crew of foreigners at her first exhibition at Galerie DuRose. François DuRose had finally agreed to mount it, owing to the success of Kiki de Montparnasse's exhibition earlier that spring, which had frankly astounded her. But if it had changed his mind, so be it. Unfortunately, the guests this evening seem to be more interested in gossiping and drinking the expensive champagne she's paid for than buying her paintings. What she wouldn't give to have Zelda here to support her in her misery!

She spots François DuRose with his arm around Kiki de Montparnasse as he listens attentively to the frostily elegant Tamara de Lempicka, who sucks on an ebony cigarette holder whenever Kiki whispers into his ear. Etta infiltrates the threesome, and, smiling with exaggerated politeness at the two women, grabs the art dealer's arm and pulls him aside.

'You're supposed to be promoting my work, not lining up your next exhibitions, François.'

'*Madame Marinetti*, I was simply engaging in conversation with two potential buyers.'

'Buyers, my foot! You know Tamara's work is selling for thousands, and even Kiki's art exhibition sold out within a week, though why anyone would buy her silly daubs is beyond me.'

'Kiki de Montparnasse is on the cusp of a brilliant career as an artist, *Madame Marinetti*. The *New Yorker* said her work gave "the impression of simplicity, faith and tenderness".'

'Is that right? There's no accounting for taste. It seems you are quite the student of Kiki's oeuvre.'

'I make it my business to know what is happening in the art world, as any good dealer would.'

Etta extends her hand to the crowd who are starting to drift out into the promises of the Paris night. 'What about my art? You know as well as I that I'm four times the painter of Kiki or Tamara de Lempicka.'

The art dealer grunts as he glances past Etta to the departing figures of the two women. Kiki releases her grip on Tamara's arm and blows him a kiss.

'*A bientôt, mesdames!*' he calls out as he waves.

'François! Forget them! This is about me.'

'*Madame Marinetti*, what do you expect me to do? I have hung your paintings and opened my gallery to all of the most glittering denizens of Paris. I cannot force people to buy.' He shrugs. 'It seems that the work of Carlo Marinetti's wife isn't as sought after as his. There are some who are saying that you are simply attempting to exploit his fame. This is a prejudice which is difficult to surmount. However, given that there appears to be a momentary trend for women's art, I felt the time was opportune to see if we could shift some of your work out of my storage facility. I wouldn't have done so if you didn't have some … skill, however oblique. I have my reputation to consider.'

'Your reputation? You're scarcely as pure as the driven snow. You know as well as I that Carlo's paintings—'

'—are still commodities. For that we should both be thankful, wouldn't you agree, *Madame Marinetti*?'

'Yes, of course, but won't you do something? It's to our mutual benefit for these paintings to sell.'

François DuRose sighs as he looks at the agitated woman. 'Fine, *Madame Marinetti*, I shall circulate and "talk up a storm" as I have heard the Americans say. They are terribly good at self-promotion. I suggest you do the same, and perhaps, if we are lucky, we shall make a few sales.'

---

A hand thrusts a coupe glass of bubbling champagne in front of Etta.

'Thought you might need this.'

Etta looks over into CJ's blue eyes. 'CJ. You came.'

'I did.'

She takes the proffered glass and sips the fizzing champagne. 'Thank you. I needed this.'

'I thought you might.'

'I wasn't sure if the invitation had reached you.'

'It did.' He takes a drink of champagne. 'I've been away, but I'm back now. Just filed my report on Lindbergh's Atlantic crossing.' He jabs a thumb toward the departing guests. 'They're probably off to track the famous aviator down now. I've heard a rumour the mayor's throwing a celebration dinner for him tonight somewhere, but the location's hush hush.'

'Rotten timing for Mr Lindbergh to choose to fly solo across the Atlantic, if you ask me,' Etta grumbles.

'What's the matter? Your work is fantastic. A star is born.'

'Hardly. How many sold stickers do you see?' She holds up four fingers. 'Four. That will just about pay for the paint and the canvases and the room at the hotel for a few weeks. Did you hear Kiki de Montparnasse sold out her doodles in hours? I'm so much better than she is. I don't understand it at all.'

'Well, Kiki is Paris's "It Girl". She's been painted and photographed by everyone from Modigliani to Man Ray. Don't expect to compete with celebrity; you won't win. It's one of the reasons your husband's work has sold so well for years, Etta. Celebrity and notoriety. Everybody loves fame.'

'Carlo's paintings sell because they're good, not just because everybody thinks he's a murderer.'

'Being a murderer helps. I'm not saying it's right. It's just the way it is.'

'Well, I'm not going to murder anyone to sell my paintings.'

'Oh, murder isn't necessary. Any kind of scandal will do.'

'What, like an illicit affair?'

CJ huffs. 'We're in Paris, Etta. Everyone has affairs. At the very least, you'd need to hook the Prince of Wales and make him abdicate for love when he becomes King of England.'

Etta laughs. 'Like that will ever happen!'

CJ shrugs. 'You'd be sure to sell your paintings.'

Etta looks at him as he lights two cigarettes. 'I painted them, you know. Carlo's paintings. The post-war ones. It was me.'

He hands her a cigarette. 'What are you talking about?'

She sucks on the cigarette and blows out a stream of smoke. '*I'm* the famous Carlo Marinetti. I'm the one who painted his "New Phase" paintings. He hasn't painted anything since before the war.'

'Seriously?'

'Yes, seriously.' She grabs at the sleeve of his jacket. 'Don't you dare write about this. Promise me you won't tell anyone, CJ.'

CJ sucks on his cigarette and tosses the butt onto the gallery's polished wooden floor, stubbing it out with his shoe. He takes Etta's champagne glass and sets it on the tray of a passing waiter along with his glass.

'Come on, let's get out of here.'

'What? Where?'

He looks at her, and his eyes seem to her to delve into the deep recesses of her soul. She swallows as excitement sends shivers through her body.

He grabs her hand and leads her out into the Paris night. 'Trust me.'

---

Etta leans over CJ in his bed as he traces her face with his forefinger. The moonlight paints the small room silver, and it occurs to her that their bodies look like two statues that have come to life. She kisses him lightly on his lips. 'What are you looking at?'

'You.'

'I shouldn't be here.'

'Who says?'

'I'm married.'

'I don't care.'

'*I* should care.'

'Do you?'

She looks at him, at the classical lines of his face, as smooth as marble in the silver moonlight. A resting Apollo. Her god of poetry. Her god of the sun.

'I don't care. Not in the least. Does that make me a bad person?'

'Probably.' He pulls her down on top of him and wraps his arms around her. He kisses her mouth, then her nose, her cheeks, her eyelids. 'I've wanted you since the first day I saw you, Etta. You feel it, too. I know you do.'

'You disappeared. You kept me waiting.'

'That was the idea. I wanted you to think about me. To dream about me. I wanted you to want me as much as I wanted you. Tell me you do, Etta. Tell me you want me.'

She leans on her elbow and runs her fingers over the lines of his face. For a moment, Carlo's face flashes into her mind, and guilt worms its way into her thoughts. She stamps out the guilt like it's an abhorrent creature.

She kisses him. 'I want you, CJ. I want you so very much.'

# Chapter Sixty-Four

Jessie & Christina

**Clover Bar, London – June 1927**

*Altumanina*
*Cairo, Egypt*

*June 2nd, 1927*

*Dear Mama,*

*I am beyond upset with you. How could you do this? Have you any idea the problems you have caused?*

*When I came back to the house this afternoon from the clinic, I walked into a terrible shouting match between Layla Khalid and our housekeeper Marta in the kitchen, with poor Shani in tears as they shouted over her. You know as well as I the tension that Layla brings to this house, but I had never experienced anything quite like this.*

*It seems that Layla walked in on Marta telling Shani the story of Jesus feeding the multitude with five loaves and two fish while she was preparing tilapia for supper, and Layla accused Marta of proselytising. Marta defended herself by revealing that Shani had been baptised a*

*Catholic under your direction when you stayed here after Shani's birth! I am speechless. Truly, Mama, how could you?*

*Shani is my and Aziz's daughter and our responsibility, not yours. Why you thought you had any right to interfere in Shani's religious affiliation is really beyond comprehension. And to drag poor Marta and her husband into the fray as your accomplices! I am absolutely furious with you!*

*Well, I hope you feel your 'duty' is done as the interfering Catholic grandmother and you won't be insisting upon Confirmation when Shani turns fourteen, because I can assure you, I will not permit it. Aziz and I are raising Shani in a family which follows both Islam and Christianity. She is as familiar with Easter as she is with Ramadan. As to which faith she will follow when she is older, this is something which Aziz and I are still working through.*

*Mama, I ask that you respect Aziz's and my roles as Shani's parents. We will address Shani's religious upbringing in a manner which we feel is best for our daughter in due course.*

*I consider this matter now closed.*

*Jessie*

# Chapter Sixty-Five

Etta

**Saint James & Albany Hotel, Paris, France – June 1927**

Etta answers the knock on the hotel door. A slender bellhop in navy livery trimmed with gold braid and white gloves thrusts a silver tray at her.

*'Un lettre exprès, madame.'*

*'Merci,'* Etta says as she takes the letter. Cousin Stefania's handwriting. She holds up a finger. *'Attends.'*

She hurries over to where she's dropped her handbag on the dressing table and shakes a few francs out of her change purse. Returning to the bellhop, she then drops the coins onto the tray where they clang and roll across the metal. The bellhop's eyebrow twitches and his lips purse.

*'Merci, madame. Vous êtes très généreuse.'*

She shuts the door and walks over to the tub chair by the window as she slits open the envelope with her red-painted thumbnail.

*Villa Serenissima*
*Capri, Italy*

*June 9th, 1927*

*Dear Etta,*

*I have enclosed another of your husband's letters. I visited Carlo last week at the prison. He asks why you don't visit him more often, and I am forced to lie and say you are busy looking after Adriana and teaching art in Capri, and that you have been unwell, but that you send your love and will visit soon.*

*You have made me a liar, Etta, covering up your stays in Paris.*

*You can imagine how that makes me feel. If you insist on staying in Paris, please let him know your address there when you next write to him.*

*There is no point of me being an intermediary in your correspondence or making him think that you are here at Villa Serenissima.*

*I will leave my note at that. I have nothing more to add than to say you have disappointed me more than I thought possible by your irresponsible behaviour. Your mother has been in correspondence with me about Adriana – your daughter, as you appear to have forgotten. She very much wishes to have Adriana attend a good Catholic girls' boarding school in England in the autumn. She has gone so far as to reserve Adriana a place, and she says she has written to you about this on numerous occasions, but has not received an answer. Please, respond to your mother and do your duty by Adriana.*

*Etta, I am old as is Liliana. Adriana needs young people her age around her. She has no friends at the school, and I don't wonder why as she has been sent home for fighting more often than is decent. Here, she has only Liliana's nephew Mario, who is now a young man of twenty-four, and, though he dotes on the child when he is on the island, he spends most of his time in Napoli pursuing interests more in keeping with a person of his age.*

*I shouldn't be surprised to hear of his engagement before the year is out, and then we shall probably not see him at all.*

*Please, Etta, for the sake of your family and your own misguided soul, come home.*

*Stefania*

Rising, she walks over to the vanity and drops Stefania's letter on top of the letters and cosmetics littering the drawer. She sits on the chair in front of the mirror and opens the envelope with Carlo's letter.

*My dearest darling Etta,*

*It has happened! I am the happiest of men today, even as I sit here on my cot in this filthy room in the prison. Someone has come forward with an alibi for me for the night of Marianna's death. I can say nothing more than that until I am released. I know many eyes read these letters before they leave the prison. There is paperwork and bureaucracy and other things, but I am coming home, this is for certain. I have not yet told Stefania as I wanted your eyes to be the first to read this. She has told me that you have gone to Paris for the month to promote 'my' paintings. Why did you not come to see me before you left?*

*Never mind,* mio angelo. *We shall be together again soon, and we can start all over as the family we always wished to be.*

*I miss you like the night misses the sun. I dream of holding you in my arms again, Etta* mia. *I dream of kissing you and whispering all the words of love I have held inside of myself these long years away from you. And my shining darling Adriana, how I intend to spoil her and love her and give her everything a father possibly can.*

*I do not know exactly when I shall be released. I expect it will take at least a month, possibly longer, but I no longer wake up in the morning with a heart filled with the blackest of despair.*

*I am coming home to you,* cara mia. *I kiss you a thousand times.*

*Your loving husband,*
*Carlo*

Her hand begins to shake and Carlo's black ink handwriting jiggles and swirls before her eyes. *Now? He's coming home now? After all these years?* Yes, she'd been sending her cousin money to pay off lawyers and judges for a retrial, but it had begun to feel like a fruitless endeavour years ago. She had accepted that it *was* a fruitless endeavour. How can he come home now, when everything is going so well for her here in Paris?

She grabs the Penhaligon's bottle and takes a drink of the sweet laudanum. She shuts her eyes and wills her heart to steady its frantic beating. Carlo. Her husband. It is difficult to imagine they'd ever been together, after eight years apart. She had tried to be a good wife, a good mother, but she simply couldn't stay on Capri, sequestered away from life like a nun. The tedium had been making her ill, she is convinced of it. It isn't in her nature to suffer and endure, not when all the excitement of Paris lies just outside her door.

The bathroom door opens. Etta looks up to see CJ in the hotel's robe drying his hair with a towel.

'That's a great bathtub in there, Etta. You should have come to join me. There was plenty of room.'

Etta smiles as she slips the letter into the drawer. 'I bathed this morning, darling. Now, where shall we go tonight? I hear Josephine Baker's show at the Folies Bergère is the bee's knees.'

CJ treads across the carpet and kisses Etta on her lips. 'Sounds good, hon.' He nuzzles her ear. 'Umm, you smell good.'

'Chanel No. 5.'

He brushes his lips along her neck. 'Do you smell like that everywhere?'

She smiles at their reflection in the mirror. 'Everywhere that counts.'

He reaches under her legs and lifts her into his arms.

'CJ! What are you doing? You've just had a bath.'

He tosses her onto the bed and falls on top of her. 'We'll just have to have another one together after.'

She traces a finger over his lips. 'After what?'

He kisses her and she pulls him down onto her body, trapping him with her legs.

'After I find out if you smell like this everywhere.'

## Chapter Sixty-Six

Etta, Celie and Jessie

**Letters – June-July 1927**

*Saint James & Albany Hotel*
*Paris, France*

*June 19th, 1927*

*Dear Celie,*

*It's me, your wayward sister, Etta. I wish so much you were here! You were always there for me when we were growing up when Mama was exasperated with me and Jessie was being mean and obtuse. You and Papa were always on my side. I miss him, don't you? Papa didn't blink an eye the time I dressed in harem pants and a feathered headdress for Jessie's and my sixteenth birthday. My, wasn't Mama incensed. Do you remember? And Jessie refused to speak to me for a week, saying I stole her thunder! I can't help it if I'm flamboyant and Jessie is as dull as dishwater. It amazes me we are twins.*

*I miss those days, Celie, when we were all a family together. Do you suppose we shall ever be together again? I still have the photo of the three of us by the waterfall in Yorkshire that you sent me a few years ago. It's on my dressing table at Cousin Stefania's in Capri. It reminds me of all those lovely days before the war.*

*I'm so very pleased you are taking photographs in your spare time. You were always so clever and talented at that. Papa said so all the time. He was ever so proud of you when you started writing for the newspaper and having your pictures published. Jessie always told me Papa spoiled me because I was his favourite, but you were really his favourite, Celie. You were always his own special girl. You should know that no matter what.*

Etta frowns. *No matter what?* No, she can't write that. She crosses it out and continues.

*Celie, I have such a terrible problem and I don't know who else to turn to. I don't know how to tell you this, or even if I should, but I'm bursting with this secret and if I don't tell you, I'm afraid it will come out at the very worst time to the very worst of people.*

*I am in love with another man. There, I've said it. His name is CJ Melton. Charles James, actually, but everyone calls him CJ. He is a journalist from America and I think about him night and day. He has brought me back to life, Celie, after all the awful years since Carlo was arrested. Eight years! I'm getting old. I'm thirty-three in August. I've given my youth to a man whom I can barely remember. Is that awful to say? I think perhaps it is, but it's the truth.*

*I loved Carlo so much once, but it was so very long ago. I've tried so hard to keep my love for him alive, but … oh, it's so difficult. And he did bring me to Italy on false pretences! I'd thought we were eloping, then, surprise! I find out he has a wife* and *a son. I should have run right back to London then and there, but I was blinded by infatuation and I was carrying his child. I was only twenty; just a girl. How is a woman meant to love the same way a girl loves?*

*And now Carlo has written me to say he's being released! It is wonderful news, of course. Someone has come forward with an alibi for him. I knew he wasn't a murderer, though now I'm afraid the value of his paintings will fall, and, with that, our income. I have learned that nothing raises prices like a scandal. He will be just another painter, and I will be just another painter's wife, which makes me so cross because I have talent, Celie. More talent even than Carlo, but no one will buy my paintings because they think I'm profiting off Carlo's fame. I'm being called a gold-digger, can you imagine?!*

*What am I going to do? Carlo thinks I have been in Capri all this time, except for this past month. Cousin Stefania told him I'm in Paris to sell more of his paintings. The truth is I've been living with CJ for the past month here at the hotel and having a simply marvellous time with him and all my lovely friends here. Am I a terrible person? I think I possibly am, but I don't want to leave, Celie. I don't want to go back to my old life in Capri. That's over for me. CJ is even talking about us going to America. Wouldn't that be an adventure?!*

*I must go. CJ and I are having dinner with Ernest Hemingway and his paramour Pauline. There are likely to be other jolly sorts there, though I miss Zelda Fitzgerald awfully since she and Scott and little Scottie left for America in December. She is terribly good fun.*

*Give my love to Lulu and Frank. You are the best, Celie.*

*Your loving sister always,*
*Etta*

*Sweet Briar Farm*
*West Lake, Alberta*
*Canada*

*July 9th, 1927*

*Dearest Etta,*

*I read your letter and I have to confess that I had to set it aside for a day while I unjumbled my thoughts. There is really only one thing I can say, and I'm afraid you won't like to hear it, but hear it you will.*

*You are married to Carlo, Etta. You've taken vows. You are his wife. He is your husband, not Mr CJ Melton, however handsome and entrancing Mr Melton is.*

*I know what it is like to love someone other than your husband. There isn't a day that goes by that Max isn't in my thoughts, but I married Frank, not Max. Marriage isn't easy, but I'm doing everything I can to honour my vows to Frank. He is a hard worker and a loving father to Lulu. Setting up this farm has been so very hard, but it is paying off now, with wheat prices doing so well. With any luck, we may manage a visit to Mama in London in a couple of years. When we do, you must come to London with Carlo and Adriana. I know she and Lulu will get on like a house on fire!*

*You must, must return to Carlo. You owe it to him and Adriana, and to yourself as well, to give your marriage a proper chance. You will regret it if you don't. You are an adult woman and you have responsibilities. If you are truly meant to be with Mr Melton, it will happen, but you must let time play its role.*

*Paris sounds like a dream and I am sure, for you, it is like living in a dream world. Be happy for the time you've spent there and the experiences you've had. Now it's time to wake up and live the life you chose when you married Carlo.*

*All my love,*
*Celie*

*Sweet Briar Farm*
*West Lake, Alberta*

*July 9th, 1927*

*Dear Jessie,*

*I've just received the most disturbing letter from Etta, and I can't keep this to myself. We three sisters must look out for each other, especially when one is on the cliff edge about to jump (I mean that figuratively, of course).*

*Carlo is being released soon – someone has come forward with an alibi for him – and you would imagine that Etta would be ecstatic about having her husband back. But Etta is ever the surprise. She has become involved with an American journalist in Paris. This, and her infatuation with the fast set there, is why she has been spending so much time in Paris, not simply to promote Carlo's paintings. Apparently, she has been hiding her long stays in Paris from Carlo who thinks she has been living with Cousin Stefania and Adriana on Capri all this time.*

*She has asked me what to do, and, of course, I told her that she must go back to her family. I reminded her of her responsibilities as a wife and mother, but you know how much she hates that word! It is almost like it acts as a prod to move her along another path. A disastrous path, Jessie.*

*I haven't written to Mama about this, and don't know if I should. I feel terribly guilty tattling on Etta, but this is a secret I couldn't keep. You are her twin, and I feel you, above anyone, might know what we might do to keep her from doing something she is bound to regret.*

*Yours ever,*
*Celie*

11.00 CAIRO 30 JULY 27
DEAR ETTA – GO HOME – ADRIANA AND CARLO
NEED YOU – ACTING
RASHLY WILL LEAD TO REGRETS – JESSIE

# Chapter Sixty-Seven

## Carlo

**Capri, Italy – August 1927**

Carlo walks down the winding lane of Via Federico Serena, here calling out a greeting to the postman, there tipping his hat to a pair of elderly women out for an afternoon stroll. The warmth of the sun that heats the flat stones under his feet and emanates from the stone garden walls hung with draperies of vine leaves and purple bougainvillea is no match for the sun beaming from his heart. *I am free! I am free!* Three small words he had thought he would never utter again in this world.

The case of the suspicious death of Marianna Ludovisi Marinetti is closed, or, rather, filed away as another unsolved case in the vast archives of Castel Capuano courthouse, an 'anonymous source' having come forward to provide an irrefutable alibi for him on the night of Marianna's death.

It had been a shock when his mother-in-law, the Marchesa Ludovisi, had visited him at the prison. How she'd sat there, in her elegant clothes and gleaming pearls, in the hard chair across the table from him in the visitors' room smoking a cigarette as the guards eyed the legendary beauty. How she'd come to tell him she was dying of lung cancer and would soon join her late husband in the Ludovisi family crypt, and that she had a confession to make.

*'You didn't see her, in the end, Carlo. You were away fighting. But I did. And Paolo as well. He hated to go to the asylum. He hated that his own mother didn't know him. She didn't know me either. She had taken to painting eyes and flowers and lemons all over the walls of her room. She was like a shadow of the girl she had once been. I couldn't bear it. How could any mother bear such a fate for her only child? So, I did it. I took a pillow and I killed Marianna, Carlo. I killed my daughter.*

*'I was too selfish to come forward when you were arrested. Too comfortable in my own life. Too afraid of life in prison. I rationalised that you were the reason my Marianna lost her hold on this world and that you deserved to rot in prison. I blamed you, Carlo, but lately, as I face the prospect of meeting God's judgement, I have begun to think about Adriana and about how she deserves none of this. So, now I am going to make it right for you both.'*

It appears the prospect of charging the dying Marchesa Ludovisi for her daughter's murder had been too much for the Napoli police to contemplate. How could they send the elegant and admired Marchesa to live out her days in the crumbling confines of the women's prison in Perugia with uneducated thieves and husband-killers?

It would have been a scandal of the highest order. The Prime Minister would no doubt have become involved. His mother-in-law was shrewder than he had taken her for, letting him rot in prison for years for her crime so that she could continue to live her life of wealth and status until she knew she was old and ill enough that a confession of murder would be unlikely to lead to her conviction. Money had no doubt changed hands; the Ludovisis had never been short of *lire*.

And, now, the Marchesa is back in the Ludovisi villa in Napoli and he is finally free, his 'alibi' manufactured to free an innocent man from prison by a system with no stomach to convict the real killer. He should hate the Marchesa even more than he hated his late father-in-law. But she is dying and she will have to prostrate herself at the foot of God soon enough. She will be judged by a greater court than any on earth.

He will see Etta and Adriana soon. In minutes. His life will start again, the life he'd dreamed of so many nights on his cot in prison. The nightmare is over. Throwing back his head, he shouts out to the cloudless blue sky, the rustling arbutus trees lining the lane, and the lone gull gliding on a thermal overhead. 'I am free! I am free!'

---

'Adriana, go to your papa,' Stefania urges the girl, who eyes the stranger warily with her large dark eyes.

Carlo opens his arms to the long-limbed twelve-year-old girl. 'It's really me, Adriana,' he says in Italian. 'Your papa. I brought you the little cat you named Alice. Do you remember? Do you still have him?'

Adriana tosses her mass of blonde curls over her shoulder and narrows her eyes. '*You* brought me Alice?'

'Yes. And we painted together here on the terrace with your mama. You were painting yellow lemons, I remember. You were very good.'

'Mario says I'm very good as well.'

'Does he now? Well, I would love to see your paintings as soon as I see your mama.'

A ginger cat eyes slinks out of the sitting room and jumps onto the plump cushion of a wicker chair.

'Alice! There you are, you naughty cat!' Adriana runs over and throws her arms around the cat. She buries her face in the soft fur and murmurs endearments to the resigned feline, her reunion with her father forgotten.

Carlo glances at Stefania Albertini. 'Where's Etta? I didn't know they were releasing me today, or I would have written.'

Stefania gestures to the sitting room doors. 'I need to talk to you, Carlo. In the sitting room.'

He follows Stefania Albertini's small round figure into the elegant, white-painted room filled with handsome Italian antiques and plush green damask furniture.

'What is it, Stefania? Where's Etta? She's back from Paris, isn't she?'

Stefania sits on a settee and folds her hands in her lap. 'Sit down, Carlo.'

Carlo frowns as he sits in an armchair. 'What is it? She is all right? She has been unwell so much this year.' His eyes widen as he grips the arms of the chair. 'She is not in the hospital, is she?'

Stefania shakes her head, her black hair, now threaded with silver and marcelled into a waved bob, glistening in the sunlight streaming in from the tall windows. 'Etta is in Paris. She has been in Paris since just before the new year.'

'What? You – you told me she had been very ill with the flu and the doctor had forbidden her to visit the prison. You told me this when you visited me—'

'No, Carlo. She is in Paris. She has been there all year.'

Carlo springs from the chair and begins to pace the room like a caged wild cat. 'But her letters were all posted from Capri. Wait, wait, let me show you.'

'That is impossible, Carlo.'

He roots around inside the kitbag he has dropped onto the floor, and tugs out several letters tied together with string.

He thrusts the bundle of letters at Stefania. 'Here. You see? All postmarked Capri. All of them sent since the new year.'

Stefania unties the string and slips a letter out of its envelope. She sets the eyeglasses hanging from a cord around her neck on her nose and scans the letter. 'It is her handwriting, but I don't know how she sent them from Capri. As I told you, she has been in Paris since just before the new year.'

He runs his hand through his hair as he paces the room. 'I thought she would be here. Why is she still in Paris?'

Stefania gestures to the armchair. 'Please, sit down, Carlo. We need to talk about Etta.'

# Chapter Sixty-Eight

Celie

**Sweet Briar Farm, West Lake, Alberta – August 1927**

The soft heat of the August sun caresses Celie's arms where she has rolled up the sleeves of her cotton dress as she picks ripe berries from the blackcurrant bushes in her garden. She sits back on her heels and looks up into the branches of the maple she'd had Frank plant their first summer on the farm. A grey squirrel, fat as a cat, chatters crossly at a crow that sits on a branch above shredding leaves, which flutter down upon the squirrel like green rain. Kip wakes up from a snooze in the tree's shade and woofs half-heartedly at the squirrel before settling back into his nap. She smiles and drops a handful of fat blackcurrants as round and shiny as black pearls into the straw basket and, whipping off her gardening hat, she shuts her eyes and lifts her face to the sun. The heat sinks into her skin, and the back of her eyelids glow red, then white, then red again as the sun's rays penetrate the thin skin.

There are moments like this when it all seems fine. Moments when a glimmer of joy shines through a crack in the concrete wall of her life. When she feels like she can reach through time to touch the person she once was, the life that could have been.

She stretches out her arms to the sun's heat. Her mother would be appalled at her wanton embrace of the sun on her skin, but she has long since given up the skin-clarifying lemon juice rubs and egg white facials of her youth to the cosmetics of sun, wind, rain and snow. She is thirty-four now; a farmer's wife, a mother, a cook, cleaner, washerwoman, needlewoman, gardener … there is no time left in the day for vanity. Her figure is edging from slender to sturdy, lines as fine as thread trace themselves around her eyes, and she plucked out her first grey hair just the week before.

Max would surely walk by her in the street now. She isn't the girl he'd known – the girl of endless dreams and earnest ambitions. All lost now to the hard realities of life on a farm in Alberta. All lost except for her surreptitious photography and the occasional anonymous article for the *West Lake News*. Since the funding for the Saturday morning English classes had been stopped at the end of June, these were the only outlets left for herself. These she clings onto like a life preserver in a churning sea. If they were taken away from her … if Frank ever—

She hears the clop of Betsy's huge feet on the dirt road and looks up to see Frank riding back from the fields. Kip jumps to his feet, barking, and bounces across the grass to the gate. She frowns. *He's early today. Lulu's still in school. What's wrong?* But there is no sense of urgency or irritation in Frank's demeanour. When he smiles at her from beneath his hat, she sees a glimmer of the young man he'd once been before the war, before hard work, long winters, and his persistent cough had taken their toll.

'Hey, there, Kip. Quiet, boy.'

He dismounts and, after looping Betsy's reins over a fence and petting the dog's head, joins Celie in the vegetable patch as Kip resumes his siesta under the tree.

'Those blackcurrants are looking good.'

'It's a good crop this year.'

He walks silently along the rows of vegetables, careful not to step on the orange marigolds Celie has planted in a battle to deter the deer and rabbits. 'Tomatoes have been good this year, too.'

'It's been a good summer.'

He wets his lips and gazes across the fence to the flat wheat ocean beyond the road. 'It looks like we'll have another decent wheat harvest next month. There was a moment back in '23 that I thought we'd have to go back to England with our tails between our legs.'

'Would that have been so bad?'

Irritation flits across Frank's face. 'We'll never go back, Celie. Never.'

'I know.'

He clears his throat. 'I, um … I put some money into the stock market a while ago. Some of the other men have been doing it and making some money, so I thought I might as well.'

Celie rises and brushes off the dirt on her apron. Finally, he's telling her. That could mean only that his investments are going well.

'Is that wise, Frank? Investing in the stock market is rather like gambling, isn't it?'

Frank clucks his tongue. 'You've been talking to Mavis, haven't you? That's just what Fred says, but the stocks I've been investing in are perfectly safe, Celie. Aeroplanes, oil, paper, chemicals … Ol' Man Forbes has put me onto his broker in Edmonton. All being well, I should be able to put in the new bathroom next spring once the mains water pipe gets out to us from the town, and get that extra storey built. Get some electricity in as well. And a truck; we can't be asking Fred for lifts everywhere for ever.'

'I'm fine with the bicycle, Frank. I just worry—'

'Don't worry,' he says sharply. He takes a deep breath and smiles apologetically. 'Celie, look, I know this move to Alberta hasn't been quite what you'd hoped—'

'There's no need, Frank—'

'No, let me say this.'

She folds her hands in front of her. 'All right.'

'Celie, I know I've … I've been …' He rubs his forehead under the brim of his hat. 'I haven't been the man I should have been for you.'

'Really, Frank—'

'Please, Celie. Let me speak.'

'Sorry.'

'I didn't know it would be this difficult. Coming out here to have our own piece of land to build a future on seemed like … it seemed like God offering me redemption for the sin of surviving the nightmare of the war. I *had* to come and you married me. So, *we* had to come.'

'We've both been doing the best we can, Frank. Lulu's the proof of that.'

Frank nods. 'Lulu's perfect.'

Celie smiles ruefully. 'Maybe not perfect. She gave Ben a black eye yesterday for breaking her pogo stick.'

Frank chuckles. 'It serves him right.'

'Thankfully, that was what Mavis said.'

Frank reaches for Celie's hand. 'What I'm trying to say, Celie …' He clears his throat. 'What I'm trying to say is, I'm sorry.'

Her hand lies limp in his grasp. She opens her mouth, but the words she is trying to say – *It's fine … I understand … There's no need* – lodge in her throat like a fishbone that refuses to budge. She slides her hand from his and picks up the basket of blackcurrants.

Frank stuffs his hands in his trouser pockets. 'Celie, I'm sorry about getting cross about that political meeting Mavis was trying to get you to go to back in the spring. I know you were upset about it. I was only thinking of you. You don't need all that agitation in your life. What can you add to it? Let those Canadian women sort out their grievances. They don't need you. Lulu and I, we need you.'

Celie nods as the joy that had filled her just moments before slides away like melted ice. She will never be able to tell him that she'd gone to that meeting, and several others since. She will never be able to share her newspaper articles nor her photography with him. He will never be a part of the things that bring her joy. She sees that now. It seems that these things, for Frank, are like illicit lovers who steal her attention away from her duties to him and Lulu and the farm. To Frank, she is a farmer's wife living in the middle of a field, and this should be enough. *He* should be enough.

She takes a deep breath and smiles at Frank. 'It's hot out here, Frank. How about we go inside and I'll make us some lemonade? Won't that be nice?'

---

That night when Celie enters the bedroom after visiting the outhouse and washing, Frank is awake on the bed, the sheet crumpled on the floor, abandoned to the night's heat. She stands in front of the mirror Frank has hung on the wall above the chest of drawers in her white cotton nightgown and brushes out her long auburn hair.

'Come to bed, Celie.'

She glances at Frank in the mirror and sets down her brush.

When she is lying on the bed, Frank reaches across and pulls her against him. He runs his fingers through her hair. 'You are the most beautiful woman I have ever seen, Celie Jeffries. Sometimes I can't believe you're my wife.'

Celie looks at him – the man she has taken as her husband, till death do they part. His dark eyes shine, and the lines which have etched themselves across his forehead and around the faded scar on his left cheek are erased in the soft moonlight so that he looks like the young soldier who had once walked into her father's photography studio, looking so handsome in his army uniform. So proud of having been promoted to second lieutenant. Maybe things will get better. If he could just be like this, maybe she could love him.

He cups her face in his hands and presses a kiss onto her lips.

'I love you, Celie. I love you so much.'

A short while later, they roll back into the familiar indentations their bodies have pressed into the mattress. Celie looks up at the ceiling, though the room is obscured in the grey night light. A soft snore breaks the night's silence. She glances over at Frank, who is lost in sleep beside her.

She'd tried. She'd tried so hard. But she'd felt nothing.

# Chapter Sixty-Nine

## Etta

**Paris, France – August 1927**

Carlo pushes through the entrance doors of the Saint James and Albany Hotel and storms across the marble floor to the reception desk. The concierge looks up from the ledger and cocks a fine eyebrow at the dishevelled man, unable to decide whether he is an intruder or a valued guest about to check in.

'*Oui, puis-je vous aider, monsieur?*'

'I'm looking for Mrs Marinetti. Etta Marinetti. She's staying here.'

Ah, of course. An Italian. '*Madame Marinetti*? I am not certain I recall—'

Carlo slams his hand down on the polished wooden reception desk. 'She is here. I am her husband, Carlo Marinetti. Tell me which room she is in, or call her down if you don't trust me.'

The concierge frowns and runs a finger along his waxed pencil moustache. 'As I was saying, I do not recall ze name of such a guest. If you wish to leave a note, I will insure zat she receives it should she check in.'

Carlo sticks his hand in his jacket pocket and takes out a wallet. He slips out a stack of one-hundred franc notes and slaps them onto the desk. 'I am looking for my wife. I know she is here.'

The concierge slides the ledger over the bank notes. He runs his finger down the guest list. 'Ah, yes. *Excusez-moi, monsieur.* It is room 204. I recall 'er now. She 'as gone to a party in the Jardin du Luxembourg by ze bandstand. She left earlier wizz a gentleman.' He wrinkles his nose. '*Un Americain* wizz a very bad tie.'

---

'CJ, darling, have another drink of champagne!' Etta says as she scoops a half-empty bottle off a table as they dance a foxtrot across the sand strewn around the bandstand. She giggles as she attempts to pour it into CJ's glass.

He laughs and grabs the bottle from her. 'You're a terrible waitress, Etta. Half of it's gone down your dress.'

She pulls CJ closer and clings to him as they follow the flow of dancers. 'Have I told you that you have the most beautiful blue eyes, CJ Melton?'

'You just did. And may I say that you have the most intoxicating dimple in your cheek when you smile? It drives me to distraction.'

Etta smiles a pearly-toothed smile. 'Does it now? Where exactly is this dimple that drives you mad with passion?'

CJ leans into her and presses a kiss onto her cheek. 'Just th—'

A hand grabs the collar of CJ's jacket and yanks him away from Etta. 'Get away from my wife!'

'Carlo!'

CJ staggers back and collects himself. The other dancers slow down to watch the altercation as the band continues playing 'Blue Skies'.

'What the— Who the hell are you?'

Carlo grabs Etta's arm. 'Come with me.'

'Carlo! Carlo, wait!' She pulls away from him. 'I was only dancing.'

'*Madonna*! He was kissing you!'

CJ steps between Etta and Carlo. 'Look, bud, I don't know who you think you are, but she's with me.'

Carlo turns to look into CJ's agitated face. 'Is that right?' He swings his arm back and throws a punch, sending CJ ploughing back into the crowd. He grabs hold of Etta's hand and pulls her away from the bandstand.

'Carlo! Wait, I can explain everything!'

Carlo glares at Etta as he pulls her across the manicured lawn. 'You will, *Etta mia*. You will explain everything, starting with who that *cazzo* is.'

---

Etta wipes at the tears streaming down her face, smudging streaks of black mascara across her cheeks.

'I told you, Carlo, he means nothing. He's just someone I met here at the gallery. He's a ... he's a buyer. I didn't want to put him off. I was trying to get him to buy more than one painting—'

'Is that what your kiss buys? Two fake Marinetti paintings? What does fucking someone buy? The whole gallery?'

'Carlo, Carlo, no, no. It's not like that. I'm so sorry. I ... I drank a bit too much. I was going to come back to the hotel after the foxtrot. Honestly, I was.'

Carlo pushes back the hair that has fallen across his forehead and glowers at his wife who is weeping into a pillow on the hotel bed.

'Stefania said you've been in Paris for months. I was worried sick about you when I thought you were so ill with the flu back on Capri and I was in the prison unable to do anything. And for you to make Stefania, who has been nothing but good to you and to me and our daughter ... to make her lie for you. Are you not ashamed?'

'I know. I know.' She sits up, clutching the pillow against her stomach. 'I didn't know what else to do, Carlo,' she chokes out between sobs. 'I was dying on Capri. It had been eight years since you'd been arrested. Eight years! I didn't know if you would ever be released. I was suffocating there.'

'You exaggerate, Etta. You are a queen of the drama.'

'No, no, I'm not. I'm trying to explain.' She throws the pillow onto the floor and walks over to the open window. She rests her hand on the sill and stares down at the chattering guests enjoying cocktails in the hotel's courtyard.

'It was like I was in a beautiful prison, Carlo, with the sea the bars of my cell. I knew if I stayed on Capri I would die. Maybe not my body, but my mind would go.' She looks back at Carlo. 'It had already begun … headaches and hallucinations. I couldn't sleep. It was just like what happened after Adriana was born. I had to leave, Carlo. I had to leave or I would lose my mind.'

Carlo presses his hands against his temples and shakes his head. He throws himself down on the settee. 'What about Adriana? Had you no thought of her?'

'Of course I thought of her. I love her, just as I love you, my darling. But I was afraid I might do her some harm. She is so disobedient. So wilful. She has become too much for me to handle.'

'So, you left her in Stefania's hands, a woman old enough to be your grandmother. You abandoned our daughter to drink champagne and dance with strange men in the City of Light.' His dark eyes narrow. 'Is that all you did, Etta?'

Etta sniffs and wipes at her nose with the back of her hand. 'What do you mean?'

'What do I mean? This for me is an answer.'

They stare at each other for a long moment. Then, Etta walks over to Carlo, who watches her approach like a hawk eyeing a snake. She reaches out and touches his face.

'I love you, Carlo. I've always loved you, ever since the first day we met at the art gallery in London. But the truth is I had given up hope.' She traces her finger over the contours of his face. 'I'd allowed myself to forget the shape of your cheekbone, the curve of your jaw, the long, strong line of your nose. I tried, for so long, to hope. Then one day I woke up to find that hope had flown away, like a feather in the wind. That's when I came to Paris. I hadn't meant to stay, but I couldn't bring myself to go back.'

'Oh, Etta.' Reaching up, he cups her hand in his. He presses his lips against her palm.

Etta leans over and rests her cheek against his hair. 'Will you forgive me? Please say you'll forgive me.'

He reaches his hands around her and presses her against him. 'Oh, Etta. *Etta mia.* I missed you so much. I forgive you. *Dio aiutami,* I forgive you.'

# Part VIII

1928

# Chapter Seventy

## Jessie

**Altumanina Health Clinic, Cairo, Egypt – March 1928**

Jessie rolls up the last of the clean bandages and places them into a drawer in the clinic's examination room. She shuts the drawer and stretches, yawning as she rubs her neck. It is late, after seven o'clock, and her stomach rumbles with hunger. She hasn't eaten or drunk a thing since the light pre-dawn Ramadan meal, and then only an omelette and some bread. It has been a long day of sprained ankles and eyesight examinations, which normally wouldn't have been an issue if Zara had been there to help organise the flow of patients. Her sister-in-law's absence, explained with a terse note of apology handed to her by Marta in the morning, had made the day especially taxing given her own rudimentary knowledge of Arabic. She'd sent Mustapha to the Anglo-American Hospital to seek out Aziz but even Aziz hadn't been able to get away from the hospital to help, owing to 'some problems in the city'. Dr Simmonds, who had been so helpful in the clinic during and after her pregnancy, had long since departed, going back to Britain with many of the other British doctors.

The clinic is seriously understaffed; there is no getting around that fact. It is difficult to entice doctors to work at the clinic for a pittance when more lucrative work is available at the private hospitals in Cairo and Alexandria. On days like today, running the clinic feels like an uphill struggle with no pinnacle in sight. If only she could train as a doctor, it would solve some of their problems. But that is not going to happen any time soon here in Cairo, especially with the political unrest being thrown up by the ongoing conflict between the Wafd Party and the Liberal Constitutionalists, the hawkish regard of the British High Commissioner Baron Lloyd on behalf of British interests in the Sudan and the Sinai, and the machinations of King Fuad to regain absolute control of the government.

She is about to switch off the light when she hears footsteps running up the chipped marble path to the clinic's door. Zara bursts into the clinic, her face bloodied and her *hijab* torn.

'Zara! Good Lord, what's happened to you?'

Zara waves her hand. 'It is nothing. It is not my blood. Please, come to the taxi quickly. I need your help.'

'Taxi? What are you talking about? Where have you been?'

'I will explain later. Please, Jessica, come!'

Jessica hurries after Zara out into the dark night where the lights from the looming shape of Altumanina throw a yellow glow over the trees and bushes of the garden. A dusty Model T Ford is waiting on the drive by the gatehouse, its headlights sending two long beams of light across the white marble gravel. A rear door is open and, as she approaches, she sees the taxi driver bending over a prone man in the back seat, trying to stem the flow of blood from a wound in the man's chest with a bloody handkerchief.

She glances at her sister-in-law. 'My God, Zara. What happened?'

'It is Isham, Jessica. Please, you must help him.'

Jessie looks back at Isham's battered body prostrated across the taxi's back seat. 'Of course. Yes. Take off your *hijab* and press it against Isham's chest. We must get Isham into the clinic. Then you can tell me everything.'

---

'We were at the student demonstrations at the House of the Nation,' Zara says as she and Jessie cut away Isham's blood-soaked clothes in the clinic's examination room. 'It was all very peaceful and respectful. I joined the students on the balcony there and I spoke about the need for the new coalition government to reach an agreement with the British to give us back the Sudan and leave our country. Then the police arrived, and they began to beat us. Isham ran up to the balcony to find me, but he was caught in the riot. I watched them beat him, Jessica. It was terrible.'

Jessie peels away Isham's shirt. She sucks in her breath. 'Zara, he's been stabbed.'

'Stabbed? That is impossible. The police do not carry knives.'

'Well, someone stabbed him.' Jessie presses her hands against the oozing wound. 'Get me the bandages and the Dakin's Solution. Quickly! Where did the driver go?'

Zara rushes around the clinic collecting the items. 'I sent him to the house to tell Mustapha to find Aziz.'

'Good.' Jessie takes the antiseptic solution from Zara and splashes it into the wound. 'It looks like the knife punctured his lung and it's collapsed. Oh, God. There's so much blood. Press a bandage against the wound. I'm washing up. We can't wait for Aziz. I have to draw out the air in his pleural cavity to release the pressure on this lung so it can expand before I can suture the wounds.'

'Jessica, do you know what you are doing?' Zara's forehead creases with worry. 'Perhaps we should wait—'

'Zara, if we wait, he will drown in his own blood. I saw Aziz deal with this dozens of times during the war. I can do this. Trust me, Zara. I can do this.'

---

Jessie inserts a large hollow needle into Isham's chest wound and slowly retracts the syringe, which fills with blood. She glances toward the door.

'What is it, Jessica? What is the matter? Should we wait for Aziz?'

'No. It's fine.' She expels the blood from the syringe into a metal bowl.

The bowl is half-full of Isham's blood when the door bursts open and Aziz rushes into the examination room followed by Mustapha and the driver.

'Jessica! What has happened?'

'Aziz, thank God. Isham's been stabbed. I think … I know he has a haemothorax. I've been trying to draw out the blood to take the pressure off his lung.'

'Put that needle down immediately, Jessica! You don't know what you are doing. You could kill him if you are not careful.'

'I'm being careful, Aziz. We couldn't wait. He was drowning in his own blood. I had to do something—'

'I said put down that needle, Jessica. You are not a doctor. I will take over from here.'

---

Aziz paces across the bedroom carpet. 'You should have waited, Jessica. You could have perforated his lung with that syringe, which could have opened the existing puncture further and flooded his lung with blood. If that had happened, he would have died. Do you understand what I am saying?'

'But that didn't happen, did it?' Jessie sits on the bed and presses the palms of her hands against her eyes. 'Aziz, I couldn't stand there watching him bleed. I had to do something. I assisted you many times during the war—'

'You *assisted* me! That is the key word, Jessica.' He thumps his chest. 'I have been trained to deal with an emergency such as this. You have not. You are a nurse. You are *not* a trained doctor. You must remember that. Isham is lucky I arrived when I did.'

Jessie bites down on her lip as she feels the blood rise in her face. 'Has it occurred to you that I might have *helped* Isham survive? I had no idea when you'd arrive. I had to do something—'

'You cleaned the wound with antiseptic and tried to staunch the flow with bandages. This was what you were trained to do. No more than that. You overstepped your boundaries, Jessica. You must never do such a thing again.'

Jessie presses her lips together. He's right, of course. She'd known what she was supposed to do for Isham from watching Aziz deal with similar injuries during the war, but she hadn't been trained under the eyes of a physician. Truthfully, she'd had a fifty/fifty chance of making a fatal error. As Aziz had said, she could have inserted the needle too deeply, flooding Isham's lung with blood, or she might have ruptured a bronchial passageway, causing a lethal fistula. She had overstepped. She should have waited. If Isham had died because of something she had done …

'Jessica, do you understand? I am serious.'

'Yes, I understand. Of course, you're right.' She looks straight into his eyes. 'But I can't promise I wouldn't do the same again in the future. It's not in me to stand aside and watch someone die when I might be able to do something … *anything* … to help.'

Aziz nods. Picking up a bag of tobacco and a rolling paper from the desk, he then begins to roll a cigarette. Jessie watches him as he lights the cigarette and sucks at it until the tip glows bright red. He blows out the smoke, and, opening up his medical bag, takes out a newspaper which he hands to Jessie.

She looks at him, puzzled. '*Le Phare Egyptien*? The French paper?'

'Turn to page 32.'

Jessie turns to the page, scanning the columns until she finds what she is certain she is meant to read.

'The Faculty of Medicine of Egyptian University,' she translates from the French, 'announces that they are accepting applications from women to study medicine from September 1928. Applicants must be aware that all teaching is undertaken in English and, therefore, applicants must be fluent.'

She looks up at Aziz. 'Are they serious?'

'It appears they are.'

She re-reads the announcement. 'Oh, my word.'

'If you wish to study medicine, I support you, Jessica. We are partners in this life.'

'You will?'

'Of course. Otherwise you will be unhappy and resentful, and I will bear the brunt of your displeasure. You see, I am simply looking out for my own interests.'

'Can we afford it, Aziz? And the clinic, what will we do about the clinic if I'm studying?'

Aziz sets the cigarette down in an ashtray and joins Jessie on the bed. 'I cannot afford for you not to study, Jessica. Can you imagine what my life would be like if you knew the university had opened medical studies to women and you weren't amongst the students?' He shudders dramatically. 'It doesn't bear thinking about.'

'And the clinic—'

'This is simply a matter of administration. We will work out a plan, don't worry about that.'

'Shani … I'm almost always home for lunch and supper with Shani.'

'Zara will help.'

Jessie nods, then her forehead furrows. 'Zara seems to have gotten herself in deep with the radical nationalists. She told me she was speaking to the crowd from the balcony of the House of the Nation just before the riot started.'

Aziz rubs his forehead. 'She and many younger Egyptians are unhappy that the Wafd Party have entered a coalition with the Liberal Constitutionalists. We had to in order to keep any kind of influence in the government of this country. She does not see what goes on behind the scenes in Parliament. She believes the coalition will keep the Wafd from honouring the promises it has made to the Egyptian people of self-government without the interference of the British. Or interference from the King, for that matter. But it is far too dangerous for her to go out to these protests. I will tell her in no uncertain terms that she is not to put herself into this kind of situation again. I will have Mustapha become her guardian angel.'

'She won't like that.'

'I am well aware. Zara can be as obstinate as our mother when she wishes.'

'What's going to happen to Isham?'

'He is lucky to be alive. It will be some weeks before he is released from the hospital. Then he will have to find other employment. He cannot stay here at Altumanina.'

'Mohammed will be devastated. As will Zara.'

'It cannot be helped. As long as he is here, Zara will be tempted to go out again.'

Aziz rises and, crossing over to the desk, picks the burnt-out cigarette from the ashtray with a book of matches. Jessie follows him out onto the balcony. The match flares bright yellow against the black sky and the cigarette tip glows red as he sucks the tobacco smoke into his lungs. She slips her arms around him and hugs his body against hers.

'Promise me, Aziz.'

He blows out a stream of smoke and rubs her back with his free hand. 'Promise you what, *habibti*?'

'Promise me you won't ever get involved in these demonstrations. Zara was lucky today. I remember when the British Army shot and killed demonstrators in Tantra during the revolution in 1919. Things can get out of control so quickly.'

'Things were different then, Jessica. The Wafd Party is in the government now. It has the best interests of the Egyptian people at its heart.'

'Until King Fuad dissolves the government again.'

'Yes, well, what do you English say? "We will cross that bridge when we come to it."'

'Aziz, I know you're a member of the Wafd Party and were instrumental in its early days, but what are you doing with them now? Is there something you haven't told me?'

Aziz kisses Jessie on the top of her head. 'I am nothing more than a Party member, Jessica. I am a doctor and a husband and a father. These are who I am. Of course I am concerned about how my country is governed, as anyone should be. I am not interested in violence and war. I saw too much of that in the Great War. I simply wish to be happy with my family.'

'That's all I wish for, too. That, and to be a doctor.'

Aziz laughs. 'Of course you do. I know that nothing will stop you now that the door has opened. This is the Jessica I love.'

# Chapter Seventy-One

Celie

**West Lake, Alberta – April 1928**

Celie stands in a mound of melting brown slush in the schoolyard of West Lake School retying one of Lulu's plaits as her daughter squirms.

'I'm eight, Mommy. I don't need you to braid my hair. It's embarrassing. What if somebody sees?'

'Somebody like Ben?'

Lulu rolls her large blue eyes. 'Mommy! Benji is just a friend.'

'Celie! Celie, the paper's out!' Celie looks over to the road to see Mavis waving a newspaper as she prods her lagging son into the schoolyard.

Celie taps Lulu on her shoulder. 'You're free to go, Miss Jeffries. I couldn't have you go into the school's spring fundraiser with half your hair flying about. How would that have looked when you're singing "Me and My Shadow" with Ben? I would have had another note from Miss Evans to add to the collection. Go in and have a practice with him. Mrs Wheatley and I will be in in a minute.'

'We don't need to practise, Mommy. All Benji has to do is copy everything I do. It's easy.'

'Practice makes perfect, Lulu. That's what your grandmother used to say to me and your aunts when we didn't want to practise piano for the church's Christmas recitals. If I had to suffer for my art, then so do you. Consider it a family tradition.'

Lulu waves at Ben. 'Come on, Benji. We have to practise again. You have to be more careful. Shadows don't stumble.'

Celie turns back to Mavis. 'Poor Ben. Lulu bosses him around awfully.'

'He has an older sister. He's used to it.' Mavis flips open the *West Lake News* and hands the paper to Celie. 'Look, it's in. Shame it's not better news. Go on. Read it out loud.'

*Women are NOT Persons in Canada*

*Yesterday, the efforts of five Canadian women, now nationally known as the Famous Five, to have the Supreme Court of Canada respond to their petition 'Does the word "Persons" in Section 24 of the British North American Act, 1867, include female persons?' were met with a resounding 'No!'*

*The Supreme Court held that women were not 'qualified persons' within the meaning set out in the British North America Act. They based their ruling on the premise that the term should be interpreted in the same way as in 1867, and that women would have been specifically mentioned were the term 'persons' to include them.*

*The five women, led by Emily Murphy, the British Empire's first female judge, and including esteemed writer and politician Nellie McClung, sent the petition to the Governor General of Canada last August asking if it was constitutionally possible to allow for the appointment of women to the Canadian Senate. It appears, with this ruling, that it is not.*

*Mrs Murphy, when contacted by this journalist after the announcement of the Supreme Court's decision, responded that the Famous Five intend to petition Prime Minister Mackenzie King to appeal the decision to the Privy Council of Great Britain in the continuing fight to assure the legal inclusion of women in the term 'persons', and establish the principle that women can hold any political office in Canada, even as the Prime Minister, should they so wish.*

Celie folds the newspaper and hands it back to Mavis. 'Put it in the beer room for me, would you, Mavis? Frank will only get riled up if I bring it home.'

'There's bound to be some heated talk around the West Lake dinner tables tonight, that's for sure, Celie. If Fred makes any joke about me not being a person, he'll have the whole apple crumble in his lap.'

'I think it's ridiculous to let some document drafted sixty years ago by old men decide the futures of modern Canadian women.'

'It's the Canadian constitution, Celie. It may not be all that easy to change it.'

'But it's wrong, Mavis, just like keeping the vote from women was wrong. And women in Québec still don't even have the vote. It's a travesty.'

Mavis tucks the newspaper under her arm. 'It's a constant battle, isn't it? One that I didn't even notice until you opened my eyes, with all your stories about the suffragettes and the munitionettes during the war.'

'Mavis, Mrs McClung is meeting with the other women of the Famous Five at Emily Murphy's house in Edmonton next month to draft the petition to the Prime Minister for him to forward to the Privy Council in Britain. She's invited me to attend to write about it and take some photographs.'

'Oh, Celie, that's wonderful!'

Celie smiles weakly. 'It is, and I'd dearly love to go, but I can't see how it's possible. How would I get to Edmonton without Frank suspecting anything?'

'Yes, of course. Well, we'll just have to think of something, won't we?'

'We?'

Mavis smiles. 'You don't think I'll let you go off to Edmonton without me, do you? What a day we would have! We can go shopping at Hudson's Bay and have lunch at Johnson's Café. Tell Frank it's your birthday treat from me and Fred.'

Celie chews her lip as she looks at her friend. It had been years since she'd been in Edmonton, not since Frank had treated her and Lulu to a day at Borden Park to try out the rollercoaster back in the summer of 1925. She smiles at the memory. If only there had been more days like that, things now wouldn't be so … difficult. And to have the opportunity to be a part of history in the making! It was just like the days when she was organising marches for the suffragists back in England. She missed those days so much. She missed being involved in important things.

'You're absolutely right, Mavis, but I'll pay my share. I have money I've saved up from teaching and writing for the paper. I'll see what I can do.'

She loops her arm through Mavis's.

'Now, let's go watch our aspiring entertainers mangle "Me and My Shadow".'

# Chapter Seventy-Two

## Etta

### Capri, Italy – May 1928

Etta pays out a handful of *lire* and takes the paper cup of lemonade from the green-tiled stand on the Via Matteotti. She giggles at the flirtations of the elderly lemonade seller.

'Your smile is as bright as the sun, miss,' he says in Italian, kissing his fingers with a smack.

'Oh, not miss. I am a married woman,' she answers in Italian.

'Then your husband is the luckiest man who walks the earth.'

'You must remind him of that when I bring him here for lemonade.'

'My beautiful lady, if he doesn't appreciate your charm and beauty, you will find an honest heart beating in my own breast.'

'I will remember that.' She toasts the seller with the cup of lemonade. 'Until we meet again.'

She picks up the canvas bag she has stuffed with art supplies and, after looping the straps over her shoulder, heads down the lane toward the Gardens of Augustus and their panoramic view of the thrusting rocks of the Faraglioni, the marina with its fishing boats and sleek yachts, and the limestone cliffs of the island's Monte Solaro.

As she steps along the narrow lane past the stone walls laden with magenta bougainvillea, she breathes in the scent of lemons and rosemary that wafts through the air. Whenever she had walked through the food markets of Paris and caught a whiff of rosemary or lemons, she had been transported back to Capri in the summer. Even in Paris, she could never quite escape Capri.

She walks through the entrance gate and follows the flower-lined path under the towering pines and rustling palms until she reaches the terrace overlooking the sea. She sets her bag down on a bench and, walking over to the iron railing, grips it and raises her face to the morning sun.

She is happy. No, no, what is happiness? What does that word mean? Her heart is so full of joy that she feels that it will burst from her body and fly through the world, trumpeting her joy like geese on the wing. Her fingers tingle, her stomach quivers, and the most private recesses of her body flutter at the mere thought of Carlo's touch. She has even managed to reduce her use of the sweet laudanum to once a day.

It had never been like this with CJ. It had been fun, absolutely. To have a man love her again, make love to her again, after so long, had been like drinking water after a tortuous thirst. She'd needed CJ. She'd needed him to help her feel alive again, and she has no regrets about the affair. Regrets are a waste of time.

She leans her elbows on the railing and looks out at the jagged rocks of the Faraglioni. What's done is done. CJ has gone back to America, and Carlo is back in her life in every possible way. She wouldn't be surprised to find herself expecting again before long. Not something Adriana would be happy about, to be sure. A thirteen-year-old girl on the cusp of womanhood, obsessed by Liliana's handsome twenty-five-year-old grandson, Mario, suddenly lumbered with an infant sibling; she can imagine Adriana's tantrums already. For Adriana, there is space for only one star in the family, and that is herself.

---

The front door of the villa slams shut and the sound of laughter drifts through the house and out onto the balcony where Etta, Carlo and Stefania (with Alice the ginger cat curled on her lap) are enjoying late afternoon *tisana* and Liliana's almond biscuits.

Mario and Adriana stumble onto the balcony followed by Mario's grandmother Liliana, who has made only the barest of concessions to modern fashion by a shortening of the hem of her black dress and the chopping of her grey-streaked black hair into a severe bob. The housekeeper's habitually taciturn expression is bright with delight as she shoos the two younger people out onto the balcony.

Mario holds up a cardboard box wrapped in string. 'I have brought you cannoli from the *pasticceria* for *dolci* tonight.'

Adriana looks up at the tall young Italian as she clings onto his arm. 'Chocolate cannoli is my favourite, Mario,' she says in Italian. 'You're so thoughtful.'

Stefania sets down her teacup. 'In English, Adriana. You must practise now that your mother is here.'

The girl, slim and long-limbed like a young deer, eyes her mother with defiant eyes so dark they are almost like black glass. She shoves her loose blonde hair over her shoulder, dislodging a red rosebud from her curls which drops to the floor like a drop of blood. She shrugs her slender shoulders.

'*Come desidera.*'

'English, Adriana,' Carlo says.

Adriana sighs dramatically. 'As you like. It's okay?' She releases her hold on Mario's arm and grabs two almond biscuits from a plate on the table.

'Adriana!' Carlo admonishes. 'You do not grab food from the table like a monkey.'

Adriana stamps her foot. 'But Papa! I like them.'

Mario leans over Adriana's shoulder and whispers in her ear.

She rolls her dark eyes and drops the biscuits into his hand. He raises an eyebrow at the sulky girl. 'Adriana?'

'*Va bene*, Mario.' She looks over at the adults. 'I am sorry. Excuse me.'

Etta smiles. 'That's all right, Adriana. You are excused. Share the biscuits with Mario.'

'Your mother is more forgiving than I am, Adriana,' Carlo says. 'If I had known your mother was in Paris all the time that I thought she was here with you, I would have insisted she come home earlier. Maybe then you would have learned manners.'

Stefania shifts uncomfortably in her chair. 'Carlo, I did the very best I could—'

'Yes, of course. I am sorry, Stefania. I did not mean it like that.'

'Carlo—'

'I am sorry, Etta. You refuse to tell me, but if I ever find out who forwarded all your letters to me in the prison, making me think you were here on Capri, I swear I will—'

'It was me.'

Five pairs of eyes turn to stare at Mario.

Carlo rises from his chair. 'What did you say?'

Adriana tugs at Mario's arm. 'No, Mario. Papa will be angry.'

'It was me, *Signor Marinetti*. I – I'm sorry. I know I should not have done it, but *Signora Etta* was so unhappy. She had always been so kind to me. She is the reason I was accepted to study at the Accademia di Belle Arti in Napoli.'

'*Piccolo stronzo!*'

'Carlo!' Stefania says. 'Your language. Please.'

Carlo throws up his hands. 'Sorry. I am sorry.'

'Carlo, it's not Mario's fault,' Etta pleads. 'Blame me if you need to blame anyone.'

Mario takes off his flat cap and holds it in his hands. '*Signor Marinetti*, when *Signora Etta* asked me to help her, I felt I had to do it. She said she had to stay in Paris to sell your paintings, but she didn't want you to worry. She would post me her letters to the flat in Napoli. Inside would be the envelopes with her letters to you to be sent to the prison. I would take these and come to Capri and post them from here. I am sorry, *Signor Marinetti*. I – I thought I was helping.'

Carlo steps toward Mario and slaps him across the face.

Etta gasps. 'Carlo! Stop it!'

Carlo clenches his hands and retreats to a vine-covered pillar. He scowls at Mario. 'Get out! Never step inside this house again!'

'No, Papa!' Adriana throws her arms around Mario. 'Don't go, Mario! Don't go!'

Mario gently disengages Adriana's hands and whispers into her ear. Liliana enfolds Adriana in her plump arms as the girl wails with all the passion of a broken heart. The front door slams.

Adriana spins around to face her father. 'I hate you, Papa! I hate you so much! I wish you were in prison for ever!'

---

Carlo joins Etta at the bedroom window and traces her naked arms with his fingers. He kisses her on the back of her neck.

'Come to bed, *mio angelo*.'

'You shouldn't have done that. You shouldn't have sent Mario away. It wasn't his fault. He only did what I asked him. I knew he wouldn't say no.'

'He is not a boy. He is a man with a mind of his own. You are my wife, and I must forgive you, but him … no, I will not forgive him for his part in this deception.'

'Both Liliana and Adriana are heartbroken—'

'I am sorry for that, but they will recover. Perhaps now Mario will understand the consequences of his gullibility.'

Etta sighs heavily and shakes her head as she stares out at the sea glittering in the moonlight. Carlo leans his chin on her shoulder and wraps his arms around her body. 'You are thinking of Adriana.'

'Yes.' Etta turns around in his embrace.

'Do not worry, *cara mia*. She is simply at that age when she is no longer a child but not yet a woman, and she hates her parents.'

'I don't know what to do with her. I'm not sure which is worse, the door slamming or the sulking. She refuses to come out to paint with me or even let me paint her portrait anymore. Did you hear the way she talked back to Cousin Stefania over supper last night about the cigarettes Liliana found in her bedside table? Accusing poor Liliana of snooping through her things!'

'I know, Etta, but I sent her to her room. She must learn that she cannot speak to her elders like that.'

'Not just to her elders, Carlo. To anyone. I had another note today from her teacher. She wants to meet with us about Adriana's behaviour. What if she's expelled?'

'If she is, we will deal with it. There are other schools—'

'Not on Capri.'

'In Napoli, or perhaps a boarding school in Rome.'

'We don't have the money for that, Carlo. Boarding schools are expensive and no one will buy our paintings now that you're no longer a murderer. Monsieur DuRose is demanding we have the ones in his warehouse shipped back here as soon as possible. Maybe we should have sent Adriana to boarding school in England last autumn as Mama wished. She said she would pay for it.'

Carlo releases Etta and strides over to the desk where he lights a cigarette. 'I will not have your mother pay for our daughter's education. Adriana is my responsibility.' He leans on the desk and looks back at his wife in her Parisian negligee, illuminated like a romantic spirit in the silver moonlight.

'I regret that you did that, Etta. It was not right to pass off your paintings as my work.'

'I had to, Carlo. We needed the money. We still need money.'

He flicks cigarette ash into an empty wineglass on the desk.

'How could you have run through so much money so quickly?'

'Are you suggesting I did nothing but flit around Paris

spending money like water? Do you have any idea how expensive all those lawyers and judges we tried to bribe were?'

'Of course.' He blows out a puff of smoke. 'But judging from your new wardrobe and the hotel receipts, you did not seem inclined to economise.'

'Oh, Carlo, you don't understand what Paris is like. I had a part to play. I was the grieving wife of a famous artist unjustly imprisoned for the murder of his first wife, who was in town to pay the bills by selling your paintings. There were gallery exhibitions and dinners and parties I had to attend. I couldn't very well go dressed as a shopgirl, could I?'

Carlo laughs and crosses the carpet back to Etta.

'I imagine you played the role well.'

Etta takes the cigarette from Carlo and inhales a long drag and blows out the smoke.

'As you say, it was like a role in a play. I had to be convincing.'

'You are smoking now? Is that where Adriana got the cigarettes from? You?'

'She must have found them in my vanity drawer. It seems there is more than one snoop in this house.'

'Don't worry about affording Adriana's education,' Carlo says as he retrieves the cigarette and stubs it out on the window sill. 'Marianna's mother came to see me when I was in prison. She told me that she left money in her will for Adriana as well as Paolo. It was a … it was a kind gesture, seeing that Adriana is no relation of hers.'

'Oh, that's good news. But we still need to find money to fund ourselves, Carlo. I sold a few of my own paintings in Paris. I thought I might … try again. Perhaps in Rome. Yes, why don't we both work toward a co-exhibition in Rome?'

Carlo holds up his damaged right hand.

'I cannot paint. You know this.'

'You just need to practise more with your left hand. You are still talented, Carlo. You simply need to train yourself—'

Carlo leans forward and kisses Etta.

'Come to bed, Etta. I don't want to talk any longer.'

He traces his lips along her neck and threads his fingers through hers.

'Come to bed and make love with me like we did in my dreams.'

# Chapter Seventy-Three

## Celie

**West Lake, Alberta – May 1928**

'It's a chilly day today, isn't it, Lulu? Wrap your muffler around your neck properly. It's dragging in the mud.'

Lulu sighs dramatically and loops the hand-knitted blue and yellow scarf half-heartedly around her neck as she follows her mother down the muddy road to Sweet Briar Farm. 'Will it ever be summer, Mommy?'

'Not at this rate, I expect.' Celie adjusts Lulu's blue felt cloche hat over her newly bobbed hair. 'The roses will be coming out in England soon. We'll visit Nanny Fry there one day and you'll see how pretty it is there in the summertime.'

Lulu squirms away from Celie and points at Fred Wheatley's truck which is parked in front of their farmhouse.

'Look, it's Uncle Fred! They're here!' She peels down the road, oblivious to the puddles that splash splotches of dirty water over her coat.

Celie holds up her daughter's hat. 'Your hat, Lulu! We're supposed to surprise Daddy together!'

She watches her daughter race up the steps to the front porch. Squaring her shoulders, she heads down the lane. She hopes it will be one of Frank's good days. He's been in such a terrible mood for the past few days that she hasn't dared mention the trip to Edmonton with Mavis, even though she'd already bought her train ticket from the money she'd saved in the Fry's Cocoa tin. But today is her birthday and the Wheatleys are here. Surely, he won't make a scene in front of them.

---

'Happy Birthday, Celie!!'

Celie laughs as she enters the sitting room. Kip scampers up to her, barking and wagging his feathery tail. 'Look at all of you Wheatleys in your Sunday best! My word, is that a bowtie, Fred? And Arthur, too? You didn't need to dress up. It's only my birthday.' She looks past their shoulders. 'Where's Frank?'

The children giggle and Mavis holds her finger to her lips and shushes them.

'Mavis? What's going on?'

The notes of a rather inept version of 'Chopsticks' plink from somewhere behind them. Lulu squeals and claps her hands. 'Mommy, it's a piano!'

'Lulu! It was supposed to be a surprise,' Ben Wheatley grumbles.

Mavis grabs Celie's hand. 'Not anymore. Make way, kids, birthday girl coming through.'

Celie gasps at the sight of a gleaming new upright piano. 'A piano, Frank?'

'It would seem so, Celie.' Frank rises from the piano bench and lifts up the lid. 'I even bought you some sheet music.' He holds up a couple sheets. '"My Blue Heaven" and "Always".'

'But a new piano, Frank. How can we afford it? Aren't we meant to be saving for the upstairs extension?'

The light in Frank's dark eyes goes out, like lit coal

extinguished by a splash of water. 'From hard-earned savings. What have you done to our daughter's hair? She looks ridiculous.'

Lulu's lower lip quivers. 'Daddy!'

Celie feels her stomach fall. She wraps her arms around Lulu. 'Lulu was the only one in the school without a bobbed haircut, Frank. Her friends were teasing her about her plaits. She poked Lizzie Philby in the eye in the schoolyard and I had to make blueberry muffins to placate Emma.'

Fred Wheatley steps forward and nudges Frank on his arm. 'What say we put on our jackets and go out back and have a beer, Frank. I brought some over from the house. Give the ladies some time to get out the sandwiches and cake.'

Mavis nods at her husband. 'Beer's a great idea, Fred. It's in the fridge.' She nudges Celie toward the piano. 'Play "My Blue Heaven", Celie. It's my absolute favourite.'

Celie unbuttons her coat and hands it to Mavis. 'All right. Then we can have some cake.' As she removes her cloche hat, she glances at Frank, who is glowering at her from the piano bench.

'Oh, Mrs Jeffries!' Fourteen-year-old Molly Wheatley gasps. 'You look just like Clara Bow!'

Frank jumps up from the bench. 'Good God, Celie! You too? What have you done to yourself and our daughter?'

'Frank, please—'

'It's ... it's ... heinous!' Pushing past Celie, he snatches his jacket and hat off the coat stand.

Fred grabs hold of Frank's arm. 'C'mon, Frank. It's not as bad as all that. It's like Celie said, the girls are all cutting their hair now. Look at Mavis and Molly. You gotta admit it's a lot more practical for working on the farm and all that.'

Frank yanks his arm away. 'Blast and set fire to it, Fred! Let go of me!' He yanks open the door and stamps out of the house.

'Daddy!' Lulu bursts into tears and runs out the door. 'Daddy!' she screams. 'I'm sorry! I'll grow my hair! I'll wear plaits! Daddy, please come back!'

'Go after him, Fred,' Mavis says. 'Talk some sense into him. Good heavens, it's only hair.'

Celie rushes out to the porch and pulls her weeping daughter into a hug. 'Let Daddy go, Lulu. He was just surprised, that's all. Your hair looks lovely. He'll come back, don't worry.' She takes a handkerchief out of her skirt pocket and wipes at Lulu's cheeks. 'Why don't you go inside and have some cake?'

Lulu glares at her mother, her face flushed and her blue eyes glistening with rage. 'I don't want cake! I hate my hair! I hate it! And I hate you!' She shoves Celie away and runs back into the house. Inside, a door slams.

Celie shivers as a chill wind whips up the porch. Why did Frank have to say those awful things? She loves the piano, of course she does. Maybe she shouldn't have questioned how he'd afforded it in front of the Wheatleys. He is so sensitive about money. Maybe she'd embarrassed him. Maybe that's what had set him off about the haircuts. Maybe it was *her* fault for being insensitive. Rubbing her arms, she steps back into the house and shuts the door.

'What's wrong with Lulu, Mrs Jeffries?' Ben Wheatley asks as she enters the kitchen. 'She doesn't want cake?'

Mavis runs a hand over Ben's tousled hair. 'I think she would love a piece of cake, Ben. Why don't you knock on her door and bring her a slice? Tell her she looks nice.'

'She always looks nice to me.'

'Go freshen up, Celie,' Mavis says as she reaches into her picnic hamper and takes out a package wrapped in tin foil. 'It'll all be fine. I'll set out the sandwiches.'

'I don't think I'll be going to Edmonton any time soon, Mavis. Not after this.'

'Edmonton isn't going anywhere. There's always another time.'

'I've already bought the ticket.'

Mavis shrugs. 'Give me the ticket and I'll get you a refund. Don't worry.'

Celie sighs. 'It looks like my newspaper career is over, not to mention playing any part in politics. I was so excited, Mavis. I thought I could be a part of something important. But it's never going to happen, is it? Not here. Not with Frank.'

Mavis slips Kip, who is eyeing her imploringly from under the table, a piece of ham. 'You still have your photography, Celie.'

'I suppose that's something. As long as Frank never finds out.' Celie eyes the wedges Molly Wheatley is carving out of the cake. 'You might want to help Molly cut the cake. Those slices look big enough to block a door.'

Mavis gasps as tall, rangy, thirteen-year-old Arthur Wheatley digs into one of the wedges with a serving spoon. 'Arthur, put down that spoon! We haven't even sung "Happy Birthday" to Mrs Jeffries yet!'

Celie nods toward the window. 'I should probably go rescue Fred from Frank.'

Mavis looks up from the slice of cake she is dividing in two. 'Sure. And, Celie, it's *your* hair. You can do what you like. You look lovely. Don't let anyone tell you that you don't. Least of all a man.'

---

Celie pushes open the barn door and steps into the cavernous interior which smells of sweet hay and warm animals. One of the cows moos and the big Percherons, Betsy and Trot, whinny at the sound of the creaking door.

'There you are.'

'Frank was just showing me the new piglets, Celie.'

Celie joins them by the pigpen. 'Yes, it seems Nigel the boar and Ethel the sow did some celebrating at New Year's.'

'At least someone at Sweet Briar was celebrating,' Frank says as he drains the last of his beer from the bottle.

Celie bites her lip and looks over at Fred, who is making an earnest inspection of the feeding trough. 'The food's ready, Fred. You might want to go before Kip and the children eat it all.'

Fred smiles at her, unable to conceal his relief. 'Sure thing. I'll be sure to keep the monsters from eating everything.'

'Thank you, Fred.'

When Fred has gone, Celie turns to face her husband. 'You hurt Lulu's feelings, Frank. She's in her room and won't come out.'

Frank rubs his forehead under his hat. 'I know. I didn't mean to. It's just … her hair, it was a shock. Then when I saw you … Your beautiful red hair, Celie. I loved to watch you brush it at night. Why did you do it?'

Celie shrugs. 'I just decided I would. It's my hair, Frank. I felt … old-fashioned.'

'I loved your hair, Celie.'

'I still have hair, Frank. So does Lulu. We're the same people. Times move on. There's hardly a woman or girl left in West Lake who hasn't already cut their hair.'

'All right. Fine. I'll apologise to Lulu.'

'Good. Thank you. Shall we go back?'

'Not yet.' His voice is emotionless. 'There's something else I want to know.'

Celie's heart judders. *Please God, don't let him have found the photograph of Hans and Max.* 'Yes?'

'What's happened to all the money in the Fry's Cocoa tin?'

'The Fry's Cocoa tin?' *How did he know about that?*

'Celie, I've known that you put your teaching money into that tin for years. The thing is, I expected it would run out after you stopped teaching last year. I thought I'd start topping it up, so you would never run out of money for the household expenses. But every time I went to top it up, there was more money in it. Where did the money come from, Celie?'

'Frank—'

'Then you started going off to all these meetings in town with Mavis, and these articles started appearing in the newspaper with some very nice pictures.' His voice is eerily quiet. 'I started to wonder if it was you, but I thought, no, Celie would tell me if she was writing for the paper again, wouldn't she? Even if I'd expressly told her not to. Or would she?'

Celie feels her heart begin to thump wildly. 'Frank. I had to. When Nellie McClung came into town and spoke about this issue about women being non-persons in the Canadian constitution, I couldn't do nothing. I *had* to write about it.'

'It's none of your business, Celie. We're British. We're not Canadians.'

'We live here, Frank. We're landed immigrants now. We'll always live here. For heaven's sake, Lulu was born here. Our daughter *is* a Canadian. Is it right that she is a non-person according to the constitution?'

'I told you not to, Celie.'

Celie stares at her husband as the long-suppressed anger bubbles up inside of her like soup about to boil over. 'So what, Frank? You don't own me. I even told Rex Majors not to put my name on those articles. I didn't want to "embarrass" you, you see. But I've had enough of hiding, Frank. If I want to write, I will. If I want to take photographs, I'll do that. If I want to go to Edmonton to meet with the Famous Five at their next meeting, which, by the way, I've been invited to cover for the newspaper, I will go. You knew the woman I was when you married me, Frank, and you've done nothing but try to suffocate me ever since. I've had enough. I'm not going to let you do that anymore.'

She turns her back on Frank and stamps across the floorboards toward the door.

'Celie! Come back here. We're not finished talking.'

She looks back at her husband. At the man she'd once thought was so polite and handsome. At the man she'd thought she could make a life with. A stranger to her.

It's over. The marriage is done. But she is a Catholic and she can't divorce. She is stuck with him for all the days she still has left on this earth. Tomorrow, when she is alone in the house, with

Lulu at school and Frank working in the fields, she will make up a bed for herself in Lulu's room until the new storey is built. Then she will have her own room till death do them part.

'I'm quite finished talking, Frank. Now, we have guests. I suggest you come back to the house and act like a host.'

---

*'Schatzi! Schatzi! Hold up the banner and I will take your picture.'*

*Celie laughs and holds up the banner she'd been making before that awful argument with Jessie about Max. How could Jessie have called her a German sympathiser? She loves Max, and he loves her. That he is standing there, now, in front of her at the suffragist march is proof enough, isn't it? All the way from the Western Front to take her picture.*

*Wait, what is he doing in London? In his German uniform? It's dangerous. He'll be arrested. She has to warn him.*

*A huge grey shadow falls over them, growing like a spreading stain, and suddenly she is jostled by the marching suffragettes as they scream and elbow their escape from the darkening sky. Then, she hears it. The low thrum of the Zeppelin's engines. She looks up and her heart stops as she watches the bomb drop—*

'Schatzi! Schatzi!'

Celie gasps and sits up against her pillow. Her body is slick with sweat, and she runs the back of her hand against her damp forehead as she gasps for breath. Beside her, Frank is as still as a corpse, though a soft snore assures her that he is deep into one of his solid sleeps. How he can sleep like that, she can't fathom. She wakes at the least sound: the brush of a branch against a window, the rattle of a loose shingle on the roof, Lulu coughing, Kip whining in his sleep, the scratch of a mouse in the kitchen.

She throws off the covers and slips her feet into the beaded moccasins Mavis had given her for her last birthday, and shrugs into her dressing gown. Her head throbs. She shouldn't have drunk those three glasses of Mavis's beer, but after her disastrous birthday, she'd felt the need to anesthetise herself. Maybe that's why she'd had such a strange dream.

She slides open the top drawer of the dresser and roots around the hairbrushes and combs, Frank's brilliantine tin, handkerchiefs and gloves in search of the aspirin bottle, but comes up empty-handed. She shuts the drawer and, pondering where it might be, remembers that Frank had used it last, when he'd come home late on Friday from Tom Philby's smelling like a still. She pulls open Frank's clothing drawer and rifles through the socks and undershirts and boxers. Her hand brushes against a small tin box. She slides it out from underneath the jumble of clothing. She glances back at her snoring husband; then, after shutting the drawer as quietly as she can manage, she slips out through the bedroom door into the kitchen.

Kip whines from the cardboard box Lulu has lined with an old blanket, and she hears the muted thump of his tail on the wool. She kneels down beside the box and pets the dog's soft head as it licks her fingers.

'Hello, sweetness,' she whispers. 'Aren't you a handsome boy.'

The dog climbs out of his bed and, resting his black and white head on Celie's lap, settles down on the kitchen floor beside her. She examines the tin box in the soft grey light filtering in from the kitchen window. There are moments in life when one wishes one could rewind the clock, erase the minutes and seconds that have led to the revelation of a secret which might have been best kept hidden. She is about to experience one of these moments, Celie thinks. And yet, she can't stop herself.

She flips open the lid with her thumb and stares at the syringe and the vials. She slides out a vial and reads the label.

MORPHINE.

She leans back against a leg of the kitchen table. Morphine. Frank is a morphine addict. That explains so much. The mood swings. The change in his personality over the years, from the considerate, loving young soldier he'd once been to the terse, humourless, tetchy farmer he'd become. Jessie had once told her about the drug abuse she'd witnessed amongst the soldiers in Egypt. Frank must have started taking it during the war.

*Well, now, Frank. We both have secrets, don't we? You're a drug addict and I'm a secret photographer who is still in love with a man whom I can never have. I won't have you making me feel guilty any longer. I am sorry for you, Frank. I can't imagine the things you saw during the war. But the war is over and I have a life to live.*

*I won't leave you, Frank. I have taken vows and I will honour them. I will survive this marriage and do my duty as your wife and Lulu's mother. More than that, I will make something of my life. I will not let you take me down with you. I am Cecelia Sirena Maria Fry and I am somebody.*

# Chapter Seventy-Four

## Jessie & Celie

**Sweet Briar Farm, West Lake, Alberta – June 1928**

Celie sits down on a wooden bench outside Forbes's General Store and, after setting down her basket of purchases, tears open the battered envelope from Egypt.

*Altumanina*
*Cairo, Egypt*

*June 20th, 1928*

*Dearest Celie,*

*Oh, Celie. I'm so very sorry to hear about your problems with Frank. I wish I could be there with you and be your sounding board like we were for each other when we were girls (even though we didn't always agree, of course!), but it sounds like you have a good friend in Mavis. She sounds like someone you can lean on, and you can always write or send me a telegram any time, you do know that, don't you? Now that there is a telephone line between the United States and the UK, who knows – one day, we might even be able to speak to each other directly! Wouldn't that be wonderful?*

*I know we are all meant to be good Catholics like Mama, but I have always thought that following Papa's Protestant religion would have been far less problematic. You would be able to divorce, for one thing.*

*Religion makes things so difficult sometimes, doesn't it? I worry about what we're going to do about Shani's faith, with Aziz being Muslim and me being a Catholic. My mother-in-law has said that Shani is meant to start her Islamic prayers when she turns seven … I just don't know what to do. I worry that her freedoms will be limited as a Muslim woman, and I wouldn't want that for my daughter when I have been free to follow my dreams all the way to Egypt. My mother-in-law and Mama have already clashed about this on several of Mama's visits. Mama even had Shani baptised as a Catholic behind my back! Isn't that outrageous? I have simply been burying my head in the sand to avoid thinking about it, but Shani is seven next June and I know I will have to deal with it all then.*

*Have you thought about returning home to London with Lulu? You know you could, if you couldn't bear it any longer. Mama has a flat in Chelsea, now, did she tell you? She stays there on the weekends with Hettie (Can you imagine? I hope it's big enough for the both of them) and shops at Harrods and drags Hettie off to shows and restaurants. Oh, to be a fly on those walls! It seems that Mama's decided she is the 'Merry Widow' and is intent on spending Papa's legacy in style. I am beginning to see who Etta inherited her dramatic side from.*

*What I am saying is that there is all sorts of room for you and Lulu at Clover Bar. If you are worried about money, I can help you. Don't let pride or silly notions like 'honour' keep you from asking. I don't want to think of you all the way out in the Canadian wilderness trapped in a dead marriage. You're not alone, Celie. We all love you. You can always ask for help if you need.*

*I'm glad you are still doing your photography, even if it is on the sly. You have always done this so brilliantly well. Thank you for the lovely picture of you and Lulu with your new haircuts! Don't you both look the bee's knees?*

*I just received a lovely watercolour self-portrait from Etta. I'm so glad she's settling back on Capri with Carlo and Adriana. I had begun to think that I would have to make my way to Paris to knock some sense into her! Her letters are jolly enough, and she is trying to teach Carlo to paint with his left hand. Carlo is anxious for them to find their own house, but Cousin Stefania is waging a war to keep them at Villa Serenissima at least until Adriana goes off to finishing school in Switzerland when she is seventeen. That, apparently, is Cousin Stefania's plan for Adriana. I get the impression from Etta's letters that Carlo is not fully on board with this. To complicate matters, Mama has been dropping hints about having them send Adriana to boarding school in England to 'polish her rough edges', which Etta thinks is a grand idea. It appears that Adriana's wild ways are causing some friction at Villa Serenissima!*

*I have begun to feel some sympathy for Mama having to bring up three girls so close together in age!*

*I have some exciting news of my own, Celie. I'm going to medical school! Here in Cairo, can you believe it? The university here has just opened its medical faculty to women students. I had been hoping to join the class this coming autumn, but we're terribly short-staffed at the clinic right now, and the political situation has been volatile with student riots, and what seems to be continuous government infighting. Zara and Aziz are involved with the nationalist Wafd Party, which pulls them away from the clinic from time to time. We've all agreed to formulate a 'let's get Jessie into medical school 1929' plan. By then, Shani will be seven, and I will have a clearer idea what direction her life will be going in as well.*

*Of course, I would have loved to start the course this year – when have you ever known me to be patient? But I want the clinic to be running smoothly when I start my studies, so I intend to find a good nurse to replace me, and a doctor who can attend the clinic full time. Zara, who administers the clinic, will have them both toeing the line before you know it!*

*Take care, Celie. Sending you and Lulu and Kip (and even Frank) all my love.*

*Jessie x*

Celie tucks the letter back into the envelope and slips it into her basket. It seems that both Jessie's and Etta's lives, and her mother's as well, are all swimming along nicely. Even Etta appears to have settled into domestic bliss in Capri, judging from the number of adjectives in her letters. She is happy for them. She is happy for anyone who manages to be happy in this world.

She'd been happy once. So long ago now that is like the fading memory of a beautiful day. Was she ever the girl who had loved the young German tutor named Max Fischer, or had that been a dream? She keeps the photograph she stole from Hans's Aunt Ursula hidden in the pocket of her best navy dress in her side of the wardrobe where she knows Frank will never find it. Max is so young in it, the photograph taken well before she had first met him in the autumn of 1912. Sixteen years ago now. She had been happy then.

Maybe, one day, she will be happy again.

# Part IX

1929

# Chapter Seventy-Five

## Etta

**Villa Serenissima, Capri, Italy – March 1929**

Etta shuffles through the letters. Bills, more bills, a postcard from Jessie from Aswan ... She turns over a long white envelope scented with Chanel No. 5 and sees the logo of the Saint James & Albany Hotel on the seal with a blue ink scribble underneath.

*Just for show! We're saving our pennies for Cannes this summer. Zxxx*

Etta smiles and heads out to the balcony. Settling herself in the cushions of a wicker chair, she tears open Zelda's letter.

*Rue de Mézières*
*Paris, France*

*March 5th, 1929*

*Dearest darling Etta,*

*I'm in Paris and you're not! Oh, sigh! The City of Light is just not the same without you. Come back, come back! Please!*

*With my darling Etta away, I have become quite obsessed with ballet and have been keeping myself very busy at Madame Egorova's ballet studio while Scott scribbles away on stories for the* Saturday Evening Post. *Horrible Ernest Hemingway says Scott is prostituting his talent for filthy lucre, but what are we meant to do? Live on air? Where would that hack be if it weren't for poor Hadley's trust fund and now evil Pauline's family money? I ask you, honestly!*

*I must love you and leave you, my dearest pet. My new ballet friend Lucienne is knocking on the door. We have a lesson at Madame Egorova's in an hour, and she is an ogress if we're late.*

*Kisses, kisses, kisses.*

*Zelda xxx*

*PS: Do try to convince your husband to bring you to Paris. Honestly, no one even remembers all that business about poor Marianna anymore. Now that Carlo isn't a murderer, no one will bother him in the least. Everyone is much more interested in trying to get a glimpse of the notorious D.H. Lawrence and his wife Frieda now!*

Had it been over a year-and-a-half since she'd left Paris with Carlo? How is it possible that that life was over? That she'll never again dance the tango with Zelda at the Dôme, pose for artistic photographs for Man Ray under Kiki de Montparnasse's glowering eye, banter with Ernest and Hadley Hemingway over drinks at La Closerie des Lilas, or spend afternoons in a haze of love in bed with CJ at the hotel? She would be lying if she said she didn't miss that carefree, hedonistic life of champagne, cigarettes, writers, artists, dancers and sex. Is she an awful person to think that? Probably, but she doesn't regret a moment of it, despite the berating she endured from her family's letters. You would never find her milking cows on a farm in Canada or bandaging up cuts and bruises in a clinic in Cairo. It's incredible how different three sisters could be.

She'd always thought she was the odd one out in the Fry family. That is, until she'd coerced Cousin Stefania into revealing her mother's illicit Italian love affair and the truth about Celie's birth – everything except who Celie's real father is. And now, when she reads her mother's letters about her new Chelsea flat and her life of theatre jaunts and cocktail parties with the likes of Noël Coward and Gertrude Lawrence – now, she understands that she is just like her mother.

She tucks the letter back into the envelope and slides it into her skirt pocket. Maybe she *will* try to persuade Carlo to visit Paris with her; tell him that they should re-establish their connection with Monsieur DuRose and excite the gallerist about the prospect of a double Marinetti exhibition.

*Yes, actually, why not?* Her heart flutters with excitement. It's a marvellous idea. She'll write Zelda back right away and tell her the plan.

She rises from the wicker chair and heads through the French doors into the sitting room toward the heavily carved antique walnut secretaire desk where Stefania keeps the Villa Serenissima writing paper. She roots around the top drawer, but finds nothing but a fountain pen, some ink cartridges, and a notebook full of Stefania's neatly handwritten household accounts. Shutting the drawer, she kneels on the frayed pile of the Persian rug and yanks at the bottom drawer. It's locked.

*Why would it be locked?* What could Stefania have that she'd wish to keep hidden from anyone? Unless … Could there be something in there about Celie's birth?

Etta leans back on her heels and scrutinises the room. *Where would Stefania hide the key? Somewhere close, but not obvious.* Her eyes scan the collection of Italian pottery behind the secretaire's glazed cabinet doors above the drawers. Rising to her feet, she opens the doors and begins a gentle examination of the Vietri sul Mare ceramics covered with exuberant lemons, sunflowers, birds and flaming suns. Inside the pannier of a turquoise ceramic donkey, she finds a small key.

When she tries it in the drawer, it turns smoothly. She pulls open the drawer, which is stuffed with manila folders tied with black ribbon. The cat rubs against her leg and she starts.

'Alice! Don't scare me like that!'

The cat sits on the rug and eyes her indifferently; he sets to grooming his paw.

She takes a breath and eases the top folder out of the drawer. She unties the string and rifles through the documents. Stefania's husband's will, their marriage certificate, a very old photograph of a young Stefania in her wedding dress … She shuts the folder and reties the ribbon. One by one, she repeats the process, until there is only one folder left.

She takes out the folder and slowly unties the ribbon. Inside there is only one document. An Italian birth certificate dated May 3rd, 1892 with five names on it:

Bambino(a): Cecelia Sirena Maria Grenville. *Grenville?*

Etta's heart thumps.

Padre: Harold James Grenville. *Harold Grenville? Who's Harold Grenville?*

Madre: Christina Maria Innocenti Bishop Grenville. *Grenville? That's a lie!*

Testimonianza: Stefania Albertini. *Of course, Stefania was a witness.*

Testimonianza: Liliana Sabbatini. *Liliana too?*

*Why does the name Harold Grenville sound familiar?* Something niggles at Etta's memory. *Harold Grenville … Harold Grenville …* She sucks in quick breath. *Of course! Harold Grenville, Lord Sherbrooke!*

She shakes her head. *Mama, Mama, Mama, that's why you always hated it when Papa brought up Lord Sherbrooke's name at the dining table when he discussed the news of the day. Celie is Lord Sherbrooke's child, which means she is heir to the Grenville fortune! Don't you think she should know that, Mama? If it were me, I'd want to know. This is too big a secret to keep buried, Mama. You have to tell Celie, and, now that I know the truth, I'll find some way to ensure that you do.*

## Chapter Seventy-Six

### Christina

**Chelsea, London – April 1929**

Christina squeezes blue ink from the eyedropper into the reservoir of her old Waterman fountain pen, unable to contain a curse as the ink splashes onto her shaking fingers in her haste.

'Sugar!'

Hettie looks up from her dusting. 'Not on your blouse again?'

'No. Just all over my fingers. It's all Etta's fault. She's quite upset me.'

Hettie grunts. 'Again?' She drops the feather duster onto the new Eileen Gray tubular steel and glass coffee table from Syrie Maugham's shop. 'I'll get the lemon juice.'

Christina bends over her stationery, too agitated for any of the normal formalities.

*Dear Etta,*

*Absolutely not! You are forbidden to say a word to anyone, especially Cecelia. Please, Etta, it would only hurt her. I sense her life in Canada has its difficulties and revealing her father's identity would only confuse matters.*

*Let me clarify a misapprehension of yours. Cecelia is* not *Lord Sherbrooke's heir. I am aware that his current wife has been unable to bring a child to term, but the matter is more complicated than it is your right to know. Suffice to say, do not fill your head nor Cecelia's with the thought that she is an heiress to a large fortune. Were anything to happen to Lord Sherbrooke, you can be certain that the McClellans will swoop in and take everything. Please disabuse yourself of coming into money via your sister.*

*I am sorry you are now in possession of this secret. Stefania, Liliana and I have done everything in our power to protect Cecelia from this information since her birth. Even your father didn't know the truth of the situation, the guilt of which I must carry till I finally shuffle off this mortal coil.*

*Etta, remember how determined you were to keep the secret of Carlo's marriage and Adriana's birth out of wedlock from me and your father? I know you were ashamed of finding yourself in such a compromising situation, just as I was back in 1892. We are quite alike, Etta. I, too, had wished to be an artist once. It's what drew me particularly to Harry Grenville. He was an artist, you see. For that one summer, he was an artist.*

*You are back where you belong now, Etta, with your husband and your daughter. Nurture your relationships with them. You have a husband who loves you, and a beautiful daughter. You are more fortunate than you realise.*

*Put Cecelia out of your mind. If and when the time comes to reveal the identity of her father to her, I will be the one to do it. This is not your story.*

*Mama*

# Chapter Seventy-Seven

Jessie

**Altumanina, Cairo, Egypt – June 1929**

'H*appy Birthday to you! Happy Birthday to you! Happy Birthday dear Shani! Happy Birthday to you!*'

Shani jumps out of her chair and dances around Jessie as she carries a large chocolate cake with seven small flickering candles. 'I'm seven! I'm seven! I'm seven!'

Aziz laughs and beckons to his daughter. 'You are, *habibti*. Come, sit down before the cake lands on the floor.'

'Remember to make a secret wish before you blow out the candles, Shani,' Zara says as she and Marta set dessert plates and forks on the table which Marta has strewn with rose petals and rosemary twigs. 'Wishes you make on your birthday are certain to come true.'

Layla Khalid frowns as she pushes her plate away. 'Don't talk nonsense, Zara. Wishes almost never come true, Shani. Life is full of disappointments. The sooner you realise that, the better.'

Jessie sets the cake on the table and looks over at her mother-in-law, who, at fifty-six, has become even more haughty in her maturing beauty. 'Layla, please, let's be happy today. Shani, blow out your candles and make any wish you like.'

Shani leans across the table and, after sucking in a deep breath, blows out all the tiny flames. 'I did it! I did it! My wish will come true!'

Zara presses a finger against her lips. 'Do not tell us what it is, *habibti*. It must be your secret.'

Layla glowers at her daughter. 'You're filling the child's head with nonsense, Zara. She is becoming far too anglicised with all this "Happy Birthday" nonsense. Aziz, we must start her prayers now she is seven.'

'There is no rush. She is a child yet.'

'A child with no faith, Aziz.' She settles a malicious gaze on Jessie. 'Unless you count—'

'Layla, Aziz and I will take care of this,' Jessie interrupts, repaying Layla with a look as icy as the Arctic. 'Shani is our daughter.'

'And my grandchild!' Layla glares at Zara. 'The only one it appears I am likely to have.'

Zara rolls her eyes as she chews on a forkful of cake. 'I am busy, Mama. I have no time for a husband.'

Layla harrumphs. 'That ridiculous clinic. It is eating your life. You are cheating me out of grandchildren, Zara. You should be ashamed of your selfishness.'

Zara's fork clatters as she drops it onto her plate. 'Yes, I work for the clinic where I can do some good during the day instead of sitting at home rejecting all the potential husbands you push at me, but I am also working for the independence of our country, where no British or French or Germans or Turks and their puppet kings have a say in how we live our lives. If I am selfish, then I am selfish for a free Egypt, not for a rich husband.'

'You are thirty-seven years old, Zara. Even if you wished it, you will not find yourself a rich husband now. At best you would be a second or third wife to an office clerk.'

Aziz holds up a hand. 'Please, this is not a subject for today.'

Zara folds her arms and glares at her brother. 'If not today, when, Aziz? You are always the conciliator, just like you are with the British and the King. King Fuad has just dismissed our Prime Minister and dissolved Parliament, and you can be certain we will be ruled by royal decree yet again. What use is a Wafd government when the King keeps dissolving it and replacing the elected Prime Minister with one of his puppets? And all the time the British intrigue to keep control of the Suez Canal. They are only too happy to stir up problems between the King and the Wafd Party if it serves their purposes. At least Isham—'

'Do not speak to me about Isham.'

Shani looks up from her cake. 'Mama, is the King bad?'

Jessie brushes her hand across Shani's dark curls. 'No, darling. He's not bad. He has a very difficult job.'

'Like Baba?'

Aziz smiles at his daughter. 'What do you mean, *habibti*?'

Shani sighs impatiently. 'Baba, you work *all* the time. You never eat supper with us.'

'Baba is a very busy doctor, darling,' Jessie says, pointedly ignoring Layla's huff of disapproval as she slides a second thin slice of cake onto Shani's plate. 'He has a lot of work to do at the hospital.'

'You work too, Mama, and you always eat supper with us.'

'That's because I'm your mama, and I work just next door. It's easy for me to come home.'

'For now, perhaps, Jessica,' Layla says as she gestures to Marta to refresh the teapot. 'What happens when you start your medical studies in September? Am I meant to eat my dinner in the sole company of a child? Has my life come to that?'

Jessie shakes her head as she lays her napkin on the table. 'Layla, we will work it all out. I'll see if I can arrange my classes to finish by four o'clock. There is no point making a problem where one doesn't currently exist.'

'It is a pity you have not been able to give Aziz a son.'

Jessie stares at her mother-in-law. 'I beg your pardon?'

Layla shrugs her elegant silk-clad shoulders. 'A man needs a son, not a physician wife. A woman has no place being a doctor. This is a man's work.'

'Layla—'

'It appears it wasn't God's will for us to have a son, Mama,' Aziz interrupts. 'And Jessica has every right to study medicine if she wishes. She has my full support, and this is all I wish to hear from you on the subject.'

Layla smiles, though her amber eyes are as cold as those of the tiger Jessie once saw in London Zoo. 'It was not God's will for Jessica to have your child, this is true, but it does not mean she should rob you of the joy of having a son.'

'Mama, that's enough!'

'You know what I say is true, Aziz.' Layla thrusts her hand at Shani, setting her bracelets jangling. 'How is this young girl to be left to run this beautiful house on her own one day? She is half English, Aziz! Shani will never be accepted as a wife to a decent Egyptian. For the sake of your father's honour and this house that he built for his family, you must marry a second wife from a good Egyptian family and have a son.'

Jessie pushes away from the table. 'Layla, honestly, it's time for you to drop this subject.'

Shani looks at her father with dollops of cocoa icing on her chin. 'Are you going to marry another lady, Baba?'

Aziz clenches his jaw. 'No, *habibti*. You and Mama are the only family I need.' He glares at his mother. 'No matter what your grandmama says.'

'We'll always be together, Baba?'

'*Inshallah, habibti*.'

Shani slides out of her chair and hugs her father. 'That was my wish, Baba. For us to be together for ever and ever. I blew out all the candles, so I know it will come true.'

---

In the bedroom, Jessie slides her arms around Aziz's back and kisses him on his neck.

'Did I tell you today that I love you?'

He turns in her arms and kisses her. 'I cannot recall it.'

'Well, I love you, Aziz Khalid. You're so good with Shani. She adores you, even if you *are* never here for supper.'

'I am sorry for that, Jessica. What with the hospital and the clinic and the work for the Wafd Party, there are not enough hours in the day.'

'I know, but you're missing Shani's childhood, and I'm missing you too.'

'I wish it could be another way, but this is the man I am. I have never tried to hide it from you.'

'I know. I love that you want to make things better for people.'

Kissing him on the cheek, she slips out of his embrace and walks over to the French doors. She throws them open, letting the warm evening breeze waft into the bedroom. Leaning against the door jamb, she looks out at the stripes of yellow and pink and orange spilling across the darkening sky.

Aziz joins her as he lights a cigarette. 'Do not listen to my mother.'

'I don't think she'll ever let up about the second wife.'

'I have no interest in a second wife.'

'Yes, I know.' She chews her lip. 'Aziz, something has been on my mind for quite a while. It's … it's very confusing.'

'What is it?'

'We haven't spoken about religion. I mean, Shani and religion. Not since just after she was born.'

'Again, do not listen to my mother. Shani is only seven. It is not required for her to start praying until she is twelve, although it is true many children start younger.'

'Don't you see? That's it exactly. Everyone is assuming Shani will be Muslim. I'm not Muslim. I can't teach her to be Muslim.' She swallows. 'I don't know that I want her to be Muslim.'

Aziz takes a long pull on the cigarette and blows out a stream of smoke. 'I didn't realise you still felt this way.'

'A couple of years ago, I saw Zara and Shani playing in the garden. Zara tied her *hijab* over Shani's hair and I felt … I felt … uncomfortable, I suppose.'

'Why?'

'It's just …' She shuts her eyes to try to make sense of the emotions tumbling around inside of her. 'I want Shani to be free to live her life however she chooses. I don't want her to have restrictions … expectations imposed upon her by others. By her … by her religion.'

'Which kind of restrictions? You see that Zara is free to do as she likes?'

'Not entirely. She has to dress a certain way, and Layla keeps harassing her to marry, and she can't go out without a male chaperone. When we go out to the souk, you insist that Mustapha shadows us wherever we go. I've seen him.'

'It is my responsibility as your husband and her brother to ensure that you are safe.' He looks at her as he puffs on the cigarette. 'You never had any restrictions when you were in London?'

'No! Never!'

'Never?'

Jessie frowns as memories of her London girlhood flash into her mind. 'Well, Mama did keep throwing poor Frank Jeffries at us as husband material until Celie took pity on him and married him. Truthfully, Mama would have been much happier if we'd all married Englishmen and settled down in London, but no one forced us to marry anyone. And we could go wherever we wanted. We had bicycles, and we took trams and buses without requiring a male chaperone. Celie worked as a photographer in Papa's shop and wrote for a newspaper, for heaven's sake. We could study whatever we wanted. We were free, Aziz. Well, as long as we got home by a certain time. Etta wasn't very good at that, I have to say, but, well, that's Etta. I want Shani to be free.'

'And you think she cannot be free as a Muslim woman in Egypt.'

'Yes.'

'I see.' Aziz stubs out the cigarette butt with his shoe. 'It is something we should have discussed before we married. I am at fault. I made an assumption … I shouldn't have.'

'It's … it's not that I'm saying no, Aziz. I need time to process this.'

'I can see that.' Aziz lights another cigarette as silence descends over them like a dense cloud. 'As I said, there is time for us to discuss this. We do not have to decide anything today.'

Jessie walks over to the white marble balustrade and looks out at the river glistening in the moonlight beyond the garden's trees. She rubs her arms as she shivers despite the warm air.

'There's something else.' She looks over at her husband. 'Aziz, my mother had Shani baptised as a Catholic when she was here after Shani's birth.'

'She what?'

'She … she convinced Marta and her husband to be godparents. I only found out a couple of years ago—'

'A couple of years ago? And you didn't tell me?'

'No, I … it was irrelevant.'

'How is our daughter's baptism into the Catholic church irrelevant? Is she not now a Catholic in the eyes of God?'

'Well, yes, I suppose so, but … Aziz, we are the ones who must decide how to go forward with Shani's religious education. My mother overstepped her bounds. Why can't Shani be a Catholic who observes Ramadan and Eid al-Adha, like me? We can teach her about Islam and Catholicism. Wouldn't that be a good idea?'

Aziz shakes his head. 'Jessica, it is not as simple as that. She cannot be both a Muslim and a Christian.'

Jessie sighs and nods. 'I know. It's why I've put off thinking about it, but we will have to address it at some point. When I found out about the baptism, I wrote my mother and told her that you and I will deal with Shani's religious upbringing when the time was right. I gave Mama quite a piece of my mind. I'm afraid she hasn't forgiven me. Her letters have been rather frosty ever since.'

Aziz runs his hand through his hair. 'Jessica, I am disappointed you didn't speak to me about this. I am Shani's father. I had a right to know this.'

'I'm sorry, Aziz. Truthfully, I'm rather surprised Layla didn't tell you herself. I threatened her with revoking the use of the car if she did. It seems she took that to heart.'

Aziz blows out a stream of smoke and stubs the cigarette butt out under his shoe. 'Is there anything else I should know?'

'No, absolutely not.' She clears her throat. 'Except, I'm worried about your mother's influence on Shani. I'll be out of the house long hours when I start at the university. Layla, well, you know your mother.'

'This I understand entirely. It seems we both have interfering mothers. We will find a way, *habibti*. I will ask Zara and Mustapha to keep an eye on my mother.'

She walks over to him and kisses him full on the lips. 'I love you so much, Aziz.'

He takes her into his embrace. 'I love you too, my darling, but do not keep secrets from me. There is no need. I will support you as long as there is breath in my body. This I promise with all my heart.'

# Chapter Seventy-Eight

## Etta

**Grotta di Matermania, Capri, Italy – August 1929**

It is a perfect summer day. Across the languid turquoise ripples of the Tyrrhenian Sea, the distant cliffs of the Amalfi Coast shimmer like a mirage in the afternoon heat. A breeze blows up to the grotto from the sea, brushing Etta's face with a cooling caress. Two gulls swoop and screech above the waves that splash and swirl at the foot of the cliff. She retreats from the cliff edge back to the grotto, conscious that the limestone has been known to loosen and crumble, plunging the foolish or the unwary into the sea with it.

Carlo's son Paolo is coming on the afternoon ferry and she doesn't know how she feels about it. The last time she'd seen him, he had been a slender boy of seventeen, sitting impatiently in the courtroom at Carlo's hearing. She had seen something of Carlo in his face, but his eyes, those aquamarine eyes as wary and unsettling as a cat's, those he must have inherited from his mother, Marianna.

'What do they say in England, *cara mia*? A penny for your thoughts?'

Etta looks over at Carlo who sits on an ancient step in the shade of the grotto. She joins him and sits beside him. 'I was just thinking about the last time I'd seen Paolo. It was nine years ago at your court hearing. He was so young.'

'He was seventeen. He is twenty-six now.'

'A man.'

'Yes, a man. Except for that one time in the courtroom, I have not seen Paolo since before the war when he was still a schoolboy in shorts and a blazer.' Carlo smiles as a memory flits through his mind. 'We had gone for the famous *gelati* at Giolitti's in Roma with my mother-in-law, the Marchesa. My father-in-law didn't come, of course. He despised me. He blamed me for ruining Marianna's life.' He shrugs. 'Perhaps I did.'

Etta squeezes Carlo's good hand. 'I'm sorry about your mother-in-law. It's a pity she wouldn't let you visit her when she was so ill.'

'Yes, well, Carolina had things to come to terms with at the end of her life. Losing her beauty to illness was probably one of them.'

'I remember her at the hearing. She was wearing a huge black hat and a veil. The judge couldn't keep his eyes off her.'

'She always had that effect on men.' He shakes his head. 'She is with the old Marchese and Marianna now in the Ludovisi vault where you can be certain I will never lie.'

'Don't talk about such things, Carlo. It's depressing. Aren't you happy Paolo is finally visiting after all this time?'

'Of course I am.' Carlo focuses an intense look on Etta. 'And you, *Etta mia*? You are not upset?'

No, she is not upset, exactly; apprehensive, that's the word. Apprehensive about how Paolo's presence might upset the harmonious life they have finally managed to attain after so many difficult years.

She smiles, turning her cheek to Carlo so that he might appreciate the full effect of her dimple. 'Don't be silly! He's your son, Carlo. He's as much a part of our family as Adriana is.' She swings her arms wide as if to embrace the blue August sky. 'I shall welcome him with open arms.'

Carlo laughs. He rests his arm around her shoulders and pulls her into an embrace. *'Ti amo, Etta mia.'*

'I love you, too, Carlo.'

A pebble skips down the cliffside path and comes to rest at the mouth of the grotto. Etta looks up the path as Carlo rises to his feet and steps into the sunlight.

'Paolo? You're here early! I was going to come meet you at the ferry.'

The young man touches the brim of his Panama hat as he steps in front of the grotto. 'Hello, Carlo. I took the earlier ferry. I am meeting friends back in Napoli for dinner tonight. The housekeeper said I would find you here.'

Etta scrutinises the handsome young man in the Panama hat, fashionable white linen single-breasted suit and two-tone shoes. It is almost like looking at the Carlo she'd first met back at the Royal Academy of Art's Summer Exhibition in 1913. The same dark hair, the same muscular build, the same nose, the same face, but those eyes ... as blue-green as the sea around the Faraglioni.

Carlo steps toward his son. 'Carlo? Why not Papa?'

'Papa? You are a stranger to me.'

'Paolo! I have tried to see you ever since I was released from prison. I have sent you letters, telegrams. I tried to place telephone calls. But you never answered anything. Not until last week.'

Paolo shrugs. 'I am here now.'

'Yes. Yes, you are here now.' Carlo opens his arms. 'Let me hug you, Paolo. Let me hug my son.'

Paolo steps back. 'Not now. Not yet.'

Carlo drops his arms. '*Va tutto bene.* I understand.'

Etta rises and steps out into the sunlight, extending her hand as she approaches Paolo. 'Paolo, it's so nice to meet you. I'm Etta. You must stay for dinner. We're all looking forward to it. Adriana especially.'

Paolo eyes Etta's outstretched hand and slides his hands into his pockets. 'So, you're the one who killed my mother.'

Etta freezes. 'I beg your pardon?'

Carlo steps toward his son. 'What do you mean by that, Paolo?'

'What do I mean by that, Carlo? We all know *she* is the one who drove my mother to madness.'

'Paolo! I don't know who put that idea into your head. Your mother was ill long before I met Etta.'

Paolo sweeps his aquamarine gaze over Etta. He shrugs. 'It is what I was told. Perhaps I was misinformed.'

Etta abandons her greeting and joins Carlo on the path. An awkward silence descends over the threesome.

Carlo gestures to the grotto with his gloved injured hand. 'Come, Paolo. Come out of the sun. Tell us about yourself. I want to know everything.'

Ignoring Carlo's invitation, Paolo strolls over to the cliff's edge and looks out at the view to the Italian mainland. 'Surely my grandmother kept you informed?'

'Yes, of course she did. You graduated with honours in mathematics from the Sapienza and you became the youngest vice-president ever at the auto company in Milan. I am so proud of you, Paolo.'

Paolo looks back at his father. 'These are the facts. I aim to be president before I am thirty-five. I intend to become the richest man in Italy.'

Etta retreats into the shade of the grotto. 'Why don't we go back to the house before it gets too hot?' she says, fanning her face. 'We can have some of Liliana's ice-cold lemonade. It's feeling like it will be baking today.'

Carlo joins Paolo by the cliff's edge and rests his good hand on the branch of a young parasol pine. 'You are ambitious, Paolo. This is a good thing. I was ambitious too, once. Now I am simply a handyman and a gardener with my family around me. I am content.'

Paolo studies his father. 'Did my grandmother write you before she died?'

'Yes, she sent me a letter … just before … She knew it would be soon.'

'What did she say?'

Carlo shrugs. 'Only that she didn't expect to see the autumn, and she asked me to do everything in my power to mend our relationship, Paolo. She said she was sorry about everything, but that she'd had no choice, and that she hoped that one day I would forgive her.'

Paolo grunts. 'When I was growing up, she used to tell me that I should let you into my life, because, after all, you are my father and blood is blood.'

'Blood *is* blood, Paolo. I love you just as I love Adriana. You are both a part of me. I would do anything for both of you.'

Paolo huffs. 'Anything? Even for my bastard sister?'

'Excuse me?' Etta says as she stamps across the path toward Paolo. 'What did you just say?'

Paolo eyes Etta coldly. 'I called her a bastard. Isn't that what she is?'

A fury like a storm takes hold of Etta; she raises her hand and slaps Paolo across his cheek.

'Etta! *Calmati*!'

'I will not be calm, Carlo!' She jabs Paolo's chest with her finger. 'Adriana is as legitimate as you are. Your father and I are married.'

Paolo laughs. 'You married *after* Adriana was born. Years after. And then my dear papa was arrested before the marriage could be consummated. Believe me, I have looked into all the details.'

Carlo's expression hardens. 'Don't disrespect Etta and your sister like that, Paolo. I understand that you are angry with me. You think I abandoned you, but this is not the case. Your grandfather never forgave me for eloping with your mother. Marianna and I were young and in love and you … you were on the way although he didn't know that at the time. He blamed me for your mother's illness, and he punished me by doing everything in his power to keep you from me. Then, when he died, I was in the jail and powerless to do anything. I had every intention of bringing you back into my life once Etta and I married. I wanted you to come to Capri, Paolo. I wanted you to be a part of our family.'

Paolo grimaces like he's bitten into a lemon. 'You think I would have wanted to be a part of your family? Living as lodgers in an old woman's decaying villa in an Italian backwater when I could live with the Ludovisis in one of the most beautiful villas in Napoli?'

Carlo expels a sigh. 'Come, please, Paolo. Let's sit in the grotto where it is cooler. We can discuss all of this rationally—'

Carlo steps away from his father. 'Do you think that is why I have come here? To reconcile with you? To be part of your *family*?' Laughing, he thrusts his hand at Etta. 'You are as delusional as your silly wife. I came here to get what is owed to me.'

'What do you mean, "what is owed to you"?'

'My grandmother left me nothing.'

Carlo frowns. 'Carolina was the wealthiest woman in Napoli. What about the villa? The Ludovisi money? She told me she would leave everything to you and Adriana equally.'

'It is all gone. It seems the Ludovisi money went to pay for my grandfather's gambling debts after he died. I discovered that my grandmother ended her days living in only one room of the villa. The other rooms were rented out to students and office clerks! It explains why she always insisted on visiting me in Milan rather than have me visit her in Napoli after my grandfather died.'

'I had no idea.'

'She was as proud as she was vain. She would never tell you such a thing. Did you know that the villa was taken from her by the government after she confessed to my mother's murder? They let her stay in that room as a favour to someone important. An old lover, no doubt. She was known to have a few.'

Etta gasps. 'She confessed to Marianna's murder?' She looks at Carlo. 'Did you know that?'

Carlo looks at Etta and nods. 'Yes, I knew it. She visited me in the prison and confessed to me. She apologised—'

'She *apologised*? She let you rot in that horrid prison for eight years, Carlo!'

Carlo rubs his forehead. 'She told me that she was consumed by guilt, and that she would confess to the police so that I could be freed. She said she did it because she couldn't bear seeing Marianna's deterioration. It appears that the police chose to conceal the Marchesa's identity in order to protect the reputation of the Ludovisi family, which is well-connected with members of the government.'

'And to have what was left of the Ludovisi fortune in return for their silence,' Paolo says. 'My grandmother was left alone in the Ludovisi villa owing to her status and the fact that she would soon be dead. It seems the police were reluctant to drag her name through the same mud as my father's.'

'How fortunate for her.'

Carlo sighs. 'It doesn't matter, Etta. It is over now.' He turns to his son. 'I am sorry, Paolo. I had no idea about this, but what do you mean about coming here for what is owed to you? Surely, you must be doing well enough at the automotive company in Milan?'

'It's not the same thing!' Paolo pounds his chest with the flat of his hand. 'I am the last Ludovisi! The money and the villa should have been mine!'

'Paolo, life is often not what you expect of it—'

Paolo jabs his finger at his father. 'No. I will not accept that. I have done nothing to deserve this.' He scrutinises his father with his pale eyes. 'You said you would do anything for your children.'

'Of course.'

'Good.' Paolo paces the limestone cliff, then he turns to face his father. 'I want you to make me your sole heir. I know you must have money. You are the infamous artist Carlo Marinetti, after all.'

'Paolo, you know I couldn't do that, even if I had the money. I have to think of your sister. She is only fourteen. We need to think of her education once she finishes school here.'

'I don't care about that daughter of a whore!'

Etta's mouth drops open and anger rips through her body like a fire. 'Take that back!'

'Paolo! Apologise to Etta!'

'What do I care about your whore wife or your bastard daughter! You want to know something, darling Papa? I didn't care about my mother, the precious Marianna, either. That crazy woman. I hated having to visit her at the asylum with my grandmother. She never recognised me. She always called me "that boy". It was insulting!'

'Paolo, you don't mean that—'

Paolo cocks a dark eyebrow at his father. 'Oh, no? All this time you thought my grandmother killed my mother, didn't you?' He laughs. 'It was a lie.'

'What do you mean?'

Paolo pounds his chest. '*I* killed her! It was *me*! I couldn't bear it anymore. She was an embarrassment. Somebody had to do something.'

Etta presses her hand against her mouth. 'Oh, my God.'

Carlo stares at his son. 'Paolo.'

Paolo smirks. 'Don't be so surprised. You seriously didn't think the Marchesa could have done it, did you?' He raises his eyebrows. 'You did, didn't you? You are more stupid than I thought.'

Carlo clenches his hands. 'You murdered Marianna? You murdered your own mother?'

Paolo shrugs. 'It was nothing. It was easy. A pillow and it was done. Unfortunately, my grandmother followed me to the asylum. She saw me leave and she went in to see my mother, but it was too late, of course. I made sure of that.'

Etta thrusts her face into Paolo's. 'You let your father and your grandmother take the blame for a murder *you* committed?'

Paolo steps away from her. 'It was only what my father

deserved for abandoning me. And then when my grandmother was dying, and her conscience began to bother her about my poor, idiot father in prison for a crime he didn't commit, why would I object to her taking the blame? She didn't want me to go to prison, you see. My whole life ahead of me. I wasn't about to rot in prison like my stupid father.'

'Paolo!'

'You want to hit me, don't you, my dear Papa? I can see it. But you can't because I am your son. The son you said you would do anything for, remember?'

'Paolo, stop this!'

'You owe me, Papa. You owe me for being a shit father. For giving me a crazy mother, a bastard sister and a whore of a stepmother.'

Carlo slams his good hand against the tree trunk. '*Pezzo di merda!*'

Paolo steps toward Carlo. '*I* am your legitimate heir, my dear Papa. I don't want there to be any confusion when you die. I know you have money. Your paintings sold like candy while you were in prison. I am your legitimate heir, and I want my due.'

'That's enough, Paolo!'

'If you don't look after me in your will, I swear I will see your whore wife and your bastard daughter out on the street. I will make sure not one penny of your legacy ever goes to either of them!'

The anger explodes inside of Carlo like a bomb. His injured hand in the leather glove balls into a fist. His arm reaches back and thrusts through the air toward his son's jaw.

Etta reaches for Carlo as a scream wrenches her body. It is like they are all moving through water, every action slowed by the weight of calamity. She sees Paolo step to one side; Carlo's stumble; his look of surprise as he reaches out for her; and then – a sight that will become the foundation of her future nightmares – Paolo's frigid blue-green eyes as her husband, the father of her child, the true love of her life, falls over the cliff's edge.

# Chapter Seventy-Nine

Jessie

**Altumanina, Cairo, Egypt – September 1929**

'Mama, why does Marta have to take me to school today? I want *you* to take me.'

Jessie loops the strap of her new leather schoolbag over her shoulder and checks her reflection in a large gilt-framed rococo antique mirror in Altumanina's large entrance hall.

'Because I'm going to school, too, Shani. We've spoken all about this. Marta will walk you to school and collect you in the afternoon. I have to go now. I mustn't keep Mustapha waiting in the car.'

'No one else's mother goes to school.'

Jessie reties Shani's school tie and tucks it into her blazer. 'That's because your mother wants to be a doctor and the other mothers don't.'

She sets a felt beret on her daughter's head and brushes an errant dark brown curl behind Shani's ear. 'Who knows? One day you might decide to be a doctor, too. Wouldn't you like your daughter to be happy about that instead of being a misery monster?'

Shani stamps her foot on the marble floor. 'I don't want to be a doctor and I'm not a misery monster! Baba says I'm a pearl.'

'You are a precious pearl, Shani,' Layla Khalid says as she enters the hall carrying scissors and a bundle of roses and dahlias. She shoots a piercing look at Jessie. 'Do not let anyone tell you otherwise.'

Marta hurries into the room after Layla, holding a vase and Shani's schoolbag, and throws Jessie a warning look.

Jessie takes Shani's schoolbag from Marta. 'I think we are all in agreement that Shani is a precious pearl, but that doesn't excuse naughty behaviour.'

'A mother has no business abandoning her child to pursue a career when she has a husband capable of supporting her,' Layla says as she lays the flowers onto the marble-topped central table. 'Just look at your poor daughter's face, Jessica. She will be in tears as soon as you leave.'

'Shani won't be in tears, will you, Shani?'

Shani shrugs as she adjusts her schoolbag strap across her school uniform.

'See, Layla? She is made of sterner stuff,' Jessie says. 'Besides, I've worked all her life. The only difference is that I'll be studying now. I'll still be home for supper every evening. Marta and I have agreed that it will be served a half-hour later so that we can all be there.' She chucks her pouting daughter under her chin. 'Possibly even Baba.'

Layla shoots a side-eyed glance at Marta, who is making a show of busily arranging the flowers into the vase. 'Is that so? We are meant to change our schedules to accommodate you, and no one saw fit to tell me? I find this quite extraordinary. It seems I am a ghost in my own house.'

'Layla, it's not that difficult a change.'

Layla yanks a purple dahlia out of the vase and jabs in a yellow rose. 'There is already one doctor in this family. There is no need for another. I am really quite astonished that you believe anyone will permit a woman to treat them.'

Jessie rolls her eyes. 'It has been the role of women to be the healers throughout history, Layla. We are living in the twentieth century, and the Egyptian University has seen fit to invite women to study medicine.'

'Absolutely ridiculous, if you ask m—'

Anger takes hold of Jessie's tongue, and the words spill out before she can stop them. 'You must keep up with the times, Layla, or you may be thought of as being old.'

Marta coughs, provoking a glare from Layla. The front door swings open and Aziz enters the hall. He smiles at the sight of his wife and daughter with their schoolbags.

'Hurry up, you two. Mustapha is waiting.'

Jessie's eyes widen in surprise. 'Aziz? What are you doing here? I thought you'd gone to the hospital after checking with the new doctor and nurse in the clinic.'

'On your first day of school, Jessica? Don't be absurd. Zara has everything under control in the clinic so don't worry about that.' He beckons to his daughter. 'Hop into the car, Shani. We'll drop you off on the way to the university. Marta can pick you up later.'

'Already your wife is disturbing your work, Aziz,' Layla says as she shoves the rejected flowers into Marta's hands. 'In my day—'

'Yes, we know, Mama,' Aziz interrupts. 'In your day, you had servants to wait on you hand and foot, but things have changed.'

Jessie ushers Shani toward the door. 'Mama apologises, Shani. You're not a misery monster.'

'A misery monster?' Aziz asks as he shuts the door behind them.

'Oh, it's a long story.' Jessie loops her arm around Aziz's elbow and takes hold of Shani's hand. 'Now, let's go to school.'

---

Jessie gazes up at the September sky and watches a lone puff of cloud scuttle across the blue. It has been a good day; the best day. Joy buzzes through her body, setting her nerves tingling. How has she any right to be this happy? How has she been so lucky in this life, when her sisters' lives have been marred by so much unhappiness?

'Mama! Mama!'

Jessie looks past the red *tarbouches* and broad shoulders of the departing medical students to see Shani waving at her from beyond the clipped trees lining the street in front of the School of Medicine. Beside her Aziz stands, tall and handsome, in his grey suit holding a large bouquet of white roses. He smiles when she sees him, and her heart leaps the way it still does whenever she catches his eye unexpectedly. She weaves through the students and joins Aziz and Shani on the pavement.

'Shani, what are you doing here? I thought Marta was picking you up from school.'

'Papa got me in the car. We brought you flowers, Mama! Papa wanted red ones but I like white better, so he bought white ones.'

Jessie's eyes meet Aziz's, and, not for the first time, she regrets the formality which must be observed between husbands and wives in public spaces. He offers her the roses and leans forward to whisper in her ear.

'We are so very proud of you, *habibti*. How was your day?'

'It was interesting. Let's just say not everyone is delighted with having women on the course.'

'It is progress, and progress sometimes rattles people. I have faith in you, Jessica. I have seen you nursing on a medical ship while we were being bombarded by the Turkish guns at Gallipoli. You are very capable of putting anyone in their place who invites it.'

'I'm afraid I've done that already. I told one of the students not to keep butting in when I was answering a question. I think he may have given me the evil eye.'

Aziz smiles under his black moustache. 'No doubt he deserved it.'

'I did meet some lovely women students. I'm sure we'll be friends.'

'I am glad of that, *habibti*.'

Shani tugs at her mother's arm. 'Baba promised to take us for *booza* in the big *souk*!'

Jessie glances at Aziz. 'Did he, now? Well, aren't we lucky? *Booza* ice cream with pistachios is my favourite.'

Shani slips her hand into Jessie's. 'Maybe I will be a doctor one day, Mama. Or a maid. Marta says I'm very good at making *basbousa* cake.'

Jessie brushes a curl off Shani's cheek. 'You can be anything you want to be, Shani. Isn't that right, Aziz?'

'Absolutely, *habibti*.' He takes hold of Shani's other hand. 'Now, shall we go get that *booza*?'

# Chapter Eighty

## Etta & Christina

**Villa Serenissima, Capri, Italy – September 1929**

Stefania stops Liliana outside the door to Etta's bedroom as the housekeeper carries away a tray of uneaten breakfast.

'How is she today?' she asks in Italian.

Liliana shakes her head. 'Not so good. I have not seen her as bad as this since Adriana was born. At times she confuses me with Carlo, and other times she thinks I am Adriana. If only we could convince Adriana to see her mother, perhaps it might help her come out of this state.'

'I agree, but Adriana is still refusing. She believes Paolo's ridiculous story that Etta pushed Carlo at the grotto.'

'You don't think she might … that she could have—'

'Liliana! How can you even think such a thing of Etta? She was in her proper mind that day. You've seen how happy she has been since she came back to Capri with Carlo. He was excited about Paolo's visit and Etta was excited for him.'

'But why won't she defend herself from Paolo's accusations?

The police are impatient to question her. They won't let us delay it much longer.'

'You have seen the state she has been in since the incident. At the burial I thought she might even throw herself into the grave with Carlo's coffin.'

Liliana shakes her head sadly. 'She will end up in the asylum like Carlo's first wife.'

'She will not! You are not to even think such a thing, Liliana. As long as I breathe, I will do everything in my power to help Etta recover and fight Paolo's accusations. He is contesting Carlo's will, did you know that?'

'Was that what was in the letter this morning? You seemed quite upset. You did not even eat your grapefruit.'

'How could I eat grapefruit when we are living through an earthquake, Liliana! Paolo is claiming that Etta's breakdown and her alleged role in Carlo's death have rendered her unfit to act as the executor of Carlo's estate, and as his eldest child, he should be appointed the executor.'

'*Madonna!*'

'Exactly. I did not trust that boy as soon as I met him. He is like a snake in a chicken coop. He cares only about himself. This is evident. He will have Adriana and Etta cut out of Carlo's will and Etta in prison for Carlo's murder if he has his way.'

'No, no, no. This cannot happen.'

'Of course it cannot happen.' She takes the breakfast tray from the housekeeper. 'Open the door, please. Etta must regain her strength. There is a fight ahead.'

---

Etta turns over on the bed and blinks at the officious woman bustling around the bedroom. She shields her eyes as sunlight pierces the room's gloom.

'Hello? Who's there?'

The woman sits on the bed by her feet, the mattress dipping

with her weight. 'It's Stefania, *cara*. Your cousin. You remember? You live in my house on Capri. I brought you some breakfast.'

Etta sits up against the pillows as the woman's dark brown eyes watch her attentively. She rubs her forehead. 'Stefania, of course. I'm sorry, I … I had an awful dream.' She looks around the room. 'Where's Carlo? Has he gone out to paint? I told him he had to start painting again with his injured hand. I told him all he needs is practice.'

Stefania regards her young cousin and pats Etta's hand. 'Why don't we have some *tisana* together? It is rosehip and orange flower, our favourite. And then perhaps you will have a little *sfogliatella* as well? Shall we ask Adriana to join us?'

'Adriana?' Etta laughs as she accepts the teacup from Stefania. 'Why would a baby want *tisana*? Really, Cousin Stefania, you don't understand babies at all, do you?'

---

**Villa Serenissima, two weeks later**

Christina sets down the steaming teacup and looks across the wicker table at her cousin, Stefania Albertini. At eighty, her cousin is as robust and handsome as she remembered, the marcelled waves of her silver-streaked black hair adding a certain cachet to the otherwise sombre attire.

'You were right to send me a telegram, Stefania. I've never seen Etta like this. It's quite frightening, really.'

'Christina, it is good that you came so quickly. I cannot put off the police much longer. I'm worried that they will arrive any day and take her into custody.'

'That is absolutely not going to happen, Stefania. I asked Mario to make reservations for Etta, Adriana and me on the ferry tomorrow morning when he met me in the marina yesterday. I have already purchased the train tickets from Naples to London.'

'So quickly? Are you certain you don't wish to rest a day or two?'

'Rest? How can I rest with Etta in this condition? I will bring her home and ensure she has the professional care she needs. Capri can only remind her of Carlo. We must get her away from here.'

'Adriana doesn't wish to go.'

'I'm afraid Adriana has no choice. I have called in some favours and have managed to get her into an excellent boarding school as soon as we arrive back in England. They have only just begun their term, so she won't have missed anything much.'

Stefania rubs the crumbs of a cannoli off her fingers with a napkin. 'You are right. Adriana needs direction. She can't be left to roam about Capri to her heart's content. She has so much energy but no focus for it.' She helps herself to another chocolate cannoli. 'Are you certain you are up to the challenge of raising another irrepressible girl, Christina? Adriana is a free spirit just like her mother.' She smiles wryly. 'And her grandmother.'

'I was never as bad as all that, Stefania.'

'No? I seem to recall you running all around the island with that young Englishman when you were only a few years older than her.'

Christina sits back in her chair and regards her cousin. 'Well, perhaps I did do that. And look what good that did me? I won't have the same thing happen to Adriana.'

---

Etta grabs hold of the rusting railing of the Capri–Napoli ferry and sucks in a deep breath of the salty air.

'It's a beautiful day today, isn't it, Mama?'

Christina looks over at her daughter, whose blonde beauty seems only to be enhanced by her fragility. 'It is that, Etta. A lovely day for an adventure. Are you ready for an adventure?'

Etta smiles and rolls her hazel eyes. 'I'm always ready for an adventure, Mama, you know that!'

'*Nonna*, is she going to be like that all the time now?'

Christina looks at her granddaughter, who is slumped over the railing beside her. She moves to brush an unruly curl that has escaped from beneath Adriana's white cloche hat away from the girl's cheek, but instead curls her fingers and rests her gloved hand on the railing. 'She won't, Adriana. I promise. Your mother just needs a good rest away from Capri.'

Adriana suddenly straightens and waves wildly at the dock where Stefania and Liliana stand watching the ferry's departure. 'Mario! Mario!'

Christina spies the tall, youthful figure in an ill-fitting grey suit waving back at Adriana. He presses his hand his to his lips and throws a kiss out across the churning wake to the ferry.

Adriana turns and focuses a penetrating dark gaze on her grandmother. 'Why do you make me leave Capri? I don't want to go to England. I am Italian, not English. I want to stay here!'

'Adriana, you will feel differently about this one day, I promise you. It is for your own good.'

'No, I won't! Never!'

The straw bag at Adriana's feet jiggles as something inside it scratches at the straw. Christina steps aside in alarm. 'My word, what is that?'

Adriana leans over and opens the bag. She pulls the disgruntled cat into her arms and kisses his thick orange fur. 'It's Alice. He would be lonely without me.'

'Adriana! What am I meant to do with a cat when you're away at school?'

Adriana thrusts the cat into Christina's arms. 'You must feed him fish and hug him and tell him I love him and that I will always come back for him, just as I will always come back for my Mario.'

'Mario is a young man, Adriana—'

Adriana regards her grandmother. 'I will marry Mario one day, *Nonna*. I will come back to Capri and I will marry him.'

# Chapter Eighty-One

Celie

**West Lake, Alberta – 29th October 1929**

Frank counts out the money for Ol' Man Forbes at the cashier's window at the Merchant Bank. He slides the notes into his wallet. 'Thank you, Harvey. See you next month.'

The young cashier pushes his horn-rimmed glasses up his nose. 'Right you are, Mr Jeffries.' He smiles at Celie who is hovering by the door. 'Don't forget supper at ours next Friday, Mrs Jeffries. Marion's making her famous pumpkin pie.'

'Oh, we'll be there, Harvey. We wouldn't miss Marion's pumpkin pie for the world.'

Outside the bank, they stand for a moment and breathe in the cold, sharp air. Frank coughs, then he coughs again. Then the coughing grabs hold of his lungs like hands squeezing air out of a balloon.

Celie pats his back. 'Frank. Do you need to sit down? We can go back into the bank—'

He reaches into his pocket and holds his handkerchief against his mouth until the coughing jag eases. He stuffs the handkerchief back in his pocket. 'It's this blasted dry air, Celie. I swear some days breathing is like trying to pull a porcupine up a paper straw. I never thought I would say it, but I miss the English rain.'

'I'll boil up some water with VapoRub when we're home for you to breathe, Frank. It always seems to help.'

They head across the road to Forbes's store. Inside, Fred Wheatley, Tom Philby, Rex Majors and Ol' Man Forbes cluster around the counter by the cash register, their heads bent over a newspaper. Frank joins them as Celie wanders over to the table where a new consignment of fabric is laid out in bolts.

'What's going on, Fred?' Frank asks. 'It's as quiet as a tomb in here.'

Fred Wheatley looks at Frank, his normally affable expression erased into one of blank shock. 'Tom's just back from Edmonton. He brought a copy of this morning's newspaper.'

'Any more news about the Famous Five?' Celie asks as she flips through the fabrics. 'The Temperance Union ladies couldn't be more delighted about the Privy Council's ruling the other week that women are actually persons in Canada. Otherwise, we'd all be going on strike and you'd have to be cooking your own dinners.'

Ol' Man Forbes shakes his head. 'It's nothing about that.'

'Yes? So? What is it?' Frank asks. 'I didn't think ice hockey season started until next month.'

'It's not about hockey, Frank,' Rex Majors says as he pushes the newspaper across the counter. Frank scans the headlines plastered across the front page of the *Edmonton Journal*.

*New York and Toronto Stock Exchanges in State of Panic*

*Slump Gathers Momentum … Wipes Out 'Paper Profits' … New Low for Favourite Stocks. Avalanche of Selling Swamps Wheat Market. Trading Floors in Leading Centres Witness Frantic Scenes as Prices Tumble …*

Celie joins the group and sets a bolt of forest green wool on the counter. 'I'll take four yards of this lovely new wool, Mr Forbes. I thought I'd make Lulu a new dress for Christmas.'

'Put it back, Celie.'

'But, Frank, she needs a new dress. The rate she's growing—'

Ol' Man Forbes clears his throat. 'I hope you haven't overstretched yourself, Frank. Things are not lookin' too good. They're runnin' around like chickens in the New York and Toronto Stock Exchanges.'

'I said put it back, Celie. Can't you hear me?'

'Honestly, Frank, the fabric isn't that expensive—'

Frank grabs the bolt of wool and, striding across the store, throws it on top of the stack of fabrics on the table. 'Blast it, Celie! I said put it back!' He stomps out of the store and slams the door behind him with so much force the bell clatters to the floor.

Celie stares at the silent men. 'I'm … I'm sorry. I don't know what's got into him.'

Ol' Man Forbes taps the newspaper. 'I think this might have something to do with it.'

Celie flicks her eyes over the article. 'Stock investments are falling?'

'Not just fallin', Celie,' Fred says. 'They're crashin' through the floor.' He rests his hand on her arm. 'Frank hasn't put everything into stocks, has he? I told him to be careful. He's kept a cash reserve?'

Panic rises inside of Celie like a tide.

'I … Of course. I'm sure …'

'I told him not to put all of his eggs into one basket, Mrs Jeffries,' Ol' Man Forbes says. 'I told him to keep some money under the mattress for a rainy day.'

'Mr Forbes, I would appreciate it if you stop giving my husband financial advice. He wouldn't be in this situation if you hadn't told him about your stockbroker in the first place.' She heads toward the door, then looks back at the store owner when her hand is on the doorknob. 'How much do we owe you, Mr Forbes?'

Ol' Man Forbes glances at the other men.

'How much do we owe you, Mr Forbes.'

The old man slides a ledger out from underneath the counter and flips it open. He pushes his spectacles up his nose. 'That'll be just shy of a hundred and fifty dollars, Mrs Jeffries.'

'A hundred and fifty do—' Celie swallows. 'How much exactly, Mr Forbes?'

Fred crosses over to Celie. 'Celie, maybe you oughtta wait to talk to Frank first.'

Celie looks past Fred at Ol' Man Forbes. 'How much exactly, Mr Forbes?'

'One hundred and -eight dollars and seventy-three cents.'

She takes her hand off the doorknob and returns to the counter. 'I need to send a telegram. I will have it paid in full by the end of next week, then I wish to close our account. We will pay in cash in the future.'

---

That afternoon, Celie walks over to the sink and looks out the window to the vast white landscape under the leaden grey sky. She swallows and grits her teeth until the pain that tears at her heart is tamed into a dull throb. Another thirty-five pounds gone from her emergency fund. There is only seventy pounds left after years of dipping into her inheritance to shore up their expenses, and now that their account at Forbes's is closed, she knows there will be more telegrams to her mother, more of her emergency money wired across the ocean and the vast mass of Canada to the Merchant Bank in West Lake, Alberta. She has no choice. She can't let them get further into debt. With any luck, the stock markets will calm down and get back to normal, and this will be nothing but a bad dream.

If she were to leave for England with Lulu now, she would still have enough money to get back home. But if the stock market doesn't recover, and Frank's creditors start demanding their money, it won't be long before what was left of her inheritance is gone. Then she'd have to ask Jessie for money, and she just can't do that. Absolutely not. This is her problem, hers and Frank's. She is his wife, she will always be his wife, and she has a duty to do what she can to help him.

She will simply have to work harder. Write more articles. See if she can take up teaching again. There must be a way out of this mess, and she will do whatever she can to find it. Sweet Briar Farm is her home now, not England, not Clover Bar, nor her mother's new flat in Chelsea. Not any life with Max Fischer. All of that is over. She is Mrs Frank Jeffries, the mother of Louisa Jeffries, of Sweet Briar Farm, West Lake, Alberta, Canada. This is her home and she will fight for it.